An Ocean Between *Us*

BY THE SAME AUTHOR

WRITING AS RAY KINGFISHER

Historical Fiction

The Sugar Men
Rosa's Gold
Beyond the Shadow of Night

General Fiction

Matchbox Memories
Tales of Loss and Guilt

WRITING AS RAY BACKLEY

Bad and Badder
Slow Burning Lies

WRITING AS RAY FRIPP

I, Smith (with Harry Dewulf)
Easy Money
E.T. the Extra Tortilla

An Ocean Between *Us*

Rachel Quinn

LAKE UNION
PUBLISHING

Published by Lake Union Publishing, Seattle

www.apub.com

Amazon, the Amazon logo, and Lake Union Publishing are trademarks of Amazon.com,
Inc., or its affiliates.

ISBN-13: 9781542040532
ISBN-10: 1542040531

Cover design by Lisa Horton

Printed in the United States of America

To the memories and spirits of:
Olive and Barney
Margaret and Con
Theresa and Brian

INTRODUCTION

This story is not a political one, but I include here just a little of the history of Ireland to help explain some of the events depicted.

In World War Two the fledgling independent state of Ireland was officially neutral. In reality, attitudes to the war raging on only a few hundred miles away were varied and ambivalent. Then again, the relationship between Ireland and Great Britain had always been close but strained, as demonstrated by the events a few decades before.

During World War One, Ireland fought for its independence *from* the United Kingdom while still fighting *for* the United Kingdom, most notably in the 1916 Easter Rising, which was severely dealt with by what the Irish Republican movement saw as imperial oppressors. The armed rebellion was put down, and executions of Irish fighters followed, but one man who narrowly escaped execution was a seasoned Republican named Éamon de Valera.

When World War One ended there was little respite for the Irish people as the War of Independence (often called the Anglo-Irish War) followed on almost immediately. Two years later this led to the signing of a treaty largely granting independence to the new 'Irish Free State', albeit with certain constraints, the most important of which was that the new state comprised only twenty-six of the thirty-two counties, leaving six of the nine counties of Ulster within the UK, creating a new province christened Northern Ireland. Thus, the two largest cities in

Ireland were now effectively in different countries: Dublin in 'the South' and Belfast in 'the North'.

Even then, the fighting didn't stop for long. In the new country there was a bitter political split between two factions: the pro-treaty (those who accepted the treaty partitioning the country) and the anti-treaty (those wanting to fight on to unite the whole island of Ireland), with tensions very soon leading to the year-long Irish Civil War. With the help of the British, the pro-treaty side won, and for the next fifteen years the country struggled to find its place in the world order just like any other newly independent state. But now it was at least a stable country.

At the outbreak of World War Two, the wounds from fighting three wars in a ten-year period were still raw, leaving little appetite for further conflict. And despite close relations between the countries on a social level, the country that now called itself simply 'Ireland' continued to deeply mistrust a Britain that many still saw as the enemy. Most notably, the memories of the feared 'Black and Tans' – Winston Churchill's often undisciplined and brutal temporary police force installed in Ireland in 1920 – still loomed large. The fact that by 1940 the same man had become the British Prime Minister only heightened mistrust, and there was a genuine suspicion that Britain might use World War Two to justify the recapture of its lost land.

Hence the country, now headed by one Éamon de Valera, stayed resolutely neutral, and the wartime years were more often referred to as 'The Emergency'.

There was always, however, an element of convenience behind the scenes. Contradicting the official government stance, many Irish men joined the British Army and fought alongside 'the enemy' in Europe, Africa and Asia, and many Irish women worked in UK armaments factories. Some say the reasons were largely financial in a poverty-ridden Ireland, but for many there turned out to be a high price to pay in more ways than one. Moreover, the idea of Irish people leaving their country in large numbers to seek a better life elsewhere was hardly new, and continued throughout and well after the war.

This story is the fictional account of one such woman, Aileen Sweeney: of her time spent in a small Irish coastal village during the war years, and of how she came to leave her country of birth and settle in New York. I have tried to keep the historical facts accurate and, most importantly, impartial. I apologize beforehand if I have fallen down on either of those counts. The one exception to accuracy is where, to avoid confusion, the country is referred to as the Republic of Ireland, when, in fact, it only became officially that in 1949.

Chapter 1

Aileen's hand fumbles to find the gap in the curtains. As she pulls the rich velvet material aside, the throw of the streetlight shows up the tree-root veins on the back of her shiny-skinned hand.

She tells herself the decades have brought wisdom, but the thought is as fleeting as any one of those years now seems. And it's only half-true. Some days she thinks there is no wisdom, only memories of paths taken.

But there's little time to dwell – she has a celebration to get ready for. Still, it's a strange feeling. Tonight is supposed to be a special night, but pondering the reasons for the celebration brings both pain and joy. It's a small dilemma compared to the trials of that faraway life.

A glance up and down the dim Long Island street breaks the barrier, and her mind goes back fifty years to when she first set foot in New York City, to when she wondered how so many people could live so close to one another. Until that day she'd been used to roaming over endless barley fields and grasslands, but here – where people were as densely packed as blades of grass on a lush lawn – she wondered how anyone could survive without being constantly annoyed by neighbours.

'Aileen,' he says, bringing her back. 'What are you looking at?'

She turns and her eyes catch the fine decor of the bedroom – the neatly ironed bedcovers and plump pillows, the fine but not extravagant prints on the violet wall, the solid oak furniture she had her eye on for months and pounced on when Raymour & Flanigan had a sale on.

'Are you okay, Aileen?'

'I was just thinking back, that's all.'

'Me too,' he says, half a cracked smile breaking through.

Aileen sits at the dresser, looking at her reflection in the mirror, at hair that was once a striking auburn but has since become overrun by marauding grey invaders. She notices him step up behind her.

'Cab's booked for six-thirty,' he says. 'We have almost an hour yet.'

Her eyes don't move from her own reflection. 'A lot of work to do on this old thing,' she says with a smirk.

'Real beauty doesn't fade.'

Now she looks at his face. There is no humour there. That's nice. But *he's* nice.

'So you say,' she replies. She picks up a hairbrush, but feels his hand – as gentle as ever, even though not as firm and steady as it once was – on the top of hers.

'Let me,' he says. 'It's been a while since I brushed your hair.'

In the mirror she sees him sit behind her on the edge of the bed, and she watches him touch the bristles of the brush to the crown of her head. He starts brushing, and she feels a tremble as his spare hand rests against the back of her neck, making the baby hairs that grow there sing with pleasure. The tremble isn't quite as delicious as it once was, but it's there. It's still there.

He guides the brush down. She closes her eyes. Gradually the smooth run of the brush becomes rougher, tugging every so often at the knots in her hair. A voice tells her she still has salt in her hair. Perhaps there's a little left from all those years ago. Then the familiar voice from a well-remembered world tuts and tells her it's dry and sticky.

And Aileen's memory of that voice takes her back to when her hair was still that striking auburn, when wrinkles were unthought of, and when life was half a century simpler.

Leetown, County Wicklow, Ireland, July 1943

'It's so damned sticky,' Aileen's mother said. 'You've got sticky hair again. Sure, that'll teach you to wash in the sea.'

Aileen couldn't take another root-tugging wrench and flinched. 'Ow!'

'Won't you keep yourself still, Aileen. Tis nobody's fault but your own.'

Aileen peered at herself in the mirror, which was leaning on the kitchen table against the wall. Well, it wasn't so much a mirror as a sharp-edged segment of one. The table was a rough slice of timber on legs – one with a rag under it to keep the whole thing from wobbling. And the wall, well, *that* was nothing but a mass of whitewashed cobblestones.

'Why didn't you rinse yourself off in the Crannagh? You should know by now that river water isn't salty.'

'I'm after forgetting.'

'Twas too far for you to walk, more like.'

'Have we any fresh water here?'

'Only the remains of what Fergus and Gerard fetched from the well this morning. Enough to boil the vegetables and for your father to wash in when he's home from the fields.'

'Ow!'

'Sure, your hair's like a windswept field of barley shoots. If you want a man to be courting you—' Aileen's mother grunted as yet another knot caused her to tug the brush down. '—you'll just have to let me do this, so you will.'

A few pulls later, a few more grimaces from both women, and the job was done.

'I think I'll be trying another colour sometime soon,' Aileen said as she caressed a sheaf of the hair teasing her shoulders.

'Different colour?' Her mother squeezed her eyes almost shut. '*Different colour?* Aach, away with ye.'

'It's true, Mammy. Up in Dublin there are people who can change the colour of a woman's hair, like how the Hollywood people—'

'Ah, the Hollywood people. I've heard all about those glamorous sorts from that newfangled wireless machine thing your daddy listens to. And I suppose you'll be pasting that muck on your face too?'

Aileen leaned toward the mirror and pressed a forefinger against the pimple that had chosen to position itself right on the centre of her chin. It was the only blemish on her skin. As long as you didn't count the butterfly of freckles around the bridge of her nose as blemishes. And Aileen didn't.

'Why, of course I will.'

'And will you be putting on the fancy clothing like your Hollywood people wear too?'

'I will.'

Her mother shook her head. 'Sure, these are awful strange times, so they are. Perhaps it's because of that there war going on in Europe – that thing in France and Germany and all those other countries I never knew existed.'

'The world's changing, Mammy. Sure, twas changing even before the war started.'

Aileen's mother took a step away and placed her fists on her hips. 'And how would you know what things were like back then? You were only fourteen.'

'And I'm eighteen now and I have my own ideas, so I have.'

'Your own ideas? Aach. All I know is that things were a lot simpler in my day. I had no fancy clothes or paint for my face, so I didn't. Back then a girl found herself a nice Wicklow man and that was that.'

'Well, it's different now. And I might not want to marry a Wicklow man anyhow.'

'Just be taking care of yourself, Aileen, that's all I'm saying. The world might be changing but some things *never* change, and young men is one of them. And when I say men I'm meaning Wicklow men or men from anywhere else in Ireland. Do you hear me?'

'I do, Mammy.'

'Good. Now I have chickens to feed and turf to fetch in.' Aileen's mother picked up a bowl of breakfast scraps and left.

Aileen rummaged around in the make-up bag she shared with her sister, Briana, and plucked out a stick of scarlet lipstick. 'And I might not even be wanting to marry an Irishman,' she muttered to herself.

A few minutes later Aileen's mother returned, three clumps of peat in the crook of her arm, to find Aileen and Briana putting the finishing touches to the pencil lines along the backs of their legs. She gave her head a dismissive shake as she loaded one clump on to the smouldering fire and set the others down on the hearth.

Pausing for breath, she looked her daughters up and down. 'Briana, you be taking care of your sister, d'you hear me?'

'Sure, I will.' Briana's eyes bobbed upward.

'And don't be doing that thing with your eyes, please. One day they'll stay up there inside your head, and then where will you be?'

'I'm sorry, Mammy, but tis only a dance on the strand. The worst that can happen is that it'll start raining and we'll both be coming home soaked.'

'As long our Aileen is safe.'

'She will be, Mammy, I promise.'

Aileen butted in. 'Sure, will you just listen to yourselves, talking about me as if I'm invisible or something. Come on and let's be going.'

She headed for the door and Briana followed.

Soon the sisters were on the coastal road that separated the row of seafront cottages from the verge of wild grasses and the beach beyond.

'Was Mammy giving you the talk about men?' Briana said as they skipped sideways to avoid Timmy Kearnan's donkey and cart.

'You mean the warning? She was so.'

'Aach, didn't I tell you she'd be doing that soon enough? She was after giving me all that when I was eighteen too, the first time I went to a dance on the strand.'

'As long as it's only the once. Mammy's stuck in her old ways, so she is.'

Briana stopped walking for a second and placed an arm around Aileen's shoulder. 'Maybe you shouldn't be so harsh on her, Aileen. She worries about you. She worries about all of us. 'Tis only natural.'

They crossed the road just before passing Cready's – Leetown's one and only store, which was a grocery selling all sorts and everything. As soon as their feet hit the sandy edges of grass, Aileen asked Briana what it was like to be courted by a man. Briana said it was 'the best feeling in the world' but also told her not to tell their mother she'd said so. They compared clothes. Aileen wore a plain green cotton dress, but Briana's dress – one she'd bought on her last trip to Dublin – was a more fancy affair, yellow and blue floral-patterned with the very fashionable nipped-in waistline. Aileen said she liked Briana's lipstick. In truth, she thought it a little too dark but didn't like to say.

They walked on past the short lane leading to the dark grey frontage of the railway station, and around the corner where the River Crannagh came into view. Two bridges straddled the river – a monstrous iron beast carried the railway, and in its dark shadow, a stone's throw from where the river widened to give itself up to the ocean, lay a footbridge of thick wooden planks. Both bridges had been there for as long as Aileen could remember, the wooden one leading to the sandiest beach for miles around.

From the near riverbank they could already hear the music, and once on the opposite side they could see the section of beach where the dance had been set up. A small band of two fiddlers, two banjo players and an accordionist stood to one side of the makeshift dance floor. Leetown's finest single lads and lasses sat around the edge on upturned wooden boxes, men on one side, women on the other.

Aileen's shoes sank a little in the sand and she stumbled once or twice.

'You'll be taking those off once you get asked to dance,' Briana said.

'Only if I *agree* to dance,' Aileen replied as they approached the wooden boxes. The remark made Briana smirk, which made Aileen giggle, and they eased themselves down next to the other girls.

A breeze that had stolen cool air from the Irish Sea hit them and Aileen folded her arms tightly against its bite. She glanced at the men on the other side, although 'boys' would have been a better description. She even recognized most of them – there was the Houlihan boy who couldn't sit still, two or three she recognized from her schooldays but whose names she'd forgotten, and then the Ellis twins, who were easy to spot even though they wore different clothes and sat well away from each other.

'Some of the lads here are younger than me,' Aileen said.

'And so?' Briana replied.

'Well, why did I have to wait until I was eighteen?'

'You're not the only one, I can tell you. Mammy and Daddy decided we're allowed here at eighteen and that's that.' Briana threw a glance of dismay across the river to the strip of cottages lining the coast road. 'But you're right, the turnout of worthwhile men is poor, so tis.'

'Sure, they should have called Leetown "Tinytown",' Aileen said, raising her voice over the music. 'I can't believe I've been waiting until I was eighteen for *this*.'

'Won't you be patient awhile? Just try to enjoy it.'

Aileen herself now peered over toward to the cottages, each one white with a thatched roof but somehow boasting its own character. Her gaze then led to the line of shingle that tapered to a point on the horizon, as though fending off the unruly ocean.

Just like the scenery, very little in Leetown had changed since Aileen was first carried down the road to church in a basket. About ten years ago the footbridge across the Crannagh had lost a few planks and so had been repaired with new ones. A few years later another cottage had been built by the McDiarmids for their son and his new wife to start a family. And the summer before last Cready's had painted the outside of their shop red, whereas it had always been green before.

Much more had happened, but those were the highlights.

For years Aileen had been dreaming of meeting a man who would take her somewhere more exciting – Dublin perhaps – although in the back of her mind she wondered whether she would end up settling for a man from Leetown or one of the many similar towns that dotted the Wicklow coast.

She looked again at the girls sitting the other side of Briana, and wondered how many of them had similar dreams, and how many would eventually lock those desires away and lose the key.

Briana had once told her she had ideas above her station, probably because she'd been the first one in the family to be so serious about what their father had called 'the school thing with all its learning and books nonsense'. Aileen had told Briana not to be so daft, that the learning and books nonsense hadn't made any difference.

Briana nudged Aileen. 'Watch out. Men approaching.'

And she was right. Well, she wasn't quite right. The boys – definitely younger than Briana and probably younger than Aileen too – were dragging their feet in the sand, heads bowed. The bigger one spoke for them both.

'Would ye . . . ?' His head twitched nervously.

'What?' Aileen said.

'Would ye . . . sure, y'know.'

'Do I?'

Briana jumped to her feet and kicked her shoes off. 'Of course we would.' She nodded to her sister. 'Just excuse the sourpuss one here, will ye.'

Briana grabbed the silent boy by the hand, and Aileen stood up too, stepping out of her shoes with a little less haste than her sister had, to take the hand of the other one. He pulled her hand to his dirty mouth, kissed it quickly, then sniffed noisily.

'Charmed, I'm sure,' Aileen said.

'Ye what?' the boy blurted.

Aileen grunted a laugh. 'Nothing. C'mon and let's dance.'

Ten minutes later a breathless Briana and Aileen sat down.

''Tis grand, is it not?' Briana said, a smile beaming from between her ruddy cheeks.

''Tis, I have to admit,' Aileen said. 'Yer man's nothing more than a wee boy. He's half a foot shorter than me, and my toes are black and blue from his shoes stepping on my feet, but I haven't laughed so much for an absolute age.'

'And while The Emergency's on, you take what laughs you can get.'

'Ah, *The Emergency*,' Aileen said, doing her best to mimic her father's deep voice. She threw her eyes upward. 'Sure, now you're after spoiling it, mentioning that.'

'Forget I said it. Let's just listen to the music.'

Aileen tried, but it wasn't easy. She didn't follow politics, leaving that to Daddy and her brothers, but everyone knew there was a war on.

Daddy had recently had what he called 'the electric' installed in Sweeney Cottage. He told everyone it was so they could get rid of the oil lamps and have switched lights, but they all knew it was so he could have a wireless machine to listen to the latest developments.

The news bulletins made them all aware of the war – *yet another unholy bloody mess*, as Daddy would say. And judging by the snippets

Aileen managed to hear, he had a point. It had been raging on for four years now, and apparently the rest of the world had gone mad, with every country declaring war on every other country and battles going on all over the place with no end in sight. But good old De Valera was resolutely keeping Ireland out of it. 'And a bloody good job too,' Daddy would say. 'The twenty-six counties have enough problems of their own without helping the bloody Brits, and sure, those bastards in London are still holding on to the six counties of the North like they own them.'

Aileen felt her shoulder being nudged by her sister, who was tapping her thighs in time with the music again and egging Aileen on to do the same. Aileen fixed a grin on to her face and obliged, humming and tapping along.

But then the music stopped, and all they could hear was the hiss and whistle of the tide. Aileen's father had told her when she was young that it was the gasp and blow of a snoring giant, and even now he occasionally mentioned it to remind her, so he said, that she was once his little girl. As Aileen smiled at the thought, a distant droning noise arrived to fill in the gaps between the giant's breaths.

All eyes turned to the road. It was a truck, its colour hard to judge, winding along the road that dropped over the hill into Leetown. A vehicle was a rare sight since fuel had been rationed. Someone said the word 'Army' and people started nodding. That would explain it. It was the Army, exempt from the rationing that normal folk had to put up with. No pony and trap for them.

The truck pulled up at the far end of the wooden footbridge and two soldiers jumped out of the back. While they shared a cigarette and surveyed the coastal scenery, two more got down from the cab and started walking – almost marching – across the footbridge and toward the makeshift dance floor.

A few of the people around Aileen took a step away, as though steeling themselves for bad news or even to run off.

But the two men stopped some distance away, and one took the lead, taking another step forward and having a good look at them all – as though assessing them, Aileen thought. She also noticed he had darker hair than the average Irishman and stood bolt upright as if to make the most of his height. 'Evening, everybody,' he shouted across casually. 'Will there be a grocery shop in this village?'

At first nobody answered, the break and suck of the waves the only sounds.

Then Aileen piped up. 'Open at this hour?' she said. 'Sure, you'll be lucky.'

Briana hissed her name, scolding her.

But the man just glanced at his fellow soldier, appearing to mumble something and laugh. Then he shouted across, 'Could somebody with a little sense just tell us where this shop is, please?'

'Just around the corner, past the Station Road,' the accordion player said. 'Red front. Name of Cready. But . . .'

'But what?'

'The girl's right. She'll be closed at this hour.'

'I wasn't asking about that,' the soldier said. 'But thank you for your help.' He turned to go, but Aileen thought she caught him staring at her for a second or two before he and his fellow soldier started walking back to the truck.

'Just who do they think they are?' Aileen said to her sister.

'They *are* the army, Aileen.'

'And so what? I mean, the nerve of it, expecting the shop to be opening up just for them, just cause they're the . . . *aaiiirmeee*. Sure, what are they going to do, break in and thieve?'

Briana's face took on a pained expression. 'Aach, who cares, Aileen? They're gone. Let's just have ourselves another dance and forget it.'

One of the banjo players tapped his fingers three times on the wooden frame of his instrument and the music restarted.

Chapter 2

Twenty minutes later, Aileen and Briana were still waiting to be asked for another dance.

'You've scared them all off,' Briana said. 'You with your talking to the soldier like that.'

'Ah, c'mon,' Aileen said. 'Why don't you and me have a dance?'

'With who?'

'With each other, y'big eejit.'

Briana folded her arms. 'It'll look like we've been at the Guinness.'

Then the sound of a truck approaching stole their attention. It was the same truck and it pulled up at the same spot just the other side of the footbridge. This time all four soldiers got out, each of the last two lugging a wooden crate. One by one the instruments fell silent as everyone watched the soldiers cross the bridge, bottles from the crates clinking all the way.

'Good evening again,' the soldier at the front said loudly, his broad frame swaggering slightly as he walked toward them. It was the dark-haired one – the one Aileen had taken a little dislike to and hoped everyone else had too. He walked on, leading the other three to the sandpit of a dance floor, and soon the crates of drinks were set down on one of the wooden boxes.

The soldier who Aileen saw as the self-appointed leader grabbed a bottle, held the top of it against the edge of the crate and brought his hand down against it. There was a little foam spillage, but it looked very much like he'd done it before. He handed the bottle to the fiddle player and offered a few words of encouragement. The fiddle player held the bottle up to him for a moment by way of thanks, then took a few slugs. He bent down, twisted the base of the bottle into the sand, and started playing again while more bottles were opened.

Briana leaned into Aileen. 'If he offers you a drink of alcohol, the answer's no.'

'Might be, might not be.'

'Aileen, I promised Mammy I'd look after you. Don't make that hard for me.'

Bottles of beer were passed around the soldiers and the other men, then a few bottles of club orange and red lemonade were lifted out of the crates and opened. The self-appointed leader cradled a few bottles in his arm, approached the girls, and offered them around. He gave the last one to Briana, then turned to Aileen and grinned.

'One minute. I'll be getting another for the wee bold lady.'

'No need,' Aileen said. 'I'll not be touching stolen property.'

The man's carefree smile started to sink away as if the sand beneath his boots was swallowing it. 'Sure, that's right, because we've gone and shot yer man and raided his shop.'

'That isn't funny,' Aileen said.

The man huffed a breath. 'You're right. And being called a thief isn't a barrel of laughs either.'

'So you didn't steal them?'

He cast a glance at his army garb. 'What do *you* think?'

'I think you think you're funny.'

'And I think you think you're special. Now, will you be having a free drink or not?'

Aileen thought for a second and nodded.

As the soldier turned to go, he pointed at one of the others. 'That's Kevan, by the way. And he wants a dance with you.' He sauntered off, his boots dragging in the sand, before Aileen could say anything.

'Do you have to be so abrasive to the man?' Briana said to her once the soldier was out of earshot. 'They do this all the time. They're only wanting a dance and a laugh is all it is.'

Aileen looked at the back of the soldier in question, then at her sister. 'Maybe. But he doesn't have to be such an arrogant one with it.'

'Aach, away with ye.' One of the other soldiers approached Briana just as Kevan offered Aileen a drink. 'And stay where I can see you,' Briana said as a parting shot.

Aileen gave a wry smile. She grabbed the bottle from Kevan and started to pour it down her throat. She faltered halfway and coughed.

'I'm Kevan.'

'I know. I'm Aileen.'

'Shall we dance?'

'Wait.' Aileen took a few breaths before downing the rest of the bottle and setting down the empty. 'C'mon,' she said, grabbing his hand.

Aileen had only ever danced properly with her brothers and father and the odd cousin, but knew a good dancer when she saw one – meaning when her toes didn't get hurt. Kevan had a nice smile too, but above that nice smile rested a big strawberry nose about twenty years too old for him. So he was a nice man and nothing more.

'Would you like to sit?' he said after a while. 'I could be getting you another drink.'

At first she hesitated, but a glance at the lonely women swayed her. Perhaps she should start to get to know him better before holding the nose thing against him.

'That'll be grand,' she said. She sat, deliberately some distance away from the other women, while he trotted across the sand and fetched another bottle.

'You're a good dancer, so y'are,' Aileen said when he returned and handed her the drink.

'Thanks. I used to go twice a week with the wife.'

Aileen choked on her first mouthful.

'Are y'all right there?' Kevan said.

'No,' she spluttered. 'You're married?'

He took a slug of the Guinness and wiped the creamy froth from the corner of his mouth with a knuckle. 'I am. Six years now and still happy.' Aileen could tell from his frown that he meant it. 'I'm sorry,' he said. 'I wasn't meaning to deceive you.'

'Ah, no.' Aileen shrugged. ''Tis only a little dance. Nothing more.'

'Grand. For myself too. I miss my wife and it's nice to meet a pretty girl.'

'Thanks. And you're a bit of a catch yourself.' She resisted the temptation to add, *in spite of the nose thing you have going on there*. To dispel the thought she said, 'Have y'any children?'

'We have. Two boys.'

'Grand.'

He looked around, his eyes finally settling on the grey cloud creeping up on them. Aileen followed his lead and watched too.

He let out a sigh. 'Sure, I've just killed the conversation, have I not?'

He was right, but he seemed a sweet sort. It didn't seem right to agree.

'Where have you come from?' she said.

'Ah, the barracks. The Curragh Camp just over the border in County Kildare. We just needed supplies. Potatoes, milk and bread.'

'And the black stuff?' She nodded to his bottle.

'Niall's idea.'

'Niall?' She looked over at the other solder – the one who'd been forward with her before. 'You're meaning that arrogant sort?'

He laughed. 'Arrogant? Sure, tis a strong word, but . . .'

'But he'll beat you up if you call him that?'

This time his laugh was a little too raucous for Aileen's liking. 'We're best pals, me and young Niall. Tis only his way. He wouldn't beat anybody up outside of battle. I'd say he was only thirsty.'

'So how did you get into the shop?'

He winked at her. 'Tis a secret.'

'Ah now, you're as bad as yer Niall fellow.'

'No, no. I'm joking. We're the army. Shops open up for us.'

'So, you didn't thieve anything?'

'Ah, c'mon now, Aileen.' He went to speak again but a raindrop hit him straight in the eye. They both looked up, neither surprised at how dark the sky had suddenly become.

'Tis warm and wet,' Kevan said as more drops hit his face. Then he looked where Aileen was looking, at the people now heading for the wooden bridge.

Aileen hurriedly shoved her feet back into her shoes. 'We have a saying about the rain in Leetown,' she said, checking the dark spots appearing ever more quickly on her dress.

'What'll that be?'

'Run!' she screamed out.

And, as the rain thickened to sheets, that was what she did. She heard Kevan laugh out loud behind her, then saw him overtake her as she approached the footbridge.

'Sure, a soldier can't be beaten by a girl!' he shouted back as he ran on to the bridge, his boots thundering across the wooden boards.

And then Aileen felt her body twist to the side. She saw the full ashen sky and gasped in shock as her back thumped on to the ground. She was now still, and could feel the rain pattering on to her face, washing off her carefully applied make-up, most likely soaking her pretty dress too. But there was something else: a burning, throbbing pain shooting across the outside of her ankle.

She lifted up her head and shoulders and stretched a supporting hand out on to the cold sand. She started to get to her feet but shrieked in pain and instinctively reached to her ankle. For a few seconds the pain kept her body rigid. It was then that she felt a warm hand on her back and heard a voice.

'Looked nasty,' the voice said, heavy and strong enough to be heard above the hiss of the rain.

She glanced up and saw Niall, the water dripping off his cap like a leaky gutter. In his hand he had one of her shoes – minus the heel.

'No wonder you stumbled and fell over,' he said. 'Right nasty thump it looked. Are you all right?'

'I'm just grand. Sure, I'm forever breaking my ankle. Twice a day, sometimes.'

'Would you like me to—'

'No, I wouldn't.'

She glared at him for a moment. *Was he trying not to laugh?* Either way, he ignored her words and went to put his arm around her. He hesitated for a moment, then removed his cap, shook the excess water off and placed it on her head.

Then she felt herself being lifted, one of his arms under her back, one under her knees. For a second it was uncomfortably close for a man she didn't know, and she knew Daddy would certainly have disapproved. After that second the pain in her ankle took over and she shrieked again.

'I'm sorry,' he said. He glanced around, first assessing the truck on the other riverbank, then the footbridge, and finally the railway bridge. 'Here, this'll do for now.' He carried her, striding along as if she were weightless, to the patch of riverbank beneath the railway bridge.

Aileen gasped and braced herself as he motioned to let her down, imagining her foot striking the earth. But it was a slow, cushioned landing, Niall's solid arms effortlessly supporting her until he'd said, 'Be sure to keep the weight off that foot, won't ye.'

'You think I should?' she replied. 'And here was me about to run home.'

'Have it your own way,' Niall said.

They sat together with their backs resting against the concrete supports, and for a moment his head was inches from hers, his shock of black hair now a solid wet lump. A hand that seemed too large for a man of his height came up to his face, and a thick thumb and forefinger pinched a stubborn dewdrop of rain from the tip of his bent nose.

He shuffled a respectable distance away from her. 'In all fairness, that was a daft thing for me to say.'

'Twas so.' Aileen dragged her eyes away from his face. Under the bridge it was dark and musty, but made for a cosy shelter, with only the occasional drip of water from above.

They stayed there for a few minutes, she gasping in pain, he looking out at the heavy rain that had turned the river's surface to a coarse mass of tiny explosions. Then she flinched a little as he reached up to her head. He plucked the cap off, stepped to the river's edge, drenching his boots in the process, and used the cap to scoop up some water. 'Here,' he said, kneeling down at her feet, 'let me look.' After rinsing the mud off her ankle, he lifted it slightly, his hand supporting the flesh of her calf, and looked at the swollen area from a few angles. 'Can you move your toes?' he said.

She did, wincing with the pain.

He nodded. 'Ah, tis only a sprain. You must have gone over on it. You've to rest it for a few days. It'll be fine after that.'

She eyed him suspiciously, not completely sure whether he was joking or serious. 'Are you a doctor?'

He shook his head firmly. 'Used to play a lot of the football and the hurling. I've seen my fair share of broken and bashed-up legs over the years.' He winked at her then added, 'None as nice as yours, I have to say.'

She shot him a glance she hoped would convey contempt.

'I'm sorry, was that too bold of me?' He spent a few moments fiddling with his soggy cap before adding, 'Would you like me to carry you home when the rain's stopped?'

'No,' she said. 'No, I wouldn't.'

'Ah, right.' He nodded a little too agreeably for Aileen's liking, his fingers nervously kneading his cap.

They spent a few more minutes motionless, he admiring the view, she resting and groaning with the pain. Then he pulled a handkerchief from his pocket, leaned down and soaked it in the river. He stepped back and started wrapping it around her ankle, tying the corners in a knot.

'That's cold,' she said.

'I know. But it'll help. Believe me.' He looked at her face, which she knew couldn't have been the prettiest sight in Wicklow, not that it mattered.

'Football and hurling?' Aileen said.

He nodded. 'Hurling's my favourite.' He tapped his nose. 'That's what happened to this.'

'Well, it's plain you weren't born with it that shape.'

'Sure, that's a little harsh.'

'Tis,' Aileen said. 'I'm sorry.'

'I'm joking.'

Aileen sighed, then tried to readjust her position, the movement making her flinch.

'Is the pain really that bad?' he said.

At first she didn't answer, but within a minute she became more conscious of him looking at her. She relaxed a little as she exhaled long and slow. 'Actually, tis waning off a bit.'

'Good.' He craned his neck to look out from under the bridge to the sky. 'Bit like the rain. Twas nothing more than a heavy shower.'

'What were you doing back there anyway?'

He frowned. 'Where?'

'Behind me. You were on the strand behind me, weren't you?'

'Sure, I was collecting up all the bottles to take back to the shop.'

'I see. To get the money back on them.'

'Ah, no. We just told yer man we'd do that for him. And I don't want to get into trouble with the army.' He kneaded his cap some more, then peered along the river which once again offered a smooth mirror to the sky.

She followed his gaze and said, 'Rain's completely stopped.'

'Now to get you home.' He stepped toward her.

'Not just yet,' she said. 'A few minutes more.'

'Grand.' He nodded. 'I'm Niall, by the way. Niall O'Rourke.'

'And I'm Miss Sweeney. But I'll let you call me Aileen.'

'In that case I think I will.'

'Ah, you should. Tis my name.'

'Aileen.' He glanced away in thought and back again. 'Tis a lovely name, all right. Is the other one your sister?'

'Does it show?'

'Sure, you could be twins – very pretty twins with that dark red hair, the button noses and the green eyes. I think you have one or two more freckles than her though.'

Aileen screwed her eyes up at him. 'Heck, you really are an extremely bold thing, aren't you?'

'I try it on. Tis only to cover up my shyness.' He winked at her again.

'And you've something wrong with your eye there – makes you look a right eejit when you close it quickly like that.'

'Ah, right. Should I stop that?'

'You should. Tell me, d'you have any sisters yourself?'

Niall started swiping a few fingers over his cap, evading her eyes. He shook his head.

'Ah, all brothers, is it then?'

Aileen waited. He went to speak, but it was only a breath, not an answer.

Then a voice calling Aileen's name made them look across the river. Niall stepped out from under the bridge and looked toward the footpath in front of the row of houses. He squinted at the sun, now low in the sky and making a bright arc under the edge of a cloud.

They heard the voice again.

'That'll be herself,' Aileen said, trying to get up. 'My sister, Briana.'

'I should be carrying you.' Niall reached out to her. 'I'm serious. You'll be needing to keep the weight off your foot for two days at the very least.'

As she raised herself on to her good foot he placed a hand around her waist. Her instinct was to resist, but a glance at the warm dusk glow resting on his face stopped her. It seemed a different face to the one she'd seen when they'd first met.

'Would you mind?' she said. ''Tis awful painful still.'

He said nothing, but swept her up as effortlessly as he had ten minutes before, and carried her over to the footbridge and then across it, to where Briana was waiting.

'What in the name of God's happened here?' Briana said. 'I turned around and you'd gone, so you had. I was sick with worry.'

'Language,' Aileen said, smirking. 'I'll tell Mammy what you said.'

'She slipped and fell,' Niall said. 'Hurt her ankle. You must be Briana. Excuse me if I don't shake your hand.'

'Is she hurt badly?'

'No. Well, not so much that she can't crack a few bad jokes.'

'He's going to carry me home,' Aileen said, pointing the way. 'Better that than I try to walk on it.'

'I see,' Briana said as they started walking. 'But Daddy won't approve of his youngest daughter turning up like this.'

'Ah, stop your worrying,' Aileen muttered.

Niall turned his head to face Briana. 'It'll be grand. I can let her down quietly just before we reach your place. Sure, she can hop the rest of the way with an arm around your shoulder.'

'And what about your truck? Won't it go without you?'

'That's hardly likely when I have the keys here in my pocket.'

'Well, if you're sure you don't mind.'

'Excuse my sister,' Aileen said. 'She thinks I'm twelve, so she does.'

He smiled. 'Tis a reassurance, having a sister to look after you.'
Aileen detected a stutter in his walk as he spoke the words, and thought
she saw a hint of pain flash across his face. Then he smiled again and
carried on. 'Sure, y'aren't living in Dublin, are ye?'

'Tis just the other end of the village,' Briana said.

'Not even a light training exercise for a big brawny soldier boy like
yourself,' Aileen added, giggling as she spoke.

Niall turned to Briana. 'Will ye get this one? I'm after saving her
from certain death and carrying her all the way home, and all she can
do is give me the lip.'

'Aileen will be Aileen. Tis what our mammy always says about her.'

'She's the black sheep of the family then?'

'More of a lamb, but yes.'

'You two,' Aileen said as they all crossed the road. 'Will ye not be
talking about me as if I'm not here.'

Niall laughed. 'Sure, my arms won't let me forget you're here.'

'Are you saying I'm heavy?'

'I'm not, but if my arms could talk, who knows what they might
say.'

She gasped. 'Ah, so now who's being full of the lip? Soldier boy
Niall, that's who.'

They reached the corner of their house, and Briana stood in front,
blocking Niall's path. 'You can let her down here,' she said. 'I'll be
taking her the rest of the way.'

'Of course.' He gently lowered her, holding her steady until she'd
planted her good foot on the ground and looped an arm around Briana.

'Thank you for your help,' Briana said, and started pulling Aileen
away – a little too quickly for Aileen's liking.

'Thank you so much for saving my life,' Aileen said to Niall
theatrically. 'What can I ever do to repay you?'

'Has she been at the drink?' Niall said to Briana.

'I'm drunk on pain is what I am,' Aileen moaned.

'Right,' Briana said. 'That's enough, the both of you. Thank you for your help, Niall, and goodnight.'

Niall pulled his cap from his pocket and fixed it on his head as he stepped back. 'Ah, twas nothing. Perhaps I'll be seeing the two of yez again sometime.'

'If I survive this mortal wound,' Aileen shouted back at him.

'Will ye shut up,' Briana said. 'Calm down or Daddy will think you really have been at the Guinness.'

A few awkward paces on, Aileen hooked her head around and looked back. There was nobody. Niall had gone, and she felt a sudden, confusing emptiness.

'C'mon,' Briana said. 'Let's get your foot rested.'

Aileen shivered.

'And you're soaked through too – aren't you cold?'

'I am, now you mention it. I just . . . I didn't realize.'

'We'll get you inside and in front of the fire.' Briana reached for the door handle and whispered, 'And no mention of soldiers, d'you hear?'

Before the door was shut behind them their mother was there, asking what had happened, helping support Aileen, eyeing her up and down, and asking again what in God's name had happened. Their father was slower, hovering a few feet away, letting his frown speak for him.

'Calm down, Mammy,' Aileen said.

Her mother addressed Briana. 'I thought I told you to look after your sister?'

'She's fine,' Briana said.

''Tis only a sprained ankle,' Aileen added. 'I'm going to live.'

Her father stepped forward. 'Don't be talking to your mother like that, Aileen.'

There was more fuss and reprimand, mostly aimed at Briana, but a few minutes later the mood had settled and the sisters were sitting on the floor next to the fire, each clasping a cup of hot milk in their hands. Frank, their youngest brother, had already gone to bed, Fergus and Gerard were playing cards with their father at the table, and their mother occupied herself wringing out the men's washed work clothes in a metal tub then draping them on a metal stand in front of the fire.

'I don't understand,' Aileen whispered to her sister. 'What did you mean by "No mention of soldiers"? What's so wrong with soldiers?'

'Ah, nothing so bad. You know what Daddy's like when he's been drinking – he can get a little angry at anything that doesn't suit him, and sometimes there's no knowing what suits him. You don't want to shock him for no good reason by mentioning the poor man bringing you home.'

'For no good reason?'

Briana tutted. 'Ah, c'mon now. You're hardly likely to be seeing him again, are you?'

'Why ever not?'

'He'll be from some barracks heaven knows where, and—'

'What are the two of yez whispering about?' their father shouted across from the table as Gerard shuffled the pack.

'Ah, nothing, Daddy. Just girl talk.'

'Not about men, is it?' Fergus said. 'You have to be looking out for yourselves these days.'

'*Men?*' their father said, almost roaring the word out. 'You'd better not be courting behind my back.'

'Not forgetting your brothers,' Fergus said, nudging Gerard, who just nodded in support. 'We'll give any man the once-over for you, just say the word.'

Gerard nodded again, then dealt out the new hand, and the trio returned their attention to the card game.

'Anyhow,' Aileen whispered to Briana, 'I might be wanting to see him again.'

'So what'll you be doing – calling him on one of those telephone things?'

'I might.'

'And where will you be doing that then?'

'Ah, won't ye shut up, Briana.'

Briana laughed. 'Sure, he's the first boy you've met from another county and you're hooked, so y'are.'

'Shut up!'

'What's this all about?' their mother said, placing a wicker basket of wet clothes on the floor. 'Now stop with your being nasty, Aileen. Tis your sister here, don't forget.'

Aileen looked straight at Briana and frowned.

'I'm sorry,' Briana replied to her mother. 'Tis my fault.'

'Well, you can both be sorry from the bedroom now,' their mother replied. 'I'll be hanging the rest of these in front of the remains of the fire. Come on, move it.'

Briana stood and helped Aileen to her feet, and their father followed suit. 'Come on, my boys,' he said to Fergus and Gerard. 'You'll have to be waiting until tomorrow to win your money back.'

Briana and Aileen headed for what the Sweeneys still called 'the children's bedroom' together with Fergus and Gerard. They all said their goodnights and asked God to bless one another, then their mother turned the lights out.

In a silent full darkness they all undressed down to their underwear. Fergus and Gerard got into one bed, the girls into the other, taking care not to disturb young Frank on a small affair in the corner.

Aileen pulled the woollen cover up to her neck to keep out the creeping night cold, and soon all she could hear was the occasional crackle from the fire in the living room. And Gerard snoring.

She said the word 'Niall' in her head over and over again, then told herself not to be so stupid and to get some sleep. But as she turned over, her thoughts switched from Niall to her brothers and sisters. Not those in the room with her, but the other ones. The older ones who had already escaped Leetown.

The oldest was Alannah, who'd married a farmer's son (and very wisely too, according to Mammy and Daddy) and moved to the west coast. Bernard was living and working 'somewhere in England', according to Mammy, to the clear disapproval of Daddy, who thought the Brits had taken enough from Ireland (not forgetting that they were still stubbornly holding on to a part of it). James and Cathleen were both working in two of the big shops in Dublin and made regular visits back home, mainly – so Aileen thought – to take delight in telling everyone how exciting the Big Smoke was, and how they couldn't possibly (that was *possibly*, like an actor would say it) consider moving back to Leetown.

Then her thoughts turned to the ones who were yet to escape. Gerard was the oldest still at home – although Fergus behaved like *he* was. To Aileen's knowledge, neither was showing any interest in leaving. Aileen had been vaguely aware of Briana having had boyfriends, but clearly none who suited her.

A doctor had told Mammy to stop having children after Aileen had been born, but she couldn't resist 'going for the ninth', and that suited Aileen down to the ground because it meant that she wasn't forever the baby of the family, as Frank was always being called. At fourteen it was starting to become a little daft.

She fell asleep wondering and dreaming what the next few years might bring – where she might travel, what sort of a man she would marry, and where she would settle.

At the Curragh Camp, County Kildare, Kevan had dropped the truck off at the compound and all four soldiers were strolling to the barracks.

'You're awful quiet, Niall,' Kevan said. 'Tisn't like you. Not at all.'

'Ah, I'm just tired.'

'What did you think of Africa falling?'

Niall's footsteps stuttered for a second. 'Africa's fallen?'

'Heck, Niall. I'm after telling you not half an hour since. I heard just before we left the barracks. The Germans and Italians have been kicked out of Africa. I must say, I got the impression you weren't listening.'

'No, in all fairness I was listening all right. I'm just after forgetting.'

'We all know what your mind is on,' one of the others said. 'The lass you carried home.'

'Sure, tis not. Tell me more about the Africa thing.'

'There's not much to tell,' Kevan said. 'They think Italy's the next target for the Allies though.'

'Italy,' Niall said. 'Right.'

'Never mind all that,' the fourth soldier said. 'Does anyone fancy an hour of cards before bed?'

They all did, although Niall needed a little persuasion.

Chapter 3

For the next few days Aileen felt an inch taller. At least, she would have done if it weren't for her bad ankle. And before long that was as right as Leetown rain. The soldier had been right. She remembered his name – Niall – but there was no missing him, only a breaking awareness of just how enjoyable life could be once she was away from the stifling blanket of her family. Niall was a just a soldier boy, one of many men. Whatever anyone told her, she would take her time and pick and choose. Of course, Mammy was quite sure she wanted Aileen to marry a Wicklow man. She'd said so. But she'd probably also said the same thing to Alannah, and she was half a world away on the other side of the country. So, Mammy was good, Mammy was helpful, but she was also happy to let her children make their own decisions. Daddy, on the other hand . . . Well, Aileen didn't even *dare* consider telling him that she had her own ideas about what sort of a man she wanted to marry.

One day when Aileen was fully recovered, the whole family had walked a mile and a half to the local peat bogs, spent an hour cutting out blocks and loading them on to a borrowed cart, and were now getting a borrowed donkey to bring the cart back to the cottage.

Aileen's father led the donkey, with her mother close by. Her brothers were walking on one side of the cart, she and Briana on the other.

'We should go in the sea when we get back,' Briana said to Aileen as they walked alongside. Aileen looked at her curiously. 'To wash off the dirt and sweat,' Briana added.

Aileen looked at the palms of her hands. 'Sure, I'm not that dirty.'

'I still think we should,' Briana said, a little more slowly and firmly.

Aileen was about to disagree because she knew the sea was freezing cold even in summer, but something was wrong. Aileen knew her sister, and she especially knew that look she was giving her.

'Ah, sure then,' she said, immediately noticing how relieved Briana looked.

When they got home they all helped load the blocks of peat into the store just outside the cottage door, and Daddy told his sons to return the donkey and cart to the McCoys at the far end of the village. Briana and Aileen said they were going to wash in the sea and left.

'I had to get you on your own,' Briana said as they crossed the road and stepped on to the grass verge.

'How so?'

Briana glanced back. 'Let's wait till we get down to the sea.'

They left their shoes on the grassy verge and headed for the water. A cool breeze made them shiver slightly, in contrast to the stillness of the peat bogs, where a breeze would have been welcome. But they padded along, doing their best to zigzag through the sandy stretches and avoid the sharp shingle.

'C'mon and tell me the big secret,' Aileen said.

They stopped just before the line of the tide.

'Yer man was asking after you.'

'What man?'

'Aileen Sweeney, you can stop that right now.' She wagged a finger at Aileen's face. 'I can see by the way you tilt your head and look all coy, you know *exactly* what man I mean.'

'You mean that soldier fellow? Sure, I've forgotten all about him.'

Briana folded her arms. 'So what was his name then?'

'Ah . . . I'm not sure. I think it might have been Niall.'

'Right, well, the man who *might have been Niall but you're not sure*, well, he crept up behind me when I was coming back from the well this morning. Said something a little too bold for my liking, so he did.'

Aileen's face dropped a little, her nostrils twitched. 'He did *what?*'

'Ah, calm down. Sure, he thought I was you. As soon as I turned around he apologized, said he'd been waiting around the corner from the cottage, waiting for you, and had forgotten how alike we looked.'

'Ah, right.'

'He said I've to ask you whether you'll meet up with him again.'

'I might.'

'You *might?* But . . .'

As Briana hesitated, Aileen broke into a gallop and headed into the sea. A piercing scream came from her as she quickly went in deeper, eventually stopping where water splashed around her knees. She rubbed her hands together in the water then looked up. A seagull banked on the breeze and seemed to squawk at her. She shouted back at it, '*Holy Mother of God, tis cold!*' and started splashing the water on to her head and neck, wiping away the sweat and dirt.

Briana appeared at her side and started washing too, preferring a whoop to protest against the chill leaching the very life from her flesh. 'Aileen will be Aileen!' she shouted.

Thirty seconds later, both girls ran back up the beach, shaking their arms in a futile attempt to dry them off. They stopped by their shoes and took a minute to wipe the excess water off their skin. Briana stood behind Aileen, wound her hair into a rope and gently squeezed the tangled mass, letting the water drip between them. Aileen was doing the same to Briana's hair when Briana spoke.

'So,' she said.

'So what?'

'So, he wants to see you again.'

'Oh, he does, does he?'

'He does. Today. Ow!'

Aileen turned her sister around to face her. 'What did you say?'

'That hurt, Aileen.'

'Never mind your hair, what about Niall?'

'Haven't I been trying to explain? I told him you weren't interested in seeing him again, but he said he'd wait for us by the bridge at midday regardless.'

'And . . . when's that?'

They both stared up at the sun, high in the sky.

'Oh heck,' Aileen said. She opened her arms wide, displaying her sodden dress and salty, matted hair. 'Look at me, I'm a mess.'

'I tried to tell you, but you wouldn't listen.'

Aileen started to run, leaving Briana to pick up the shoes and chase her across the grass verge, over the road and into the cottage.

Their mother, busy peeling potatoes, froze for a second and watched them bolt inside and run to the fire. 'What in the name of all that's holy is going on here?' she sang.

'I have to go out, Mammy,' Aileen said.

'We both do,' Briana added quickly. 'We've . . . we've arranged to meet a few friends from the village and . . . ah . . . we forgot with all the turf-cutting and things.'

Their mother gave them each a puzzled look, then slowly returned to peeling.

'Mammy, do I have a clean dress?' Aileen said.

'You need a clean dress just to see a few friends?'

Aileen didn't know how to answer that, and her mother continued before she got the chance.

'No matter. You could take a look in the press.'

Aileen jumped up and went into the bedroom, to the closet she shared with the other four – although Aileen and Briana used most of the space. She heard mumbling from her mother and sister, but didn't care to worry about that.

Twenty minutes later, wearing a clean dress and with her hair brushed as best she could – well, as best *Briana* could – with a brief slap of face powder and a swipe of lipstick, Aileen headed for the bridge, Briana in tow.

'Do you think Mammy suspects?' she said to Briana.

Briana giggled. 'Suspects? D'you think she's daft? As soon as you went to the press she whispered, "Is it a boy?" to me.'

Aileen stopped. 'And what did you say?'

'Relax, Aileen. It's nothing to worry about. I told her it was a man, not a boy, and she told me to look after you.'

'Ah, right.'

'And don't say it like that. You know I would anyway. And remember, you're after telling me how you're not really interested in this Niall fellow, but when it comes to actually meeting him – oh well, then you go off like a crazy thing and fret about how you look and your wet dress and your hair . . . and . . . are you laughing at me, Aileen? Why are you laughing?'

Aileen's twitching lips gave way to a loose shriek.

'What is it now? What did I say?'

'Ah, Briana, you're like an old mother hen, so y'are.'

They started walking again, Aileen taking long, leisurely strides, a red-faced Briana almost strutting to keep up.

'I'm sorry,' Aileen said as they approached the corner toward the end of the village. 'I know you're only trying to look after me.'

'I am. And while I'm being mother hen, don't agree to meet him again straight away.'

'What?'

'Turn him down at first.'

'Why?'

'Because good girls keep them waiting a little.'

Before Aileen had a chance to reply, the footbridge came into view, and they saw a figure leaning against the handrail.

Aileen's pace quickened. 'Do you have to stay with us?' she said. 'Sure, you could go home. I'll be all right on my own.'

Briana shook her head. ''Tis the way. I can't be leaving the two of you alone – not until yer man's met Daddy and Daddy says he's good enough to be courting you.'

'Right. So, just be quiet and pretend you aren't here.'

A few seconds later Niall stepped away from the handrail, one hand holding his cap, the other flattening down his dense, black hair.

'So you came,' he said as Aileen approached.

Aileen waited until she was closer before saying, 'I thought I might,' and swaying her shoulders a little. She looked at the sky. ''Tis drying and I have nothing else on today.' She heard Briana tut but didn't react.

Niall stepped forward and gave Aileen a kiss on the cheek. 'And one for the lovely chaperone too,' he said, doing likewise to Briana.

'Let's go for a walk on the strand,' Aileen said.

They crossed the bridge and started walking slowly along the beach, Niall and Aileen sticking close, her shoulder occasionally touching his arm, while Briana stayed a few yards further out.

'So, tell me about your family,' Niall said. 'Apart from the lovely Briana here.'

Aileen told him about the ones who had flown the nest, the ones who probably should have flown the nest by now, herself and young Frank, and finally the ones who owned the nest.

'So, what's your da like?' Niall said.

'You're wanting to meet him?'

'I might. Depends how yerself behaves.' He grinned.

'And what about you? No sisters, only brothers, isn't that it?'

His grin fell away, replaced by a hint of sourness. 'Didn't I tell you? I'm an only child.'

'Oh.'

''Tis very unusual, I know. My da, he . . . ah . . . he died while Ma was with child.'

'You mean, expecting you?'

He started laughing again. 'Ah, that'll be a yes to that one.'

'Sure, I'm embarrassed now. You've embarrassed me. I'm going all blushed. Am I going all blushed?' She covered her face with a hand for a moment. 'I'm sorry. You're an only child and your mother was with child and . . . yes, of course. Sorry for being such an eejit. I'm not always like that.'

'I'm sure you're not.'

'And I'm sorry about your father. What happened to him?'

'Oh, he was a soldier – got killed fighting in the war.'

'Aach, that's terrible.'

'Sure twas, but I'm grand now.'

'You must miss him.'

Niall turned to Briana. 'Sure, your sister's on top form today, isn't she?'

'Ah, no,' Aileen said. 'I see that you never met him, but you can still miss a person you've never met.'

He narrowed his eyes at her. 'Now, you're either wriggling your way out of that one or you're a very deep person.'

'Deep?'

'Complicated.'

Aileen thought for a moment then nodded. 'I think I like that. Sure, who wants to be plain and simple? There's no point in being just the same as all the others. Complicated I'll take as flattery – as if you'll be wanting to court me.'

He stopped walking for a moment to look her up and down. 'Mmm . . . sure, I fancy giving you a chance, all right.'

She tilted her head to one side. 'A regular charmer, so y'are. But *I* might not even want to give *you* a chance.'

''Tis up to you if you want to miss out.'

'Ha? Me miss out? Now you're flattering yourself, mister soldier boy. I have so many admirers I can't count them all.'

'So, would you like me to court you?'

'Ah, no. Tis up to you to ask me properly. Tis the way things are.'

Niall took her hand, lifted it up as if it were a delicate work of art, and kissed it. 'Yes,' he said, his face now taking on a straight and solemn expression. 'I'd like to court you, and yes, I'd like to do it properly, so I need to meet your da.'

The gesture caught Aileen off guard. Here she was, trying to be casual and full of good humour, and he sprang something just a little too serious. *Meeting Daddy? Really?* Of course, despite the jokes, she wanted to be courted by Niall, but in the back of her mind there was a darker feeling – a fear. Of what she wasn't sure, but Daddy could be very harsh when he wanted to be. And then there was Briana's advice to turn him down the first time. She didn't want to do that. Briana could take her own advice.

'I don't know,' she said eventually. 'I'm not sure.'

Niall frowned. 'What's wrong?' He turned his back on Briana and stepped up close to Aileen, so close that for a fleeting moment the smell of his sweat and the starch of his uniform overpowered the fresh sea air. It didn't make sense, but somehow Aileen liked the smell. He hooked his head back to check Briana was some distance away. 'Leave the jokes, Aileen,' Niall said in a rasping whisper. 'I don't know what it is, and I could be wrong, but I think you're lovely. Sure, you're a real beauty, but—'

Aileen filled his pause with a thank you, aware that her voice was wavering, almost warbling, as she felt weak, but also enthused, her head fizzing with excitement but her mouth shy.

'—but there's something else,' he continued. 'You're different. I mean, in a good way. We have a good laugh, we get on like good friends. And I'd like to meet you again – meet you alone. I can take care of you, best behaviour and everything. What do you say?'

Aileen gulped. It was serious – at that precise moment it was strangely more serious than anything she'd ever known. This was no longer about having a laugh and a joke, she was being taken seriously as a woman. It felt good, uplifting even – as though her body was about to float off the very sand she stood on. Either that or she was about to faint.

The only reason she didn't was probably Briana suddenly shouting, 'What are the two of yez whispering about?' from further down the beach, which startled her.

Or it could have been Niall's warm smile and honest eyes set in that jet-black frame of hair, or even his hand, quietly strong as it had crept unnoticed around her torso, pulling her closer as they walked on.

'Could I give you a kiss?' he said.

She felt the flesh on her face glow warm. 'Of course not,' she heard herself say. 'I hardly know you.' Then she realized it was said more by instinctive reaction than any conscious wish. It was too early. Good girls left them waiting a little.

'That's a shame,' he said, disappointed but covering himself with another one of those winks in her direction.

Aileen stopped walking, faced him directly, and saw it again: a kindness in his eyes, a depth to his smile she hadn't seen in anyone before. 'Ah, go on then,' she said.

Good girl or not, what was the harm?

He took a step closer to her, closer than any man had ever been since she used to fight with her brothers – brothers who had only been boys at the time. He raised a hand and she felt the back of his fingers brush against her cheekbone. She had to force a dry swallow and realized her smile had vanished, replaced by a fear that she felt invigorating – a fear of want, a fear of the new. She sensed his forefinger circle the skin on the side of her neck and drift around to the nape. The tender fledgling hairs on the back of her neck bristled with a rare pleasure as he ran his fingertips lightly over them. Then she felt his firm hold, gently pulling her toward him, guiding her lips toward his. The kiss warmed her lips, but moreover sent a tremor throughout her body, weakening it, making her limbs go limp.

'Are you all right?' he said.

Her tongue flicked out and licked her lips, tasting where his kiss had been. She needed a couple of breaths before speaking. 'Grand,' she said in a broken, fluttering voice.

'Grand,' he repeated, his eyes lingering on her face. '*Now*, could I ask your da permission to court you?'

That was twice he'd asked. It seemed impolite to put him off again, and heck, *she didn't want to*. And if she wanted to be courted there was no choice in the matter – Daddy would have to approve. It was the way. Briana and everyone else had told her so.

'We'll see,' she said.

'Oh,' he said quietly. 'But I thought . . .'

'I said, *we'll see*.' And while his puppy-dog eyes were fixed on her face, she winked at him. It was instinctive, bold, and something Mammy would have been shocked to see.

Niall's head rolled back a fraction. 'Ah . . . I see.' He nodded between laughs. 'Do you have a wee problem with your eye there?'

'Perhaps I have. It's such a bad habit. I can't think where I picked it up from.'

Niall's laughter deepened.

An hour later, in the neighbouring county of Kildare, Niall took the truck back to the compound at the Curragh Camp and headed back to the barracks. At first he ambled, hands in pockets. There were a few greetings from fellow soldiers, including one or two knowing winks. He drew his hands from his pockets, took a few stiff breaths, and in the space of a few steps his amble turned to a confident stride past the canteen toward his dormitory.

'Tis himself,' Kevan said as Niall shut the door behind him.

'Certainly is.'

'Grand.' Kevan lowered his voice. 'There's something I need to ask you.'

Niall smiled as he leaned back on the doorframe and gazed into space. 'Whether I had a nice walk along the strand with the sweetest girl in County Wicklow?'

'Ah, no, Niall. Please don't tell me you're seeing the girl from the dance?'

'Do I detect a spot of jealousy?' Niall said. 'Jealous of me being a bachelor and yourself being . . .' He noticed Kevan's worried expression and his grin cracked. 'What?' he said. 'What is it?'

Kevan's boots clumped over the wooden floorboards. He opened the door and ushered Niall out first. 'C'mon,' he said as they both stepped out. 'Let's take a walk.'

Kevan headed for the recreation ground and Niall followed.

'This is hard for me, Niall. I've been volunteered by Jimmy and Dermot to talk to you.'

Chapter 4

Mr Sweeney nodded, as though weighing up a matter of life and death, then took a moment to warm his hands above the glowing peat fire.

'A soldier, y'say?'

'Stationed somewhere in County Kildare,' Briana replied.

'Ah, yes. They have the barracks there, sure they do. But . . . you don't think Aileen's a little too young to be courting?'

'She's eighteen, Daddy.'

'But she's a daft eighteen sometimes.'

'Ah, no. She's bold beyond her years, knows her own mind.'

'There's that, all right. Aileen will be Aileen.' He pointed his thumb at her. 'And tell me, what do *you* think of this fella?'

'He seems a grand sort.'

'And Aileen likes him, does she?'

'Oh, she does. They make a right pair, the two of them, if you know what I mean.'

'Because that's important to me.' He shifted in his seat. 'I don't want to see my own daughter getting let down by a man.'

'I don't think he's that sort, Daddy. He seems very nice.'

'You can never tell. But if he's a soldier . . . mmm, he'll be earning a steady shilling if nothing else. And he'd have to be fit and healthy to be a soldier. Does he look fit and healthy?'

'Sure, he's not what you'd call a tall man, but he has broad shoulders and he's fierce strong with it.'

'Good.' Her father sighed, as if that was his final word.

'So, you'll be happy to meet him?'

'I will.'

'Will you be here tomorrow evening?'

'Ah, well . . . mmm.'

'What?'

He gazed into the fire and paused for thought. 'Tis fine, so it is. I was going to see a farmer about swapping a couple of our chickens for a leg of pork, but a man wanting to be courting my youngest daughter is more important. Never let it be said that I don't care about my own daughter's future.' He looked up at Briana and took a moment to draw breath. 'And what about yourself, Briana? You're almost twenty-one now and not yet married.'

'Ah, I have enough time yet, Daddy.' She let out a nervous giggle. 'I'm busy looking after Aileen first. After that I can be searching for a husband of my own.'

'As long as he's better than the last two fellas you picked.'

Briana forced a smile she knew to be crooked. 'Anyway, shall I be asking Mammy to lay an extra place for tomorrow's tea?'

'Aye, you should do that. We might even have one of the chickens.'

'Thank you, Daddy. I'll . . . I'll just go and tell Aileen.'

But she had no need: Aileen was waiting just inside the bedroom listening to every word, hoping and praying that Daddy would agree to have Niall round for tea.

When Briana went in, Aileen gave her an open-mouthed grin and started doing an impromptu jig on the spot.

Briana had to smile. 'Ye daft article, ye.'

The next evening, the table was covered with a cloth, the cutlery was a little more neatly laid out than usual, and the butter was fresh from Cready's that day rather than the suspiciously yellow substance that they were all used to. It was clearly a special occasion, and by the look in their eyes, Aileen's brothers were anticipating a bigger and better meal than usual.

All the men had their hair combed flat, the women wore their second-best dresses, and little Frank had even washed his hands – an event as rare as hens' teeth, Mammy had said, after which Frank said she should know about that as she'd only that afternoon wrung the neck of one, gutted and plucked it. By now she'd roasted the creature and wasn't too far away from serving it up with a big pot of carrots and two huge pots of potatoes.

Daddy, Fergus and Gerard were sitting at the dinner table playing cards, something which spoiled the atmosphere according to Mammy, but when the knock on the door came they hurriedly gathered the cards up and put them away.

Mammy, Briana and Aileen exchanged expectant glances. Everyone knew whose duty it was to let guests into the cottage, and Mammy took off her apron and patted her hair as she stepped over and reached for the handle, letting out a barely audible cough as she opened the door.

And Niall was there, uniform and all, neat hair and all, clean face and all. Best of all, a bunch of lilies and roses sprouted from his fist. He'd obviously made a big effort, and Aileen could feel her excitement fit to burst out of her body, only just managing to keep control. Niall was also still, having the good sense to wait until he was asked before entering the cottage, although he took his cap off in expectation.

'These are for you, Mrs Sweeney,' he said. 'Well, for the house, I suppose.'

'Ah, they're beautiful, so they are. Lovely colours.' She turned to show them to her husband, who nodded and said, 'Grand.'

A few minutes later, after Niall had shaken everyone's hand, he sat down with Aileen's father at the table.

'Tis grand to meet you, Mr O'Rourke. I've heard a lot about you.'

'I hope it hasn't put you off,' Niall replied. 'And please, call me Niall. I'm quite an average man, and I'm only wanting your permission to court your daughter.'

'Average?'

'I mean, I haven't got wealth or anything. But I'm a hard worker and I have high hopes.'

Mr Sweeney nodded, then leaned forward to listen better. 'Tell me more about your background, son.'

And while Mammy looked after the food, the world stopped turning for the rest of them as they listened to the soldier man talking to the head of the house. A smile to all of them signified Niall had finished his speech.

'You must earn a shilling or two from the army?' Mr Sweeney said, then quickly held a hand up as if to take back the question. 'No, tisn't my intention to pry, but tis a secure job with decent money, I'd be guessing.'

Niall nodded. 'It's enough.'

'And tell me, do you save or spend, generally?'

'Well, ah . . .' Niall struggled to continue. 'Y'see, I send most of it back to my ma, my da being . . .'

'In the war. So I heard. Twas a terrible thing, that war to kick the Brits out of here. I remember it well.'

'Ah, no.' Niall smiled awkwardly. 'Twas the Great War, toward the end of it. 1918.'

'Ah, well . . . I see.' Daddy looked down and nodded a few times. 'I suppose a soldier is a soldier – we were all the same country back in them days whether we like it or not. And it must have been a terrible time for your ma.'

'Oh, she still talks about it, all right – the day she got the news.'

'And how is she keeping now?'

'She's grand, thank you for asking, Mr Sweeney.'

There was more talk of what Niall had done in the army – which seemed to be very little – before they were interrupted by Mammy serving up the tea. The two oldest boys got a leg each, Niall, Aileen, Briana and Frank shared the breast, and the parents settled for a wing each. On each plate, however, the piece of chicken was lost among a large pile of boiled carrots and a mountain range of half-mashed boiled potatoes with a river of molten butter running through it.

They all closed their eyes and said grace, after which the glasses were filled with water and the gravy boat was passed around.

Aileen, seated across the table from Niall, caught his eye and nodded madly at him. He looked to Briana for advice and she nodded just as vigorously.

They started eating, but Niall paused, cutlery in hand. 'So, Mr Sweeney, how would you feel about me courting Aileen?'

Everyone stopped what they were doing and looked at the head of the house.

Mr Sweeney took a long pause before pronouncing, 'Ah, twill be grand by me, son.'

Briana bowed her head, trying to hide a self-satisfied smile. Aileen and Niall stared at each other for a few seconds, until Aileen dared a quick grin, unseen by the others. Niall smiled back and everyone carried on eating.

'So, Mr Sweeney,' Niall said. 'What is it do you do for a living?'

'Oh, I just do a bit of helping out.'

Niall nodded, waiting for more, but it didn't come. 'Helping out?' he said. 'What exactly . . . ah . . .'

For a moment, knives stopped cutting and jaws stopping chewing. All eyes were on Niall.

'Aach, it doesn't matter,' he quickly added. 'Sure, as long as it pays the bills.'

'There's no shame in not having a trade.'

'Ah, now I wasn't suggesting otherwise, Mr Sweeney.'

'Of course you weren't. And we manage. A little labouring, a few errands here and there. We grow a lot of our own vegetables and keep chickens. We manage.'

'Tis a lovely cottage you have here,' Niall said, which earned another approving grin from Aileen.

Toward the end of the meal, as the plates became empty and the stomachs full, Mr Sweeney placed down his knife and fork and turned to Niall. 'So, what do you think of that there trouble going on beyond?' he said.

Niall took a moment to hurriedly finish his last mouthful before saying, 'You mean, the war?'

Mr Sweeney nodded. 'The thing they have with Germany.'

'Ah, tis very worrying, all right. But they say the tide is turning. The Germans and Italians have been pushed out of North Africa. They say Italy's likely to fall before the end of the year.'

'I can't say I follow it in too much detail, but tell me—' Mr Sweeney lowered his voice. '—is there any truth in the rumours?'

'Rumours?'

'I thought you might know, you being with the army and all that.'

Niall didn't speak, but glanced around the table for help, which was not forthcoming. 'I'm . . . I'm sorry,' he eventually said. 'I don't know what you mean, Mr Sweeney.'

'You can tell us, son. The rumours that the Irish Army are taking precautions to defend our country.'

'You mean, in case the Germans invade?'

Mr Sweeney laughed. 'Not at all. In case the *British* invade. Sure, they'd say it was strategic, like, to stop us siding with the Germans.'

Niall hesitated, shrugging awkwardly. 'Ah, I'm sure we wouldn't be wanting to do that – siding with the Germans.'

'And why not? Why not if it would save us from the unholy Brits?'

This time there was a longer pause, and it was left for Mrs Sweeney to break the silence. 'Could we talk about something else?' she said. 'I'm sure Niall doesn't really want to be grilled about them there political things, do you, son?'

Niall smiled, but it was a stiff smile. 'I'm just a soldier, I don't know too much about the politics, but I know they're . . . complicated.'

'What do you think of Leetown?' Mrs Sweeney said. ''Tis grand, is it not?'

'Ah, tis a lovely little place,' Niall said, the words now coming more freely. 'The long strand, the river, the fields. Some nice views all round, so there are.' He looked around the table, his eyes settling on Fergus and Gerard. 'Tell me, do you lads do much fishing?'

And so the talk turned to daily habits, how well-built the wooden bridge was, how many animals people kept out in their backyards, how unreliable the trains were of late, the whereabouts of the older Sweeney children, and how Cready's had started selling some peculiar things of late since that modern thing called 'the electric' had been installed, such as ice cream. Mr Sweeney became a little subdued, obviously preferring to talk politics, but the rest of them were happier discussing the history, residents and weather of Leetown – especially those mists that rolled in from the Irish Sea like platoons of silent ghosts – before conversation turned back to Niall's hopes and fears for the future.

As for hopes, he told them he didn't have much in the way of ambition, only to have paid work for as long as possible, to care for his ma, and one day – and there he stole a glance at Aileen – to settle down.

Aileen noted that if there were any fears he kept them to himself, which she took as a good sign, and the conversation thinned to a healthy silence while they waited for young Frank to finish eating.

'Thank you very much, Mrs Sweeney,' Niall said as she started clearing the table. 'That was delicious.'

'You'll not get spuds much better than Ma's,' Fergus said.

'I can well believe that,' Niall replied. Then he noticed young Frank staring at him. He smiled back.

'How did your da die?' Frank asked.

'Frank!' his mother said. 'Sure, don't you know that's a rude question.'

'Sorry, Ma.' Frank bowed his head a little.

'He's already told you,' she added. 'He died in the Great War.'

'No,' he moaned. 'I mean, *how* – what happened to him?'

'Ah, Frank. Won't ye just stop it now.'

'Tis grand,' Niall said, his head bobbing between them like an unwilling referee. 'I don't mind talking about it. Twas a long time ago, sure twas.'

'Well . . .' She scowled at Frank. 'Don't feel obliged to.'

'No, really. Twas one of the last campaigns, which only made it worse for Ma. He'd only just been home on weekend leave before going to the front, and told Ma the word was that the Germans were on the back foot, that they didn't have much fight left in them. He went out to fight near a place called Amiens in northern France. The Allies were advancing, the Germans were retreating. It all seemed easy. But the Germans, y'see, they laid booby-traps as they left.'

'What's a booby-trap?' Frank said.

Niall turned a little red. Aileen glared at her mother.

'That's enough, Frank,' Mrs Sweeney said. 'We know enough, we don't need the nasty details.' She stood up and patted Niall on the shoulder. 'Niall,' she said softly, 'would you be liking some apple and blackberry pie?'

'Apple pie?' Fergus blurted out from down the table. 'We're having apple and blackberry pie? Jesus.'

She stepped across to him and gave him a crack across the back of the head with the palm of her hand. 'I'll thank you not to speak like that at the dinner table in front of a guest.'

Fergus flinched, then rubbed his head as he pulled himself back up straight. She gave him another crack – even harder this time – before reaching for the last plates.

'Ow!'

'Sure, now I think of it, you're not to use that word in vain at all. Now, behave yourself. We have company.'

The apple pie was served, the three boys shovelling it into their mouths as if it were a winner-takes-all race.

'So, Niall, son,' Mr Sweeney said, 'where are you going to be taking my daughter?'

'I was thinking of the cinema up in Dublin.'

'The *what*?'

'You know, that there picture house thing.'

'With the movies – the moving picture things?'

'Aye, or perhaps a show. It all depends when I can get the leave.'

'Ah, grand.' Mr Sweeney peered down the table. 'Have you been to a show before, Aileen?'

'I have not.'

'I didn't think so.'

Aileen got up from her seat, put her arms around her father and kissed him on the cheek. 'Thank you, Daddy,' she said.

'An apple-and-custard-flavoured kiss? Just what I need.' He laughed and said, 'Aileen will be Aileen.'

Chapter 5

Long Island, New York City, 1995

Aileen peeks behind the curtain of the living room again. This time she rushes into the hallway to get her coat.

'Cab's here!' she hollers just before she opens the front door.

'Arturo's?' the man in the woolly hat says.

'You know it?'

'Kinda my job, lady. Italian, just off West Forty-fifth.'

She nods and steps outside, buttoning her thick coat up against the wind. She turns and stares at the open door, her eyes searching for him. Seconds later he appears, slips his coat on, and soon the two of them are in the back of the cab.

He leans forward, his head inches from the driver's ear, and is about to speak.

'He knows where he's going,' Aileen says.

'Oh, right.' He smiles and sits back.

They both do nothing more than gaze out of the window, until the Long Island Expressway approaches Queens, and the scene is flecked with a fog of tiny snowdrops.

'Why did we do it in winter?' Aileen asks, as much to herself as anyone.

'Do what?' he asks back.

'Get married. We should have waited until summer. If I'd realized we were going to spend the next fifty years celebrating our anniversary when there's snow on the ground or cold, hard rain lashing down I'd have insisted on getting married in June or July.'

He shows her a crooked smile. 'Forty-nine, actually. And as I recall, you seemed to be in a rush at the time.'

'Aah,' she says, fluttering her eyelashes at him, 'he remembers.'

'Just about. That was a lot of years ago.'

'Well, I prefer to count the passing of time in terms of children. I like to think we got married four children and seven grandchildren ago. Makes me feel not so old.'

'Aileen will be Aileen,' he says with a chuckle.

They pass through a few junctions without comment and are perfectly comfortable with that. He peers through the haze and makes a joke about how the snow saved everyone having to buy confetti on *that* day. She tuts – she's heard it before. She's heard them all before. But that doesn't stop her smiling and giving him a loving glance.

Then he turns to her and says, 'You really miss the kids coming to our anniversary dinners, don't you?'

She shrugs. 'A little, not a lot. Next year's the big one though. Perhaps we could push the boat out, hire a hall or something – invite people in our old neighbourhood, people we used to work with, people from the Irish Club.' She tilts her head in thought for a second. 'But I do like the routine of going to Arturo's. Same day every year, same table.'

'Same menu,' he adds.

'And I swear that chunk of parmigiana is the same one every year too. The waiter grates a little more off but it always stays the same size. It's the everlasting cheese.' She grasps his hand and gives it a little shake. 'Joking aside, I really do enjoy it. We've had some memorable anniversary dinners over the years. It's the one time a year we get to talk about –well, you know – what happened all those years ago.'

'You like to reminisce. I get it.'

'It's more than that. I find it . . . I don't know . . . comforting.'

'You're getting sentimental in your old age.'

'Well, once a year I deserve it.'

'You do, Aileen. You do.'

Leetown, County Wicklow, July 1943

The truck pulled up outside Sweeney Cottage and Niall jumped out confidently and strolled to the front door.

He straightened his tie, checked his boots for scuffs, knocked on the door and fixed on his broadest smile.

Thirty seconds later the smile had unfixed itself and his teeth were gritted in frustration. He'd borrowed an army truck and driven to Leetown to tell Aileen when he'd be taking her to the bright city lights of Dublin.

And nobody was in.

He cursed under his breath. The idea had been to see Aileen again, to arrange the date personally. At least he'd had the foresight to bring a pencil and notebook. He really, really wanted to see Aileen today, but accepted he might just have to leave a note.

He knocked on the door once more, louder this time. Again there was no reply. Again he cursed. He heard a creak and turned to see a window of the next house swing open.

An old man's face appeared. 'They're out cutting turf,' he said.

Before Niall could ask when they might be back, the window was closed. Niall got out his pencil and notebook.

When the Sweeneys returned, Fergus was first to spot the note, and picked it up while the others removed their shoes at the door.

He said the first few words aloud, which were 'My dear Aileen', and laughed so much he couldn't read out the rest.

Briana grabbed the note. 'It's from Niall,' she said excitedly.

Aileen scurried over and snatched it from her sister's hand, her eyes scanning it feverishly. 'Next Saturday,' she said.

The two sisters jumped up and down with glee a couple of times.

'Will the two of yez calm down,' their father said. 'The way you're carrying on you'd think she was courting one o' them there Rockefeller fellas.'

Aileen and Briana exchanged glances. Briana chewed on her lip to control her amusement. There was no such attempt from Aileen, her face turning a darker shade of pink as she chuckled away to herself.

'What?' their father said. 'What's so funny?'

'Ah, tis nothing.' They both carried on laughing as they almost bounced out of the house and started walking toward the beach.

'Sure, you'll have to wear your second-best dress,' Briana said.

'I will.'

'And I'll help with your make-up. Can I help with your make-up?'

'Of course you can.'

'I can't wait. I'm so excited for you, Aileen.'

They crossed the road, and as their bare feet hit the sand, Aileen halted and turned to her sister. 'Briana,' she said, her face losing all traces of humour, 'why is it you're not married yet?'

Briana's jaw fell open and she took a step back. 'Heck, Aileen, that's a big question.'

'I'm sorry, I was just wondering. It's grand you're helping me so much, but what about yourself?'

'Aach, you don't want to be worrying yourself about that, Aileen. You've more important things to think about.'

'I'm serious. If you don't want to tell me, that's grand. But you're almost three years older than me, and I . . .'

Aileen's words petered out as Briana walked away from her and toward the sea. She followed and soon they were both shin-deep in the freezing water, some distance apart.

'I'm sorry,' Aileen shouted across. ''Twas only something I wondered.'

'And you don't want to make the same mistake as me, is that it?'

'Well . . . I don't know,' Aileen said. 'I'm not sure what you mean.'

She sidled along toward Briana so they didn't have to shout. They both knelt down in the shallow tidal water and started rinsing the sweat and black peat dust off their skin and out of their hair.

'If you want my advice,' Briana said, 'don't appear desperate at first, but when you get a man's interest, hold on to him, get away from here as soon as you can, and don't look over your shoulder as you leave.'

'You're not serious?'

'I am so, Aileen. You might only get one or two chances, and remember that Daddy will always take them on.'

'I still don't understand.'

'It's simple,' Briana said. 'If any man falls out with Daddy, he'll never let you even see him again, let alone marry him, and that'll be that.'

They heard shouts over the rush of the breaking tides, and turned to see their three brothers running down the beach toward them.

'Is that what happened to you?' Aileen said.

Briana nodded. 'Twice, if you really must know.'

Aileen tried to think back. There were vague muggy memories of arguments and tears. 'I think I remember the one,' she said. 'The red-haired chap.'

'Michael Delaney from up the road in Bevanstown.' Briana threw a wistful glance toward the next village along the coast. 'I loved him, I really did. He made me laugh the way Niall does you. I felt alive and special when he was around me, like someone cared for me in a way Mammy and Daddy don't. I knew he'd treat me well. I had grand dreams for us, so I did.'

'And what happened?'

The shouts from their brothers made them flinch. As usual, the boys ran straight into the water at full pelt, not caring who they splashed. Then Fergus paused to lean down and cup his hands in the water, throwing it over his two sisters, whooping as he did so. They both screamed and he laughed. Then he joined his brothers, splashing and shouting the cold away.

'C'mon,' Briana said, nodding back to the cottage.

They started walking.

Aileen said nothing, waiting for Briana to answer her question, to tell her what had happened with Michael Delaney.

'Twas politics,' Briana said eventually. 'Michael and Daddy had a few drinks, started discussing the treaty.'

'The what?'

'The treaty with the Brits to give up the six counties. Daddy was anti, said it was our island and we should have it all. Michael was pro, said they should just accept the deal and get on with it. They ended up almost fighting, so they did.' She shook her head dolefully.

Aileen leaned across and gave her sister's shoulder a squeeze. 'I'm sorry.'

'Ah, I'm grand now, so I am.'

'Good. But . . . you said it happened twice.'

A sad smile played on Briana's lips. 'The second one was Johnny Lynch from Dublin. I wasn't quite so mad about him, but I would have accepted him. There was something there and I knew it would grow.'

'Something?'

Briana shot her sister a grave look. 'You know when it's there, Aileen. You know.'

Aileen nodded. 'I think I see. So, what happened with this Johnny fella?'

'You were probably still too young to take any interest in what happened. Again, Daddy liked him at the start, but they soon fell out. Daddy always finds a way to have an argument. In the end he threatened to take his belt to me if I ever met with Johnny again.'

The two sisters didn't exchange another word until they reached the road.

'I'm sorry,' Aileen said again.

'Ah, tis me who should be sorry,' Briana said.

'And why's that?'

'I've ruined your day out.'

'Aach, nonsense. Better to be warned.'

'Well, yes, consider yourself warned. Alannah knew what she was doing when she moved away from here. She told me the same thing as I told you and I ignored her.'

Aileen said nothing. They went inside and spent the next hour sitting by the fire drying off.

The next Saturday, Briana and Aileen arranged to have the bedroom to themselves. Briana did Aileen's make-up while their mother pressed Aileen's second-best dress. Briana lent Aileen some shoes as Aileen's had been ruined that day on the beach when she'd fallen over. They were a tiny bit too big, but some straw padding sorted that out. Briana told her that little extra length made Aileen look slightly more elegant. They even roped in young Frank to polish them so they ended up looking even shinier than when they were brand new. Then again, he'd been told they would have to be like a pair of mirrors for him to earn his bottle of lemonade.

'Are you sure about these shoes?' Aileen said to her sister as she walked up and down the gap between the beds.

'Just get out there. He might turn up at any moment.'

They killed time playing cards with Frank at the table. He'd won all three hands when they heard a truck pull up outside. Aileen stood up and ran her hands along her hair and down her dress before striding to the door.

'Sit down,' Briana said.

'But that could be—'

'Calm down, Aileen. Give the poor man time to knock.'

Aileen took a deep breath, nodded and returned to the table.

When the rap on the door came, Briana told Frank to open it and see who it was.

'Why me?' he said.

'Do you want that bottle of lemonade or not?'

He answered the door and the sisters could hear Niall's voice.

'Who is it?' Briana shouted across the room.

'Yer man Niall,' Frank replied.

'Well, invite him in, won't you?' she said, motioning for Aileen to stand up.

Niall was over immediately, lifting Aileen's hand to kiss it.

Aileen giggled at the gesture. 'Sure, I never knew this was the eighteenth century.'

'Ah, don't,' Briana said to her. ''Tis nice.'

'Well, I thought so too,' Niall said, and kissed Aileen on the cheek. 'Are you ready?' he said. He looked her up and down. 'Listen to me and my stupid questions.'

'D'you like it?' Aileen said, giving a twirl.

'You look a million dollars, so ye do. Really.'

'You don't look so bad yourself,' Briana said.

'Ah, my one and only suit and my one and only pair of shoes.' He looked down at the brown pinstripe suit framing a white shirt and dark green tie. He jerked up his toes to draw attention to the brown brogues, almost as shiny as the shoes Aileen wore. Then he lifted up the black trilby hat in his hand and gave the top of it a wipe.

'And your one and only hat?' Aileen asked.

'Not even that,' he said. 'Borrowed.'

She giggled and put a hand up to cover her mouth.

'Don't take any notice of her,' Briana said. 'You look lovely.'

'Lovely if you're in Hollywood,' Aileen said with a wry grin.

'Ah, no,' he said. ''Tis what they're all wearing up in Dublin nowadays. Wait and see for yourself.'

'All right, I'll believe you for now.'

'Are you ready?'

'I am. I was just wondering whether I can bear to be seen with someone the spit of Jimmy Cagney.'

He laughed. 'And here was me going for the look of Clark Gable or Cary Grant.'

'And me that Katharine Hepburn.' Aileen turned side-on and posed with a hand behind her head.

Briana tutted and shook her head. 'Will the two of yez cut out the double act. I'm not sure about Clark Gable and Katharine Hepburn – tis more like watching Laurel and Hardy.'

Aileen burst out laughing, but had enough control to notice Niall looking at her in a way that made something inside of her seem lighter than air.

'I have a feeling I'm going to enjoy our first official engagement,' he said.

'I'm sure you will,' Briana said, straight-faced. 'Tell me, will you be getting the train in?'

'Ah, well now.' He glanced at Aileen and gave a mock scowl. 'That's the bit that lets us down a little.'

'Let me guess,' Aileen said. 'The coach and horses you booked didn't show up?'

Niall pointed at her. 'You're good. You're very good. How did you know that? I swear to holy God above I booked the gold-encrusted coach along with the four white horses and the driver with the tall hat.'

'They must have got lost on the way,' Aileen said.

'That'll be it. Sure, Leetown's easy to miss.'

'That's enough,' Briana said, unsuccessfully trying to stifle her smile. 'I'm getting caught in the crossfire here. Are the two of you going now or what?'

'I'm sorry,' Niall said. He turned to Aileen. 'I've got the truck outside. It's not a horse and carriage, but it's dry and you won't have to wait.'

'Sounds grand.' Aileen grabbed her coat. She kissed her mother and sister goodbye and climbed into the truck. Minutes later they were out of Leetown and away from the salty air.

'Do they not mind you taking a girl out in army property?' Aileen said.

'In all fairness, they don't have much use for it.' A few seconds later he added, 'They don't have much use for an army, now I think of it.'

'Don't you like being a soldier?'

'In all fairness, 'tis a little boring at times. We don't have much to do.'

Aileen's eyes locked on to his. 'You like that phrase, don't you? *In all fairness.*'

He took his eyes off the road for a second and flashed a smile at her. 'Sure, I like to be fair,' he replied. 'In all fairness, of course.'

The Curragh Camp was almost silent by the time Niall returned the truck to the compound later that night.

The evening had gone better than he'd dared hope for. But now he felt a little sickness in his heart. He'd made a deal with himself that he was going to tell Aileen, but only when the time was right. The problem was that from the initial meeting at the cottage to the moment he'd dropped her back there, that smile of hers and her wit had both captivated him and derailed his plans. The meal, the movie, the walk along the Liffey, the journeys to and from Leetown – these had all felt more than perfect and there had been no 'right time' to tell her. And Niall knew that wasn't right.

He took a long sigh before opening the door to the barracks, hoping Kevan, Jimmy and Dermot had all gone to bed.

But they were tucked away in a smoky corner around a card table.

Nobody spoke until Niall had sat down on the edge of his bed.

'So?' Kevan said.

'So what?' Niall replied, a sharp edge to his words.

'So, did you tell her yet?'

'I didn't want to spoil her day out.'

'Or yours?' Jimmy said.

Niall nodded. 'That's true, in all fairness.' He reached down and started unlacing his boots. 'Although I did try to mention it once or twice.'

'What stopped you?'

And Niall could hardly say he was lying, that he didn't try to mention it at all, or that it was as if he'd been hypnotized by Aileen.

'The thing is,' he said, 'I don't know *how* to tell her.'

'But you know what you *should* tell her,' Dermot said.

'I do. And I feel terrible about it. But it's easier said than done. I was going to say it once or twice, but then her face was lighting my life up and I . . . I just couldn't. The words stuck in my throat.'

'Ah, she's one girl among thousands,' Kevan said. 'I remember her, and you're right about her being pretty and all. But don't be falling for the girl, Niall. Not at a time like this.'

'You know, I think I already have.'

'There'll be no backing out now,' Jimmy said. 'You've given your word. We all have.'

'I know, I know. And don't be thinking like that. Any soldier is a man of his word and I'm a soldier.'

'So, when are you going to tell her?' Kevan said.

'When I've worked something out,' Niall replied. 'I have an idea but I need to sleep on it.' He lay back on the bed and placed his cap on his face as a shield from the light.

Chapter 6

For the next few days Aileen could hardly keep a smile off her face.

Even when she and Briana went with their two eldest brothers to help bale hay at O'Reilly's fields, the grimace of exertion was somehow laced with pleasure. Briana told her she'd noticed. Fergus and Gerard probably noticed, but only Briana remarked on it, and if there was any jealousy it didn't show.

At the end of the day they all walked home from O'Reilly's, took some cooling water from the stone jug, and sat resting their weary limbs. Aileen had just closed her eyes ready for a catnap when Daddy, who had been unusually quiet, approached her.

'Aileen,' he said, 'would you do me a favour and come outside for a moment, please?' He smiled as he spoke, but it was an awkward smile, and he was just a little watery-eyed.

'What is it, Daddy?'

'Just . . .' He nodded to the door, and a few seconds later they were alone together in the backyard.

'I need to talk to you,' he said.

'What's wrong?' Aileen replied.

He spoke softly, quickly wiping a tear from his eye. 'Ah, nothing's wrong, sweetheart.'

Aileen thought otherwise. It was the first time she'd ever seen her father shed a tear except in anger.

He took a few breaths. 'It's about this Niall fellow.'

'What about him?'

He laughed nervously. 'Well, do you like him?'

'I do.'

'I mean, do you *really* like him?'

She started breathing heavily, could feel her chest tightening. 'I do, Daddy. Sure, you must know that.'

'Good.' He smiled again and seemed reluctant to continue. ''Tis good. But . . . listen to me, Aileen. He's meeting you at the bridge.'

'What? But . . . when?'

'Now.'

'This minute?'

'Aye.'

'What does he want?'

Her father hesitated. Then he pointed to the road. 'Just go, Aileen. Go now.'

'Oh.' She stood, not quite knowing what to say. 'So . . .'

'Go on,' he said.

The smile took some time to spread across her face, but then she stepped forward and kissed her father on the cheek. 'Thank you, Daddy.' Then she turned and started running.

She darted around the corner on to the road, across it and along the sandy grasses lining the top of the beach. She ran past the red shopfront of Cready's, past the last few cottages in the village, then across the junction with Station Road.

There she stopped for a second. An army truck was parked up on the verge next to the railway bridge, but she hardly saw it, being more interested in the figure leaning against the handrail of the wooden bridge, just where he'd been a few weeks before. On spotting Aileen, he stepped away from the handrail and waved to her.

A rush hit Aileen – a rush of something she'd never known before. She took a few steps forward. Briana had told her to play it calm, not to let a man know how keen you were. Yes, that was it. Take it easy, walk over to him calmly and ask him why he'd turned up out of the blue like this.

The rush had other ideas. Whatever Briana had said, the rush was going to ignore it. The rush was either going to make her faint or make her run.

She broke into a gallop, down the road, along the footpath, toward the man in the army uniform fidgeting with his cap, and didn't stop until she reached him. She jumped up and threw her arms around his neck, kissing him full and strong on the lips as she sensed the fairground thrill of her body being swung around. She felt the firm hold of his hands on her hips, guiding her to a gentle halt, and soon her feet were once more planted on the wooden planks of the bridge.

'That's what I call a welcome,' he said, grinning.

'Oh, Jesus, I've missed you, Niall.' She leaned up on tiptoe and kissed him again, this time grabbing his head and not letting go until she felt the need for another breath. Then she saw him blink a few times, saw a sadness overwhelm his hazel eyes. 'What is it?' she said.

'Daddy told me to come here and meet you.'

'Come on,' he said. 'Let's take a walk.' He held her hand and started walking across the bridge.

She resisted. 'No, Niall. Tell me, tell me *now*. What's this all about?'

He swallowed. 'I'll tell you, but let's go for a walk first. I need a walk.'

She didn't move, but he said, 'Please,' and reluctantly she let herself be led over the bridge and down to the sandy area of beach where they'd first met. They walked down to the shore, to where the receding tide had left the sand rippled but firm.

They walked on, the only sound the breaking of the waves, Niall looking straight ahead, Aileen glancing up at him every so often.

'So?' she said.

He pointed ahead. 'Let's walk on a little more.'

She leapt in front of him and planted her feet as solidly as she could manage. 'Niall O'Rourke,' she said, her voice raised above the crash of the breaking tide. 'Tell me right now what this is all about, d'you hear me?'

He let out a long breath, then nervously brought a hand up to wipe his chin. He pointed a few yards up the beach, to a section of tree branch that the tide had brought in, and they sat together, looking out to sea.

'I've known a couple of girls,' he said. 'I've told you that. I've not made a secret of it. But you're something special – that's no secret either.'

Aileen said nothing, just kept her lips tightly sealed to make sure she stayed silent, to let him say whatever it was that was so important.

'Aileen, I love you, but I've had to make the hardest decision of my life. And as long as I live I don't think I'll make a harder one.'

Aileen opened her eyes fully to let the breeze dry the wetness gathering there.

It didn't work. She wiped a tear away and sniffed.

'It's something Kevan and myself have been talking about for a while – a year or so.' He turned to the side, held her head, one hand behind her neck, touching the hairs, making her tingle. He kissed her slowly, the wetness making her taste the saltiness of the air. 'As God is my witness, I'll never know if I'm right or not, and I only hope you can forgive me.'

Now she saw tears drop down his face. She pressed her face against his shoulder, hugged him, but stayed silent.

'Kevan and myself and a couple of others, we're . . . we're joining the British Army.'

She pulled away and looked up to him. 'You're *what?*' She checked herself and placed a finger on his lips. 'No. Please. Don't speak. Just hold me.'

Aileen put her head back on his shoulder, holding on to him as he held her, wishing they could stay there until the sea was dry. They rocked gently, as one, and watched the tide for a few minutes.

'Nothing will change, you know,' he said. 'I'll still feel the same about you.'

'How do you know that?'

'Because I do.'

'But how d'you know you'll still want me when you get back?'

'Ah, well. That brings me to the other thing.'

'Oh, Niall. I can't take any more.' She pulled away and took a handkerchief out to wipe her tears away.

'There's something else I have to tell you,' he said. 'No, I mean, *ask* you.'

'What?'

He fumbled in his jacket pocket. 'I want to know – no, I *need* to know.'

'Know what?'

'I need to know whether you'll wait for me.'

'But—'

Now it was his turn to place a finger on her lips, silencing her.

He knelt beside her in the sand, opened the tiny box and showed her the contents. 'Will you wait for me, and do me the honour of becoming my wife when I return? I give you my word that when I come back I'll make you happier than any other man ever could, happier than you could be even in your best dreams. Aileen Sweeney, will you marry me?'

A couple of raindrops hit his face.

She swallowed, then said quietly, 'Can I speak now?'

'I'd like that.' He waited, open-mouthed, staring at her.

As more raindrops fell on them both, she held his head with both hands and kissed him on the lips, feeling his arms pull her in. 'Yes,' she said, 'I'll wait for you. I'll wait for you however long this damn war lasts – forever if I need to. I'll be here, and I promise we'll be married when you get back.'

'Really?' He grinned, his eyes now alive, his tears mingling with the rain, and he threw his head back and laughed to the skies. He plucked the ring from the box and placed it on her finger. She lifted her hand up so the struggling sunlight caught the brilliant green stone, dazzling them both for a second. Then Niall grabbed her and lifted her up, twirling her around as he shouted for joy, as she shouted for joy.

The rain started to get heavier, now soaking their hair and shoulders.

'The bridge,' Aileen said.

They held hands and ran back to the railway bridge, soon reaching the sheltered section of riverbank where he'd carried her the first time they'd met.

They collapsed on to the grass. Niall took out a handkerchief and wiped her face dry, not once taking his eyes off hers.

'I know tisn't perfect, but I meant everything I said. As God is my witness I'll make you happy, Aileen. I really will.'

He went to kiss her again, but she resisted, and they lay together, their faces inches apart.

'I want to marry you, Niall,' she whispered, curling a tuft of his dark hair with her forefinger. 'And I'll want to marry you whatever you do, but . . .'

'But what?'

'Don't go to war, Niall. Please. Stay here.'

He motioned for her to come closer, and held her in his arms, squeezing the breath out of her. 'I'm so sorry,' he said. 'But tis done. I've agreed and I can't go back on my word.'

She drew back and looked up to him. 'And . . . was it all done and agreed before you met me?'

There was no answer.

'Was it, Niall?'

He shook his head. 'When we pulled up to the strand dance that evening, twas only an idea between us. But we've all talked about it a lot, and I had to make a decision a few days ago. I suppose the truth is that I could see it coming and I . . . I'm sorry, I should have told you earlier.'

'And if you could choose again? If you had to make that choice right now?'

He sighed. 'It's hard, Aileen. We've all been following the war, what's been going on in Europe and the Far East – Africa too. The whole thing's a mess. And in all fairness to me and the rest of the lads, we're . . . well, we're fighters. I don't expect you to understand, but you see, we joined the army to see battle, to fight, not to spend twenty years doing drills and exercises.'

'And what about fighting here, defending our own country?'

He sighed. 'We all know the facts, Aileen. Everybody in the army knows. If Hitler can overrun all those countries so easily, and if he takes Britain . . . Well, there'll be no battle in our country to speak of – we'll stand no chance.' He gave his head a sad shake. 'No, the best way of defending our country is to join the Brits. None of us likes it. It's just a fact of war. What the Germans do, they call it "blitzkrieg", faster and more brutal than any army that's gone before. And really, only a fool would think Ireland could defend itself against that. We've all thought it through. Even the money's better than what the Irish Army are paying us.'

'*The money?*' She looked away, at the rain dancing on the river. 'You're doing this for the money?'

'Look at me, Aileen.'

'No.'

'Please.'

'I'm in love with you, Niall. That doesn't mean I'm a fool.'

'And I won't treat you like one. I won't lie. For some of the men the extra money's important, for some it isn't. Some have got families to feed. And we all know the risks. In the end, what's common to us all is that we're soldiers. Fighting is what we do for a living, what we *choose* to do. And me? I'll be able to save more up for us – for when we're married.'

'Does Daddy know you're doing this?'

'He doesn't.' A shaft of pain hit Niall's face. 'I was back there just now asking him if I could marry you, but I know how he feels about the Brits, and I didn't want to do anything to upset him. How do you think he'll take it?'

She shrugged. 'Aach, I daren't think about that. But I do know he needs to be told at some point. He'll be asking when the wedding is, so he will.'

'Aye, I know. But I was hoping he might be persuaded – persuaded that me joining the Brits is the right thing to do.'

'Let me talk to him first.'

'Ah, no. Sure, that's not right. I can't—'

'Niall, I'll talk to him. I'll explain it to him. I can tell when he's in a good mood.'

Niall thought about it for a moment and shook his head. 'No, I can't let you be doing that. I have to tell him myself. Perhaps I can take him for a drink, to celebrate, and to thank him.'

'Well . . .'

'I need to do it myself, Aileen. If I'm off to fight on the front line, there's no way I should be running away from your da.'

Reluctantly, she nodded. 'So, that's it?'

'I'm afraid it is.'

'So, when will you be going?'

'We're catching the train up to the North the Saturday after next.'

'*What?*' She shot him another worried glance.

'I'm sorry. It's sudden, I know. But there's no point in waiting now we've all decided.'

'Will I . . . will I see you before you go?'

'Well, you will if . . . if you want to.'

'Of course I do.'

'Grand.' He nodded uncertainly. 'I wanted to see you on Saturday. Would you like that?'

She closed her eyes and nodded.

'Grand. I'll take you out on Saturday whether I can get leave or not, and when I bring you back I'll break the news to your da. I swear I will. And if he doesn't like it . . . well, we'll sort out that mess when it rears its head.'

'Ah, that'll be a relaxing evening, so it will.'

Niall laughed softly, forcing Aileen to smile, and he wiped a few tears from her face. 'You'll be fine because you've got spirit. And we'll be fine.' He cupped her chin in his thumb and forefinger, holding her still while he kissed her once more.

They waited, lying together, until the rain stopped.

'I have to go,' Niall said. 'They'll be sending a search party out for me if I'm here much longer. I don't want to rock the boat just yet.'

They walked slowly over the bridge back to the coast road, and at the other side they embraced once more. Aileen almost asked him again – considered pleading with him not to join the army, to carry on the way things were. But something told her the words would be wasted, so instead they shared a final kiss, and she watched him climb into the truck and drive away, one hand waving out of the side window.

And when the truck disappeared over the brow of the hill she was alone.

She started walking along the grass between road and beach, but couldn't quite face going home yet, so sat awhile on the sand, letting the sun's gentle evening rays dry off her hair and the shoulders of her cardigan, and thinking.

Briana had egged her on to see Niall. But she'd only seen him a few times, so could she really be sure he was the man she wanted to marry? Briana had her heart in the right place, there was no doubt about that. But was Briana somehow trying to deal with her own missed opportunities? And how would Daddy react to the news about Niall joining the British Army? Most importantly, what if he didn't come back from the war?

That last thought made her burst into tears.

Briana didn't matter. Daddy and his stupid politics didn't matter. Nothing else mattered. She knew only that she missed Niall, that when she was with him she felt alive – happy and woozy like a drunk but somehow with her senses heightened, not dampened. So yes, she'd only seen him a few times, but that didn't matter. She felt like she'd known him forever, that somehow they were long-lost friends, and he clearly felt the same. Briana had said on a few occasions what a good double act they were, and that felt good. When Niall wasn't there she felt half a person, and spent most of her waking moments looking forward to the next time she saw him.

No, whether she liked it or not she had to admit that she was in love or obsessed or infatuated – or whatever those Hollywood films called it. *She wanted to be with him, and nothing less would do.*

So she would cope – how, she didn't know – but she would cope with life while he was away fighting. She would wait as long as was needed – three months, six months, perhaps even a whole year. She would wait, she would marry him, they would find a cottage of their own in Leetown or somewhere nearby, and that would be that.

She dried her eyes, took a few deep breaths, and went home.

'Are y'all right?' Aileen's father said, turning the wireless down as she entered a few minutes later.

'I just want to go to bed.'

Her mother stepped over and made a point of looking at Aileen's left hand, then at her husband, then at Aileen's hand again. She pointed to the wireless. 'Turn that thing off, Dan.'

He did and faced Aileen. 'Are you sure there isn't . . . ah . . . something you're wanting to tell us?'

Aileen shook her head and said, 'I don't feel well,' then headed straight for the bedroom.

'But, Aileen,' her mother said, 'you've had no tea.'

Aileen said she wasn't hungry and went into her bedroom. At least she was on her own: that was a small relief. She didn't know or care where the others were – although she felt horrible for even thinking such a thing. She got into bed and pulled the covers over her head.

Then she heard the creak of the door opening. It closed gently and she felt a weight settle itself on the bed. She took the cover off her head.

'Oh, Aileen,' her mother said. 'What's wrong? What happened?'

Aileen felt her face tighten again, and more tears came.

Her mother grabbed her hand again and took a closer look at the engagement ring with its tiny flash of green. 'Your daddy told me about Niall, and here's the ring. I . . . I don't understand. You should be happy.'

She pulled her hand away. 'Mammy, please. Just leave me alone.'

'But . . . did he do something?'

'I want to be alone, Mammy.'

'Oh, Aileen.' Her mother said nothing more for a few moments, just gave Aileen pitying looks. Eventually she said, 'Are you sure?'

Aileen nodded, and heard her mother slowly get up and walk out of the room, closing the door quietly behind her.

After that, Aileen fell asleep.

Chapter 7

The next morning Aileen was woken by the noise of her three brothers getting up and getting dressed.

There was a second when she was sure Niall hadn't told her – a second when he wasn't going to join the British Army after all. But Fergus opened a window and the cool morning mist on her face put paid to those thoughts.

Then the three boys left the room, as they always did, to give the girls some privacy to get dressed.

Briana, lying behind her, put a hand on her shoulder. 'Are you all right, Aileen?' she whispered. 'Mammy told me about yesterday, that Niall came to the house to talk to Daddy.'

Aileen got up and sat on the edge of the bed. Briana shuffled over and sat next to her. 'Mammy's really upset, Daddy's gone all quiet, and the rest of us are confused as heck.'

Aileen glanced at her, but looked down to her bare feet and said nothing.

'What in the name of God happened, Aileen?'

'I can't say.'

Briana held her hand. 'How so?'

'I know you mean well, Briana, but you'll know what's happened in time. It's just . . . you need to let things be for a while.'

'All right.' Briana nodded slowly. 'If that's what you prefer.'

A few minutes later the family were all sitting around the breakfast table.

But something was wrong.

As usual, the room was thick with the aromas of porridge and freshly baked soda bread. Cups of black tea were dotted around the table. But this morning there was no talk of what everyone was up to today, of the latest village gossip, of what weather they were all hoping for. Today no words were spoken, and nobody would look directly at Aileen.

Her mother came over and put a plate of two fried eggs in front of her. 'Eat that, Aileen. You must be famished, what with you missing your tea last night.'

'Thank you, Mammy.'

Aileen waited a moment, then picked out a chunk of soda bread and placed it on her plate. She sliced one of the eggs, dipped the bread in the runny yolk, and started nibbling on it.

Still, nobody else spoke.

Then, to her left, her father mumbled something to himself. While Aileen ate one of the eggs the air was filled with clinks and crunches and slurps. No words. She looked down at the remaining egg, now all alone.

Her father groaned and dropped his cutlery down on his plate.

Fergus, Gerard and Briana glanced over, but young Frank didn't dare. They all started to eat more quickly, keeping their eyes down.

Daddy mumbled something again, this time with a little more aggression.

Aileen felt sick, and placed her knife and fork down, next to the other egg.

'Are you not that hungry yet?' her mother said softly.

Aileen shook her head, and opened her mouth.

Before she could speak, the flat of her father's hand slammed against the table.

'This is enough, Aileen,' he boomed across to her. 'For God's sake tell us what happened last night.'

He waited. There was no reply. Only Aileen dared look him in the eye.

'Tell me why you're upset,' he said.

'I'm not upset. I'm . . . I'm happy.'

'Ha!' He looked up and around the room. '*Happy?* Jesus Christ almighty.' He waited, but she was still silent. 'Right,' he said. 'I didn't want to do this, but you've forced me into it, girl. Yesterday Niall asked me for permission to propose to you.'

Briana choked and coughed. The boys gawped across, first at Aileen, then at their father.

'I told him, yes, of course, because he seems like a good man and all that, and you told me you liked him. So as your father I have the right to know. What in God's name happened?'

'I'm confused, Daddy. Just stop it.'

'Confused? Are you? Are you *really*? The thing is, I sent you to see him, and I expected you to run home with tears of joy and the biggest smile on your face I'd ever seen. But no, you're with the misery and all that, behaving like he's said he never wants to see you again. Then again, of course, you have his ring on your finger. And you say *you're* confused?'

'Daddy. Please. Just stop asking me or I'll be away for a walk.'

'Oh no, you won't, girl.' He thumped all four fingertips of his right hand on to his chest. 'Not until I know what's going on, you won't.'

'You can't stop her going for a walk,' Briana said.

He glared at her, baring his teeth. 'Oh yes, I can. She's my daughter and until she's married she'll do what I tell her to do. And so will you, for that matter.'

'But she's upset.'

'*Be quiet!* He turned back to Aileen. 'Now tell me what's going on. If that man has ruined what should be one of the happiest days of your life, I want to know what he did.'

'But I can't talk about it.'

'Well, I say you can. If any man breaks my daughter's heart I need to know about it.' He waited, then pointed to his three sons. 'You, you and you, go to the bedroom.'

They stood up, leaving their food half-eaten, and silently filed into the bedroom.

'Now, does that help?'

Aileen shook her head.

'If I have to get someone to take me to the Curragh Camp, find yer man and ask him myself, then that's what I'll do. D'you hear me, Aileen?'

'I'm not talking about it, Daddy. I just *won't*!'

'Daddy,' Briana said, 'perhaps another day might be better.'

Now he picked up a knife and pointed it at her. 'I won't be telling you again, Briana. Stay out of it.' He turned back to Aileen. 'Now you – just tell me.'

'I shan't,' Aileen said, standing up. 'And that'll be the end of it.'

Her father stood up too, his face now red and starting to bead with sweat. 'Perhaps my belt might change your mind, girl.'

He started to unbuckle. Briana stood up too and shouted out, 'No!' But her words were ignored.

Aileen started to cry again, she ran for the door but her father grabbed her hand. He pulled and shook her arm until their faces were inches apart.

'Tell me!' he bawled out. 'Tell me! Tell me this minute, girl!'

'Yes, yes, yes!' Aileen shouted back at his face, her own a mess of tears. 'He asked me to marry him and I said yes. So I'll be marrying him. I'll be marrying him as soon as he gets back.'

'*Gets back?* Gets back from where?'

'He's joining the British Army to fight in the war, and before you say anything I'm hating him for doing it more than you can imagine. But I love him too and I'll be marrying him when the war's over.' She gasped for breath, snatching her wrist out of her father's grasp. '*Are you happy now?*' she shouted at his frozen, shocked face.

She turned and ran to the bedroom, smashing the door against the wall as she opened it. She ran past her brothers, all sitting patiently on the bed, and jumped back into her bed, pulling the covers up over her head.

She lay there sobbing for some time, then was disturbed by the shouts. There was no way she could blot them out – they were too loud, too angry. She was sure everyone in Leetown could hear the racket coming from the next room.

'The British Army?' her father said. '*The British Army?* The turncoat bastard's joining the Brits?'

She heard a crash – the sound of plates and cutlery skidding along the table and crashing against the wall.

'Ah, no,' he bawled. 'Damn everything, I can't live with that. I can't let a daughter of mine marry a man like that.'

Then Briana's voice: 'Is that all you have to say?'

'I'm warning you, Briana!'

'But she's upset to tears, Daddy. She's had her heart broken and all you can think of is your precious politics?'

'Don't you DARE speak to your father like that!'

'Ah, you're PATHETIC, so y'are.'

'And you've had enough warnings. Come here!'

More noises of crockery or ornaments or something being smashed, of chairs falling to the floor, and of Briana screaming.

Then came another sound, one from Aileen's mother. But this wasn't any *Mammy* Aileen had ever heard before. It had to be her, but then again it was such a powerful screech it scared Aileen more than her father had. 'PUT THE BELT AWAY!' it said. 'DAN! PUT IT AWAY!' Then, not so piercing but still a shout: 'Briana, go to your bedroom!'

Then the bedroom door flew open again, and Briana's heaving, whimpering body joined Aileen. They held each other.

'I'm so sorry,' Aileen said. 'Oh God, I'm so sorry.'

They stayed together in bed for the rest of the morning, only rousing themselves when they were certain all the men had left the house.

'Are y'all right?' Aileen whispered. 'Did Daddy hurt you?'

'He didn't get the chance, thanks be to God.'

'Grand.' They both shuffled up the bed, sitting at the top with their shoulders resting uncomfortably on the wall. To Aileen it felt as if the rough cobbles at her back were punishing her, like she was once again a naughty ten-year-old sent to bed. But more than that, it felt as if her life and dreams had been turned upside down and given a few kicks by a prize stallion.

'What'll I do?' she said, almost groaning the words out.

Briana gave her a look of pity. 'You have to decide yourself, Aileen. You're the only one who can work out whether you want him more than you want Daddy's blessing.'

'Do you think he'll come round?'

The pain on Briana's face was her only answer. 'Come on,' she said. 'Whatever else has happened, we have to eat.'

She coaxed Aileen off the bed and into the living room. The hunched figure of their mother stood over the metal washtub, her shoulders yawing from side to side in time with the scrubbing of clothes. She stopped for a few seconds, hooking her head around to offer them a disdainful stare, then returned to the scrubbing.

Briana took a step toward her. 'Mammy, have we got any—'

'You know where to find it all.'

Together, and almost silently, they got soda bread, butter, plates and knives out of the cupboard, and sat at the table, eating not speaking, occasionally glancing at their mother.

Eventually, their mother wrung out the workshirt she was washing, grunting as she put her back into it, then wiped her well-developed forearm across her brow and walked over. 'I can only hope you're happy with yourselves,' she said. 'Upsetting your father like that – and the boys too.'

Aileen and Briana stopped eating to glance at each other. Aileen drew breath to answer, but Briana silenced her with a small shake of the head.

'I'll assume you'll not be seeing the fella again.'

Aileen felt her mother's stare burning into her and took a moment to respond. 'Well, you assume wrong,' she said blankly.

'Aileen,' Briana hissed. 'Don't say that. Let me—'

'Oh, dear God,' their mother said, shaking her head. 'Aileen, just tell everyone you'll not be seeing the man again, and after a while you'll believe it yourself.'

'Why should I?'

Mammy looked at Briana, thrusting a finger toward Aileen. 'Tell your sister, will you?'

Briana swapped her gaze from her sister to her mother and back. She let out a long sigh. 'Perhaps Mammy's right, Aileen,' she said. 'It won't feel like it now, but there will be other men. And if Niall goes away you'll be forgetting about him soon enough.'

Aileen choked, almost being sick. She threw her chair back and ran to the bedroom, slamming the door behind her and throwing herself on to the bed.

The door soon opened again, her mother's imposing figure almost filling the gap. 'Now don't you be misbehaving like that, Aileen. You're a grown woman now, not a child.'

Aileen was now crying. Her words were almost whimpers. 'But I love him, Mammy. I love him.'

'Love? Aach, what's love? You're a pretty girl, Aileen. Sure, there'll be other men – men who care enough about you not to risk their lives. I mean, what sort of a life would he be able to give you anyway?' She heaved a sorry sigh, leaning on one hip. 'I'm sorry, darling, but it's for the best. We all know that, and in time you'll accept it too.'

Briana appeared behind her, and she stood aside, ushering her toward Aileen.

'It'll be all right soon enough,' Briana said. 'You'll get over him and move on to some other fella, so you will.'

Aileen lifted her blouse up to her face and covered it, weeping. Then she looked up to see her mother give her head a rueful shake.

'You need to grow up, young lady. Life's hard sometimes, tis the way, but sulking does nobody any favours.' She turned and wandered away, and moments later Aileen heard the scrub of brush on cloth resume.

Briana shut the door and sat next to her sister, resting a hand on her shoulder. 'Shh,' she said, holding her face inches away from Aileen's. 'Don't listen to Mammy,' she whispered slowly and clearly. 'You do what you damn well want to, d'you hear me?'

Aileen's face froze for a moment, staring at her sister.

'I had to go along with her,' Briana said. 'I felt awful. I'm sorry.'

A smile broke through Aileen's tears, and she grabbed and hugged her sister. 'Thank you,' she whispered. 'Thank you so much.'

'We have fresh water this morning, so wash your face and let's go for a walk on the strand. There's a little sun today.'

'So there is,' Aileen replied.

'I'm sorry I doubted you,' Aileen said a few minutes later as they walked along the deserted beach, heading for Bevanstown, the next village along the coast.

'Aach, away with ye,' Briana replied. 'Mammy likes to think she's the boss, just like Daddy does. The truth's somewhere else.'

They walked on, letting the sharp salty breeze clear their heads. As they approached Bevanstown, Aileen pointed to the haphazard train of houses facing the shore. 'So, this Michael Delaney fellow, the one you were talking about, does he still live there?'

'Ah, he's long gone, so he is.'

'Do you know where he went?'

Briana looked away, far out to sea, then shook her head. A few paces on she stopped and took another look at the houses. 'Ah, who am I kidding?' she said. 'Of course I know what happened to him. After Daddy put a stop to him seeing me I used to walk up this way a couple of times a week, passing through Bevanstown, hoping I'd bump into him, that we'd strike up a conversation. I used to go back home and dream that had really happened. Later on, the dream became that we were secretly seeing each other every week, lying together between the sand dunes up here and talking. And then that we were secretly in love and he'd vowed to marry me and sweep me away from here, to our own cottage, to somewhere Daddy didn't know about.'

'Oh, Briana. That's the saddest thing.'

'I thought the dreams were going to turn me mad, so I did. I knew I couldn't forget about him and I had to do something. So I started asking around, and found out he'd gone to London. Something small in politics there, so they say. And that sounds about right, he was always interested that way. For almost a year I kept asking how he was. Then the dreams came back – dreams that I'd gone to London with him and we were living together in a big house there. The dreams only stopped when I met Johnny from Dublin. That might have been the appeal. He helped me forget. He wasn't so clever, but it was there, Aileen. I know we could have been happy together. So then I had dreams about him, that we were going to be married and move away.' She showed Aileen a pained smile. 'And then he had the arguments with Daddy.'

'Have you never thought of going up there, finding out if he still lives there?'

'To Dublin?' Briana laughed. 'I tried that, so I did, a few months later. I said I was going to visit our Cathleen and James up there. Well,

I did see them, of course I did – and they were both living in fairly horrible conditions, I can tell you. But then I looked for Johnny. Apparently he went to Scotland, then England, working with the road gangs, laying the black stuff. Found a wife somewhere in the Midlands and settled there, so they said. It made me so unhappy to know that. I wondered whether there was something wrong with me – that I was cursed.'

'Don't you be saying that, Briana. And I'm sorry. You've not had much luck with the men, have you?'

'Oh, I still have my hopes. I'm hardly an old maid and I haven't given up by any means. I just feel sorry for myself sometimes.'

They walked on a little more, just past Bevanstown, to where the coastal cottages at the top of the beach thinned out, giving way to mounds of sand sprouting long grasses.

'C'mon,' Briana said, heading up there. 'Do me a favour and come over here with me. I find it peaceful.'

Soon they were both sitting shoulder to shoulder between the huge sand dunes, sheltered from the coastal breeze. Compared to walking along the beach there was an eerie quietness.

Briana closed her eyes. ''Tis good here. I can pretend things are different. Better.' She said nothing more, just breathed long, slow breaths.

Aileen closed her eyes too. She was quiet, but not for long. 'There's something else,' she said. 'Something I didn't tell anyone.'

Briana quickly opened her eyes, her face stern, and drew her head back ever so slightly. 'Ah, no, Aileen. Don't tell me . . . you're not . . . you didn't let him . . . ?'

'Aach, shut up.' Aileen giggled a little and blushed. 'He's not like that.' She straightened her face, now trying to look as serious as Briana. 'No, I . . . I'm to see Niall again on Saturday, for the last time before he goes away.'

'And so, how are you going to manage that?'

'He says he's going to come to the cottage. He says he's going to tell Daddy – break the news, so he puts it – that he's joining the British Army.'

'Oh heck, that doesn't sound good, Aileen. That doesn't sound good at all.'

'I wish I could tell him Daddy already knows.'

'And there's no way of contacting him?'

Aileen shook her head.

'So, what are you going to do?'

'Well . . . you've been so good to me, Briana, and I thought . . . well, I was thinking . . .'

A crooked smile drew itself on Briana's face, and she nodded. 'Ah, I get it now. You need my help.'

'But I'll owe you a favour in return.'

Briana put an arm around her sister. 'We'll work something out, so we will.'

Chapter 8

Saturday morning came around sooner than Aileen expected, but she and Briana had agreed that they had to catch Niall before he reached the house. While the men were out, they would wait at the front door, and when the men were at home, they would wait along the road.

That way they would warn Niall that their father already knew what he had come to tell him, and that he didn't like it one bit.

The plan worked well until the men arrived back from a hard morning's work helping out at O'Dowd's farm. Aileen and Briana were about to leave the house when their mother called them back. 'The boys are starving,' she said, 'so we'll be eating early today.'

Both sisters said they weren't hungry.

'No matter,' they were told. 'There'll be nothing more until tonight, so you'll eat now, so you will.'

'It'll be half an hour,' Briana whispered to Aileen. 'What are the chances he'll turn up in that time?'

Aileen's only reply was to give Briana a slightly anguished look.

'What else can we do?' Briana said. 'Tell the truth?'

A few minutes later the whole family sat down at the table.

Aileen felt sick. The aroma of peat-toasted barmbrack and hot butter didn't help, and as it turned out, she never got to taste it. Everyone heard the sound, the chug and rattle of the truck pulling up outside. But nobody spoke. They all stilled themselves and stared at the door. Aileen expected the knock but when it came it still jolted her.

'Will that be who it sounds like?' Aileen's father said.

'Who else do we know with a truck like that?' Fergus replied.

Daddy got to his feet. 'Let me see who tis.'

'No,' Briana said. 'I'll go.'

Daddy gave Aileen a barely disguised scowl, then said to Briana, 'All right. If tis himself you can tell him to go away, that he's no longer welcome here.' He turned to Aileen. 'And you. Go to your bedroom.'

'Why?' Aileen said.

'Don't disobey me, Aileen.'

Aileen said nothing more, but huffed a breath and reluctantly headed for her room.

Outside the front door of Sweeney Cottage, a nervous but optimistic Niall was about to knock at the door again when he heard footsteps from the other side. He pulled his jacket straight, flattened his hair with the palm of his hand, and cleared his throat.

'Hello, Briana,' he said, smiling. His smile quickly fell away. 'What is it?' he said. 'What's happened?'

'Oh, Niall. Why did you do it?'

'Do what?' He tried to look beyond her but she pulled the door to. 'Is Aileen in? I'd like to see her if that's all right.'

'It's probably not for the best, Niall.'

'I don't understand.'

'Aileen told everyone you're joining the British Army.'

'Oh.'

Before Niall could say more, there was a shout of, 'What's happening?' from behind Briana.

'Is that your father?' Niall said.

'It bloody well is,' came the reply, the angry-faced figure pushing Briana aside.

Niall instinctively took half a pace backward. 'Ah, Mr Sweeney,' he said. 'Is it all right if I see Aileen, please?'

'No, it damn well isn't, and what's more it never will be. You're not fit to utter my daughter's name, and I can guarantee there's no way you're marrying her while I have two fists. Do you understand that?'

Niall took a few seconds to compose his thoughts. 'I gather you know about me joining the British Army.'

'That's right. And you can gather this too. You're a traitor to your country and you can just stay away from my family and stay away from my house.'

As he took a step toward Niall, Briana moved between them and grabbed Niall by the arm. 'You'd better go, Niall. Please.'

'But . . .' Niall stared at her, then at her father.

'I'd take my daughter's advice if I were you,' he growled.

'Daddy, go inside.'

'Shut up, Briana. I'll not take orders from my own daughter.'

'I'm only asking, Daddy. Please. We don't want a fight. I'll make sure Niall goes away if you just get inside and let me talk to him.'

After a few heavy breaths and a spit on the ground, Mr Sweeney gave in and the door slammed shut.

'Just go,' Briana said to Niall.

'Why should I?' he said, breathing heavily. There was no reply, and although he took his time, after a minute or two he traipsed back to the truck, Briana following.

'At least tell me how she is,' he said.

'She's upset, no thanks to you.'

'I'm not giving up on her, you know.'

Briana glanced back to the cottage and lowered her voice. 'For what it's worth, Niall, I hope you don't.'

'Thank you. Tell her if she wants to see me before I go, I'll be at Amiens Street Station next Saturday. I'll be there early on Saturday morning and I'll wait for her until my train leaves.'

'We'll see. Now go, before you get yourself lynched.'

Niall jumped into the truck, took a final look at the cottage, and drove off.

Briana went back inside and the meal continued, but words were limited to the necessary, with nothing approaching what could be called conversation.

After the meal, Aileen and Briana went for a walk. And they talked. They agreed that this time their plan would have to be better.

The evening meal continued where the previous one had left off, with little or no conversation. After the food had been dished out and grace had been said, the only sounds were the tap of cutlery on crockery and the occasional cough or slurp.

Toward the end, Briana asked Aileen to pass her the salt. She did, and as Briana took it she made a point of grabbing Aileen's hand and examining it.

'Your ring,' she said. 'What's happened to your engagement ring?'

'In the sea,' Aileen said, snapping the words out. She scanned the faces looking in her direction. 'I threw it in the sea. Is everyone happy now?'

Briana pulled a sullen face. 'Are you sure you should have done that?'

Aileen didn't reply, but kept her eyes low and carried on eating.

Their father cleared his throat. 'Is that true, Aileen?'

'What do you think?' she replied without even looking at him.

'I'll ignore your insolence,' he said, 'but that's good.' He reached for a slice of bread and started wiping it around the edges of his plate.

'Good?' Fergus said. 'Sure, it might have been worth something. She could have taken it to Dublin and sold it.' He put a chunk of potato into his mouth, then spoke again. 'Ah, no,' he said. ''Twas probably worthless, just like the rotten man who gave it to her.'

Aileen dropped her knife and fork, which clattered on her plate, throwing spatters of potato and gravy on to the table. She stood up, kicked her chair back and headed for the bedroom.

Out of the corner of her eye she saw her mother lean over to Fergus and raise her hand. She heard the crack of hand on skull, followed by a yelp from Fergus.

The next few days were tense ones. At mealtimes – or even in between them – there was very little in the way of conversation among the Sweeney family members. And hardly a word was spoken while Aileen was around.

Her mother spoke the most to her, her father hardly at all. Fergus and Gerard spoke about her, although never using her name.

Frank hadn't spoken at all – not one word in three days – and so the next morning, when Briana was alone in the house with her mother, she said she was worried about the 'poor little lad'.

'Aach, he'll be all right,' her mother replied.

'I'm not so certain,' Briana insisted.

'Sure, he's at a funny age.'

'Oh, I know that. But . . .'

'But what?'

'Well, what with the funny age he is, don't you think the last thing he wants is to have all this trouble around him, to have to listen to arguments all the time.'

Her mother went to speak, but instead thought for a moment as she nodded her head, weighing Briana's comment up before speaking. 'Sure, he'll be grand given time,' she said with a dismissive wave of her hand.

'But Mammy, you have to admit the atmosphere is awful tense these last few days.'

Her mother gave her a suspicious look. 'Ah, well, there's nothing that can be done about that, is there?'

'Ah, I don't know, Mammy. I suppose . . . well, no, tis too much trouble.'

'What?'

'No, tis only an idea. Well, more of a thought. I was just wondering . . .'

'Spit it out, girl.'

'It's just . . . I haven't seen Cathleen or James for months. Twould be grand to go up to Dublin. I could take Aileen too, give her a break from the house.'

Her mother stared into space for a moment. 'I suppose it might help. Mmm . . . twould calm the waters a little, I'd say.'

'Just what I was thinking, Mammy. And it would give you and the boys some breathing space, let you get things back to normal.'

'Aye.' She nodded, slowly at first, then faster. 'Aye, right. Tis a grand idea. You can go up tomorrow.'

'Right. Tomorrow it is. We can—' Briana stopped herself. 'Ah, no. For one thing, I really want my best clothes and they're not washed and ironed. For another, Cathleen and James will be working tomorrow.'

'Mmm . . . So why don't you go on Saturday?'

'You think that would be best?'

'Of course. And that's the day your father and your brothers are most likely to be cluttering up the house, shuffling around and moaning like they do.'

'Right,' Briana said. 'Saturday it is.'

It was overcast when the train pulled out of Leetown Station early on Saturday morning. Aileen and Briana, sitting opposite each other, said nothing until the edge of the village was out of view, when the sun started to glint off the window as if the train had just come out of a tunnel.

'Do you think it's safe now?' Aileen said.

''Twas safe as soon as we got on to the train,' Briana replied.

Aileen gave her shoulders a gleeful shrug. A smile she'd kept locked away for days appeared on her face as she opened her handbag. Moments later the engagement ring was back on her finger. Where it belonged. She held her hand out so the emerald caught the sunlight now streaming through the window.

'Briana,' she said. 'I just—'

'And don't be going thanking me again, ye daft thing.' Briana allowed herself a smirk. 'Anyway, 'twas easy. The hardest part was getting little Frank to stay quiet about it. I had to buy him another whole bottle of lemonade, the greedy thing.'

'Aren't you the conniving sort.'

Briana widened her eyes. 'And aren't you a pot calling a kettle black.'

The two of them shared a giggle, and Aileen carried on admiring her ring while Briana watched the countryside of Wicklow race by, neither of them speaking for another few minutes. Then Briana said, 'Ah, go on then,' and leaned forward to take another look at the ring. 'Oh heck, it is beautiful, I'll give you that. I've never seen such a bright green in a stone before. 'Tis as if it's throwing out its own light. You're a very lucky woman, Aileen.'

To Aileen, the rest of the train journey seemed to last as long as one of Father Kinross's legendary sermons, although whenever she glanced across she got the impression Briana was enjoying the ride and could have happily sat there for hours.

But eventually the train pulled into Amiens Street Station, and Aileen's foot was the first to hit the platform. Her eyes darted around the station concourse, then fell on a group of men she vaguely recognized.

Yes, those two were the same she'd seen with Niall the first time they'd met. She started running and the one with his back to her turned.

He caught her and spun her around. It was becoming a habit, and as addictive as a fairground ride. Except that this time it felt like the last ride of the day. Aileen's feet hit the ground and she felt his hand slip behind her neck again, as if he knew what to do. She felt his fingertips dance on the baby hair at the top of her neck, and it was still delicious.

But there was something else. A mix of fear and confusion on his face.

'What?' she said. 'What's wrong?'

He shook his head. 'Nothing's wrong.'

But there was, she could tell. She waited, staring him out.

'I have an hour. I mean, *we* have an hour.'

'Oh.'

'I'm sorry, Aileen. My pals all wanted to go earlier. I persuaded them we should catch a later train so I could have some time with you.'

Aileen glanced behind him. Yes, that one was Kevan; the other two, she didn't know. But they all nodded politely and said hello. She said hello back and half-heartedly thanked them for staying later.

Then a flustered Briana arrived.

'We only have an hour,' Aileen told her.

Briana greeted the others, then said, 'Well, I'd suggest you get going while I busy myself looking around the shops. I'll meet you here in an hour and we'll go to see Cathleen.'

Ten minutes later Aileen and Niall were strolling along the north bank of the Liffey. They talked of what they were going to do when Niall returned, the sort of house they were going to live in, how they would both work before starting a family, and whether they would live in Leetown or elsewhere in Wicklow or even in another country entirely. There was no talk of arguments or what to do about Aileen's family or of her father's opinions. For an hour those problems were a world away.

Whenever they passed a clock – be it outside a jewellers or coffee shop, or on the frontage of a public building – Aileen stared and willed the time to slow down or stop. The train journey had taken an age, the minutes languidly strolling by, but this was the opposite. There was a falseness to their conversation because the time was racing by so quickly. They talked as if there were no problems and they lived in paradise. The truth was that her family might never accept him, that they had very little money, and most of all . . . the biggest thing . . .

She could forget all those minor problems for Niall's sake, but not that biggest thing. She was no educated woman but she knew this was a war – a horrible, bloody war that many soldiers wouldn't return from. Yes, that was the biggest problem of all. He could easily return wounded and not in a fit state to work or be a father. Or even worse.

No. She had to cut down that falseness. She had to plead with him one more time to see sense, to stay out of the war.

She pulled his arm so they stopped walking, and stepped in front of him. 'Listen to me, Niall.'

He smiled, sadness apparent in his eyes, but said nothing.

Aileen took a breath but struggled to phrase the sentence. It didn't sound right. She could say, *What am I going to do if you don't return?* But would that help? Was that the right thing to say in their final ten minutes together?

'Listen,' she eventually said. 'I have something to say.'

His hand rose to her head and he pushed his fingers through her hair. 'I'd listen to you all day long if I could, Aileen, and one day I will. I promise.'

Her throat stalled, the words caught in a tug of war.

'What is it?' he said.

She threw her head on to his chest and her arms around his waist. 'Niall O'Rourke. Just promise me you'll look after yourself and come back in one piece.'

She felt his warming embrace. And she felt she would be safe and at peace – for another ten minutes at least.

'I'll certainly try my best,' he whispered.

'And write.'

'Definitely.'

'I mean, write to me. You'll be able to write, won't you? They'll have pencils and paper, won't they? They'll let you—'

'Shh,' he said. 'I'll write. Of course I will. And when I tell you my service number you'll be able to write back. And even if I can't write for some time, remember that I love you and I won't stop loving you, no matter where they send me.' She felt his solid arms squeeze her, almost crushing the breath out of her chest. And it was the most wonderful feeling.

Then he spoke like a child. 'Bloody hell, Aileen, I'm going to miss you.'

'I'll be here,' she whispered back. 'I'll wait for you forever, if that's how long it takes.'

The remaining few minutes went by in a blink, and before Aileen knew what was happening she'd waved Niall goodbye, his Belfast train had pulled out, and she was walking toward Cathleen's place with Briana.

'I'm sorry,' Briana said quietly. 'It was a shame it was only for an hour, but at least you saw him before he left.'

Aileen didn't reply. Her head was muggy with confusion. There had been a brief exhilaration at seeing Niall again, but also a clear grief that resisted attempts to be talked away. She was now on her own. The man she loved was going to war, and only the Lord knew when he would return. It could be many months, or even years.

And, of course, there was a chance he wouldn't return at all.

She had no idea how she would cope with Niall's absence, but she knew she would have to. For the first time since she'd waved Niall goodbye she glanced at Briana.

She still had her sister. Yes, Briana would keep her sane.

Chapter 9

A month went by, slowly at first, but more easily once Aileen had come to terms with her situation. She wouldn't see Niall for some time and could mention his name only to Briana. There was no other option.

She found work where she could – cleaning at the church or the railway station, mucking out livestock or helping with the harvest on one of the many local farms – and put her wishes and dreams to one side; they would keep.

Toward the end of that month, however, there was one thing she was finding hard to accept: she hadn't yet received a letter from Niall. Yes, she understood it was a war, but then another few weeks came and went with no letter, and her disappointment deepened so much that she could no longer keep her tears at bay. The address – Aileen Sweeney, Sweeney Cottage, Leetown, County Wicklow – was hard to get wrong. It crossed her mind that perhaps he was working on some top-secret mission where they wouldn't allow him to write, or that there was a shortage of paper or stamps, or even that he was too busy with exercises and manoeuvres. In short, anything but the unthinkable.

She occasionally confided her concerns to Briana, who told her to be patient, that she couldn't do anything about it, that she didn't know his situation, and that there would be a good explanation.

By October 1943 almost three months had passed since Aileen had said goodbye to Niall. She kept telling herself to keep calm, but concern and disappointment were now turning into deep fear. While fetching water from the well with Briana one morning, she mentioned her fears. Briana told her again to be patient, that it was a war, that during a war things like sending letters to loved ones took second place, and that anything could have happened.

'Like what?' Aileen said.

'Like . . .'

'He's been captured?'

'Well, no.'

'Or else he's been . . .'

'Aileen,' Briana said as earnestly as Aileen had ever heard her speak. 'I don't know what's happened to Niall, but I can assure you that no good ever came from worrying. You *will* find out one day. You *will*. And when that happens, you'll feel foolish for doubting him.'

Aileen agreed. At least she told Briana she agreed.

Soon afterward, early one morning while the family were getting comfortable at the table, there was a knock at the door. A knock and a tuneful whistle, to be precise.

Aileen's mother got up and answered it. The others could just make out a postman, still straddling his bicycle, holding out a letter.

'For Aileen?' she was heard to ask as she took the letter.

Aileen had hardly woken up yet, but on hearing her name it felt as though iced water had been poured down the back of her blouse.

She stood, but Fergus was at the door first, leaning past his mother.

'Where's Michael?' he asked the postman.

'Ah, he's sick today,' the man replied, before saying a cheerful goodbye and cycling off, whistling to himself.

Fergus shut the door and went to grab the letter from his mother's hands.

She was too quick and slapped his hand with her spare one for good measure. 'What're ye doing, Fergus? The letter's for our Aileen, not you.'

He went to speak, but merely gave Aileen a glance of disdain before stomping back to the breakfast table. To Aileen, none of that mattered. Nobody ever wrote to her. She grabbed the letter from her mother and ripped it open. She read the first few words of the letter, gasped and ran out of the door.

She ran across the road, frantically scanning the lines, checking the length of the letter, and only occasionally looking where she was going. She collapsed on to the sand as soon as she reached it.

Then she started reading it properly.

15 October 1943

My dearest Aileen,

I'm so sorry it has been a couple of weeks since my last letter. And I have to tell you I still haven't received one from you yet. I'm assuming that the Forces mail system is getting things mixed up. Perhaps there is another Niall O'Rourke somewhere in the British Army wondering why you're writing to him. Ha ha. But just in case you've forgotten or have lost it, I've put my service number and address at the end of this letter again. I'm sorry – that sounds terrible. In all seriousness, I'm sure you have written letters and they're stuck at Aldershot.

Anyway. So. I am on my way back from the Dodecanese and my leg has been patched up as good as the Navy medics can manage. I told you before that the place here is hotter than I ever thought any place could be, but I have to say, now we're retreating, I can see it's a beautiful part of the world, all deep blue lagoon sorts of places and sand that looks pure white when the full sun hits it.

I also have some bad news. I lost another of my friends yesterday. It was Billy, the man I told you about who was a carpenter in London before being conscripted into the army. I didn't see it, but they say he took a bullet to the head. It's terrible, and I'm as upset as anything, but the blessing is that he didn't suffer.

I have to finish now. I can't write too much as I need to rest, and more importantly, I have to pass the pencil on to the next invalid, or he's said he'll hit my bad leg with his good arm. As you might imagine, there's a grand spirit in here. And there needs to be. It's hell on the front line, and everyone suffers, even the men who aren't injured, if that makes sense.

Aileen, they are a good bunch of lads here, but once or twice it's been hard for me to find the will to live. The one thing that keeps me going is the thought of seeing you again. I hope everything is all right with your mother and father. As I've said before, I look forward to a time when they can accept me into your family.

As always, I'm missing you and love you very much,

Your loving fiancé,
Niall.

P.S. Please write.

Aileen read the whole letter twice again and held it to her chest, grinning up at the clouds. He'd written. *He had written.* Wherever he was – and she had absolutely no idea where the heck that was – he'd taken the trouble to write words on paper and to get someone to post the letter. Yes, he had a leg injury of some sort, but he was alive and he was coming home.

She bathed in the moment, sighing to herself, but then her smile flattened and an anger of sorts took over. Her first letter from Niall should have been a special moment, but something or someone had spoiled that moment. She looked ahead at the ocean. Today there was little wind and the tide looked as if it didn't really want to exert itself. The sound of the waves lazily breaking was regular and soporific enough to calm anyone under normal circumstances. But these weren't normal circumstances.

What the heck was going on?

Quite a few things didn't make sense. One word in particular didn't make sense. 'Dodeca-*what*?' she said aloud. 'Where the blazes is that?'

Anyhow, that was the least of her problems. It was clear that not only had Niall written to her before, but that he'd expected her to write and she hadn't. That was a terrible thing to do to Niall.

She read the letter again, her vision blurring as tears formed. But no. She wasn't going to have this. Something was going on and she had a good idea who was behind it. She sniffed, wiped away the tears, and started marching back home.

They were still at the table when she got there, her mother's mouth full of buttered soda bread, Fergus with a large slice in his hand. Aileen walked right up to him and slapped the hand, causing him to drop it.

'Hey!' he shouted. 'What're ye doing?'

'No, Fergus. What the heck are *you* doing?'

'Trying to eat me some breakfast is what I'm doing and I'll thank ye to leave me alone.'

She stood there, arms on hips, bearing down on him with her nostrils twitching, her eyes narrowed in suspicion.

'What?' he said.

'Why did you ask the postie where Michael was?'

He shrugged. 'Ah, I dunno. Get outta here. Let me eat.' He picked up the slice of bread he'd dropped. It was almost touching his teeth when Aileen grabbed it and threw it across the room.

'Aileen!' her mother said. 'Now stop that.'

'He's done something, Mammy. I know he has. I don't know how, but he's been stopping my letters from Niall.'

Fergus held a buttered finger up to her. 'Aha! So, you admit it. You're still speaking to yer traitor man?'

'*Aha!*' Aileen shouted back. 'So, *you* admit you've been reading my letters?'

Fergus turned to his father.

'It's for the best,' their father declared with a sour grimace.

'Dan!' Aileen's mother said. 'Ah, not you as well.'

He shifted uncomfortably in his seat. 'I have a duty to know what kind of man is writing to my own daughter, have I not?'

Aileen was too shocked to speak, but turned to her mother for support.

'But, Dan, you can't be taking the poor girl's letters.'

'You don't understand these things, Maureen. You're best staying out of it.'

'Is that against the law?' she replied.

'How can it be against the law? I'm the head of this house, Michael the postie's a public servant and yer man's a deserter.'

'He has a name,' Aileen said.

'Well, I'd rather not use it in my house if you don't mind.'

Briana, silent up until now, spoke up. 'Daddy, that isn't right. Aileen's eighteen, so she is. She can make her own decisions. And you can't be going opening her mail.' She and her father stared at each other like two stag deer locking antlers, neither yielding. 'And it's your own daughter,' Briana added for good measure.

Aileen looked around the table. Fergus was scowling, Gerard was keeping his head down. Poor little Frank was almost in tears.

Eventually Aileen's father spoke in an almost presidential manner. 'Look. She's been told she can't see him as long as she lives here. So, it's an utter waste of time them talking or writing to each other. And I'll thank the rest of yez to keep out of it.'

Aileen glanced at her mother, who returned the glance and let out a long, frustrated sigh before starting to collect the dirty plates and cups.

'I can't live like this,' Aileen said, shaking her head and not bothering to hold back the tears. She turned and walked slowly to the bedroom, shutting the door gently behind her.

She got into bed and pulled the covers over her head. Her body now curled up into a ball and she let her sobs come freely. There was no point in holding her emotions back.

There was no point in anything. Not anymore.

By the time Aileen heard the bedroom door open and close she'd stopped crying and drifted off to sleep, imagining a better world for herself, so the noise startled her even though it obviously wasn't intended to.

It would be Briana. Good old Briana, ever the peacemaker. Well, today that wouldn't wash. Aileen had been thinking of possibilities, and now it was about time she thought of them more as serious options.

She was shocked when she heard her father's voice – edged with an uncharacteristic softness. He eased himself on to the bed next to her.

'I'm sorry, Aileen. I know it sounds bad, taking your letters and all that.'

'Sure, you're right there.'

'But . . .' He went to put his arm around her and found a hand rising up to stop him. He relented and let his hands rest on his thighs. 'You know we only have your best interests at heart, Aileen. The man's no good for you.'

Aileen glared at him. 'You don't really believe that, Daddy, do you?'

He looked away from her face and let his head hang down.

'It's your politics, that's all it is.'

'Politics is important, Aileen. I . . . I wouldn't expect you to understand, but a man's politics is a measure of that man, it shows what sort of character he has. And that's important in the long run.' He paused, then returned his gaze to her. 'You deserve better, Aileen. There are plenty of good men around – a few of them in this village. I mean, this deserter fellow, why do you have to stay in touch with him? I don't understand. I mean that. I really don't get it.'

'You don't have to understand something to accept it, Daddy.'

'Aach, that's all muddled talk. He's no good for you. I can see that and your mother can see it too, she just doesn't like to tell you to your face.'

'Have you thought you might be being unfair about him?'

'Aileen, you'll get over him. You'll find another man to marry, I know you will.'

'But I don't want that, Daddy. Can't you understand? I want *Niall.*'

He shook his head. 'Well, I'm sorry, but you'll not be doing that while you live under this roof.'

'Right,' she said. 'I understand.'

'Grand,' he replied, then got up and left the room.

'Grand,' Aileen said to herself when he'd gone.

At around the same time, Niall was arriving back at Aldershot barracks.

The plan he'd agreed three months before with Kevan, Jimmy and Dermot hadn't quite gone like clockwork. They'd joined up in Belfast assuming they would be assigned to the same company – or at least the same battalion. But there had been little or no choice. Once a man signed his name on the dotted line he belonged to the army and had to go where the powers that be thought best. They all accepted that.

So Niall had gone to Aldershot alone and had no idea where the others had ended up. So much for their plan.

After four weeks' basic training and another four of battle exercises on Salisbury Plain, Niall had been sent to the Dodecanese islands, held by Italy for many years, and, after the surrender of Italy in September 1943, fought over by German and British forces.

The German forces won, forcing the British to hastily flee the area, and Niall was one of the casualties. A desperate retreat under heavy gunfire; a stumble racing across rocky terrain; an awkward fall was all it took. Getting back to Aldershot barracks felt like a nightmare had ended. He was safe – relatively – and settled into hospital to recover from a serious leg fracture.

The doctors explained and the nurses were diligent, but Niall's mind was elsewhere. During his days on the ship only one thought had made the physical pain bearable: that Aileen would have written to him by now, that he would have at least one letter from her and probably more waiting for him at Aldershot. But there were none.

He had to be content with letters from his mother. And that was no bad thing. A man could always rely on his mother.

Those letters turned out to be scant consolation. He couldn't get Aileen out of his mind – that pretty girl from Leetown he loved and was engaged to marry. There would be an explanation as to why she hadn't written. There *would* be. Niall wasn't prone to stubbornness, but he told himself he would keep trying as long as he lived. So one of the first things he did on his return to Aldershot was to write to her again.

Chapter 10

As the cab approaches the bridge leading to Manhattan Island, Aileen notices that the snow has settled like a light dusting of sugar over the streets and rooftops. She checks her watch. He notices, tells her it'll be fine, and his hand gives hers the briefest of squeezes.

'And another thing,' he says, 'this is the one time of the year you get to think about yourself. I always said you spend too long worrying about the kids.'

'The kids?' Aileen says. 'Oh, I've moved on from them.'

'Well, that's good to hear.'

'I have grandkids to worry about now.'

'Right.' He laughs. 'Except, of course, I know you haven't stopped worrying about our own kids.'

'No, of course I haven't. And why should I? That would be unnatural. Surely you worry about them too?'

The short pause as he draws breath doesn't go unnoticed and Aileen jumps in with, 'Well, do you?'

A thoughtful sigh is his initial answer. Then he says, 'Well, let's see. First we have Michael and his third failed business.'

'You leave Michael alone. He's a trier, and with four children he puts our other three kids to shame.'

'Then there's Victoria, who married that pudding brain of a dreamer.'

'You mean the Victoria who is, I can assure you, very happy with Carl.' She draws in a little breath and mutters, 'Although you're right about his pudding brain. I pray to God young Jake has inherited her brains and not his.'

'Jenny had her problems as a teenager.'

'Don't remind me.'

'I'll never forget her first few boyfriends.'

'You and me both. Scared half to death I was. But considering what I was like at eighteen, it's a kind of poetic justice of a kind, I guess.'

'She did good in the end,' he says. 'Getting married and having Jenny Junior really made her blossom.'

'And you can't say *she* married a pudding brain.'

He shakes his head. 'I can't. I have to admit I've had the occasional argument with Robert over the years, but—'

'*Occasional?*'

'Well, all water under the bridge now. I know he's a smart cookie and I know he takes care of Jenny – *both* Jennies.' They exchange a smile, interrupted by a jerk from the car. 'And as for young Kelvin, well, we both know he was blessed from an early age. Academic, popular with women, good at every sport he tried.'

'All of that can be a curse though.'

'*What?*' he snaps.

'I mean it. It's easy to assume you'll always have those virtues, that the doors they open will stay open. Doesn't work that way. Decades go by in a flash and before you know it both you and the world have changed.'

'Jeez – that I agree with.'

Aileen nods. 'Indeed. So, I'm glad he settled down with Patricia.'

'Well, she sure put him in his place once or twice – and probably more we don't know of.'

'And she gave him a son. Little Ryan certainly changed him, and they're both young enough to have more.'

'Yes, well,' he says. 'Anyway, to answer your question—'

'What question?'

'Whether I worry or not.'

'Oh, I know you worry.'

He frowns. 'So why did you ask?'

'Because you kept yammering on about me worrying, but I know you worry too but you usually won't admit it, so I wanted you to remind yourself of that fact.'

His frown turns to a look of extreme confusion and he spends a few seconds squinting at the cab's headlining. Then he says, 'I guess that's the kind of reasoning I've come to expect from you over all these years.'

'Oh, darling,' Aileen says, 'you say the most romantic things.'

He puts on an exaggerated Irish accent. 'Aileen will be Aileen.' The corners of his mouth twitch and even his nose quivers as he tries to keep a straight face.

Aileen starts to laugh and he loses the battle. They both lose control. Aileen catches sight of the cab driver glancing at them and trying to suppress a sneer.

The cab crosses over East River and Aileen happens to look through the window toward the far side, where two lovers kiss as they stroll along the footpath at the side of the bridge. Aileen's laughter quickly subsides as she's taken back to a very different bridge, in another country, in a time so far back it might as well be another life.

Leetown, County Wicklow, October 1943

Once Aileen had received that one letter from Niall she knew his service number, so she wrote back telling him to address his future letters to Briana for safety.

So Briana had her uses. But Briana could also be confusing. There was the Autumn Strand Dance – the final one of the year before it became too cold. Briana had egged Aileen on to come along and she'd eventually agreed. Many local men attended – some mere boys, some who Aileen would have seen as quite handsome and full of charm if it weren't for Niall and the bitterness in her heart. Briana pointed many of them out – isn't that one smart; hasn't he lovely blond hair; the tall one with the blue eyes – and Aileen felt the need to show a little disdain each time. Aileen wondered whether Briana was really on her side, or whether she was testing her.

For the rest of 1943, as the days became shorter, the wireless was on more than off. The Irish stations apparently didn't like referring to the war at all – only to 'The Emergency'. It was the British – the BBC – that most people listened to for news of the conflict. It was strange, Aileen thought, that the likes of Daddy and Fergus kept moaning about Britain but were happy to listen to the very same country's broadcasts. On one occasion Aileen's mother asked why they listened to something they always complained was British propaganda. The reply was that it gave them something to talk about.

Aileen liked to listen too – initially in the hope of hearing the word 'Dodecanese' and having some idea where it was. More importantly, she sensed that the whole family – the whole country, even – had a reluctant but understandable curiosity for what was happening in Europe.

She'd heard the stuffy official government announcements on the BBC before, but, like others, preferred listening to discussion and comment by BBC staff. Now, however, one particular type of announcement piqued her interest. It was a request of sorts. For most Irish people the request might have been merely a way to earn money, but for Aileen it was a way out – a way out of Leetown and a chance to escape her father's ironclad opinions.

For weeks she agonized over this request, keeping her thoughts to herself, not even mentioning it in her letters to Niall.

By December, the Leetown sky was so dark and low that it threatened to take the thatch off Sweeney Cottage, and in one letter from Niall, Aileen got the news she was half-fearing but half-expecting: he wasn't coming home to Ireland on Christmas leave because he was still in hospital recovering from his leg injury. It was difficult news to accept, but Niall had inadvertently given Aileen hope. It was due to him that she'd started listening to the broadcasts in the first place – those broadcasts that had made the request she agonized so much over.

And now, with Christmas approaching, she had made up her mind. The more immediate problem was telling her family of her decision.

Telling her mother was an ordeal best left alone for now. No, Briana would be her sounding board. There was no rush, and one mild day the week before Christmas the two sisters were on the beach, washing themselves in the shin-deep water. At this time of year the washes were shorter and the run back to the cottage fire – now blazing – was faster.

Aileen told Briana to stop splashing, to listen, that she had something to ask her. So Briana stood still and Aileen unburdened herself of her plans.

'You're going to *Belfast*?' Briana said. 'But why Belfast?'

'Because they need the labour, of course – women to make things in factories, even some in the Forces themselves.'

Briana's face reddened at the thought.

Aileen held up a hand. 'Ah, no. I'm not talking about joining the Forces, only working in the factories. 'Tis good money.'

'And what will Daddy think? Have you thought of that?'

'I have.' Aileen splashed water over her body and shivered. 'I'll say I'm helping fellow Irish men and women.'

'But Aileen, ye can't go.'

'Why not?'

'Because . . . well . . . because I'll miss you, ye daft eejit.'

'Ah, thanks, Briana, and I'll miss you too, but it won't be forever, only until the war is over at the very most.'

'And have you thought how long that could be?'

'I haven't.'

'Well, perhaps you should. And what about the bombs? Half the place is in ruins, so I hear.'

'Sure, twas bombed years ago. And that's why they need the labour. Half the people are busy rebuilding the place, half busy making things for the war effort.'

'Making what?'

'Armaments, uniforms, parachutes, medical equipment. They give you a job and arrange some lodgings, so he said.'

'So who said?'

'The man on the wireless.'

'The *British* man on the wireless? And you believed him?'

'Don't be starting, Briana.'

'Ah, no, I'm sorry. That'll be me listening to Daddy too much. I know what you mean. I was talking to a woman in Cready's whose cousin has gone up there. But I can just hear what Daddy will say.' Briana put on as gruff a voice as she could muster: '*Sure, it's a fool who believes the word of the British government.*'

The laughter warmed up both women for a few seconds, but Briana stopped quickly enough and told Aileen she was serious, that he wouldn't like it at all.

Aileen thought for a moment. 'I'll just have to deal with Daddy when I really have to and not before.'

'All right,' Briana said.

Aileen expected more, but Briana's reaction hadn't been too negative, although sometimes with Briana it was hard to tell.

They washed in silence, save the barely suppressed screams at the cold, then Briana waded over and gave her sister a hug. 'Do it,' she said. 'I think you should go.'

'You're not against the idea?'

'I am a little. I'll get awful lonely without you, so I will, but . . . ah, no, you might be happier up there. Aren't you the lovesick one stuck in Leetown? A little time in a big city might show you Niall isn't everything.'

Aileen scowled at the remark.

'I'm sorry,' Briana said. 'I didn't mean it like that. I just meant—'

'Briana. You're not . . . jealous, are you?'

Briana nodded toward the cottage. 'Freezing is what I am. C'mon, let's get in front of that fire.'

'Why don't you come with me?' Aileen blurted out.

Briana's mouth fell open on hearing the words, but no answer came and she looked away – out to sea, back to the row of cottages and up to Bevanstown.

'I'm serious, Briana. Twould be company. For the two of us.'

'I'll see. Perhaps. Or perhaps another time – I'll think about it.'

Aileen tutted and threw her gaze to the sky.

'What?' Briana said.

'Your problem is that you're always thinking but never doing. Twould be so much better if we went up there together. I know you've thought about moving out of Leetown once or twice. Why not now?'

'I'm . . . I'm . . .'

'Scared?'

Briana sighed. 'Aileen, d'you not think I've wanted to get out of this place before?'

'And so?'

'I'm worried for Mammy.'

'No, you're not. You're scared, aren't you?'

'Perhaps I am. But whatever it is, it's just the way I am.'

'What does that mean?'

Briana, eyes low and pain drawn on her face, didn't reply.

'So, what if I were to say I'd only go if you came with me?'

'Oh heck, Aileen. Please don't be like me.'

'Like you?'

'Weak. Don't be weak.'

'I won't, Briana. Believe me, I won't. But I'm thinking of you too. I mean, are you really going to just stay here and wait for a man to come and sweep you away?'

'You don't understand, Aileen. It's harder for me. You were right when you talked about this being Tinytown. It's stifling, so it is. But the longer you stay here, the more fear you have, the more time Tinytown has to put its hooks in your back.'

'So, you're just going to wait here and do nothing for the rest of your life?'

Briana thought for a few seconds, then shook her head. 'I'm just not as strong as you, Aileen. And now I'm freezing. C'mon and let's get to that fire.' She shivered and broke into a run.

Aileen knew Briana's words should have made her think long and hard about how to tell her father of her plans. She knew that more than anything. But the days passed and it seemed mean to spoil Christmas for everyone, so she left it until the last week of the year, when the time seemed right, while she and her mother were alone, collecting water from the well up the lane.

'Belfast?' Aileen's mother stopped pumping the well.

'I need to do it, Mammy,' Aileen said.

Her mother's face was visibly shaking. 'But . . . but why Belfast? Why not Dublin?'

'They have jobs in Belfast.'

'They have *bombs* in Belfast.'

'That was a few years ago.'

Aileen's mother started to pump again, driving the handle back and forth furiously until the bucket was full, then spent a few moments staring at it. 'It's still a city at war, Aileen.'

'The *world* is at war, Mammy.'

'Well, I don't care about the world. I care about my daughter.' She swapped the full bucket for an empty one and gestured for Aileen to take her turn.

Aileen took a breath and set to work. 'I'm going, Mammy,' she said between grunts. 'Would you prefer it if I went to London or Birmingham or Liverpool?'

'Pah! I can't see your father being too pleased about any of those.'

'That's the point, Mammy. To him it's Ireland. I'll be helping Irish people. I'm trying, Mammy. I'm trying hard to please everyone.'

A flat smile slowly appeared on her mother's lips. 'I suppose I can see your point there.' She nodded. 'Let's get these buckets back to the cottage and I'll think about it.'

Aileen grabbed a handle on each side. 'You can think about it, Mammy. But I'm going.'

'On your own?'

'On my own. And I'm not going to tell Daddy.'

'What?'

'You can tell him if you want to, Mammy. I won't be.'

'Right.' Her mother nodded to herself. 'Right you are.'

Chapter 11

Belfast, Northern Ireland, January 1944

One chilly winter afternoon a nervous Aileen stepped off the train at Great Victoria Street Station, the case she'd borrowed from her mother grasped tightly in her hand. The air was distinctly cooler than back down south and that helped, somehow awakening her, invigorating her.

The journey from Leetown had been uneventful, although the leaving of the village had been a blur at the time. Her mother had wished her well, the boys of the household too, despite their disagreements. Only Briana and their mother saw her off at the station. A wordless wait on the platform, a long hug from the mammy she would miss, and a longer hug from the sister she would miss even more. And then, at the last moment, as Aileen stepped toward the carriage, Briana hugged her again and managed to thrust something into her coat pocket.

'It came yesterday,' she whispered. 'I thought you'd appreciate something to read on the journey so I kept it back.'

Aileen wanted to thank her sister, but was also angry for a moment. If Niall had written her a letter she wanted to read it *as soon as possible*. But this was no time for anger, and then the whistle sounded and the feeling was gone. She waved her mother and sister goodbye, and as the train started moving the enormity of her decision hit home. She would no longer be able to talk to Briana, let alone share an embrace or go for a walk together along the shore or across the River Crannagh.

As the train pulled away from Leetown, Aileen felt her heart resist the motion like a leaden weight. She waved out of the carriage window until she was merely waving to the arc of the train as it pulled away and across the river, past the beach where she'd first met Niall.

Niall.

She sat and hurriedly opened the letter. Better that than cry.

> 10 January 1944
>
> My dearest Aileen,
>
> If you are reading this, it means you are still in Leetown and your lovely sister is still passing on my mail. Please tell me your new address in Belfast and I will write there directly.
>
> I'm supposing that going straight from little Leetown to Belfast will be hard for you. You will have to put up with the noise and traffic and sheer number of people, but I'm sure there will be compensations in the way of shops, cinemas, dances and suchlike. I wrote in an earlier letter how I visited London with a few of the chaps (I was based in Aldershot at the time so it wasn't far). At first it was just too much for me. I hated it and longed for a deserted field like back home or a beach like at Leetown. But after a while there was a sort of beauty to it with so many lights reflecting off the river at night. You don't see things like that in a small place.
>
> If there's one practical piece of advice I can give you, it would be never to forget that there will always be a train back to Leetown should you need it. But hopefully you won't need to heed that advice, Belfast

will be to your liking and you'll make friends there. I wish you the best of luck. You are a brave woman and should be proud of yourself for helping the war effort. I'm certainly proud of you. I absolutely detest being away from you, but the more I learn about the war and what that man Hitler is doing, the more I feel I did the right thing in joining the British Army.

Anyway, to more mundane matters. I'm still in Aldershot, a patient in the Cambridge Military Hospital. If you don't know, Aldershot is in Hampshire and nowhere near Cambridge at all. And this is a country where they make jokes about the Irish being odd!

And I'm still bedridden – me and my bust leg. They say it was a bad break and it's still very painful if I try to move. The good news is that the doctors tell me it should mend stronger and better than it was before. The bad news is I'm in and out of sleep with the pain, although thankfully they've stopped giving me morphine – it was giving me hellish nightmares of the day I broke my leg.

The nurses occasionally sneak me in a little brandy to help with the pain. I keep telling them I prefer the black stuff. I don't think they know what I mean. You can't always get Guinness here, and when you do it doesn't quite taste the same as back home. I miss it, but not half as much as I miss you, Aileen.

Anyway, I'm really tired now, so I'll sign off.

I still miss you every day, and whenever I wake up you are in my first thoughts.

Your loving fiancé,

Niall.

Aileen had read the letter countless times on the journey, and now that journey was behind her. In truth – or *in all fairness*, as Niall would have put it – she was halfway between nervous and scared. But she took a few steps along the station platform and told herself that Niall was right – there was a train back home if she needed it, and there always would be. That fleeting thought of Niall reminded her that he was enduring much greater hardships. If he could do what he was doing, then she could work in a factory.

Just as she'd heard on the wireless, the posters were everywhere and they guided her out of the station and to the building where she would be allocated a job and somewhere to live.

After queuing up there, she had a short conversation about what work she would prefer.

'Dressings and materials it is,' the man said, which didn't make much sense to Aileen. But she was given a small map of directions to her workplace and lodgings, and set off.

This was going to be a completely new way of life. She would have regular money coming in, but more responsibility: she would have to pay for her food and lodgings. This was a big city with no family to give her eggs and no local farms to provide a joint of pork in return for labour. And the first step in this new life was turning up for work. On time. As she walked through the Belfast streets she noticed it was just like Dublin in one important respect: there were clocks everywhere here, so turning up for work would be easy. She headed for the factory.

Aileen had been adamant in her desire not to get into an argument with her father before leaving Leetown, and the parting had gone as well as she could have expected: few words had been exchanged, but none of them angry. That, she hoped, was because she'd told him she wouldn't be working on weapons or their components, so he had no need to concern himself that she was helping to arm the Brits. It had been Briana's idea to emphasize that so as not to burn her bridges. She really missed Briana, who had given her valuable advice: keep Leetown as a refuge in case she wasn't happy in Belfast, because she'd have to go back there some day anyway. Avoiding a big bust-up would also make life a little easier for Mammy and Briana, which was no bad thing.

Aileen saw no reason to renege on that agreement, and so turned up to work at the gates of a modern, square-fronted building where they manufactured bandages, dressings and blankets for the Forces.

There was no induction period. There were no training sessions. A stern woman who didn't introduce herself took Aileen's name and address and led her to an empty seat in a room where women – a couple of hundred, Aileen estimated – busied themselves cutting pieces of lint bandage from a large roll and packaging them into gummed envelopes. To the right of each woman was a large wooden box into which the completed packages were being thrown.

Aileen sat down, spent a few minutes looking around and getting herself comfortable on the seat, then leaned over to the woman alongside her. 'What are we supposed to do?' she said.

The woman pointed to a table in the corner of the room. 'Get your envelopes from there.' She nodded to the reel of material in front of Aileen. 'Cut that there lint to the right size and put the piece in the envelope. The size you need is printed on the envelope.' She pointed to the teacup in front of Aileen and then to the corner of the room again. 'Fill that cup over at that sink and use the water to gum down the envelope. The more lint you get through, the more you get paid, but be sure to seal the envelope tight else you get your wages docked.'

The woman then returned to doing exactly those tasks herself, at a speed Aileen would have thought impossible had she not seen it with her own eyes. Each envelope made a scuffing sound as it was tossed into the box, and the combined sound wasn't unlike the hiss of an ocean. It sounded almost homely.

Aileen did as she was told and tossed the first of her envelopes into the cardboard box at her side. She was just a beginner and was probably the slowest woman there, but before long the bottom of the box was no longer visible.

Just as she was starting to get the hang of the work, a loud horn sounded. There were cheers from the women and they all jumped off their chairs, grabbed their coats and handbags and headed for the exit. Aileen put her coat on and steeled herself to make conversation with her neighbour while she turned around to pick up her case, but by the time she turned back the woman was gone.

Aileen followed the throng out into the darkness and stood shivering under a streetlight as she got her scrap of paper out and tried to get her bearings. She glanced back along the way she'd come only a few hours before, toward the railway station, where there was probably a train that would take her back home. She dismissed the thought and fifteen minutes later found herself standing outside 22 Kingdom Avenue, a neat and tidy but rather austere-looking terraced house. She glanced back along the street, then up at the house again, still unsure of how this was all working out. However, she had to admit that it all looked solid and well maintained, even if rather unfriendly.

She knew from her older sister Cathleen that in towns and cities people tended to lock their doors even when they were at home, so she gave the painted wood a couple of raps with her knuckles rather than try the handle.

The face that greeted her when the door opened couldn't have been more different to the property itself. The woman was middle-aged and smiled sweetly as she spoke.

'Can I help you?' she said in a soft voice that was as different to a Wicklow accent as Aileen had ever heard. Well, apart from in the films and on the BBC wireless broadcasts.

'I'm Aileen.' She offered the official slip of paper. 'They sent me from the—'

'Ah, yes!' It was then that the woman started to bow as though in deference, her face blushing as she grinned in welcome, said she'd been expecting her and introduced herself as Mrs McDonald. She told Aileen to come in and asked where she'd come from, whether she'd had a good journey, where she was working and whether it had got colder outside since the sun had gone down. Somewhere between the words she managed to grab Aileen's case by stealth as much as force before Aileen realized what had happened.

They carried on talking – at least Mrs McDonald talked and Aileen tried to interject the occasional word – as they went upstairs.

'Doreen will be home in a few minutes,' Mrs McDonald said as she opened a door at the back of the house and ushered Aileen through. 'You don't mind sharing, do you?'

'Oh, I'm used to sharing a bed,' Aileen said.

Mrs McDonald giggled, her shoulders twitching despite her attempts to suppress her amusement, as she placed Aileen's case on a bed. 'Anyway, you must be very tired. Tea isn't too far away but I'll let you settle in first.' She left and shut the door behind her.

Aileen stood in the silence and glanced around.

There were two beds in the room, a few feet apart, with a night table between. A wardrobe, a vanity table, an armchair and a window framed by floral curtains completed the inventory – apart from a picture of a galleon being tossed around an ocean. There were also the floorboards. Aileen had been upstairs in buildings before, but not very often, and had certainly never slept so far above the ground. It seemed unnatural and unnerving. But the most important aspect of the room was the two beds. Aileen still had no idea how many people she would be sharing the room with – or the bed, but either way it looked like paradise.

She kicked her shoes off and sat on the bed. It was softer than the one she shared with Briana back home and more comfortable by some distance. She lay down, curling a side of the bedcover over her and closed her eyes. Just to rest them.

The light was still on, but it had been an exhausting day. Aileen had travelled to somewhere that either was or wasn't a different country depending on your politics, had worked attentively for three hours, and was now lying on an unfamiliar bed, in an unfamiliar room, in an unfamiliar house. In an unfamiliar city.

She was asleep within a minute.

The creak of the door woke Aileen up. She lifted her head but needed to screw her eyes up against the stark light to see what was happening. A figure appeared to glide across the room in front of her and settle on the other bed. It was a woman – younger than Aileen by the looks of it.

'Hello there,' Aileen said.

'Hello.'

The voice was light and nervous, the body language timid. This wasn't a woman, it was a girl.

'I'm Aileen.'

The girl turned to face Aileen but kept her head bowed, her eyes down. 'I'm Doreen.'

Aileen tried to catch her eye and let out a light laugh. 'Aileen and Doreen. We could be sisters.'

No reaction. Not even a smile.

'Your mammy said you'd be here soon enough.'

'She's my aunt.'

'Ah, right.' Aileen waved a finger around the room. 'Is it only the two of us sharing this room?'

A single nod.

Aileen thought for a moment. 'Listen, Doreen. If you'd rather I didn't stay here, I wouldn't mind, honestly. I mean, if—'

'No.'

Aileen waited for more explanation, but none came. 'Right,' she said. 'Good.'

'Aunt Susan and Uncle Jack say we owe it to you.'

'Well . . . I wouldn't quite say that. You don't really know me, so you can't owe me anything.'

Doreen gave a half-hearted, glum nod. Then there was a knock on the door. Aileen looked at Doreen, but there was no reaction.

'Come in,' Aileen said.

Mrs McDonald's head appeared around the door. 'Tea's almost ready,' she sang, 'if you'd both like to come down.'

'Thank you,' Aileen said. 'We'll be down in a minute.'

Before the meal was served, Aileen was introduced to Mr McDonald. She decided to stick with calling them Mr and Mrs McDonald rather than Jack and Susan until she was told otherwise. A large bowl of mashed potatoes and a smaller one containing peas and chopped carrots were placed in the middle of the table, and four plates of belly pork, steaming and shiny wet with grease, were set down. After saying grace, they helped themselves to potatoes and vegetables, with Mr McDonald insisting he went last. There was a little small talk about how work had been that day for Mr McDonald, who was a wages clerk at a local factory, and what sort of a place Leetown was, but the meal was mostly eaten in a pleasant silence.

'Is that an engagement ring I see on you?' Mrs McDonald said as Aileen was finishing.

'It is,' she replied. 'Oh, I was meaning to say, do you mind if my fiancé and my family write to me here?'

'Well, you live here, don't you?'

'Thank you, Mrs McDonald.'

'Have you any paper for me to write and tell him the address?' Aileen asked. 'I'll give you the money for it when I get paid.'

'Ah, no, you won't,' Mrs McDonald said. 'It's only paper.' She pointed to a small cupboard in the corner of the room. 'Help yourself. There's envelopes too. I don't think we have any stamps though.'

'That's grand,' Aileen said. 'I can buy stamps tomorrow. I should write to Mammy and Daddy too as soon as I can, so they know I'm safe and sound. They worry about me.'

At this, Mr and Mrs McDonald stared at each other and Doreen got up and quickly left the room, a few chunks of food left uneaten on her plate. Her feet could be heard thumping up the stairs.

Mr McDonald tutted, Mrs McDonald gave Aileen another sweet smile – although this time it came out a little twisted – and Aileen didn't know what to do.

'Is Doreen all right?' Aileen said after a few moments.

Mr McDonald ignored the question.

'She'll be fine,' Mrs McDonald said. 'She'll be . . . fine.'

Afterward, Aileen offered to help clear the table, but Mrs McDonald was having none of it and told her to make herself comfortable in the living room. Mr McDonald led the way, switching the wireless on as Aileen headed for an armchair. But as he reached for his pipe and tobacco she veered to the door, excused herself and went up to her bedroom.

Doreen was lying motionless on her bed, curled up like an infant, so Aileen crept over to her own bed, pulled Niall's letter out from her luggage and read it just once more before tucking it under her pillow. Later, after writing letters back home and to Niall, she slept with her head above his letter. And she slept well.

The next day Aileen was woken up early, and after washing they all ate a breakfast of fried bacon, egg and potato farls. Doreen was still quiet but seemed in better spirits, and the upset of the previous night wasn't mentioned. Aileen walked to the factory, taking a short detour to post her letters, much happier for telling her parents and Niall her address.

One thing she wasn't happy about was Doreen. The girl hadn't spoken more than a few words, so there was something going on there. But whatever it was, it wasn't Aileen's problem. They shared a bedroom, so if Doreen wanted to confide in her she would do so in her own time. Aileen had enough problems to cope with, getting used to a new city and her first-ever regular job.

At the factory, she filled her cup with water, grabbed an armful of envelopes, sat down and started work. After a while the work became automatic and her mind drifted. She reflected that she was glad she'd held firm and not turned back and gone home. Whatever was going on where she was staying, it could have been a lot worse and she felt lucky to be living with such a kind and hospitable family. It was strange not having to fetch fresh water from the well every day, but that was a chore she would not miss.

What she *was* already missing was her sister. Having a whole bed to herself had been a welcome luxury for one night, especially with Niall's letter close by, but she still missed Briana. She missed the warmth of a body next to her, someone to hold when she felt downhearted. And now, only one day after leaving home, and despite the welcoming family she was staying with, there was a creeping sense of a loneliness to come.

Chapter 12

Aileen's first few days in Belfast were pretty much the same. She would wake up, wash, eat breakfast, go to work, come home, have tea, listen to the wireless, try to avoid Mr McDonald's pipe smoke, then go to bed.

But that was good. Aileen was starting to feel at home in a noisy, bustling city that at first felt like it could have swallowed her whole. She was a little bored at times, but felt secure. There was still hardly anything in the way of conversation from Doreen. Yes, she was young – fifteen, so Mrs McDonald had told her – but even for a young girl she seemed distant, like she didn't belong, or didn't *want* to belong. Aileen mentioned the weather, how good Mrs McDonald's cooking was, where she was working, and more. But Doreen, although never rude, seemed uninterested in talking. Presumably in friendship too. Aileen's initial urge to ask her what was wrong, to find out whether she'd done anything to offend or upset her, had now subsided. But *something* was wrong, and she decided she would ask the obliging Mrs McDonald. But only if it came up in conversation – there was no point in prying.

On the Thursday, Aileen got paid. It was her first proper pay packet. After years of being given a few pennies here, a few pints of milk there, or a mutton chop elsewhere for helping out on a farm, it felt good. It felt official. Grown up.

As soon as she got home she asked Mrs McDonald what the weekly rent was.

'Ah, no,' she was told. 'Forget that.'

'But I'd like to pay you,' Aileen said. 'Tis only fair.'

Mrs McDonald simply shook her head, forcing that same twisted smile, and walked away mumbling something about having housework to do.

The thought of insisting or even simply asking again felt awkward, so Aileen said nothing. There was a little embarrassment among the polite conversation during tea – that much was clear from the quietness of Mrs McDonald and the occasional knowing glances Mr McDonald gave her and Aileen. But he said nothing, and the next evening tea was again punctuated with polite conversation.

'So, Aileen,' Mr McDonald said as they all tucked into plates of boiled cabbage, roast parsnips and shepherd's pie that they'd been warned contained no meat. 'What are you up to at the weekend?'

'I'm working tomorrow, Mr McDonald.'

'Ah, they have you working six days a week. I see.'

And then, after a few seconds of silence punctuated only by clicks of cutlery on crockery, Aileen spoke.

'What about you, Mr McDonald?'

'Seven days for me. But we have a long break on a Sunday for Mass.' He took a gulp of water, swallowed and gave Aileen a sideways look. 'Talking of which, I'm supposing you'll be attending the Catholic church?'

'Jack,' his wife said, a hint of scolding in her voice.

'Sure, I'm only asking the girl.'

'Well, what do you expect her to do?'

'Please,' Aileen said. 'It's grand. I've already seen where my church is.'

'Of course,' Jack said. 'I was only, you know . . . well, I was going to tell you where it was, just in case you didn't know.'

'Thank you.' Aileen smiled but kept her eyes low. 'This is very nice, Mrs McDonald,' she added. 'Lovely mash.'

'I had a little spare butter, so I did,' Mrs McDonald replied, 'and a spare egg, and besides that a half-pint of milk on the turn, so there's stewed apple with a little custard for afters.'

'Grand,' Mr McDonald said.

The next day Aileen went into work, lining up to collect her envelopes and cup of water as usual. She set them down on her desk and went to take off her coat. She stopped for a moment, surprised to see a different woman sitting next to her.

'I'm Mary,' the woman said. 'And yes, I am quite contrary, before you ask.' She giggled. 'People do. They make that joke. Mary, Mary, quite contrary.'

Mary looked older than Aileen, fuller in the face and with an extra line or two of experience. She also wore a skirt quite a few inches shorter than Aileen would have dared to wear.

'Hello, Mary. I'm Aileen. Nice to meet you.'

'I certainly hope it will be. And that sounds like a southern accent you have there. Is that right?'

'Tis. County Wicklow.'

'Ah, well. The more the merrier, Aileen. We need all the help we can get here to cope with Herr bloody Hitler and his followers.'

A whistle sounded, and the conversation died down to a murmur as the women started cutting the lint and filling their envelopes. Even Mary, who sounded like she was never going to stop talking, quietened down to concentrate on keeping her work rate up.

They had a tea break halfway through the morning and it was as though Mary had been given fresh batteries.

'How long have you worked here, Aileen?' she said as they stood outside for a few minutes to get out of the stale air. 'You look like you've been here a month, I would say. Wouldn't bet my life on it, but if I did I'd be wagering on a month. Is that right? About a month?'

'Only about a week,' Aileen tutted, 'but it *feels* like a month.'

Mary plucked a packet of cigarettes from her handbag and offered one to Aileen.

'Ah, no,' Aileen said. 'But thanks.'

Mary shrugged. 'You're better off without them anyhow.' She lit up and took a long drag, then held her arm out fully before tapping the ash off the end. 'And what are you doing with yourself after work tonight?'

The directness of the question stumped Aileen. She hadn't thought of doing anything differently to every other night she'd been in Belfast. This was a big city. There were no evening walks along the beach, no open-air dances. She just shrugged.

'You could always come with me for a drink,' Mary said. 'How would you like that, Aileen? We could pick ourselves up some GIs.'

'Some what?'

'You know, the American soldiers and sailors. You must have seen them.' She twirled a hand toward the factory floor. 'Stuck inside there all day perhaps you haven't noticed, but you can hardly move for them in the city.'

'Ah, yes,' Aileen said. 'I see what you mean. It's been on the wireless, so it has. Three hundred thousand of them, so they say.'

Mary frowned. 'Sure, you know more about them than I do.'

'I wouldn't say that.' Judging by Mary's high heels, short skirt and pose, it seemed a fair assumption.

'So, anyway, what is it you usually do with yourself when you have time off?'

'Well, ah . . .' Aileen struggled to answer for a few seconds. 'I'm still getting my bearings, getting used to living in a city.'

'So, c'mon, what d'you say about the two of us going out tonight?'

'Ah, well, we'll see.'

Mary's elbow nudged her. 'Go on.'

'I'm supposed to be saving my money.'

Mary spluttered a laugh out as she exhaled smoke. 'Saving your money? Are you joking? Stick with me, Aileen. I know which pubs and dances are full of GIs. You'll never need to buy yourself a drink while you're there.' She thought for a moment. 'Or stockings. Or chocolate. Or chewing gum.'

'I'll think on it,' Aileen said.

The cigarette stub glowed as it fell to the ground, only to be twisted out by the toe of Mary's shoe. 'Suit yourself,' she said. 'But you're only going to have the one life.' She nodded for them both to go back inside and they started work again.

It was only toward the end of the day, when Aileen's work rate was slowing and after a lot of thought, that she leaned across to Mary and said, 'All right then.'

'What?'

'Tonight. We'll go out somewhere. If the offer's still there.'

Mary laughed sharply – a deep, raucous cackle. 'That's grand.'

'And thanks for asking me.'

'I knew you would. Sure, we'll have a grand time.'

'Do you ever go to the cinema?' Aileen asked.

Mary nodded slowly. 'Ah, sometimes. The old Yanks like that, reminds them of home, I suppose. And, of course, they pay for it. And ice cream too, at the intermission.'

'You make it sound like you do it all the time.'

Mary raised her eyebrows and returned to her work.

At the end of the working day they made arrangements to meet outside the factory, from where Mary would lead them into the city centre and to the pubs frequented by GIs.

Aileen went home, had tea, and was getting herself ready for going out when Mrs McDonald entered the room.

'Are you going out somewhere?' Mrs McDonald said with another one of her special, distinctly forced smiles.

Aileen, sitting in front of the mirror, brushing her hair out in front of the mirror, replied, 'Just with one of the women from work. To a pub or a dance, I think.'

Mrs McDonald sat down next to her and was clearly about to place a hand on her knee but thought better of it. 'You will be careful there, won't you?'

Aileen immediately stopped combing. 'What . . . what do you mean?'

'What with you being . . .' A nod to the ring on Aileen's finger completed the sentence.

'Ah, sure, I'll be grand, Mrs McDonald. I won't go doing anything daft.'

'Yes, but . . . those American men.'

'What about them?'

Mrs McDonald glanced behind her at the open door and lowered her voice. 'They can be very . . . very brazen. You know, where the women are concerned.'

'Brazen?'

'Well, I don't know how I can put it, but a girl's head can be easily turned. They're fine men, so they are. They're brave sorts – they must be to do what they do. But they have money too, and they're not afraid to use it to get what they want.' She widened her eyes. 'If you know what I mean.'

Aileen nodded. 'That's all right, Mrs McDonald. Thank you very much for warning me. I'll try my best to be careful.'

'Good.' Mrs McDonald took Aileen's hand and gave it a gentle squeeze, then stood and headed for the door.

'Mrs McDonald?' Aileen said.

'Yes, dear?'

Now Aileen lowered her voice to little more than a whisper. 'Have I done anything to upset Doreen?'

'Aach, no.'

'Doesn't she like sharing a room with me?'

Mrs McDonald shook her head. 'She's had . . . she's just had a hard time of it. It's only her way. You've done nothing wrong.'

For a moment Aileen was going to ask the question that had been on the tip of her tongue a few times: what had happened to Doreen's parents? But a part of her didn't want to know the answer. 'All right.' She nodded. 'She's nice, so she is. I'm sure we'll get along grand. In time.'

'I'm sure.' Mrs McDonald smiled and left the room, only to reappear almost immediately. 'Oh, I nearly forgot. This came for you today.' She took a letter from her apron pocket and dropped it on the bed.

Before Mrs McDonald had reached the top of the stairs outside, Aileen had ripped open the envelope and was reading.

18 January 1944

My dearest Aileen,

Thank you so much for letting me know where to write to you. And, of course, for your letters. They really are the tonic I need. I'm so relieved you've found good lodgings and are enjoying the job although, like you say, it's early days yet. How is life in Belfast? Have you had time to go into the city?

I'm not really in any great pain at the moment as my leg is still in a cast, so my main problem is boredom. I've tried reading books, but I can't do that all day because it gives me a headache. I can, however, read your letters over and over again, so please write again soon if you have the time.

I'm trying to keep myself fit by using dumb-bells. I'll wager I could be like that Charles Atlas fellow by the time I'm finished – in the arms at least.

And I have to be grateful. Doctors keep stressing that I will make a full recovery, but the man in the next bed, Neville, lost both of his legs while fighting in Italy. He says he didn't know anything about it and didn't feel any pain, he just sensed a flash and then woke up to find himself being carried on a stretcher. He later found out a bomb dropped by the Luftwaffe caused a wall to fall on his legs, crushing them both. I dread to think what sort of life he will have when he goes home. He laughs and jokes during the day – such a jolly sort – but when the lights go out I've heard him crying. I feel so sorry for him, but I also know there are many even worse off.

I'm sorry if all of that sounds a bit depressing. Rest assured I am in good spirits considering my situation and trying not to let my boredom show.

I think of you constantly.

Your loving fiancé,

Niall.

P.S. I found out why this is called the Cambridge Military Hospital. It was named after the Duke of Cambridge, who was the top army fellow when it opened.

Chapter 13

Aileen and Mary walked into the pub, the Red Lion, just off one of the main crossroads in Belfast city centre. Mary glanced around, covering all the corners, while Aileen shrank in embarrassment, wondering what Mammy and Daddy would think of her strolling into a pub – especially one so dimly lit and so full of middle-aged men propping up the bar.

The floorboards were bare but at least they looked clean, and Aileen had just about come to terms with the idea of finding a seat when Mary gave her head the briefest of shakes and said, 'Mmm . . . no.'

'What?' Aileen replied.

'No Americans.'

'Do we need Americans?'

'*What?*' Mary looked her up and down, curling up a lip.

'No. I mean, we could have a drink here – just one – and have a talk. I hardly know you.'

'I haven't much to tell,' Mary said, heading for the door. 'C'mon.'

Outside, Mary cast the same expert eye around the streets. 'Must be a dance on,' she said. Then she set off at speed, like one of those torpedoes they'd mentioned on the wireless, and Aileen struggled to keep up.

'How much is it to get in?' Aileen whispered as they queued up outside the dance hall a few minutes later.

Mary shook her head in despair.

'What? I'm only asking.'

'They don't charge the women,' Mary said. 'We're bait, you might say.'

Aileen thought for a moment. And what she thought was that she didn't much care for the idea of being 'bait'. She also thought of Niall, still recovering in some military hospital in England. She dismissed her thoughts of guilt. No. It was only Mary being daft. There was no harm. She was just going to meet people. Niall wouldn't mind; he'd even mentioned going out of a night and had done so himself in London.

The room was huge – bigger than Leetown's church. A jazz band was playing at the far end – very American, Aileen thought. To her right was a bar. To her left, a wooden dance floor was flanked on each side by a dozen or so tables, each with four chairs. Many of those tables were full – mostly occupied by two women and two uniformed GIs.

'C'mon,' Mary said, raising her voice over the blaring music, 'let's grab ourselves a table.'

Aileen followed and they sat, patiently, all the while looking around the room. Aileen was staring half in fear at the men, all smartly dressed, all holding glasses or bottles of beer. Mary was clearly just scanning the uniforms.

They had to wait about six minutes. It was no more than that; Aileen was used to timing eggs boiling, so she knew.

'Over there,' Mary said, nudging Aileen.

Aileen looked across the floor to the two men leaning against the bar. Both were holding bottles. They were talking, but they were looking directly at Mary or Aileen – it wasn't clear which man was eyeing up which woman.

'Wave to them,' Mary whispered.

But Aileen simply gulped, her mouth getting dryer by the second. So Mary waved.

One of the men took his elbow off the bar, his spare hand instinctively tucking his shirt into his trousers. Another few words were exchanged between them and they started the walk. But it was more of a swagger than a walk.

'I'll have the light-haired one,' Mary managed to whisper to Aileen. 'The one with the good teeth.'

Aileen was too scared to care which one sat next to her.

As it turned out, the men had their own ideas, the slightly shorter but stockier man with brown hair choosing to sit next to Mary. He also did the talking. He tilted his sailor's cap to one side while he said, 'Well, hello, ladies of Ulster.'

Aileen said nothing and Mary was clearly too preoccupied to care.

'I'm Steve. This is my friend Marvin.'

Aileen and Mary introduced themselves.

Marvin, sitting next to Aileen, nodded politely and said, 'Nice to meet you both.'

But from then on it was all Steve. He asked Mary and Aileen what they wanted to drink – Aileen asked for a lemonade, Mary the same but with vodka – and told Marvin to go and get them.

While he was gone, Aileen listened to Mary and Steve talk. By now, Mary had clearly forgotten that this was Steve and she'd previously chosen Marvin, and was matching him sentence for sentence.

'Aileen, isn't it?' Marvin said when he sat down with the drinks a few minutes later.

She nodded and noticed his broad smile which appeared fixed, all the better to show off unnaturally white teeth. His eyes were alive with a bluish-grey colour but also warm, his eyelids drooping ever so slightly, his blond hair cropped short but thick.

'So, Aileen, tell me something about yourself.'

'What would you like to know?'

He seemed taken aback, which was after all the desired effect. He still kept those teeth on display. And she still didn't smile, not wanting to encourage him.

'Are you from Belfast?'

'I'm from the South.'

'South Belfast?'

'Southern Ireland.'

He nodded. Aileen saw his eyes work their way over her face. And she didn't much care for the experience.

'I'm from New York,' he said.

'Right.'

His smile dropped for a second and he softened his voice. 'You know, you should really lighten up a little.'

'Why's that?' Aileen said, almost snapping the words out.

He thought about it for a moment and the glance at her torso was very quick. 'Because you're a very attractive young woman and you might enjoy yourself if you were to lighten up a little.'

Aileen had to gulp to believe the nerve of the man. She looked to the side, where Steve and Mary were almost in each other's faces and, more importantly, Steve's hand had planted itself firmly on to Mary's knee.

'Hey, Aileen,' Marvin said, hooking a thumb in Steve's direction. 'That isn't me. Don't get all frightened. I only wanna talk. Really. And I'm sorry for calling you an attractive young woman – perhaps that was a little forward of me.'

Aileen took a swig of lemonade. 'So, you're from New York?'

'Much better,' he said, the smile widening again.

'I know that place from the films – Central Park and the Statue of Liberty.'

He shook his head. 'No, I'm from upstate.'

'I thought you said you were from New York?'

His jaw twitched as he struggled to contain a laugh, and his mouth fell open as he lost the battle and chuckled away to himself. 'Hey, I'm sorry. I'm from New York State but not the city.'

'Ah, right.'

'You don't know the place. It's an easy mistake.'

Aileen kept her face straight. He apologized again.

'So, does that mean you live near Hollywood?' she said. 'Where they make the films – the *movies* as you say?'

His face cracked into discomfort. 'Uh, no. That's . . . that's the other side of the country.'

Aileen raised her eyebrows at him and for a moment they were still and silent. And then it was Aileen's turn to laugh, covering her mouth with her hand as she stared at him, his face getting redder by the second.

He nodded slowly. 'Ah, I get it. You knew that one, right?'

She carried on laughing, but eventually it subsided. 'Los Angeles,' she said. 'Which is in California. I read about it.'

'You're cute,' he said, frowning but smiling. 'You're cute. And I like that.'

Aileen had never been called 'cute' before. Even Niall hadn't used that word and she had to admit that it felt nice, but just then her attention was diverted by Steve and Mary getting up from their seats.

'We're just going out for a walk,' Steve said, not even trying to disguise his leer.

Mary leaned across to Aileen. 'I might not be back for some time. Will you be all right for getting home on your own?'

'I think I can remember. I'll be off soon anyway.'

'Good.' Mary allowed herself to be pulled away by Steve – although she was laughing as it happened, and a minute later they were gone.

Aileen swirled the inch of lemonade left in her glass and drank it.

'Would you like another?' Marvin said.

Aileen shook her head.

'Or something stronger? One with vodka in if you prefer?'

'I don't drink alcohol.'

He nodded acceptance. 'Mmm, beauty *and* wisdom.'

'Ah,' Aileen replied, 'money *and* flattery.'

'You really are determined to give as good as you get, aren't you?'

'I try to,' she said. 'Anyhow, I'd better be going now.'

'Would you like me to walk you home?'

'I'd expect nothing less of a gentleman. You could even lend me your coat.'

Marvin quickly finished his drink and stood up. 'Oh, sure, of course.'

'I'm joking,' she said. 'I already have a coat. But walking me home would be grand if you don't mind.'

The walk took about twenty minutes, during which they talked some more. Marvin ran through the different foods available back home that he couldn't buy in Belfast, how many theatres there were in New York City, how dramatic the unspoilt countryside was upstate, and how his uncle in the city had lined up a good job for him when the war was over.

Aileen didn't say much. There wasn't much she *could* say about life in Leetown after hearing about the famous actors and actresses Marvin had seen on his many visits to Broadway.

They stood outside 22 Kingdom Avenue and Aileen thanked Marvin for walking her home.

'Well, thank you for your company,' he said. 'It was short, but I hope it was as sweet for you as it was for me.'

She thought for a second. 'Mmm . . . We didn't quite hit it off like Steve and Mary, but it was grand. So thank you.'

'Just my luck,' Marvin mumbled. 'You take a guy along for the ride and . . .' He shook his head and the sentence was left unfinished.

'What?'

'Nothing.' He stood tall, hands on hips, and sighed. 'Well, I didn't want to say but I . . . uh . . . I spotted you, thought you were the most beautiful woman in the room and asked Steve to come along with me to . . .'

'To separate me from Mary?'

'I'm just being on the level with you, Aileen.'

'If it's possible to be on the level about being underhand and devious.'

Half his mouth smiled. 'Oh, you're good. You're very good.' Aileen didn't react and his lopsided smile fell away. 'Look, I've come clean. I'm an honest guy. And, uh, I'd like to see you again. If, that is, you'd like to see me again.'

'Ah, I don't think so, Marvin.'

She turned to walk to the front door but he stepped in front of her. 'Please. Just one more time. Didn't we eventually get along together okay?'

He stood close, forcing Aileen to look up. This close, she could tell he was almost a foot taller than her, and his jaw full of those perfectly arranged teeth now looked as square as his shoulders. With those eyes somehow looking sorry below that shock of short-cropped blond hair, he managed to look manly but also like a lost little boy.

'All right,' Aileen found herself saying before she could think. 'Only the once.'

'Next Saturday?' he said.

'Yes. Next Saturday.'

'Great. I'll be here at seven, yeah?'

'Yes. Grand.'

He stepped away and Aileen went inside.

She shut the door behind her and leaned on it, wondering why the heck she'd agreed to see him again.

Mrs McDonald's head popped around the edge of the door. 'Did you have a nice time?' she said.

'I did, thank you, Mrs McDonald.'

'And who was the fine gentleman in the uniform?'

'Oh, he's just a friend,' Aileen said. 'Just a friend.'

Mrs McDonald gave a tight-lipped smile and nodded slowly. 'Ah, good. That's good. If he's a friend you know you're welcome to invite him in, don't you?'

'Thank you, Mrs McDonald. We'll see.'

The next Monday, Aileen was almost disappointed to find that she'd been moved to another desk, well away from Mary. It was only during the morning tea break that Aileen felt a tap on her shoulder.

'Coming out for some fresh air, Aileen?'

'Mary? I'm sorry. They told me to sit here and—'

'They like to swap us all about. Keeps us from chattering too much. C'mon.' She hooked her head toward the back door and a few minutes later they were outside and Mary was lighting up a cigarette. She took a long drag and tilted her head back to blow the smoke straight up. 'Did you get back home all right on Saturday?' she said.

'I did.'

'Good.'

'And what about you?'

'What about me?'

'Did you enjoy your evening with Steve?'

'Ah, I did that, all right.'

'Where did you go?'

'Go?' Another pause to smoke. 'I spent most of the time in the back of a truck.'

Aileen giggled. 'Mary, you're awful bold, so y'are.'

'Do I shock you?'

'Ah, no,' Aileen lied. 'Sure, it does nobody any harm.' *Except yourself*, she wanted to add.

'What about you? Did Square Marvin take you anywhere nice?'

'*Square* Marvin?'

'That's what they call him, the rest of the American sailor fellows.'

'What does that mean?'

Mary shrugged. 'Boring, I suppose. Did you find him boring?'

'I didn't, no. We had a good talk, but I was a little tired so I came home early.'

'Early?'

'About eight.'

'*Eight?*' Mary laughed, but with a bitter undertone, Aileen thought. 'You're joking.'

'No, I mean nine – nearer half nine, really.'

'You don't know what you missed, girl.'

'What did I miss?'

Mary lifted her cigarette up a few inches. 'Twenty of these, some chewing gum, and some prime American beef.'

'Beef?'

'As in *flesh*.'

Now Aileen couldn't hide her shock and felt her face warming. Mary clearly noticed the blushing and looked her up and down, her smile only disappearing when her lips locked on to her cigarette.

'Mary?' Aileen eventually said.

'What?'

'Well, if you don't mind me asking . . .'

'C'mon. Spit it out, girl.'

'Do you do that sort of thing all the time?'

'Whenever the opportunity arises. And whenever I want to.'

'Don't you think . . . perhaps it's dangerous?'

'Perhaps danger is exactly what I like.'

'No, but, I mean, when you go with one of those men, do you, I mean, when you're alone with him, do you let him . . . ?'

Mary blew out a cloud of smoke and tilted her head toward a rare gleam of sunshine. 'Like I said, if the opportunity arises and if I want to, then yes.' She aimed a look at Aileen and shrugged. 'But not always.'

'Do your mammy or daddy know what you do?'

'Well . . .' Mary smiled, but Aileen thought it a sad smile. 'Mammy got done by the Blitz, so she did. And Daddy? Well, he might as well have gone with her.'

'Why's that?' Aileen said, immediately regretting it.

'He got injured. Badly. In the head. Ended up in a special hospital. I visit him when I can, but there's hardly any point – he hardly knows who I am. The stairs don't go all the way to the attic, you might say.'

It was a terrible thing to say about your own daddy, Aileen thought, but she also thought better of saying that to Mary. All she said was, 'Oh, I'm sorry.'

'So life's for living. That's what I tell myself. And I have a good time.'

'But . . . I know it's awful about your mammy and daddy, but don't you worry you'll never find a husband?'

'Oh, I already found one of those, all right.'

'You did? Really?'

'Yes, really.' Mary took another few breaths while fixing her gaze to the distance. She gulped and her jaw trembled slightly as she spoke. 'We were married for seven and a half months. Two hundred and twenty-six days it was; I remember counting them all. And even now I feel as though I can remember every last glorious one of them. He was such a lovely man. William, his name was. Everyone else called him Bill, but I called him Will and he liked that. He bought me flowers every Sunday. Whenever I found something funny and was about to laugh, he got there first, as though God had put the same sense of humour in our heads. And there was never a cross look between us in all that time, never mind a cross word.'

'So . . . are you still . . . ?'

Mary took a deep breath, her nostrils dilating. 'I begged him not to go. I'd had this dream a few nights before, but he told me not to be so daft, that he had to go, that it was orders. He told me he'd be back before I knew it.'

'What happened to him?'

'Dunkirk.' She wiped a tear from her cheek and sniffed. 'Dunkirk happened to him.'

'Oh, Mary. I'm so sorry. It must have been terrible for you.'

She nodded, and now Aileen saw frown lines on Mary's face that hadn't been there before. 'More than I could describe to you, Aileen. I wanted to die – and I mean really die – for a few weeks, and it was months before . . . I . . .' She sucked sharply on the cigarette, then dropped it, even though it was only half smoked. 'C'mon,' she said. 'Back to work.'

'But the whistle hasn't gone.'

'C'mon.' Mary marched back inside.

Chapter 14

25 January 1944

My dearest Aileen,

I'm afraid I can only manage a short letter today. This morning I took my first steps without help and I just had to tell you. Well, I say without help, but in all fairness I'm using crutches. It sounds stupid, but it feels grand just to be able to get around under my own steam. I'm overjoyed, and the doctors say the more walking I do the stronger my bone will get. I do find it tiring though. That's right, walking twenty yards has me exhausted.

The nurses here are real grand (and pretty, although none of them are as pretty as you).

I feel alive again.

Thank you so much for your last letter. I hope things are still going well for you in Belfast. And good luck with the girl you share a room with. Of course, I don't know why she's so quiet, but I think there are a lot of troubled people around these days due to the unpleasantness of the war.

Please remember that I only live for the day I see you again.

Your loving fiancé,

Niall.

Marvin knocked on the front door of the house at exactly seven o'clock. Aileen had come home from work, eaten and was almost ready to go out, but it was then that Mrs McDonald chose to hand her the letter from Niall. It was a short letter, but she'd read it four times, imagining Niall hobbling about and getting bored, and had lost track of the time.

So it was left to Mrs McDonald to get the door. Marvin stepped inside and held on to his small bunch of flowers for the full eight minutes Aileen kept him waiting. Mrs McDonald remarked how hard it was to get fresh flowers of late, then kept him talking for all of those eight minutes, three times remarking how smart all GIs seemed to be, and so was duly rewarded when the flowers were handed from Marvin to Aileen and then on to her. She was as thrilled as if they'd been bought for her, and left to put them in a vase.

'You didn't need to do that,' Aileen remarked as she and Marvin left the house and headed for the city centre.

Marvin frowned at her.

'The flowers,' she said.

'They were for you.'

Aileen frowned at him. 'I think we worked that out,' she said. 'And thank you, they were lovely, so they were, but I don't want people getting the wrong idea, especially Mrs McDonald.'

He asked where Aileen wanted to go, and she suggested the Red Lion – the only pub she'd been in before. Soon they were sitting at a table in a darkened corner – Marvin, Aileen, a pint of Guinness and a glass of lemonade.

Marvin took a sip and licked the creamy line from his top lip. 'So what do you do?' he said.

'Do?' Aileen asked.

'For a living.'

'Aren't I after telling you? I work at the dressings and materials factory.'

'I meant back home. Back in . . .' He pulled a crooked face. 'I'm sorry. I forgot.'

'Leetown, County Wicklow.'

'Yeah. What do you do there?'

'I . . . I don't do much, to tell you the truth. There aren't enough jobs to go around. I do a bit of cleaning when I can and help out on farms.'

He laughed as he looked her up and down.

'Why are you laughing?'

'I'm sorry,' he said. 'I just can't imagine you as a farmhand.'

'Why ever not?'

'Well, because you're far too pretty.'

'Sure, will you stop that?' She curled a lip at him in admonishment. 'Farm work is all there is – harvesting and dealing with animals, usually either the in-end or the out-end, if you know what I mean.'

Marvin almost choked on his second sip of beer, and had to cough a few times to recover. 'The in-end or the out-end?' he said, grinning. 'Did you really say that?'

'I do what I get paid to do – although I usually get paid in pints of milk or bacon or cuts of beef.'

'Sounds like a beautiful place, this Leetown.'

'You should visit, after the war is over.'

'When you've gone back there, you mean?'

'Preferably,' she said. 'Otherwise you won't be seeing me there because I'll still be here.'

He stared into space for a moment. 'I think I follow.'

They talked more about what Marvin had done back in Upstate New York, and what went on in Leetown, but mostly Aileen listened to Marvin talking about how he missed the dairy cattle, apple orchards and vegetable patches of his family farm, and how he would have to stop working once in a while just to admire the sun glinting off the Hudson, a mighty and lazy silver ribbon of a river dotted with steamships at any time of the day. He also bought two more drinks, and Aileen told him about Niall, and how her family weren't exactly keen on him because he'd joined the British Army, and how they were engaged to be married despite that. Marvin didn't seem to listen much to that part, and twenty minutes later both glasses were empty again, and Aileen let out a deep breath and smiled at him.

'Would you like another drink?' he said.

She shook her head. 'Thank you, but you could walk me home.'

'You sure? I could get you something different?'

'Thank you, but no.'

He nodded. 'To tell you the truth, I didn't really want another drink anyway. Come on, I'll take you home.'

He stood and held up her coat, and after a casual stroll and more talk they reached 22 Kingdom Avenue. There, Marvin pulled something from his pocket and handed it to her. 'Here,' he said.

'Chewing gum?' she said. 'I . . . I don't think I've ever tried it.'

'Well, now's your chance.'

'I'll try it later. But thanks, Marvin. That's very kind of you.'

He looked over at the house. 'You gonna invite me in?'

'I'm a little tired.' She tried to smile sweetly at him.

'Oh,' he said. 'Well, okay.' He shrugged and smiled back, swapping his weight from foot to foot. 'So I guess this is where we say goodnight,' he said. 'Did you have a good time?'

'I did,' Aileen said. 'I enjoyed talking with you.'

'Perhaps we could do it again.'

'Perhaps.'

He held an arm around her shoulder and leaned in. Aileen saw his face coming toward her, then felt his lips touch hers and stay there. She pushed him away and made a noise she hoped would put him off. It did.

'What?' he said. 'What is it?'

Aileen gave him a sour look. 'No, Marvin. Really – I only wanted a bit of company.'

'I could be company.'

'I think you know what I mean.'

'You don't like me? I thought we were getting on pretty swell.'

Aileen held her hand up to him, the stone of her engagement ring glinting in the moonlight. 'So you haven't noticed this? You didn't hear me talk about Niall?'

He shrugged, his face dropping slightly in disappointment. 'So you're engaged? So what?'

'But . . . I'm *engaged*. To be *married*.'

'Jeez, Aileen. I'm asking you to have a little fun – not to marry me.'

'But doesn't it bother you?'

He shrugged. 'Well, I don't mind if you don't.'

Aileen looked up at the square jaw, the bright teeth still peeping through a thin smile, the neatly trimmed hair. Somehow the face didn't seem quite so handsome now.

'You know, Marvin, sometimes you're a lovely man, but I think I *do* mind.'

Finally, Marvin seemed deflated. 'Oh,' he said, 'I'm sorry. I just thought . . .'

'What, Marvin? What did you think?'

'If you must know, I thought we were just two lonely souls, miles away from home, trying to make friends.'

'Perhaps you're right, Marvin, perhaps you're right. But we're clearly from very different parts of the world.'

Aileen turned and strutted to the front door. There were more words from Marvin but she didn't listen to them. A few seconds later she was standing at the foot of the stairs and could no longer hear his voice. Perhaps she'd been a little harsh, lost her temper with him even. It might just have been his way – how things happened where he came from. Well, at least he was no longer under any illusions.

Aileen's body jolted at the sight of Mrs McDonald's head poking out into the hallway.

'Are you all right, Aileen?'

'I'm grand, thank you, Mrs McDonald.'

'You . . . ah . . . you don't look so well.'

All Aileen could manage was a nod.

'Listen, Aileen. It's none of my business, but . . . well, what I mean is, was he a bit brazen with you, this Marvin fellow?'

'You're right, Mrs McDonald. It's none—' She stopped herself saying it by taking a sharp breath. *No, it wasn't Mrs McDonald's fault.* 'Thank you for asking,' she said after calming herself, 'but I'm grand. Marvin's just a friend. Well, he *was* a friend.'

Mrs McDonald's lips pursed and tightened like a string bag. 'Very well,' she said. 'Can I get you a cup of hot milk?'

Aileen nodded, and was ushered into the living room.

Thursday came around again, and with it Aileen's next payday. As soon as she got back to her lodgings she went into the backyard, where Mrs McDonald was busy shoving sheets through a mangle, beads of sweat forming on her brow despite the chilly February air.

'Mrs McDonald, I need to talk to you.'

'That's sounds a little serious, so it does,' she replied jovially, half laughing as she spoke.

'It's about the rent.'

'Oh.' Mrs McDonald stood still, holding a sheet. 'But I've told you, there's no rent to pay.'

'And I think I should insist. I can afford it. I'm not spending any of the money I'm earning.'

'Ha! Isn't *that* a good thing.'

'But I'd really prefer to pay you rent.'

'No. It's grand. We have the room.'

'But the heat, the hot water. Even if I only pay for my food.'

For the first time since Aileen had met her, Mrs McDonald's face was completely devoid of humour or warmth, and it took Aileen aback. *Had she offended her?* She certainly felt like she'd offended Doreen. Perhaps there was something about Belfast people she'd misunderstood.

Mrs McDonald dropped the sheet she was holding into the wicker basket and stepped toward the door. 'Let's go inside. Quick. My Jack is due back soon.' She gestured to the dining table and both women sat down, Aileen more than a little unsure and starting to regret her approach.

Mrs McDonald's face was still blank and lifeless. She looked away from Aileen, down to her lap, and drew breath.

'You won't remember the Blitz,' she said.

'Wasn't that in London?'

Mrs McDonald's jowls trembled, and it took a few seconds to get them back under control. 'We had our own. Perhaps the Germans didn't want us to feel left out.' She excused herself and hurriedly fetched a cup of water, sitting and taking a gulp before continuing. 'Twas soon after Easter, three years back this April. Little Doreen didn't live here back then; she was at home in Crown Street. But on that day she was out playing in Jubilee Park with her friends, so she was. Others weren't so lucky.'

As Mrs McDonald steadied herself to continue, Aileen said, 'You mean . . . her mammy and daddy?'

Mrs McDonald closed her eyes as she spoke. 'My sister. Her husband. Two sons.'

'Oh dear, Mrs McDonald. Oh God, I'm sorry. I didn't realize, so I didn't. Were they all . . . ?'

Mrs McDonald gave a single nod, her eyes squeezed shut in pain. She took a minute to compose herself. 'When I think of Doreen, that little girl lost, I can feel my heart screaming inside of me.'

'I'm so sorry. Poor Doreen.'

Mrs McDonald shook her head. 'You weren't to know. We felt incredibly lucky, Jack and myself living here. And that was all it was – luck. We're not too far from certain factories, you see. But for the grace of God we could easily have been bombed too.' She took a weary breath. 'Like I say, we were spared here, but we could feel the shock of the explosions, we felt the heat of burning buildings – well, no, entire *streets* were burning. It seemed as though the whole city was alight. I hope I never go to hell, but I've tasted it. *I've tasted it*, so I have. In the end, they say we lost almost a thousand people. A huge number of houses were left as wrecks – just uninhabitable – and half the city was like a desert of bricks. A lot of it still is.'

Mrs McDonald fell silent, and Aileen didn't dare break that silence.

After a few moments Mrs McDonald turned and eyed the clock. 'And I suppose you'll be wondering what this has to do with yourself.'

'I suppose I am, yes.'

'You see, when the Luftwaffe did their worst, we were at their mercy. We weren't prepared for that scale of attack – nobody could have been. It was so brutal, so relentless. They showed us no mercy. And as the fires burned, Jack and I changed. At first, once the planes left the smoke-heavy air above Belfast, we were so relieved they'd spared us. But then we realized there was so much more to come. The fires raged and we feared they'd engulf the whole of our street and everyone in it. 'Twas then that the fire engines turned up.' She edged closer to Aileen, looked her in the eye. 'You see, we're Protestants, for the Union, loyal to the king and proud to be British, so we are. But the . . . the Catholics in the South – your country – they sent up fire engines and firemen, from Dublin and places in between. They all pitched in to put the fires out. We'll never know if they made the difference, but our house survived and we survived. And then, when it was all over, some of the houses over the border took in homeless and looked after them. A lot of these people were in little more than underwear with no belongings in the world, and some with no family either. Poor Doreen was due to be one of them. Well, Jack and myself never managed to have children, and Doreen was always the closest thing we ever had to a daughter, so we said no, that she was our family now, that we'd take care of her. But the offer from across the border was there, and it was appreciated.'

She took a long, calming sigh and a sip of water before continuing. 'Moving on to more recent times, when the authorities were looking for volunteers to take in workers – the people like yourself coming up from the South to help with the war effort – we were so grateful for what your people did during the Blitz that we jumped at the chance, and put our names down, so we did.'

A key rattled in the door. Both women heard it. Neither moved.

'And that's why, my dear Aileen, while I breathe I shan't be taking a penny of rent from you.'

The sound of footsteps came from the hallway. Then a cheery whistle echoed around the house.

'We'll not talk about this again, Aileen, but I'll tell you this. You keep your money. Take it back home when this horrible war is over. Spend it wisely, and spend it on what *you* want to spend it on. Spend it on something that'll make you happy. Will you promise me that?'

'I will,' Aileen said, her voice quavering with emotion. 'I promise.'

Mrs McDonald wiped her face clean of tears just as the door opened. Mr McDonald stood there, briefcase in hand.

'What's she got you doing now?' he said to Aileen.

Aileen's attention swapped between them.

'I was just telling her to be careful out there of an evening,' Mrs McDonald said.

'Ah, good.' Mr McDonald leaned down and kissed her. 'Are you all right, Susan? You look like you've been . . .'

'I'm fine, I'm fine. I had a splash of soapy water in my eyes a few minutes back, so I did.'

'Ah, right. So, what's for tea?'

Chapter 15

Aileen came to accept without question what Mrs McDonald had told her about the rent and Doreen, and put the matters behind her. Working at the factory wasn't exactly hard work – not compared with mucking out a cowshed or baling hay – but it had started to become a habit. A boring habit. She'd also started to realize that sitting at home with the McDonalds every evening, reading and listening to the wireless, wasn't going to alleviate the boredom. Twice Mary had asked her to go out for a drink again, and twice Aileen had declined. She'd done that because the last thing she wanted was another Marvin. Yes, Marvin had been pleasant company, but she didn't like the boldness and brashness of the man, and Niall certainly wouldn't have approved. She'd told him in her last letter that she'd gone out for a drink just to get to know the other women in the factory, to make friends in the new city, but hadn't mentioned GIs or Marvin or even Mary.

She got home the next Friday, still having those second thoughts about turning down Mary's offer, to find another letter from Niall placed on her pillow by Mrs McDonald. Perhaps it was a sign – a sign of support for her decision not to go out with Mary. She ripped open the envelope before she'd even kicked her shoes off.

7 February 1944

My dearest Aileen,

Thank you so much for your last letter. It's good that you're going out of an evening. You shouldn't feel guilty about that because you're doing a grand job for the war effort all week, so you've earned it. And Belfast must be an exciting city. Oh, Aileen, I wish I was closer and could take you out to the cinema or the theatre or just for a drink. Even to see your face would make my heart sing with happiness.

I'm still making good progress. I'm now out of the hospital and back in normal barracks, although on lighter duties. I'm not long back from walking almost half a mile. Can you believe that? In a few weeks I'm going to try some gentle running to get myself fitter. Hopefully at some stage in the future when I'm better I can apply for leave. My mother also writes to me and she's awful lonely. Of course, when I do come over I'll see you one way or another, even if I have to travel up to Belfast.

It was funny. I felt so tired halfway through my walk, as though I needed to stop and rest. Then a strange thing happened. My mind wandered, and for a while I imagined that I wasn't on my own, that you were right by my side, holding my hand, and that we were walking across that bridge and over the sand at Leetown. That sounds a little daft, but it made a big difference to the way I felt. I had more energy. Yes, thinking you were with me somehow made my walk easier. And when I came back I realized that thinking of you makes this whole job of war a little easier to bear. So don't ever think that you and the other women don't play their part in this fight.

Anyway, I'm so tired after the walk that I need another rest, so I'll sign off for now.

Your loving fiancé,

Niall.

The letter made Aileen think. Perhaps Niall wouldn't mind her going out. At least, he wouldn't like her sitting in the house getting bored – he'd said as much in his letter. And she would only be going out for a talk with a woman from the factory. More importantly, she *did* work hard during the week and deserved a little relaxation occasionally. Why, Niall had been out drinking with other soldiers – once to London, so he'd said.

Yes, perhaps she should go out with Mary again, but avoid getting involved with those Americans. She might even show Mary that there was more to life than cigarettes, chewing gum and American 'beef'.

By the time she started work the next day she'd convinced herself it was okay. During the morning break she sidled along to Mary, started up a conversation, and it was arranged.

That evening they went out again, but to a different pub, although Mary had chosen it. It wasn't what Aileen had in mind. It was much more boisterous than the Red Lion – certainly too noisy to talk to each other.

But Aileen told herself not to be a stick in the mud, to sit and try at least to hold a conversation with Mary. Yes, the laughter of the drunken men at the bar seemed devilish, but they would probably leave. So, on Aileen's insistence, they bought their own drinks – a lemonade for Aileen, a lemonade with gin for Mary – and sat down. Even then, Aileen wanted to sit at a table far away from the men at the bar, but Mary insisted otherwise.

After a few questions from Aileen on where Mary lived and what else she liked doing of a weekend, and a few non-committal answers from Mary, who kept glancing toward the bar, a group of four men wandered over. Whereas Mary had barely uttered a word to Aileen, she couldn't stop talking now – 'A tall, handsome sort like yourself', or 'Texas? You're from Texas where the big cowboys are?', or 'That would be for you to find out', or even 'What sort of a girl do you think I am?' – delivered with one raised eyebrow.

It was as if Aileen wasn't there.

When Mary got up to leave with one of them, this time she didn't turn to Aileen and ask whether she was all right for getting home on her own; she was obviously more interested in nylon stockings and chewing gum.

Now the three remaining men sat down at the table next to Aileen – sitting on chairs the wrong way and leaning their forearms on the backrest like they did in the films. They started talking to her, asking where she was from and telling her what a pretty face she had and, very soon after that, what shapely legs she had. Later on she would think to herself that these were probably decent men, but as Aileen's mother had once told her, alcohol can smother decency.

Aileen made her excuses and left. But she didn't know the way home, and meandered through the streets for half an hour getting increasingly anxious. She was relieved to see the Red Lion, from where she knew she could find her way back. Before she reached Kingdom Avenue the heavens opened. She was soaked through by the time she got to number 22, but sat on the second step of the stairs for a few minutes, her mind racing with the possibilities of what could have happened to her.

She decided to be polite to Mary at work, but not to go out with her again. And this time she wouldn't change her mind.

For the next few weeks Aileen spent six days out of seven working at the factory, and every evening saving the money she'd earned, usually listening to the wireless or reading, occasionally playing cards with Mr and Mrs McDonald and Doreen. There was always the cinema, but she couldn't go on her own. Mr and Mrs McDonald had made it plain that they didn't understand the interest, Mr McDonald especially questioning why anyone would pay money to watch people pretending to be other people. She'd asked Doreen to go with her on more than one occasion, telling her which stars were in the latest film, even offering to pay for her. But Doreen didn't want to go.

Saturday evenings were particularly difficult. Aileen would try not to think of the few occasions she'd gone to pubs in the city centre. She had to admit that the hubbub, the slightly seedy characters and the conversation in such an atmosphere – all of these held an attraction, made her feel alive in some way. What was even harder to accept was that in some strange way she missed Marvin – or perhaps merely his conversation.

Sundays were for Mass, rest, and Mrs McDonald's roast dinners. It was also a day when Aileen took time to think about Niall, to read all his letters again, and to write back to him as well as to write to Briana and her parents.

On one such day, a dark-skied one in early April, Aileen had got soaked on the walk back from early Mass, so she spent the rest of the morning drying out – and letting her coat dry by the fire – while she composed a letter to Niall.

After the Sunday roast they all sat down to digest, to listen to the wireless and to read. But an hour later, the stifling nature of life at 22 Kingdom Avenue – the smoke from Mr McDonald's pipe and the click of Mrs McDonald's knitting needles – was starting to bear down on her. Not wanting to appear ungrateful, Aileen sat down next to the window with another library book, but was secretly wishing away the torrents of rain falling outside. Halfway through the first chapter her wish came true, and the rain was replaced by a golden sheet of light, the dark wetness on every surface reflecting the sun in every direction.

Aileen spent a few moments taking in the glorious, glowing, almost living entity, then stood. 'I'm just going out,' she said.

'For a walk?' Mr McDonald asked.

Aileen grabbed her coat, now dry. 'I have a letter to post.'

'Grand,' Mrs McDonald said, not looking up from her knitting.

Then something occurred to Aileen. She pointed upstairs and said, 'Do you think Doreen would like to come out for a walk with me?'

Mr and Mrs McDonald looked at each other – their looks had started to take on the feel of a secret code to Aileen – and it was left for Mrs McDonald to reply. 'I don't think so,' she said. 'It's a very delicate time of year for the poor wee girl. 'Tis three years ago almost to the day.'

'The Blitz. Of course.' Aileen took a breath and forced a smile on to her face. 'Well, I'll see you later. I fancy a walk into town and my letter will go more quickly that way.' She looked outside again just to make sure, and yes, the sky was clear blue with a golden sheen.

A few minutes later Aileen was two streets away and well on her way into the city centre. She posted the letter at the central post office and turned back, now a little relieved that the sun, low in the sky and direct, was behind her rather than in her face.

It was Sunday evening, much quieter than Saturday evening thankfully, and there were few people around. That probably made him easier to spot. He was walking straight toward her but it took a few seconds for her to recognize him. He didn't look quite as tall, probably because his head was bowed low. So low that he walked straight past her.

She turned and said, 'Marvin?'

He turned back and squinted to see. 'Aileen? Is that you?' A smile appeared. 'I'm . . . I'm sorry. I didn't mean to be rude, ignoring you or anything.'

'That's all right.'

The stoop disappeared. He seemed to jump up, like a firecracker igniting. 'It was in my eye.'

'What?'

'The, uh . . . the sun.' He pointed to it.

'It's all right,' she said. 'I know where the sun is.'

The grin got even broader, showing off those perfect teeth again. 'Hey, your sense of humour hasn't changed at all, has it?'

'I'm sorry. And yes, the sun's lovely this evening.'

'How are you? Are you . . . grand?'

Aileen couldn't help but smile. 'I am,' she said.

'Say, what are you doing on your own in town?'

'Ah, I'm just after posting a letter and now I'm walking home.'

He looked up and down the street then at the sky, which was streaked in a golden orange hue. 'Would you like me to walk you home?'

'Ah . . . well, all right. Yes, thank you.'

They started walking, Marvin keeping what Aileen's mother would call 'a respectable distance' away from her.

'So what are you doing on your own?' Aileen asked.

'Ah, nothing. Returning to base.'

'You're not out with your sailor friends?'

He shrugged his square shoulders. 'They're all getting drunk. I don't want to.'

'But you do drink alcohol. I saw you.'

'Oh, I like a beer. Don't even mind two beers. Not so sure about getting all liquored up.'

'So, what are you going to do?'

'Oh, probably go back to base and read my book.' He stilled himself, as if expecting a reaction. 'Yeah, I know, I sound like a sixty-year-old. Sorry.'

Aileen frowned at him. 'There's no need to apologize. And I know plenty of sixty-year-olds who get half-cut – as we say over here – most nights of the week. And they don't look so great for the habit, sure they don't.'

Marvin broke into laughter, then stopped when he got a curious stare from Aileen.

'Sorry,' he said. 'Take it as flattery. I just love the way you talk. It's like poetry.'

'Funny kind of poetry.'

'What if I said your voice was music to my ears,' Marvin said theatrically. 'That any better?'

'Sounds like a bit more of that flattery of yours.'

'Hey, I'm sorry.' He blushed slightly. 'And I guess I have something else to apologize for too.'

'Such as what?'

'Oh, my behaviour a few weeks back. But you are a beautiful Irish girl and I guess I thought it part of my official duty to try my luck.'

'Well, I forgive you, if that helps.'

'And how is your Niall guy? You heard from him lately?'

'He's just out of hospital, back at his barracks. And yes, we still write to each other every week.'

Marvin nodded, trying to grin but faltering. 'Good,' he said. 'Good. He's a brave man. You should be proud of him.'

'I am.'

There was an awkward silence for a minute or two. Aileen sensed Marvin was either upset or afraid of upsetting her. Most likely the latter.

'Did you say you read books?' she said.

He nodded. 'Yeah. I prefer movies though, and music. You?'

'I read books, but I love movies – *the films*, as we say. And I like music – listening, that is, not playing.'

'Oh, same here. I can't play anything – although I hope to learn one day. I like concerts though. Not too keen on classical: I prefer big band music.'

'You mean, like Glenn Miller?'

Marvin stopped on a street corner, almost shocked. 'Glenn Miller? Are you kidding me? He produces some great music, real foot-tapping tunes. *You* like swing music too?'

'Only everything I've heard. The family I lodge with listen to him a lot on the wireless. I suppose it sort of rubbed off on me.'

Marvin started laughing and shook his head a few times.

'What's funny?'

He looked down, his fingers playing with his cap for a second or two. 'It's just strange. I remember you saying we were two people from very different parts of the world. It's just, well, it seems like we have quite a lot in common after all.'

They stood there, neither speaking for a few moments.

'C'mon,' Aileen said eventually, 'I should be getting home.'

But Marvin didn't seem to want to move. 'You know . . .' He hesitated, swaying his head from side to side.

'What?' Aileen said. 'What is it?'

'Well . . . I'm starting to think we got off on the wrong foot before. And I completely accept that you're promised to another man. I just wondered whether . . .'

'Whether what?'

'You see, there's a swing band playing at one of the concert halls next Saturday night. I was going to go, but I didn't like the idea of going on my own. I wondered whether . . .'

Aileen was already shaking her head.

'I mean purely as friends, you understand. Just company, two people who happen to be music lovers.'

'Not really, Marvin.'

'I'd pay for everything and I wouldn't expect anything in return. Really.'

Aileen stood and thought.

'Hey, perhaps I shouldn't have asked. I'm sorry.'

'Just the two of us?' Aileen shook her head again. 'I think people might talk.'

Marvin nodded toward a striking gap in the row of houses some distance ahead of them, where a mound of rubble spewed out on to the street. 'I could be wrong, but I'd say people around here have more important things to worry about. And if they haven't, they darned well should.'

Aileen started walking on and Marvin followed.

'Just as friends?' Aileen said.

'Sure.'

'Well, I suppose I can't see why not.'

Marvin jerked upright. 'So is that a yes?'

'It is.'

'Hey, that's just swell. I guess I'll pick you up around seven, if that's okay?'

Aileen nodded. 'That'll be grand.'

Chapter 16

Aileen spent the next few days convincing herself that she would be doing nothing wrong in going to the concert with Marvin. They were friends and only friends, and she deserved a night out. Telling Mrs McDonald what she was doing was easier than she expected, with just a little pursing of the lips to show disapproval.

When Aileen got home from work on Saturday there was another letter on her pillow. She felt awkward, as though bees rather than butterflies had taken occupancy of her stomach. She told herself again that she was doing no wrong, and hurriedly ripped open the envelope.

2 April 1944

My dearest Aileen,

Just a quick note to tell you that I might have some news to tell you soon. I don't say 'good news' because the circumstances are unfortunate.

I've applied for leave to come back home because I've received word that my ma has been taken ill. She's had a few too many giddy turns and the doctor says her heart is weak and she has to get more rest. I'm only glad I send my money to her and she could afford a doctor when many aren't so lucky. Of course, if I'm granted leave I plan to visit you too, depending, of course, on what happens to Ma.

Progress with my leg is still good. I have not tried the running I mentioned yet, but those crutches that were my best friends for a while are now long-lost relatives, and the doctor says I'm doing well.

I'll let you know as soon as I hear anything about the leave. I can't wait to see you again. As always, I miss you.

Your loving fiancé,
Niall.

P.S. I'm sorry if this letter sounds a bit miserable. There was something else I didn't know whether to tell you, but here goes. Do you remember Neville? The fellow in the next bed when I was in the hospital? We started to become good pals, and I visited him as often as I could after I got out. He's Scottish and has no relatives nearby so I thought I'd be good company. Last week I went in and his bed was empty. At first I was pleased because I thought he must have got out. He did, in a manner of speaking. He got blood poisoning and passed on. At least he's no longer in pain.

As always, Aileen read the letter twice more. This time it was different. She didn't get a warm feeling inside, but instead was conscious of the time and of Marvin, who would be at this very moment on his way to Kingdom Avenue.

She had never been one for dithering. Not until now. It seemed disrespectful to go out enjoying herself after receiving this particular letter.

Then again, it had been planned many days ago. So no. She would try to lock away any feelings of guilt, and she would go out with Marvin and try to enjoy herself. Niall would want that.

A dutiful five minutes before seven there was a knock at the door. Aileen hurried downstairs to open it. This time there were no flowers, and there was no flattery – humorous or otherwise.

'Are you okay, Aileen?' Marvin said. 'You don't look so well.'

'I'm not, to tell you the truth.'

Marvin's brow shrank a little more. 'You wanna call it off? That's not a problem, really.'

'And you'll go to the concert on your own?'

'Uh . . . yeah. I'll go on my own. I don't mind.'

'But you won't go, will you?'

He stood, hands fidgeting, clearly unsure how to answer. 'Uh . . . no,' he eventually muttered. 'But really, I don't mind. Did you get some bad news?'

'I . . . ah . . . I got a letter from Niall. He's grand, but the letter was a bit upsetting.'

'I see.' Marvin nodded gravely. 'Look, tell me to mind my own business, but I know a bar that's quiet. If you want, we could talk. I mean, you could tell me about the letter. I *am* in the Forces. I know what happens.'

'And have you ever had someone you know get killed?' As soon as the words were out, Aileen saw a shaft of pain crack Marvin's face. 'I'm sorry,' she said, 'that was a horrible question. Ignore me.'

'No, no. It's fine. But you might as well know something.' He gulped and drew breath. 'I had a brother in the army, name of Earl. Now I don't.' He went to speak again, but struggled to control himself, his cheeks reddening and one hand nervously rubbing the back of his neck.

Aileen laid a hand on his arm. 'Don't say any more, not just yet.' She grabbed her coat from the coat stand. 'C'mon, let's go. Sounds like we could both do with a little enjoyment to take our minds off things.'

'The concert?'

'Yes. Let's forget about our troubles.'

'Are you sure?'

'It's not going to harm anyone, is it?'

So they went to the concert, and Aileen enjoyed it so much that they returned the following Saturday. On that occasion Marvin told Aileen more about Upstate New York, about the family farm in the small town overlooking the Hudson River, and about how the men would go into what they called the 'Wilderness' on hunting expeditions. Aileen could hardly compete with that, but when coaxed described the lakes, forests and craggy landscapes that made up the Wicklow Mountains.

Aileen was asked to, and accepted, invitations to a third and fourth concert. It was just before that fourth concert that Niall's next letter arrived. Aileen had been asking Mrs McDonald every few days throughout that time whether there had been a letter for her, because for Niall to take three weeks to write again was rare, and – though Aileen never admitted it openly – a little disappointing.

When it did come, Aileen's disappointment quickly turned to confusion.

22 April 1944

My dearest Aileen,

This is a real hard letter to write. I have some bad news. They tell me all leave has been cancelled, and they can't tell me why. I suppose now I am almost back to full strength and fitness they are wanting to send me somewhere.

In all fairness it's what I'm here to do, and I have to say I feel so much better physically. I can run for miles and my leg feels like there was never anything wrong with it, so I shouldn't grumble. But I was upset about the leave being cancelled. That's why I haven't written in a while, because I didn't know how to break the news to you and I suppose I was hoping they might change their minds – that there might be some major change in the war and they would let me come back. I found out a little more about what's going on back home too. Some of Ma's neighbours won't speak to her anymore because they found out I've joined the British Army. That seems awful spiteful of them because it was me who joined up, not her. The only good news is that she's feeling a little better, thanks to the rest she's getting and due to some medicine the doctor is making her take.

Aileen, don't think that any of that means I don't think of you. You are constantly in my thoughts and I want to promise you that one day we'll be together. We'll get married, I give you my word. I'm sorry this letter is so short. I really haven't much more to tell you as I don't know what's happening, except that it feels like it will be important, and we're spending a lot of time doing exercises.

I miss you so much.
Your loving fiancé,
Niall.

For the next few Saturday evenings Marvin would pick Aileen up and the pair would go to the cinema, or perhaps attend a concert, and once went to see a play that neither of them understood the point of but both laughed at afterward.

Marvin was true to his word about behaving, as he put it, like a gentleman, but what he and Aileen lacked in physical contact they more than made up for in conversation. She didn't talk about Niall's letters and he didn't talk about his brother, but they talked about the concert or the movie, about other movies Aileen and Marvin had seen – eight in Aileen's case and 'more than I can remember' in Marvin's. Marvin also talked about his family back home, and Aileen got the impression he really missed them but didn't want to admit it.

On the last Saturday in May, however, things were different. Marvin picked her up as usual, but let Aileen do all the talking on the walk into town. She obliged, out of nervousness more than any desire to control the conversation. They both knew – the whole of Belfast knew – that a cloud was descending, and silence would have only added to the dour atmosphere.

Aileen had heard the rumours that something important was about to happen, and Niall's letters made the rumours more believable. She'd also heard that General Eisenhower had recently visited Belfast to inspect the Forces and to witness what the wireless called 'an armada of ships' berthed in Belfast Lough. Aileen followed the goings-on in Europe as closely as the wireless broadcasts allowed, and there seemed a mood that a tide was about to turn, and that the Forces were going to try to capitalize on recent successful battles.

Aileen told Marvin she wanted to see *Casablanca*, even though Marvin had told her weeks before he'd already seen it (and had told her what happened). But Marvin kindly checked the newspapers only to find out it wasn't being shown. Instead, they went to see *The Philadelphia Story*, with Cary Grant, Katharine Hepburn and James Stewart all at the top of their comedy game. Aileen was enthused, as she always was by movies, but Marvin hardly reacted throughout the screening. On the way out, when

Aileen asked Marvin whether he'd ever been to Philadelphia, he merely shook his head blankly. And when she commented over a drink afterward that she thought Katharine Hepburn's performance was the best she'd ever seen, he was distant and not at all talkative.

'What did you think?' Aileen asked.

'Huh?' he said.

'What did you think of the film? Of Katharine Hepburn's acting?'

'Oh, I . . . uh . . . I enjoyed it.' He nodded encouragingly. 'It was good.'

She searched his face for clues. 'Are you all right, Marvin?'

'Oh, sure.'

'Were you wanting to go to a concert instead?'

At first he smiled and shook his head, but the smile fell away and his face spoke of trouble – his mouth flat and his forehead heavy. 'It's nothing like that,' he said. 'But . . . actually, no, I'm not all right.'

Aileen said nothing to fill the silence, but waited.

'We leave soon,' he said, then sighed as though those three words explained it all.

'What . . . what d'you mean? Leave for where?'

He shrugged, his shoulders slow to return. 'We don't get to know that. We've been told we sail in the week. I guess they might tell us more in the next few days, but then again they might not. What they *have* said is that this will be our last weekend in Belfast.'

'Oh.' Aileen gulped. She reached out across the table and laid her hand on top of Marvin's. She felt a tremble – her hand or his, she wasn't sure.

'Shouldn't come as a great surprise,' he said, smiling sadly. 'We gotta push into occupied territory sometime, and we need ships to get our guys there. It's what I'm in the navy for.'

'So . . . will I see you again?'

'Guess that depends on what Adolf and his pals have in store for us.' Now he held her hand, squeezing it gently. 'But I certainly hope so.'

'Bloody hell, Marvin,' she muttered.

The words caused him to widen his eyes in shock.

'Sorry,' she said. 'Just something I picked up from the women at the factory.' She shook her head. 'I can't tell you how much I've enjoyed these past couple of months, Marvin – well, the Saturdays at least. I spend all week looking forward to our Saturday evening.' She took a deep breath. 'I . . . I don't want you to go.'

'Hey, that means a lot to me, Aileen. More than you know.' He shifted uncomfortably in his seat and leaned forward, both forearms on the table between them. 'And there's something else I wanted to say to you.'

'You know you can tell me anything, Marvin.'

He lowered his voice. 'Well, this is something you might not like. It's . . . well . . . I've really enjoyed the time I've spent with you. You say you've always looked forward to our Saturdays, but you can't begin to imagine what they've meant to me. The only thing I didn't like – I hated, in fact – is the deceit, the idea that we're only friends.'

'Oh, but Marvin, we've talked about this.'

He nodded and held up a hand to silence her. 'I know, I know. But please, don't get yourself worked up about it. I'm just a lovestruck old fool, and you must know I'd prefer it this way than not to see you at all. As I've always told you, you have Niall, and I . . . I accept the situation.' He paused for a long breath. 'But wherever I'm going, you know there's a chance I might not return, don't you?'

'Don't say that, Marvin.' Aileen felt tears welling up, her vision starting to blur, her voice cracking.

He gave her hand a gentle squeeze. 'Hey, hey, hey. Don't upset yourself. I told you. I'm resigned to the way things are between us. I just wanted you to know, in case I don't come back, that I'm in love with you and I have been from the moment I set eyes on you because you're a remarkably attractive woman and a lovely, strong person. I just wanted to wish you all the best in life. While I still can.'

Aileen could only stare at him, her jaw lifeless. Then she started crying.

Marvin got out a handkerchief and handed it to her. 'I'm sorry,' he whispered. 'I know this isn't what you want to hear. But it's the truth, and I felt I had to say something or go out of my mind.'

Neither of them spoke for a few minutes while Aileen stemmed the flow of tears.

'This really isn't like you,' Marvin eventually said.

'I know. I'm strong.' Aileen sniffed. 'You said so, so it must be true.'

He smiled, although he was clearly struggling to reach for a beacon of happiness through a fog of sadness.

'Ah, Marvin. You just bring the sentimental eejit out in me, so ye do.'

Marvin's smile grew, and Aileen started laughing even as she was wiping her eyes dry.

'Oh, I reckon if anyone's the "eejit", it's me.' He laughed too until they both stopped, then asked if she was feeling better.

She nodded. 'Would you mind walking me home now?'

Without a word, he got up and held her coat out for her.

'I feel scared for you,' Aileen said a few minutes later as they crossed the road.

'Well, don't. I feel scared enough for myself. But hey, it's a war. There's no rule book.'

They talked some more about when the war might end, although neither of them had any sensible answer. It had already lasted five long years, with too many losses on all sides. There had been so many confident predictions by experts and drunken old men alike, first that the war would be over before the end of 1940, then that it wouldn't last until 1942. But now, with the summer of 1944 upon them, people were beginning to think it might just go on forever.

They reached 22 Kingdom Avenue.

'I guess this is it then,' Marvin said.

'A bit like *Casablanca*,' Aileen muttered.

'You haven't seen it, if you remember.'

'But you told me what happened, if you remember. You spoilt it for me really.' She laughed. But he didn't. She laid a hand on his arm, gently caressing. 'Marvin, I have to thank you for everything. You're a lovely man. One day you'll make some lucky woman a grand husband, so you will.'

He nodded, his eyes now glassy, and whispered, 'Yeah.'

'You'll have to come down to Leetown when you get back, when the war's . . . you know. You could meet the family, my mammy and Briana.'

'I'd really like that.'

'You'd like Briana.'

He nodded. Aileen saw fear and regret in his eyes. His hand came toward her and started caressing her hair. And then, before she could think, his face was in front of hers. There was still time to react, to pull away, but she didn't.

And then the taste of beer and chewing gum hit her lips. It was a flavour she had never thought in a million years she would find pleasant, but for just a second it was one she wanted to bottle and keep. She felt his hand drift down, dipping under her hair and on to the back of her neck. He was as gentle as a kitten, but still he held her close, and she felt no urge to do anything other than be there for him, to let him kiss her for as long as he wanted to.

His lips were smothering hers, and she could feel his fingertips brushing against the baby hairs on the back of her neck.

And then, just as it was starting to feel like heaven, their lips parted, and he drew his hand away.

'I'm sorry,' he whispered, and slowly stepped back. 'I'm really sorry. Goodbye, Aileen.' He took a few more steps back, gave her one last look, then turned and started walking away.

Aileen watched him until he was no more than a dot that turned around the corner at the end of Kingdom Avenue.

The next day Aileen attended early Mass, and spent the rest of the morning writing a long letter to Niall, and trying not to concern herself with what she would do with her Saturdays from now on.

Then Mr and Mrs McDonald said they were going to Belfast Lough to see the ships. Aileen said she would like to go too, and to her surprise so did Doreen.

When they got there, it looked as though the entire population of Belfast had had the same idea. There were more people than Aileen had ever seen gathered in one place, and there seemed more ships than she thought existed – a carpet of them covering the sea up to the horizon and to the land left and right. Aileen had only seen small fishing boats in real life, so the size of some of the ships was hardly believable – they were like floating towns. And there were many smaller ones too. Mr McDonald reeled off names like battleship, cruiser, cargo ship, passenger ship and escort craft. But Aileen could only stare at a sea turned metal-grey.

It was around ten days later – after all the news reports of the D-Day landings – that Aileen visited the same place by herself straight from work, and it was now a ghostly vision. Only a handful of tiny boats remained, moored alone and awkward on the edges, and the water had returned to its usual murky green hue.

Somehow life in Belfast wouldn't be the same without the troops. The lough was calm, the air quiet. Marvin had left Belfast.

Aileen couldn't help thinking that he'd taken a little of her with him.

When she got home that same day, however, her feelings of anxiety were heightened by the contents of the letter that was waiting on her bed.

2 June 1944

My dearest Aileen,

I'm really sorry for the rush, but I need to make this another short letter. We have all been training hard with no spare time.

This morning we all found out the reason for the ban on leave. Tomorrow we are being transported to the south coast. We have been told we are on red alert or standby or whatever you want to call it, which means we could be ordered to battle at any moment. The rumour is that it's very big, involving every last soldier we have.

Nobody really knows what it's all about. Then again, I'm sure we all know, we just don't talk about it to each other. That helps keep our spirits up. The chaps all keep joking and playing tricks on each other, but just below the surface we all know.

I promise I will write again when I know anything more. I have to admit that when I'm alone I feel scared. The only thing that makes me feel a little reassured is the thought of returning home to Ireland and to you.

Your loving fiancé,

Niall.

Aileen read the letter again and again through tears. When he'd written the letter, Niall hadn't known why he was being transported to the English south coast, but now the world knew. Similarly, Marvin wouldn't have fully known what awaited him. Even now there was little on the wireless apart from updates on the D-Day landings – wave after wave of Allied troops landing on the beaches of Northern France. Thousands of ships had departed from ports all over the UK and carried hundreds of thousands of men there, Marvin and Niall just two of them. Aileen feared for the lives of both of them, one more so than the other.

Normandy, France, June 1944

This was the moment. It happened in the middle of the night and made Niall's hands shake with fear.

He and his fellow soldiers had been hearing about the D-Day operation for days. The wireless announcements were bullish, but in private there were murmurings that the Allied landings on Normandy's beaches had been harder than envisaged, with more casualties than the Allied leaders had foreseen. The German defences along the coast were extensive and well organized: underwater obstacles dotted with mines, camouflaged tank traps, arrays of clifftop concrete pillboxes spewing fire down on to the beaches. Allied planes had done their best to counteract the measures, but still the Allies' targets for advancing into France were not being met – at least in the time periods they had planned.

However, with the help of the French resistance sabotaging the rail network and the electricity supplies, the Allies eventually made headway, pushing German forces away from the coast, leaving the beaches free and relatively safe for successive waves of Allied troops and vehicles.

Niall and the rest of his company were given no warning. They were woken in the middle of the night – at least, those who had been able to sleep – and boarded a commandeered passenger liner. By sunrise they were wading out of the sea and on to a Normandy beach.

The air was filled with the noise of confusion: the great ship engines rumbling as they idled, the popping of distant gunfire, the slop of seawater on hull and soldier, the occasional exploding shell, the shouted orders from the beach. It was as though all these noises were fighting their own battle.

As Niall reached dry land the shouts were clearer: 'Keep between the markers!'

But it was only a reminder. They all knew. They'd been briefed on how the Germans – or more likely their slave labourers – had placed obstacles on certain areas of the beach, and how the other sections – those walkways between the obstacles that Allied soldiers would naturally take – had been mined.

Niall looked left and right, seeing debris and craters. These were the results of unfortunate men discovering the German defences, although the tides had done their best to hide the grislier reminders with sand. He trudged on up the beach toward the grassy banks beyond.

The first few hours on French soil were ones of cold sweat that felt wasted: a hike over flat scrubland, a tense walk over a brick bridge that might explode, or even the well-planned capture of a farmhouse that turned out to be deserted after all, but not so much as a glimpse of the enemy.

They reached a settlement of hundreds of Allied troops, and there was a break for food and rest, during which time they were briefed on the plan to take Douzier, a small town which most definitely *was* in German hands, with wooden lookout towers and manned gun emplacements clearly visible from half a mile away.

More Allied troops gathered there over the next few days, and when the time came, it seemed clear that they would outnumber and easily outgun the Germans.

They were wrong. The Germans held out for six days before retreating, burning a quarter of Douzier to the ground. The Allied troops were left to put out the fires, and Niall felt his life in more danger from that task than it had been in taking the town.

Over the next few days and weeks, the fear of losing his life gradually drifted to the back of Niall's mind.

Chapter 17

Belfast, Northern Ireland, mid-June 1944

The D-Day landings were now old news, and the BBC was reporting on the progress of the Allies through German-occupied France. Aileen waited for another letter, hoping that perhaps Niall had been spared the invasion, had somehow been deemed unfit to fight. Anything would be preferable to the hell of the D-Day landings and fighting in France. But even to know that he *had* gone would be a blessed relief.

The letter came just after breakfast one morning as she was about to leave for work. She hurried upstairs to read it in the privacy of her bedroom. The handwriting was more jittery than in any of Niall's other letters, which only added to her concerns.

> 8 June 1944
>
> My dearest Aileen,
>
> Very soon I will be going to France. And I'm sorry to say this letter is another short one and might be the last I'll send for a while. Also, I probably won't get another from you.
>
> I'm assuming by the time you get to read this letter that you will have heard the news of the troops landing in France. Some of the men who crewed the

ships back to England have been telling stories. They say they could hardly see the ocean because there were so many ships of every variety, a hundred thousand men or more were crawling up along every beach for miles, and the sky was alive with planes. They say it was like a vision of hell with all the gunfire and explosions. They also say that the whole exercise is a success – that the Germans are on the run.

And we are sending thousands more every day. Me and the other lads are all fidgety. Nobody talks much. We don't even joke. We know it's our turn any moment now. We've been told to eat as much as we can and rest as much as we can. But it's hard to get to sleep when you know what's lying just around the corner. I haven't told anybody here but I'm so very frightened of what might happen when I get my orders to go.

Please pray for me, Aileen. And remember that whatever happens to me over there, I will always love you.

Your loving fiancé,

Niall.

P.S. I don't know whether to say this, or even how to say it. My mind is like a whirling dervish and I just can't keep still. I only hope you can still read my writing and that it all makes sense. My muscles are full of energy and I'm bursting to get going, but in spite of all that I'm also scared and confused. There's something I have to tell you. It's this. If anything should happen to me over there, well, I hope you find love with another man, and if you want my blessing to do that, you have it.

P.P.S. I think I should apologize. I know that what I've written is not the sort of thing you want to hear. But in all fairness this is what I joined up to do, and what I was trying to do in the Dodecanese. Besides, I'm a tough old sod and I promise you I will take care of myself.

Not for the first time in June 1944, Aileen went to bed, curled up and wept.

She only surfaced when she heard the creak of the door opening and the clink of cup on saucer, and quickly sat up on the side of the bed, wiping her eyes.

'Thought you could do with a cuppa,' Mrs McDonald said as she sat next to Aileen. 'I know it's none of my business . . .' She paused expectantly.

'It's Niall,' Aileen said hoarsely.

'He went as part of the D-Day landings thing?'

Aileen nodded.

'And you've no idea where he is?'

She shook her head.

'Sure, tis a horrible thing, war. And don't we know it here. He's doing a good thing, Aileen – all you can do is hold yourself together and hope.' She held Aileen's hand and squeezed it tightly. 'And be grateful for the little pleasures you have.' She eyed the cup of tea. 'Perhaps you should give work a miss today.'

'Thank you, Mrs McDonald.'

Mrs McDonald left the room and Aileen started drinking the hot sweet tea. The heat brought comfort, the sweetness acceptance. One thing was certain: there was, indeed, nothing Aileen could now do. She could pray and she could hope, but she would have to wait. Writing to Niall was pointless – by all accounts he was by now deep inside France.

But there was one other thing she could do. She could work. Mammy always told her that sulking does nobody any favours. And besides, if Niall was doing what he and thousands of other men were doing, then at least Aileen could do what thousands of other women were doing and go to work. So she did, and – after apologizing for being late – didn't utter a single word all day.

Aileen worked the summer months in the factory, walking there and back rain or shine. She told herself it was to enjoy the morning and evening sunshine, but she knew it was to make the hours pass more quickly, so she had less spare time to think and to find things to do by herself.

The war prospects were looking good, with Allied advances on all sides and what the man on the wireless called the 'end of the longest fight' within reach. Aileen didn't offer to pay rent again, but she managed to persuade Mrs McDonald that every other Saturday night they would go to the cinema, and that the McDonalds and Aileen would alternate paying for the four of them. To Aileen's surprise and joy, even Doreen and Mr McDonald were enthusiastic about the idea. Nevertheless, as the weeks and months went by, Aileen was putting away a considerable sum from her wages – more than she would ever spend, the way things were going.

There was little point in writing to Niall, but she decided to write anyway, not expecting a reply. She exchanged letters with Briana more often, keeping up with events in Leetown and telling Briana that very little exciting was happening in her life apart from the cinema evenings.

One bright Sunday in August 1944, when the sun was still high in the sky and the breeze was warm and gentle, she decided she needed to go for a walk – to go anywhere to break the boredom. She went to her room to change out of her best clothes, still left on from Mass that morning. Doreen was sitting up on her bed, book in hand.

Aileen spoke the words instinctively as she was thinking them. 'Would you like to come for a walk, Doreen?'

It didn't seem a lost cause. Doreen had now turned sixteen and wasn't what Aileen would call outgoing, but was just a little more talkative, especially on nights out at the cinema.

Doreen's eyes now darted away from the page for half a second to acknowledge the question. She shook her head and continued reading.

A part of Aileen was disappointed. She'd managed to engage Doreen in conversation a few times now, but Mrs McDonald's words of warning had always made her wary of appearing to be forceful. The two men in Aileen's life and her family were all out of reach so it was partly selfish, but she figured it would hardly do Doreen any harm to have a friend either.

'I was thinking,' she said, 'we could go to the cinema tonight, just the two of us. Would you like that?'

This time Doreen didn't look up at all. 'Thank you. No.'

'Ah, c'mon. Why not just take a walk outside with me? The sun on your face is lovely, so it is.'

Doreen shook her head.

'I'll even give you a strip of chewing gum my American friend gave me. It's double mint. How about that?'

Now Doreen looked up. She said nothing, but there was a pleading in her eyes.

Aileen sat down next to her. Their shoulders touched. Aileen wanted to tell Doreen she could be her little sister, that when she was a girl she had always wanted a little sister and that she got young Frank instead. But, of course, Doreen had been someone's sister a few years ago, so those comments wouldn't have helped.

'Tell me,' she said, 'don't you get awful bored spending so much time up here, day after day, just reading books?' She waited, this time staring at Doreen.

Eventually Doreen's mouth opened. 'I don't think about that too much.'

'And lonely too. Do you never think you'd like to meet other people?'

'I see Aunt Susan and Uncle Jack.'

'I mean, besides them.'

Doreen's eyes glazed over and she took a long breath. 'I miss my mammy and daddy and my brothers.' Before Aileen could think how to reply, Doreen added, 'Don't you miss your family?'

Aileen shrugged and said, 'They're there for me if I need them. I know that much.'

'I used to think that,' Doreen said. 'Well, you do when you're a child. You think they'll always be there for you. You think your family is permanent, set in stone, indestructible, like an immovable object. You never think that . . .'

Aileen barely heard the rest. Her mind was back in Leetown, walking along the beach with that coarse gritty sand biting into the flesh between her toes. She heard Briana screaming – half in joy, half in anger – as young Frank splashed her with freezing water. She was in Cready's, listening to her mammy swapping gossip over the counter. She was watching a tiny fragment of peat glow and die, feeling the warmth from its larger mass crisping her salt-laden frock as she sat with the rest of her family, waiting for tea, ingesting that aroma of burning peat mixed with mutton stew mixed with fresh barmbrack.

'I'm sorry,' she heard Doreen say in her delicate voice.

The words brought Aileen back to Belfast. They also made her dismiss her thoughts as nonsense or at least weakness.

'I'm sorry, Aileen.'

Aileen pulled herself together with a deep breath. 'Sorry?' she said. 'Sure, what have you to be sorry about?'

'You looked upset. Did I say the wrong thing?'

'Aach, no.' Aileen dismissed the idea with a wave of her hand. 'No, you didn't. I was just thinking about back home. You know an awful lot of big words for a sixteen-year-old, don't you?'

Doreen blushed.

Aileen nodded toward the book. 'It's all that reading you do, I'll be supposing. You just made me think, that's all. You have a point. I do miss my family, especially my sister.' She felt a melancholy smile drift on to her face.

'Actually,' Doreen said. 'Now I think about it, I would like to go out somewhere.'

'Ah . . . what?'

'If you don't mind.'

'Of course not. That's grand. Get a little sun on your skin, yes?'

'Could we go to Jubilee Park?'

'Jubilee Park?' Aileen said. 'Isn't that where . . . ?' Her throat locked at the prospect of finishing the sentence.

'But I'd like to visit Crown Street first, if you don't mind. Just for a few minutes.'

'Crown Street?'

'It's where I used to live.'

'Ah, right.' Aileen slowly nodded. 'Of course we can go there. That'll be grand.'

Twenty minutes later, Aileen and Doreen stood at the top of Crown Street, behind wooden barriers on to which KEEP OUT signs had been nailed. Aileen had seen many bombed houses on her travels through Belfast, but never *whole streets* that had been destroyed.

These were no houses. There weren't even *walls*. Yes, it had been a few years since the Blitz, and any walls left standing after the bombs had probably now been demolished. But the devastation was still apparent.

A few craters broke up the road surface here and there, and much of the area lay covered in mounds of brick, wood and concrete bulldozed into neat piles – piles that seemed to sit there like proud testaments to the destructive power of mankind.

'They took away all the useful things,' Doreen said.

'What?'

'Anything metal was taken away to be used for the war effort. Things people could use, like chairs and clothes, all disappeared because people helped themselves. Some people got hurt taking things, so they had to put up these barriers. Just before Christmas Aunt Susan took me shopping into the city, and I saw a woman wearing Mammy's best coat. I knew it was Mammy's because I helped her sew patches on the elbows and I got one of them all crooked.'

'That's terrible,' Aileen said.

'I used to think that too.' Doreen stared ahead, a look of defiance on her face. 'Perhaps that's why I didn't want to go out.'

'You mean, you thought you might see more reminders of your family?'

'Yes. But I've had time to think about it. What happened was terrible, you're right, but what happened to Mammy's coat wasn't terrible. She didn't need it anymore. 'Twas a good coat, nice and warm. And if it helped someone stay warm over winter . . . well, I think Mammy would have liked that.'

'That's a lovely thing to say, Doreen.'

'But I do miss them all.'

While Aileen was still scanning the wreckage, a door opened behind them and they turned to see a woman stepping out of her house, a rug in one hand and a beater in the other.

The woman was middle-aged, with a rotund torso and grey-tinged hair wrapped in a bun tied with twine. For the shortest and silliest of moments Aileen thought it was her mother.

A whack of beater on rug, a plume of dust from which the woman recoiled, and Aileen was again brought back from her faraway thoughts.

'Can we go to the park now?' Doreen asked.

'We can.'

They started walking, and Aileen gave the woman at the door a last look. This time she couldn't dismiss the idea; it may well have been a weakness but it definitely wasn't nonsense. She was homesick.

A hundred yards of thought later, she realized that she'd made her point – she'd shown herself and her family that she could break away, and she'd learned an awful lot. But there was another aspect. She missed Briana even more than Mammy. She even missed Daddy and the boys just a little if she was honest. They were her family, and, as Doreen had reminded her, they were not set in stone or indestructible or permanent.

Young Doreen might have been only sixteen, she might have had a coat of shyness, but in some ways she was stronger than Aileen. She had no choice but to be strong. She had no choice because she had no family. But she had her Aunt Susan and her Uncle Jack, and with their love and care she would survive without Aileen.

At Jubilee Park, they strolled between flower beds that had been converted into rows of carrots and parsnips and potatoes. They still looked pretty, Aileen thought. She also thought it was a beautiful day, with the sun high and the ground dry. She had enjoyed living in Belfast, but even after all this time it still wasn't home. She wasn't sure whether she'd fallen in love with Marvin, but she was sure she'd ever so slightly fallen in love with the McDonalds and Doreen. She would miss them all, family or not.

By the time she and Doreen walked out of the park, she'd made her mind up.

She was going back to Leetown.

Chapter 18

The taking of the town of Douzier had become the blueprint for future battles. By late August 1944, more and more French towns and cities had fallen to the Allies, and Paris had been liberated. There were casualties – tragic to their loved ones but mere dents in the war machine. Niall saw death and injury aplenty, but by skill or the grace of God escaped unharmed for month after month. And there was reward for every town freed as the French hailed the Allies. Men who had previously only had a taste for beer were plied with wine. Niall was a Guinness man through and through but was starting to get a taste for the grape.

To Niall, the coastal landings now seemed years ago, and his previous life in Ireland a distant memory. The Allied troops were now approaching the Belgian border, and the capture of the small but well-defended town of Saint-Jean was their next target.

It was just after dawn. They were advancing from lowlands just outside the town. The fear was like a nagging pain – a warning something unpleasant might be imminent – but Niall was now well used to managing such feelings. Of more immediate concern was the mud caking their boots, gathering in clumps as though trying to pull their feet down and hold them back. Niall cursed the decision to attack during rain after a wet night. *How were they expected to shoot with any accuracy – or even to look*

in all directions – when they were sliding all over the place with every step?
This was nothing like any of the training-ground practices in England.

About a dozen of them were caught in a particularly troublesome area – almost a swamp – when the order was given to retreat. So they turned back, but each step was only half a step, and soon they fell behind. And then the rain turned heavier, like horizontal waves penning them in.

Niall and four other men stopped and grouped together. They talked of heading for a small copse nearby for temporary shelter, but decided to press on, and within fifteen minutes they were hopelessly adrift, lost from the pack. They walked on aimlessly, reaching a gate next to a road. Smiles broke out as they heard vehicles approaching. One of them joked that it was generous of the corporals to lay on chauffeurs.

By the time they realized the trucks were of the enemy variety it was too late. They stopped sharply at the gate and half a dozen German soldiers spilled out. Niall's comrades turned and started running for cover, slopping and lurching in the muddy field. Their erratic movements only served to make target practice for the German soldiers more entertaining.

Niall made a dash for a nearby tree – perhaps to shoot from its cover, perhaps merely to hide – but he was too slow in the mud and was forced to stand there, hands aloft, cursing his useless feet, watching the men take potshots at his comrades. For a second he considered charging at one of them, or at the very least asking if they really had to shoot men who were running away. A sideways glance from one of them dissuaded him, but his scowl had been noticed, answered by the steel muzzle of a pistol. It felt cold and wet on his temple, digging into the skin. Words were shouted at him in German. As the rain continued to lash down, the water at his feet now an inch deep, Niall could do no more than bow his head and keep his hands up.

It was only when he'd been shoved into the back of the truck and driven away that he dared believe he would probably be living for a while longer. Perhaps it would be moments, perhaps years. It was hard to tell. The German soldier – a good few inches taller than Niall and muscle-bound with it – still held the pistol against his head, the muzzle doing its best to create a small indent in his skull.

Within minutes the truck came to an abrupt halt. Niall heard an angry exchange just outside. The canvas door was pulled aside for him and the German soldier to get down, and there was more arguing, a finger occasionally being pointed in Niall's direction. There were sighs and nods, and finally an arm was flung out in the direction of a drab building across the road.

With the pistol still at his temple and a meaty hand pulling him along by the shoulder, Niall was forced toward the building. Although it was dark inside, the place clearly had a character every bit as austere as its exterior. A panicking Niall was forced into one corner of the building, past vertical bars. By the time he realized it was a jail cell, the pistol had parted company from his skull and the door had been bolted. Seconds later, all shouts were distant and he was alone.

With his adrenaline now subsiding, Niall became aware of his shin stinging. Yes, now he remembered – the crack as he was forced into the back of the truck, stumbling as he tried to keep his hands in the air. Also, his temple was still hurting, and his shoulder was stiff from being pushed and pulled along by that monster German soldier like a recalcitrant puppy.

A few windmill turns of his arm brought some feeling back to his shoulder. He tapped fingertips to his temple and viewed the results. It hurt but there was no blood. That was good. A tug on his trouser leg revealed a nasty graze along three or four inches of his shin bone. For all the danger he was in, the stinging from this was now causing him the most pain. He spat on his fingers and pasted the saliva on to the wound, wincing at even more pain.

He told himself to ignore it, and cast his eyes around his new surroundings. As seconds turned to minutes his eyes became more accustomed to the darkness. Metal bars shone in the light that slunk through the cracks in the doorway and the one tiny window set up high. The bars were on two sides of the cell, with two walls behind him. He could almost touch opposite sides at the same time with his fingertips. The floor was dusty earth, and the cell contained no chair or bed. There was, however, a bucket in the corner. The cell covered about a quarter of the whole room – beyond the cell were a desk and chair to one side, a counter to the other. He was alone in the only jail cell of the town police station.

Niall sat on the floor to think, his back against the rough brick wall, his shoulder blades rubbing awkwardly against the ragged mortar lines. There were two positives. For one thing, he hadn't been shot or seriously injured – not yet. There must have been a good reason for that, but what was that reason? More importantly, how long would it remain a good reason? Secondly, the first proper flush of winter hadn't yet descended, so the cage he was locked up in wasn't cold. Two big positives. Niall was nothing if not an optimist.

He waited, ears pricked for any sound, eyes fixed on the door ahead of him, but inevitably his well of attention eventually ran dry. It was quiet, dim and a little on the warm side, and he could feel himself nodding off. There was, for the moment, nothing more for him to do. In fact, it was warm enough for him to remove his jacket and roll it up to make a pillow of sorts.

He lay down on the dry earth, shut his eyes, and was soon walking along a beach – one covered in natural ridges of sand rather than craters or obstacles. Cool, refreshing water was bringing his tired feet back to life, while Aileen's warm embrace enveloped his arm as they strolled along together.

It was the first time he'd been alone for months, and in this unlikely peace he fell asleep.

Leetown, County Wicklow, August 1944

Aileen's train dropped her off at Leetown, and she was halfway along Station Road by the time she heard the toot as it pulled out.

Saying goodbye to Mr and Mrs McDonald hadn't been easy; saying goodbye to Doreen had made her shed a tear. Doreen said she'd be fine, and looked as though she meant it.

Aileen somehow felt different, as if her time in Belfast had changed her. Perhaps it was wishful thinking. Perhaps she would find out over the next few days.

She hadn't written to say she would be arriving home, and a small part of her wondered whether her half of the bed would still be available. On the seafront road she slowed her pace, taking time to appreciate the coastal views and the never-changing shush of the tide, as well as the air – fresher than in Belfast. She took a deep breath of it. Yes, it was so much cleaner than in the city and had more of that bracing, salty tang that spoke of home.

There was a sense that things might have changed, but nothing on her walk home supported that view: Cready's, a pony and trap at the roadside, the grass verge sprinkled with sand, an old man with a walking stick, one or two people washing themselves down at the water's edge. She could have been returning after a day away for all it mattered.

At her front door she listened for noises, but heard nothing. Perhaps they were all out helping on nearby farms or digging turf. A faint smell of meat stimulated her senses, perhaps leftovers. Mammy's mutton stew with turnips, onions and carrots – there was nothing like it.

As her hand headed for the door handle she paused to think. Although nothing in the village seemed to have changed, perhaps one or two attitudes had. Or perhaps not. She would have to face that issue head-on in time.

She opened the door and took a step inside.

They were all there, gathered around the table, quietly eating. Briana, Mammy, Daddy, Gerard, Fergus and little Frank. Heads turned, spoons were stilled.

Aileen sensed tears welling up, then felt her arms tremble, her face tingle as it reddened, and finally nothing but convulsions of sadness. She cried like the lost soul she had become.

Her mother was the first to get up and run to her. But the others followed, telling her in turn how they'd missed her, and asking for details of her adventures 'away'. Even Fergus and Daddy were welcoming, their usual brashness quietened by concern.

Had they all changed?

Saint-Jean, near the France–Belgium border, August 1944

Niall could only wish he was back in Leetown. Or at home in County Kildare. Or anywhere in the world but a tiny jail cell in Saint-Jean.

He'd slept passably considering he had bare dirt for a bed, but was woken by noises from outside – shouts and the thumping of boots. He woke up so suddenly that his head jerked and hit the wall – a timely reminder that alertness was now required.

Beyond the bars the door opened, letting sharp yellowy light flood the room, momentarily blinding Niall. He got to his feet and squinted to see, but didn't quite follow what happened next. The hinges of the cell door squealed horribly, what seemed like a rasping puff of dust was thrown to the back of the cell, the door lock clanged, and it was over. The German soldiers had gone, the stark light was gone, and there was a figure on the floor next to Niall.

He stared for a few moments, then said, 'Are you all right?'

'Been better,' came the reply, so chirpy it took Niall by surprise. The man stood up, stumbling with dizziness, then brushed the dirt off his uniform. 'So 'ow long you been 'ere?' he asked casually.

There was only a little light in the room, but Niall could still make out that they shared the same colour of uniform. He also noticed that the man was a little taller than him and quite thickset, his voice a little more high-pitched than it had a right to be.

'I don't know,' Niall replied.

'You don't know?'

'I fell asleep. But I haven't eaten, so it can't have been more than a few hours.'

'You a Paddy?' the man said.

'And what of it?'

The man laughed. Niall made a point of not joining in, although that was hard; the grin that went with the laughter was endearing. The man held up a hand to placate Niall.

'Just placing the accent, that's all. You're from the South, aren't you – the Free State?'

Niall nodded. 'The Republic, you mean.'

'If you like. No offence. Just a hobby of mine, accents.' He held a hand out. 'Peter,' he said. 'Private Wilkins if we're being formal, which I sincerely 'ope we're not – originally of Dagenham.'

Niall shook Peter's hand. 'Niall O'Rourke, County Kildare. Where did you say you were from?'

'Dagenham. Just to the east o' London.'

'Ah, right.' Now Niall could see the man's face a little more clearly. 'What do you have there?' he said. 'On your face.'

Peter wiped his fingertips on his cheek, leaving three broad smudges of white, then licked them. 'Cocoa,' he said.

Niall gave him a suspicious stare.

He laughed, showing that a little cocoa had also found its way on to his teeth. 'Best thing there is for those pre-dawn raids. Well, *cheapest* thing there, is truth be told. Standard issue for paratroopers.'

'You're a paratrooper? Heck.'

'For my sins.' Peter tutted. 'Just my ruddy luck too. Three years' training, and as soon as I opens my parachute I gets a freak gust of wind. Only came down in the ruddy town square, didn't I? They could see me a ruddy mile off. Bastards had enough time to set up a welcome party for me.' He glanced around the cell. 'Anyway, less of the "heck" malarkey, if you don't mind. We all play our parts.' He walked around the perimeter of the cell, absent-mindedly trailing his knuckles across the bars as he went.

'I was wondering,' Niall said. 'Why haven't they killed us?'

Peter shrugged. 'Your guess is as good as mine. They shouldn't, of course – Geneva Conventions and all that. But we *are* lucky – I mean, I *feel* lucky. When I was floating down toward them I had half a mind to go for my gun and shoot myself.'

'And what stopped you?'

Peter's smile widened, and he shrugged. 'Blind faith, I suppose. Sometimes you just gotta go with it and believe in luck – that it averages out, I mean. I had so much bad luck with that gust of wind sending my parachute off target, I figured I was due a barrelful of good luck.' He tapped a few of the bars again, looking to the top and bottom. 'Me and you, Niall O'Rourke, we'll be fine here. I feel it in my bones. If they were going to kill us they'd have done it by now.' He sat down at the back of the cell, his back against the wall, and let out an exhausted sigh.

'On the other hand,' Niall said, 'if we were genuinely lucky they'd have given us beds.'

Peter pursed his lips, weighing up the idea, then gave a dejected nod. 'Fair point, fair point. Still, it's warm and dry.' He turned to face Niall, then screwed his eyes up in puzzlement. 'There's one thing I never understood about you lads, if you don't mind me asking.'

'Sure, go ahead.'

'Tell me, why did you volunteer?'

Niall drew breath. 'Well, I know it sounds stupid, but sometimes—'

At that moment they both heard a noise from outside – right outside the station door. It opened and four German soldiers strode in – two privates and two men who looked like generals or sergeants, maybe. The privates stood to attention while the other men talked, all the time looking Niall and Peter up and down. A fifth soldier entered carrying a tray of food and drink. Niall and Peter approached the cell door, but the privates stepped forward and took aim. One of them shouted something.

'What?' Peter said to him. 'What are you saying?'

'I think he wants us to step away to the back of the cell,' Niall said, pulling on Peter's arm.

'Well, why doesn't he bloody well say so?' Peter shook his arm away from Niall's grasp, not taking his eyes off the German who'd been shouting. Slowly he stepped back, and both prisoners stood with their backs against the brickwork while the fifth German unlocked the cell door and placed the tray inside. Only once the door was locked and the Germans had left did Niall and Peter step forward.

The bread was stale, but edible. The cheese was like no cheese Niall had ever eaten before – soft and jelly-like. The water was lacking only in quantity.

When they'd finished, Peter offered the tray of crumbs and smudges of cheese to Niall, who shook his head. 'Well, I ain't proud,' Peter said, and licked the thing clean.

The tray was turned and slid between the bars, the metal mugs just about fitting through. A few belches later, both men sat back into positions that had now – even after only a few hours – become customary, their shoulder blades scraping against the wall.

Peter let out a satisfied sigh, then glanced at Niall, noticing the expression on his face. 'What?' he said.

'Aren't you worried?'

'Oh, I've got a feeling we'll both be all right.'

'What makes you say that?'

Peter drew a long breath. 'The big boss is Feldwebel Brandt – that's Sergeant Brandt to you and me. He said they're gonna use us as bargaining tools, so he wants to keep us alive, which means keeping us fed and watered, and not thumping us about too much. They're hoping they can swap us for German prisoners taken by the Allies. Fingers crossed we'll be out of here within days.'

'What? How do you . . . ?' Niall thought for a moment. 'You speak German?'

Peter put a finger to his lips. 'They don't know that,' he whispered. 'And it's gotta stay that way.'

Niall couldn't help but smile. 'You crafty sod.'

They laughed.

For the rest of that day the men talked almost incessantly. They were only rarely disturbed, twice when water was brought to them, and on the few occasions that sounds of distant gunfire and shouts from outside halted their conversation.

It was a day when each man told the other his life story.

Peter had a wife and three children back in Dagenham. The youngest, Lily for short, but more often *Lily with the long blonde hair and a missing front tooth*, was too young to understand what her father was doing. The other two, Beryl and John, idolized their father. They both talked about joining the Forces when they grew up. John wanted to join the RAF as a pilot; his father hadn't the heart to tell him his short-sightedness would make that difficult. Beryl wanted to be a Wren, although her mother was trying to guide her toward nursing.

Peter's wife, Cynthia, had the sharpest dimples he'd ever seen. Making her smile was so rewarding that he even listed it as one of his hobbies, alongside pigeon racing and cricket –supporting Essex and playing for his local team. It had come as no surprise to be told while training for the paratroopers that he had much better than average hand-to-eye coordination.

To Niall he seemed a simple man at heart, pleased and proud to do his duty for king and country, but ultimately just as concerned that his children grew up happy and healthy, and that his wife didn't go without the one or two luxuries that helped her stop worrying about him – if only for a short time. Niall remarked on the contrast between those two aims – fighting and caring for his family – but Peter insisted the objectives were one and the same: that if Hitler was allowed to succeed he feared for his children's futures.

Peter's plans for after the war were just as modest. He wanted to find a good job with a good pension, race pigeons, start playing with the local cricket club again, and give the children the occasional week at the seaside that would leave them with fond memories for the rest of their lives.

Looking further ahead, his big wish was not to work himself into the ground like his father had done, but to retire to the seaside. There were one or two likely spots along the Essex coast. In truth, that was *Cynthia's* wish, but Peter wanted to make her happy, so that had become their plan.

Niall and Peter both spoke of their schooldays, their families, and their war exploits so far, and by the end of the day Niall felt as though he knew Peter as well as he knew himself.

The bucket got used more than once, something else that provided a little humour for both men.

As the sun was setting outside, more food was provided. More stale bread, more soft cheese, and this time an apple each.

'We must be in their good books,' Peter remarked as the tray was laid down.

An hour after nightfall Niall's ears were ringing with Peter's voice, and his throat was sore from talking. Both men fell silent, as if they had said all they needed to say.

But Peter did say a little more. He said he was whacked out and was going to get some shut-eye. He pulled his boots off, arranged them on their sides, one on top of the other, then lay down on his side with his head resting on their muddy leather.

'You never did finish telling me,' he said as he closed his eyes, 'why you volunteered to join the British Army when you coulda just as easily stayed at 'ome.'

'Well,' Niall said. He managed to get another sentence out before Peter's snoring told him more words would be wasted. Niall lay down too and was soon asleep. Distant gunfire woke him up once or twice, but there was nothing he could do, nowhere he could run to. He would just have to trust in Peter's theory of luck, so fell back to sleep quickly every time he was disturbed.

The next morning, both men were woken up by the same group of officials as on the first day. Again, Sergeant Brandt and his colleague spoke while breakfast was passed to Niall and Peter, leaving shortly afterward.

Niall started eating, but Peter didn't seem to be hungry. Also he didn't speak. Or smile.

'What is it?' Niall said. 'What were they saying?'

Peter struggled to speak. 'They . . . they, erm . . .'

'They what?'

Peter gave a sceptical smile. 'Brandt said the prisoner swap didn't work. They wanted five German POWs for each of us.'

'*What?*' Niall screeched.

'Exactly. The Allies refused, which is understandable.'

'So . . . we just stay here?'

Peter stared straight ahead for a moment.

'What else did they say?'

'I got the impression they're planning to move on tonight.'

'Move on?'

'To retreat from the town. Don't know whether you noticed, but the gunfire's getting closer.'

'I thought so. Didn't like to say. But what about us? Did they say any more?'

Now Peter's face seemed to sag a little. 'Your guess is as good as mine,' he said. 'Well, that is, as long as your guess is that they won't take us with them.'

Niall said nothing.

For the rest of that day, with sounds of battle getting ever louder, the conversation between Niall and Peter didn't come quite so easily. There was talk, but it was stilted, with neither man able to concentrate for more than a few minutes. As the sun started to descend and no food came to them, both men fell silent.

As darkness came, Niall said, 'We're going to die, aren't we?'

Peter didn't even look at Niall, let alone reply.

The crackle of gunfire became louder, and just as the explosions threatened to shake the very building apart, the German soldiers returned.

There was still no food, and the German faces were sullen, staring right through Niall and Peter as they opened the cell door, strode in, and shoved both men up against the wall. This time Niall was aware of the rough mortar grinding against his shoulder blades for only a split second – mere physical pain was neither here nor there.

There were five of them: the two senior men, including Sergeant Brandt with his pistol at the ready, and three ordinary soldiers, rifles in hand. The senior men exchanged a few words. Niall heard Peter curse on hearing them. Sergeant Brandt stepped forward and held his left hand against Niall's neck, pinning him to the wall. Niall saw the other hand come up, the one with the pistol. He could hardly put up a fight, not with two rifles also pointed at him.

With the muzzle right between his eyes, he almost fainted, struggling to focus on the hand at the other end, its trigger finger twitching randomly.

Chapter 19

Leetown, County Wicklow, August 1944

Aileen had been back home for a day. So far, it had been all smiles and questions on what Belfast was like. They asked about the house she'd stayed in, the factory she'd worked in, what films she'd seen, who she'd met, the cars she'd seen in the city and so on. There was no undercurrent – as far as she could tell – suggesting she'd done anything wrong by going there.

It was the next morning before she and Briana managed to leave the cottage for a walk on the beach to talk. Speaking to the whole of her family had been just a little stilted, almost formal, and she'd been too busy answering questions to ask any. It would be different, just her and Briana on their own.

'So, are you pleased to be back?' Briana asked as they walked down to the shore. 'I mean, really, genuinely happy?'

'Ah, tis grand,' Aileen replied. She knew how it sounded as soon as she'd said it.

'You don't sound certain?'

'Tis mixed feelings, I suppose. You'd understand if you'd come with me.'

'Ah, right.'

'Ah, no, I didn't mean it like that, Briana. You know that.'

Pain etched itself on Briana's forehead. 'Aileen, you'll never know how much I thought about joining you up there.'

'Does that mean you regret not coming with me?'

Briana glanced down at her feet, dragging in the wet sand. Then she stared at Aileen, squinting at the morning sun beyond.

Aileen stopped walking. 'Ah, bloody hell, Briana. Sure, why didn't you come with me? I feel terrible now.'

'*Bloody hell?*' Briana echoed, narrowing her eyes at her sister.

'Sorry. Tis something I picked up in Belfast.'

'Be sure not to go saying that in front of Mammy or Daddy.'

'Well, *of course not*. Being in Belfast hasn't made me stupid, Briana.'

'But it's certainly changed you, all right. Everyone in the family has noticed, sure they have.'

'Really?'

'Yes, really. And I'm still trying to find out whether it's for the better.'

Aileen thought for a moment as they paddled along the shallow water toward Bevanstown. 'Ah, definitely for the better. It's hard to explain, but I'm seeing Leetown in a completely new light, almost as though I haven't been here before.'

'And your family? Do you see *us* in a new light?'

'Mmm . . . you know, I think I do. I'd find it hard to leave this place for good – it'll always be home. But Belfast certainly opened my eyes a bit, so it did.'

'Grand,' Briana said. 'Grand.'

'So . . . are you a little jealous?'

'Stop it, Aileen. You know I am.'

'So, twas horrible here without your little sister, was it?'

'I'll tell you one thing, it was certainly horrible sharing a bed with young Frank. He's at that . . . y'know, that funny age boys go through.'

Aileen held the palm of her hand up. 'Ah, no. I'm not wanting to know about that.'

'Sure, I didn't want to know either. But never mind boys, what about men? Are you still writing to Niall?'

'Of course I am.' There was a little more vitriol in the words than Aileen intended.

'I'm sorry. I was meaning, how is he?'

'Well . . .' Aileen walked on a few paces before continuing. 'He was in the D-Day landings thing. I haven't received a letter from him since then. I just hope . . .'

'Oh, I'm sorry, Aileen. Perhaps you don't want to talk about Niall.'

'Not really. I just want to wait and pray for him. I have absolutely no idea whether he's alive or . . . whether he's injured or captured or whatever.' She looked straight ahead, not wanting Briana to see the fear in her eyes.

Saint-Jean, near the France–Belgium border, August 1944

In the jail cell, Niall's eyes were wide with terror – still staring at the hand pressing the pistol to his head, its trigger finger twitching.

'Stop it,' he said. 'Don't do this, please.' His arms shook uncontrollably, his head a little too. But the worst thing was his voice, straining and warbling as though he was eight or nine and being threatened in the playground. 'Take us with you,' he said. 'Please. We'll . . . we'll do anything.'

Brandt tutted, a look of disgust on his face. 'Why can't you take it like a man?' he said in almost perfect English, and in a voice so gentle it magnified the menace. 'My God, you are a coward, aren't you?' He pulled the pistol away and instead brought his head up to Niall's so their noses were almost touching, their foreheads inches apart. 'A typical *cowardly* Englishman.'

Niall gulped. The man had a point. Perhaps he was going to die, but there was no reason to die a coward. From deep down in his guts, he somehow summoned up a little energy. 'I'm not an Englishman,' he said, his voice strengthening with every word.

Brandt shrugged. 'All right, a *British* man. You prefer that?'

Niall reached a hand up and grabbed the man's wrist, wrestling the hand away from his throat. 'I'm not British either.'

Brandt laughed. 'What is this? Is it a . . . how would you say, a comedy joke?'

'He's Irish,' Peter said. 'Can't you tell by the way he talks?'

'You think I'm stupid? You think I know nothing of my enemy? I know about Ireland. American forces are stationed there.'

'Only in the North. He's from the South.'

'The . . . Free . . .' Brandt was confused for a moment.

'The Irish Free State,' Niall said. 'The Republic, we prefer to say.'

'Tell me the truth,' Brandt said, still glaring at Niall. 'Is that where you are from?'

Niall nodded. 'Aren't I just after telling you? County Kildare, just south of Dublin.'

Brandt paused, then took a step back. He exchanged a few words with his compatriot while Niall looked to Peter for some sort of guidance as to what they were saying.

Before Peter could react, Brandt stepped back to Niall.

'Why are you in the British Army?' he said. 'It does not make sense.'

Niall hesitated. It was a hard question to answer in the circumstances. It was hard to think of *any* logical answer to *anything* when his words might well be the last ones he ever uttered.

'For the money,' he said. 'That's all. Just the pay. If you want the truth, I hate the British as much as you do.'

Brandt's brow creased up. He briefly glanced at Peter then said to Niall, 'You really hate the British?'

'Not half,' Peter interjected. 'We've almost come to blows in here, him and me. He told me the British killed his father, see. He was in the IRA. Good riddance to him too, I say. Bloody Paddies. And we hate them as much as they hate us.'

Brandt turned to Niall. 'Is this true about your father?'

Niall nodded. ''Tis. He, ah . . . he died fighting against the British for independence.'

'And this man still knows people in the IRA,' Peter added. 'He's no friend of mine, but he could be useful to you, I suppose.'

Brandt opened his mouth to speak, but closed it again and glanced back at the other official. He stepped back to talk to him.

Niall looked to his side. But Peter was looking straight ahead, his face expressionless.

Brandt returned to Niall. 'Very well,' he said. 'We will see. We might have uses for you.'

Then he turned to Peter and grasped him by the neck.

'I could be useful to you too,' Peter said. 'Fluent German. I could translate.'

Brandt brought his revolver to Peter's forehead and said, 'We don't need translators.'

He pulled the trigger, and in a split second all Peter's dreams – of playing cricket on lazy Sunday afternoons, of racing pigeons, of watching his children grow up and have their own families, and of retiring with his wife to the seaside – vanished in a blast of cordite.

Niall found himself staring at a blood-soaked crater in the wall.

'Out!' Brandt barked at him. 'Now!'

Niall didn't move – couldn't even *breathe* – could only stare to his side, at his friend. He didn't know Cynthia, Beryl, John, or Lily with the long blonde hair and a missing front tooth. But for a moment he cried for them.

The building shook as a bomb of some sort exploded nearby.

Brandt held his pistol up to Niall's head. 'Last chance.'

Niall gulped, then nodded. Taking shallow breaths, he managed to stagger out of the jailhouse and into the street, followed closely by the three German soldiers, their rifles inches from his back.

He took deep, greedy gulps of the fresh air, and his body eventually stopped trembling. He looked up to see the night sky flashing orange and yellow with the reflected light of exploding shells and gunfire. To his left lay the road by which he'd been driven into the village only a day before. To his right was a steady stream of people and vehicles heading out of the town, fleeing the inevitable march of the British Army. Beyond all of that, flames from burning buildings licked the sky, children screamed for their lives, and people raced around like wild animals.

He was manhandled on to a truck and spent the next ten minutes with a rifle inches from his chest. With each lurch of the truck the rifle rapped on to his ribs and toyed with his mind. How many times until the soldier's finger was jolted the wrong way? And arguing was pointless. Even if the man understood English, Peter's theory of luck told him to accept when he was winning.

Peter.

Niall could hardly believe he'd only known the man for one day. He would miss him.

The gunfire was now more distant but still frightening. For a moment he thought about asking the soldier where he was being taken. But he stayed silent.

Then the truck stopped. Moments later the canvas cover at the back was flung open and they were all told to get out.

Niall stepped down and looked around. Once again, a current of cold fear travelled up his spine. This was no town. It was the middle of nowhere. Why had he been ordered off the truck? It didn't make sense. If they were going to shoot him . . .

And then all became clear. Niall and the German soldiers walked around to the front of the truck. Sergeant Brandt stepped down from the cab to join them.

A large tree branch had fallen across the road.

'Help us,' Brandt said.

Niall and the three soldiers bent down to grab the branch.

Then all hell broke loose.

There was gunfire, shouting, and a few seconds later Niall found himself kneeling, but leaning back awkwardly against the branch, a rifle sticking into his neck, pinning him in place. His hands were aloft, although he couldn't remember having put them there. At the other end of the rifle was a figure – and it wasn't a German soldier.

He glanced around. Two of the German soldiers lay motionless on their bellies, their limbs splayed out unnaturally. It was dark, but pools of liquid around their torsos reflected the moonlight. There were other people – all with woollen hats and scarves covering the lower halves of their faces. Sergeant Brandt and the other German soldier were still standing, but had rifles pointed at them and held their hands aloft.

The figure standing over Niall leaned in to get a better look at his uniform, but kept the rifle poised. 'You are British, yes?' The accent was heavy, the voice as hazy as a September sunset.

Niall nodded. 'I'm British,' he blurted out. 'Yes, I'm British.'

The scarf was pulled aside, letting long black hair cascade down.

'French Resistance?' Niall said.

'Who else?' she replied. She stepped back to let him get up.

'Thank you,' Niall said. 'Thank you so much.'

She said something in French to one of the other Resistance people, who came over.

'This is Eugene,' she said. 'He will take you along a footpath to the British Army position.'

'What about your new prisoners?' Niall said, looking at the two Germans.

'What do you think?' she whispered. 'Should we kill them?'

Niall looked over at them, at their faces, now stricken with dread of a fate unknown – a feeling Niall knew all too well. 'No,' he said. 'I don't think you should. I think you should treat them as well as you can.'

She shrugged and said, 'I will decide. But now you must go. Join your army.'

'Of course. Thank you again.' He looked toward Eugene, who turned and started walking. Niall started to follow, then stepped sideways to face Sergeant Brandt. 'I just thought you should know,' he said. 'My father didn't die fighting the British. He died fighting the Germans.'

He waited for a reaction from Brandt, but there was none. He hurried along after Eugene.

Leetown, County Wicklow, into 1945

For the Sweeneys – for all people in the Irish Republic for that matter – 'The Emergency' meant rationing and general food shortages. The autumn months of 1944 brought welcome potato and apple harvests, but the winter months, when little grew even in Ireland's mild climate, were times of hardship. Food stocks dwindled, rivers were plundered for fish, and almost every part of farmyard animals was cooked and eaten. And still, belts felt looser.

By the spring of 1945 there was finally hope that the war would end very soon. British wireless broadcasts kept the Irish people up to date with progress – and there had been a lot. Advances were slow, with colossal casualties on both sides, but it was progress.

On the Western Front, Allied troops had long since recaptured France. By early February Belgium was entirely in Allied hands. In the Netherlands only small pockets of territory were occupied by stubborn

German forces. And inroads had been made into Germany itself. On the Eastern Front, the Soviets had made equally significant advances.

In the summer of 1945 the war finally ended, although hardships in Ireland and Great Britain were to continue for many years. The huge logistical task of sending soldiers into battle across the globe ceased, but the process of gradually winding down the Forces and sending millions of soldiers home was only starting. It would end up taking many months.

Chapter 20

'How long now to Arturo's?' Aileen says, leaning forward.

The cab driver cocks his head to the side. 'I'd say about twenty minutes. That okay?'

'That's just fine,' the man sitting behind him replies.

Aileen checks her watch and says quietly, 'Aren't we late?'

'Who cares?' he replies. 'It's our wedding anniversary. We're entitled to be a little late.'

In front of them, the cab driver groans to himself in frustration. 'Too many cars,' he mutters, 'not enough road.'

'They're probably there already,' Aileen says. 'I wouldn't want to keep them waiting.'

'Mmm . . . I know. But it's a nice place to be kept waiting in.'

'I guess so.' Aileen nods acceptance. Arturo's is more pizza hotel than Plaza Hotel, but it's cosy, quiet, and has long since been a tradition for their wedding anniversaries. Their children went with them in the early days, but not now.

'Couldn't we walk from here?' she whispers to her side. 'It'd be quicker.'

A quick shake of his head dismisses the idea. A few silent minutes go by, and they're only a few yards further forward. Aileen catches his eye and raises her eyebrows. He understands. He leans forward and points, making sure his hand has caught the driver's eye. 'Just drop us off at the lights up there. We can cut through and walk the rest.'

'You sure, buddy?'

'We're sure,' Aileen says before her husband can reply.

He sits back and turns to Aileen. 'I guess from your clock-watching you're looking forward to it.'

'No more than any other year.' She turns and looks directly at him, her eyes holding on to his for a few seconds. 'It's good to reminisce. Don't you think it puts things into some sort of perspective when you remember how things were?'

He nods thoughtfully. 'You're right. Life's so fast. Jeez, the whole thing goes by so *fast*. But you know I don't like to dwell on the past.'

'Don't you think you get to the stage where the past is pretty much all you have left?'

'That's morbid, Aileen. I like to look forward. We have a future to plan.'

'Ah, yes. Wills and probate, hip operations, incontinence devices, nursing homes, dribble rags.'

'Hey, I'm trying my best to be all sympathetic here, and you know that doesn't come so easy to me. On the other hand, I guess I can see what you mean. It's good to think back, to remember who we once were – as long as it's only once a year.' He frowns and thinks for a moment. 'What's a dribble rag?'

'Can't you guess?'

'Well, I *could*. I just never heard the phrase before.'

'Me neither.'

'Right.' He grunts a laugh.

The cab stops. They pay the driver and clamber outside.

'Are you sure you can walk the rest of the way?' Aileen says.

'Hey, you're the one who's complaining about being old.'

'*Celebrating* being old, if you don't mind. And if you feel so young and full of energy why don't you offer to give me a piggyback?'

'That's very funny,' he says as he zips his jacket up around his neck.

The cab drives off, and a chilly breeze seems to sweep them up toward what the sign describes as ARTURO'S FINEST ITALIAN RESTAURANT.

Dublin, Ireland, September 1945

It was early one morning when the overnight ship docked in Dublin. The previous night, as the ship prepared to leave Liverpool, Niall had fallen in with some other soldiers returning home to the Irish Republic after fighting for the British Army. They were easy to spot: young, fit, smartly dressed, and with an obvious but unspoken foreboding about what awaited them back home. Over a few drinks in the bar they exchanged their experiences.

Liam had served in North Africa – the dryness and the heat had been such that he struggled to complete basic physical exercises. They all said it was normal – especially so for an Irishman. But he got progressively weaker, with chills, headaches and fever, and at one stage was hardly able to move. After months of appearing to recover but falling ill again, he was eventually diagnosed with relapsing fever, and made a recovery of sorts with medical attention. Despite not feeling anywhere near healthy, he didn't argue when he was sent to the front line and then on to Sicily and Italy. Although Niall thought he looked fit and well, Liam said he'd never felt completely the same since the illness, and that he was looking forward to the wet, mild weather of his homeland.

Jack had been posted to Burma to fight the Japanese. He also looked fit and well, but there was a twitching unease on his face when he spoke of his capture and incarceration in a POW camp. He said in a mere three months his body had been ravaged so much by malnutrition and disease – coupled with hard labour for every waking hour – that he had made his mind up. He'd made peace with his maker and was going to force a guard to shoot him. But the guard saw through his plan, and so merely beat him. Only the liberation of the camp by British troops saved his life. Like Liam, he was sure his body would never fully recover. He shed a tear when he told the others how much he was looking forward to planting his boot on Irish soil, and swore to God never to leave it again.

Pearse, like Niall, had served in France, taking part in the D-Day landings and the push through Belgium and into Holland. In Belgium he'd sustained a bad bullet wound to his leg. Bandaged up but in growing pain, he fought on, but was taken to hospital after the liberation with a serious infection. Yes, he now appeared fit and well too, but a rap of his knuckles on his wooden stump showed that he too would never be quite the same again. Nevertheless, his spirits were good, which buoyed everyone else.

Barry was also a D-Day survivor, and had continued fighting into Germany. He thanked God he hadn't been injured. He'd shot German soldiers, thrown grenades into rooms where they were known to be hiding, and on three occasions had used a knife to kill. He also said he'd seen the results of many of his actions at close hand. He couldn't shake away memories of those sights, but tried not to consider that the men he'd killed left behind mothers, wives and children. He now wanted to forget all of that, to return to his wife and family, and to tend to his smallholding. He did, however, let slip that he had just lately started suffering from nightmares. But they would go in time, he was sure. Yes, they would. Until then he would simply ignore them. At least he had his health.

Niall gave a potted history of his exploits too, of his capture and subsequent escape, of his own relentless push toward Germany, of the friends of many nations he'd lost, sometimes listening to their final desperate words. He too was relieved that he'd survived the war unscathed. Blessed, he thought he'd been. He didn't mention the conversations he'd had with fellow soldiers who had walked into Bergen-Belsen concentration camp after the German surrender. *They might ask questions*, he told himself.

The five of them stopped off at a café in the dockside area of Dublin for a farewell fry-up breakfast, and all wished one another the best before going their own ways. Before they parted, one of them suggested they meet up again. They all agreed, but no details were exchanged, no plans made. The truth was that although Niall had enjoyed the men's company and listened intently to each of their stories, he didn't want to see them again. There was guilt at that, but he knew they all felt the same. It was over. The world was now at peace. They were all young men with the best years of their lives ahead of them. Like Niall, they probably had people to meet and things to do – normal things like feeding livestock, playing with their children or making a little money.

After a detour to buy a small bunch of flowers, Niall headed for the station and took the first train to Leetown.

He knew trouble lay ahead, but at least he'd met Mr Sweeney before – and had even had a couple of cordial conversations with him before the falling out. Aileen had told him of the further rows she'd had with him, but Niall was certain that in spite of their political differences Mr Sweeney was a reasonable man who only wanted his daughter to be happy.

And if Niall could face up to a German soldier – if he could feel the cold, hard steel of a pistol pressed against his temple and survive the ordeal – then coping with an angry, middle-aged Wicklow man shouldn't be beyond him. The war was now over and it was a time to heal old wounds. All people – British and Irish included – should be celebrating the end of the costliest conflict the world had ever known.

Yes, he would simply apologize for any offence caused, tell Mr Sweeney he'd now left the British Army and still wanted to marry his daughter, and they would plan the wedding. And he would have to talk to Mrs Sweeney too. She was sure to be excited about her daughter getting married. With that formality complete, he could start seeing Aileen again with no subterfuge – no messages passed on via Aileen's sister or secretly arranged liaisons – and become her husband.

After the tough years of fighting, of travelling and living in squalor, after the utter repulsiveness of witnessing his friends being killed and maimed, the occasions that he too could so easily have been one of the casualties – after all of that, life was now getting so much better, with everything to look forward to. More importantly, after all the letters he and Aileen had exchanged, he knew she was waiting for him, and that they were going to be together.

The train crossed the Crannagh and he leaned over to see. Yes, the wooden footbridge was still there, linking the village to the sandy beach on the other side of the estuary where he'd first met Aileen. He grinned, wiped a hand over his jaw to hide his joy from the other passengers, and headed for the doors with his duffel bag slung over his shoulder.

He managed to open the door and jump off the train before it had come to a standstill, and soon the hissing clouds of steam were far behind him. He positively skipped along Station Road to the coast road, where he took a lungful of sea air but didn't stop, just turned and carried on walking briskly, which was a legacy of all that good exercise, those healthy rations and, he had to admit, good luck.

At such a pace, it took only a couple of minutes to reach Sweeney Cottage. He glanced down at himself, and how smart he looked in his demob suit. Yes, that would do. That would impress Mr Sweeney.

He took his flat cap off, pasted his hair down neatly, glanced down to check his tie was straight, then gave the front door a few confident taps with his knuckles.

He could feel his breathing running away from him and tried to tame it. As he stepped uneasily from one foot to the other, he took a few swallows to wet his dry throat and wiped his clammy palms on his jacket.

God, it was like being with that German soldier again.

Then the handle rattled and the door started to open. He took a sharp breath, stood up straight, and put on his warmest smile.

'Mrs Sweeney,' he said. But she said nothing. *Perhaps she'd forgotten him.* 'Hello again. It's Niall, Niall O'Rourke.'

She stood there, her eyes shocked, her mouth not knowing what to do.

'We . . . we met some time ago,' he added.

He offered the flowers. She didn't react at first, her glazed eyes looking him up and down. Then she took the flowers.

'Thank you,' she said flatly. She looked back into the cottage, then at Niall, then back again.

'Who is it?' someone shouted out. Niall recognized the voice.

'I'll not be wanting any trouble,' she said to Niall.

This was far from the welcome Niall had expected. 'You won't be getting any from me,' he said. 'Sure, all I want is to see Aileen.'

Another figure appeared from the shadows behind her. Then it grew a little taller as it spoke. 'Holy mother of . . .'

'Hello again, Mr Sweeney,' Niall said, firmly but calmly.

Mr Sweeney looked at his wife, then at the flowers. He snatched them from her hand and flung them out on to the road. 'I thought I recognized the voice,' he said, 'but I told myself no – he wouldn't have the nerve to turn up here again.'

'I've come here in good faith, Mr Sweeney. I don't mean any—'

'Well, you can just go away this second in good faith. Aileen doesn't want to see you anymore, so get yourself away and make sure you don't come back either.'

Niall tried to glance over Mr Sweeney's shoulder, but he stepped to the side, blocking the view as he clearly struggled to control his anger.

But Niall's heart was anything but faint. 'Look,' he said, 'if I could just come inside and talk.'

It was then that they all heard the voice, and Niall couldn't hold back.

'Aileen!' he shouted out. 'Aileen, it's me!'

Aileen spoke again, but her mother turned back to face her, and Niall heard a half-whispered argument coming from inside the cottage.

He took a step forward but quickly felt the hand of Mr Sweeney holding him back, and then pushing him away toward the road. Mr Sweeney shut the door and didn't shout, but spoke loudly. 'I'll not tell ye again. Stay away from my daughter. She doesn't want to know you.'

'If I could just speak to her for a few moments? Please.'

'No, you can't. Go away.' He stood firm, his ruddy face trembling and his nostrils twitching.

Niall took a few deep breaths and stood equally firm, hands poised at his sides, fingers twitching, trying to control his own temper, trying to hold his tongue. 'So, what if we were to talk? You and me. Man to man.'

Mr Sweeney shook his head.

Niall huffed a few times and gave a shout out to the skies. This was too much. He cursed loudly. 'Do you have any idea what I've been through?' he said.

'No. And I don't care. You're a traitor, so y'are. You're a deserter. That's a fact, a fact ye can't deny.'

'Please, Mr Sweeney . . .'

Before Niall got another word out, the raging figure stepped forward and pushed him in the chest again. 'You and your damn British suit. You think you look *so good*. Well, you don't. The likes of you should be in prison. So our government has gone all soft and decided not to do that. All right. But while I have breath in me, you will *not* see my daughter and you will *not* be welcome in my house. Do you understand?'

'But don't—'

'Do you understand that?

He grabbed Niall by the throat, but Niall stood his ground. Whether he could have fought the man off wasn't the point here, but the hand around his throat clearly belonged to a labourer. A few seconds later Mr Sweeney let go, but not before he'd shoved Niall even further away. 'Let me go one step further, just to be sure your thick head gets the message. I don't care whether you're a soldier or even Joe Louis himself – if you're not out of my sight in ten seconds, I'll *kill ye* with me bare hands. And the same goes if I ever see you in this village again.'

'I'm not giving up, Mr Sweeney.'

'And I'm counting. Eight seconds.'

Niall took a few steps back, for the first time giving the man a glare of defiance. 'I won't give up,' he said quietly. He turned and started walking toward the railway station. As he passed Cready's, he stopped still for a few moments and turned around.

Perhaps he should go back right now, to sort the matter out once and for all.

But no. The man was over twice his age and a fight wouldn't help – whoever won. No. The time wasn't right. With a heavy and still thumping heart, he trudged to the station and caught a train back to Dublin. He wasn't sure when the right time might be, but he knew he would be back some day.

By the time Aileen awoke the next morning everyone else had got up and eaten breakfast. Only Briana spoke to her – to ask her how she was and whether she was hungry. She didn't answer, but nevertheless Briana brought her a small bowl of porridge, which she ate in silence.

Aileen hadn't spoken to anyone since the altercation the day before. And that only seemed reasonable. She'd been physically stopped from going outside to see Niall, it had all been too much, and she'd gone to bed while the others had talked, eaten, and – in Fergus and Gerard's case – spent a couple of hours playing cards.

After breakfast, the whole family except for Mrs Sweeney were due to help a local farmer harvest his potatoes and carrots in return for a share of the spoils.

Aileen, however, now sitting on the floor in front of the fire, showed no signs of getting ready to leave. Even when the others were putting their coats and boots on she hardly moved, looking into the fire, trying to blot out the previous day.

Aileen's mother, as always, was in charge of provisions for the family, and as she put the package in the sack she made a point of saying she'd included enough buttered barmbrack and apples for six. At this announcement a few faces glanced in Aileen's direction, but nobody spoke.

The three men and young Frank had their coats on and were about to leave. There was still an atmosphere, only now the atmosphere said *someone needs to talk to Aileen*. None of the men had spoken to her, so it was again left to Aileen's mother.

'Briana, Aileen, will the two of yez be getting ready and helping with the harvest?'

Aileen was motionless, and Briana looked as though she couldn't think what to say.

'Farmer O'Hara needs all the help he can get,' their mother added. 'And the more we help, the more he'll give us in return.'

Still, Aileen didn't drag her gaze away from the glowing peat bricks.

'What about you, Briana? This is important; this is about food. Can you not be helping out?'

Briana looked over toward her father and brothers, and then at Aileen. 'I'll stay with Aileen,' she said.

'Don't stay on my account,' Aileen replied.

Briana thought for a few moments, then said, 'No. I'll stay here. I'm sorry, Daddy.'

Their father and three brothers said nothing, but left the cottage, leaving Mrs Sweeney washing up the breakfast utensils.

'At least we know you can still speak,' Briana said a few minutes later.

Aileen turned and peered at her with heavy, red-rimmed eyes, then turned back to the fire.

'C'mon,' Briana said, 'let's get you out of here for a walk.'

Aileen gave her head the subtlest of shakes.

Briana knelt down next to her. 'We can walk up to Bevanstown if you like – get some fresh air in your head.'

'No.'

'Ah, it'll do you good. You know it will.'

Aileen looked at her for some time, then glanced over to their mother and murmured, 'Well, all right.'

Briana smiled in encouragement, but Aileen's face was still veiled in sadness.

Ten minutes later they were walking along the sand and shingle shoreline, halfway between the two villages.

'You'll have to be speaking to everyone at some stage, you know,' Briana said. 'If you keep all those thoughts inside your head, you'll be sending yourself crazy. Tis like having a bad dose of wind.'

The corners of Aileen's lips started to twitch upward.

'Aha, I saw that,' Briana pointed to her jaw. 'Twas a smile and no mistake.'

'Make the most of it. You'll not be seeing many more from me.'

'I know you're upset, but you have to recover, get over it.'

Aileen stopped walking and put her fists into her hips. 'Get over it? *Get over it*, did ye say? I cried my damned eyes out yesterday, Briana.'

'I know. We all know. We heard you.'

'And do you blame me? I haven't seen Niall for two whole years now, but I've thought of him absolutely every day and we've sent each other letters. I've dreamed of nothing else but the day I meet him again. And when he finally comes here, Daddy does his dictator routine and doesn't even let me *see* him.'

'All the more reason why you have to pull yourself together. You have to plan your next step.'

'My next step?'

'Unless you want to give up on him. Do you want to give up on him?'

Aileen went to answer but stalled.

'Ah, c'mon,' Briana said. 'You're not serious?'

Aileen said nothing, but started walking on, and Briana followed.

'I'm confused is what I am,' Aileen said after a few paces.

'Confused? Confused about what?'

'It's been two years, Briana. I'm just worried.'

'Worried about what?'

'Well, y'know, worried he might have changed.'

Briana's face soured a little. 'Ah, no. People don't change that much. He can't be like a different man, sure he can't.'

'But I've been working in Belfast, I've had my eyes opened to a few things, so I have. I feel different. Do you think I'm different?'

'Mmm . . . You're my little sister, and you always will be. You've just grown up a bit more, that's all.'

'But that's the point. If *I've* changed, I wonder what's happened to Niall. He was away longer than me and he's been at war, not working in a factory. Y'see, I saw some footage in the picture house in Belfast, about what's been happening in those countries beyond.'

Briana pulled a face. 'You mean, they've filmed people killing each other?'

'Not exactly, but . . . aach, I can't talk about it, Briana. It upset me just to look at it, but God only knows how it affected people who were actually there.'

'But he's a soldier. Surely he should be able to cope with that sort of thing?'

'Says a woman who never—'

'Aileen. It's simple. You have a decision to make. Yes, Niall might have changed a little, I admit that. But if you do as Mammy and Daddy want and you never see him again, you'll never know. You won't find out if he's still the same man you fell in love with and whether you still love each other. So, you have to decide. Do you want to know?'

Aileen took a few seconds to think, then said, 'Well . . .'

'The thing is, is it still there?'

'Is *what* still *where*?'

'Oh, for heaven's sake, Aileen. You know what I mean. Does your chest go all light and fluttery when you think of his face? Does your heart still ache for him like it did two years ago? *Is it still there?*'

'Oh yes,' Aileen said. 'Oh, by God, all of that and so much more. I find it hard to think of anything else. I'm going out of my mind thinking of him and I'm not sure how much I can take.'

'Well, that means it's still there.' Briana grabbed her hand and pulled. 'C'mon, let's lie down behind the dunes again. I'll race you.'

She ran, Aileen ran after her, and within a few minutes they were lying on their backs behind the grassy sandbanks, squinting at the sun.

'So, you think I'll be doing the right thing?' Aileen asked. 'I mean, if I go against Mammy and Daddy and see him again?'

Briana lifted her head and torso off the sand and leaned on one arm, facing her. 'Remember, my little sister, I've seen the two of you together. You're very annoying and very irritating and you both get up my nose more than anything I've ever known, so you do. But the two of you have something between you that I can't put into words and I don't think you can either. You belong together, Aileen.'

'But what can I do? Daddy says I'm not to meet him, I'm sure Fergus and Gerard will both fall into line behind him, and Mammy and Frank won't say anything to upset anyone.'

'I'll tell you what you're going to do,' Briana said. 'You're going to do whatever you need to do.'

Aileen sighed wearily, drew a hand across her forehead and sat up in the sand. 'And will you be helping me?' she said.

'Ah, no. Sure, you're on your own there, Aileen.' Briana's eyes scanned the skies. Then she started giggling and shoved Aileen's shoulder. 'Well, what d'you think, ye big eejit? You're my little sister. *Of course* I'll be helping you.'

Aileen joined in the laughter, and pulled her sister's supporting arm away so she fell back on to the sand.

Briana shrieked and took a few moments to shake the sand from her hair. ''Tis awful grand to see you happy,' she said.

'Sure, I've a long way to go before I can be that.'

But as soon as the words left Aileen's lips she knew that wasn't quite true. A little hope was keeping her warm inside.

Chapter 21

It was now just over a week since the fracas of Niall's visit. The fighting in Europe and the Far East might have been over, but the Sweeneys were still a family at war. Aileen and Briana were on one side, their father and two older brothers on the other, and very few words were tossed over the barricades. Little Frank was now taller than the women of the household but was still a boy inside and in danger from the crossfire. For this reason as much as any other, Mrs Sweeney pained herself to keep a delicate truce.

Aileen had been trying to keep herself as busy as possible, and was sweeping the side yard clear when a squeal of bicycle brakes from the roadside made her and the nearby chickens jump. She looked just in time to see the front of a bicycle wheel poke itself around the corner, then she heard a knock on the door followed by a cordial exchange of greetings. Moments later the bicycle and the postman came into full view, wobbling past the cottage and along the coast road. Aileen carried on sweeping.

A minute later the door was flung open, cracking against the wall, and the chickens once again squawked and jumped up into aborted flight. Briana strode out, heading straight for Aileen, and Aileen opened her mouth to ask what was happening. The sight of white paper clasped in Briana's hand made the words jam in Aileen's throat. She gulped and let the broom fall from her hands. Neither of them spoke, but both instinctively headed across the road toward the beach.

'What did he say?' Aileen said as soon as their feet hit sand.

'This time the letter really is to me, but you have a right to read it.' Briana glanced back to the cottage. 'Wait till we get to the dunes.'

'Ah, please, Briana. I'm not sure I *can* wait.'

'C'mon.' Briana broke into a run.

Aileen caught up and stopped at the very first hollow they came to, pulling Briana down with her on to the sand, and snatched the letter. Watched only by Briana and a few inquisitive seagulls, she read it.

> 15 September 1945
>
> Hello, Briana,
>
> First of all, I have to thank you for passing my letters on to Aileen these last couple of years. But this one is for you, because I know how much you care for your sister and I need you to talk to her for me.
>
> I'm assuming you know what happened when I tried to see Aileen yesterday, and I've had a long, hard think about my future and Aileen's future. Out on the battlefield, sometimes it's only the thoughts of women back home that keep the men going. I've lost count of the number of times I saw men almost give up and give in, only to get a letter from a wife or girlfriend and realize what they were doing it all for.
>
> So, whatever Aileen's thoughts of me are, I want to thank her for those letters that made me carry on. Please tell her how grateful I am.
>
> Of course, once a soldier returns home there's a different kind of reality to deal with. Concerns that seem petty compared to battlefield problems take on more importance, and family loyalties have to be

respected. Whatever my situation is, I know Aileen's family mean everything to her, and I have never wanted to cause any falling out. And so I want you to find out whether Aileen still wants to marry me, or even wants to see me again. Please tell her that I'll understand if she doesn't want anything to do with me. If that is so, please don't tell her that I think of her every hour of every day, or that my heart aches for her company, or that I long to hear her warming laugh and look into those magical eyes and touch her wavy auburn hair.

I'm in Dublin, but I haven't what you might call an address just yet so she can't write back, but if she wants to see me again tell her I'll be at Tara Street Station at noon on the last two Saturdays of September, and will watch out for her on every afternoon train coming up from Wicklow. If she doesn't turn up I'll have my answer, and although I'll be as sorry as any man could ever be, I'll wish her and you all the best. May God bless you both.

Once again, Briana, thank you for being the go-between for the last couple of years.

Niall.

Aileen clutched the letter to her chest and breathed deeply, her eyes closed and a lazy smile on her face. The smile gradually contorted as she tried to keep her emotions inside, but she failed and sobbed in Briana's arms for a few minutes.

'I know it's a mess, Aileen,' Briana said, 'but he *does* want to see you again.'

'I know,' Aileen replied, pulsing the words out between gulps.

Briana held her until the tears subsided. She dried her eyes and took a few deep breaths to compose herself.

Then a look of fear took over Aileen's face. 'What date is it?' she said.

Briana thought for a moment, scanning the letter again. 'Oh heck, Aileen. You're right. There's only one Saturday left.'

'And how am I going to get out there?'

'We can sort something out, Aileen. I'm sure we can.'

'You know Mammy and Daddy are awful suspicious of everything I do and everywhere I go?'

Briana was deep in thought.

'It's like being a prisoner, Briana. You know that. Oh heck, what am I going to do?'

The question went unanswered, so Aileen shook her sister by the shoulder. 'Briana?'

'Aren't I always telling you to calm down. I know how much this means to you. We'll work out a way to get there, sure we will. You just have to be patient.'

'I can be patient, all right, but what am I going to do? How am I going to get there? Tell me, Briana, *tell me.*'

Briana rolled her eyes. 'I don't know. I'm thinking. For the moment let's get back home before they send out a search party.'

Aileen took more calming breaths. 'But you'll tell me as soon as you've thought of something?'

'Of course I will.' Briana stood up. 'C'mon. Now wipe your face dry and hide that letter.'

By the time they reached home the whole family was in the living room, their mother peeling potatoes, and their father and the boys playing cards at the table. But all eyes then turned to the sisters. Their father held a gaze with their mother. Aileen knew this game – all the children did. He hadn't the nerve to do the interrogation himself.

'Where have you been?' their mother asked.

'For a walk,' Aileen said.

'Along the strand,' Briana added.

Aileen's parents locked eyes again. Her father shrugged. More stony-faced looks were exchanged, then the card game and the potato peeling resumed. Whether they guessed something was afoot Aileen didn't know, but there were no more questions.

Over the next few days Aileen felt a peculiar sort of restriction – even worse than before. Whenever she so much as approached the door she was asked where she was going. Usually her mother asked, occasionally it was her father. At least that made him talk to her.

Fergus had spoken to her only once. Aileen had asked why he was being so horrible to her. She needed to ask three times before she received a response.

'That man's a deserter,' he said. 'He's brought shame on himself and we all get the idea you still want to see him, so you're bringing shame on all the family. Think of the silent treatment as your penance for sin.'

Aileen found it hard to stop herself arguing. But no. She'd heard the discussions the boys had had with their father. If she were to argue, she would tell them that she'd seen the ruined parts of Belfast, that she'd known people who had lost loved ones to the bombs and bullets, that she'd heard of the horrible things that had happened in those camps, and that she could be certain that *Niall had done a good thing*. They would laugh bitterly at her and say he was a deserter, a traitor, a fool who'd helped the *bloody Brits* instead of letting them fall, a man who should, by rights, be in prison. The argument would continue in the same vein, and she would get angry and be goaded into saying more than she should, that she was going to see Niall again and they could whistle if they didn't like it.

No, that would be very bad. Tempting, but bad. No, she could hold her tongue for a few days.

She did, however, occasionally have private moments, such as when she was alone in the bedroom, when she would shut the door and clench her fists and perform a solitary jig, shaking with excitement.

Oh, how she wanted to tell them, just to see how they would react. And *oh*, *oh*, how she longed to see Niall again.

She would tell them one day, when Niall had married her and taken her far away – perhaps to another county where it didn't matter what they thought. It would happen. Briana would help her see to that.

And Briana did, although it took a few days for her to put her plan into action. When she finally did, Aileen struggled to keep still, to keep quiet, to pretend she had no idea what was going on.

'Have you heard from our Cathleen lately?' Briana said to her mother one morning while they were washing clothes together.

Her mother's face adopted a pained expression. 'I got a letter only the other day. She's doing grand, so she is.'

'Really?' Briana said. 'Oh, well. Yes, tis grand. I'm happy for her.'

She watched her mother pound her fists on a dress with a little more vigour than usual. And she waited.

'Ah, no,' her mother said. 'I can't lie about my own daughter. She seemed very down in the mouth, so she did.'

'I have to say, she seemed a little lonely when I saw her last.'

'Is that so?'

Briana nodded sadly.

'Well, I've told her she can't move back down here, sure I have. It was her choice to move up to the Big Smoke, and that meant we could move young Frank out of our bedroom and into yours. We can't go back on that.'

'Oh, I don't think she'd be wanting that.'

Briana's mother thought for a second before snapping, 'Why? What did she say to you?'

'Ah, only that she was looking forward to seeing me and Aileen again.' Briana left it at that, and carried on wringing out clothes in measured silence. Eventually the reply came.

'Perhaps you should go up and see her again.'

'You think so?'

'Have you any money left for the train fare?'

'Ah, no. I suppose I could borrow some from Aileen and just go on my own.' Briana left the sentence hanging. There was a long pause.

'Aach, twould be unfair like that. The two of you should go together.'

'You wouldn't mind?'

Her mother smiled and nodded. 'As long as that's the only place you go. Cathleen might be a grown woman, but she's still my daughter and I'll always worry about her.'

Just around the corner, crouching by the fire and hanging on every nuance of every word, Aileen pinched her thigh to stop herself from showing any reaction.

'Thank you, Mammy,' Briana said, and went over to Aileen.

'Did you hear that, Aileen?' she said. 'Mammy says we can go to Dublin together.'

Aileen bit her tongue and tried her best to sound pleasantly surprised. 'Ah, grand,' she replied. Then, with her voice a little louder, she said, 'Thank you, Mammy.'

Her father, sitting next to the fire, put his reaction into a grunt, then switched on the wireless. Her three brothers, playing cards, were oblivious.

It was only much later – when the boys were playing football on the beach, their father was on the toilet in the backyard, and their mother had gone to Cready's to buy ham – that the lid truly came off Aileen's excitement. She hugged Briana, let a shriek explode from her mouth, and with a rare exuberance danced up and down the room.

The next Saturday morning they set off, their mother even accompanying them to Leetown Station, just to be sure they got on to the train safely.

'Tell her I'll see her soon,' she said to Aileen and Briana, who were squeezing together to poke their heads out of the same window.

'I will, Mammy,' Briana said. 'I'll give her your love and tell her you were too busy this time.'

'Ah, you do that, please.'

They settled into their seats, the train pulled out, and Aileen put her engagement ring back on again, which in turn put a wide, proud grin on her face. There was little conversation between the two of them as the train followed the coast through the north of Wicklow, although Aileen's fidgeting got worse as they entered County Dublin.

Twice Aileen asked whether Briana had checked and double-checked the arrival time, and twice Briana told her it didn't matter – that the train was arriving before noon, that they would wait for Niall or even surprise him. The plan was for Briana to help Aileen find Niall, then go to Cathleen's place, after which they would reunite at the station for the return journey, back to a family that would be none the wiser.

The train chugged through the south side of the city, past the dreariness of the Dún Laoghaire dockside district, and almost to the banks of the Liffey, before pulling into Tara Street Station. And when that happened Aileen was waiting at the door, rattling the handle to open it well before the train came to a halt.

She cursed the door, which promptly opened, then jumped out on to the platform.

'Won't ye calm down,' Briana said once she'd caught up. 'He probably won't be here just yet.'

'He's not coming. I just know it.'

'Will he be wearing his uniform?' Briana said, looking around too, her eyes hopping along the hordes of travellers.

'Why would he be wearing his uniform? He'll be wearing his suit – the one the Brits give their soldiers when they leave the army. I only caught a glance when he came to the house, but he looked so handsome in it, so he did.' She tutted. 'Uniform. *Honestly.*'

'I don't know. I was just asking.'

'Well, ask something helpful, why don't ye?' Now Aileen looked at her sister for the first time since getting off the train. 'Ah, I'm sorry,' she said. 'I'm just being a bit . . . y'know.'

'Selfish.'

'That's right.'

They caught each other's glances and shared a brief laugh.

'Let's go and search,' Briana said. 'You take a look over the far side in the ticket office and I'll have a quick look in the waiting room.' She started walking, but her words hadn't registered with Aileen, who was too busy squinting toward the ticket office, not daring to think she recognized the dark-haired man who was returning her gaze.

And then Aileen was gone.

Chapter 22

Niall was outside the ticket office waving a large piece of cloth in the air as he walked toward Aileen, but had to drop it and brace himself as she rushed toward him. He caught her in his arms and swung her around, just as he had on that day on the wooden bridge across the Crannagh over two years ago.

To Aileen they were one whirling being, their lips pressed together, their arms locked around each other, trying to squeeze and pull themselves even closer, just as she'd been dreaming of for those same two years.

The hoot of a train brought her back to reality, and she pulled her lips from his.

'Oh God, Aileen – you came! *You came!*' Niall's voice was slightly deeper than she remembered, and weather-worn like an old shed.

'Nothing would have stopped me,' she answered. 'Let me look at you, so I can believe you're really here.' She couldn't resist another kiss, then stood back, still holding his hands, and inspected every inch of him. After all he'd been through – the travelling, the broken leg, the fighting, the fellow soldiers he'd known and lost, and God knows what else – this was just Niall, *her* Niall.

'Hello, Niall,' she chirped, conscious of the grin that grew crooked as she tried to rein it in.

'Hello, Aileen,' he said, with a twitch of his eyebrows.

She looked more closely, and noticed more changes. There were one or two extra lines on his face, and his hair desperately needed a comb. The uniform had been replaced by clothes that weren't so distinguished. Underneath his black jacket, with its pockets bulging, his white shirt was covered in dark smudges. His baggy trousers were shiny just below the knees, and a toe peeked out from a hole in the point of one shoe. But more than anything else there was experience in his eyes, and that only made her love him even more. She ran her fingers through that wild, black hair and wanted to do it again and again.

A hint of sadness or even pain trying to hide itself in his lopsided smile made her stop. Now she could see he was also a little thinner than she remembered, probably fitter, she thought, and his hair needed a cut as much as a comb. But all of that was understandable – normal even, considering what he'd been through. Aileen didn't know much about war. A broken leg she could understand, guns and bombs she could only imagine, although she'd seen their after-effects in Belfast.

'I got your message,' she said. 'The letter you sent to Briana.'

'That'll be why you're here.' Now his smile was warmer, more like the Niall she knew. 'You look like a million dollars, Aileen,' he said, hauling the words from his soul, his eyes fixed on her face. 'I had to see you again, but I didn't want to upset your family by going to Leetown.'

'I don't care about my family, Niall.' She checked herself. 'Well, of course I do, but I like to think I don't. If you know what I mean. I mean, *I* know what I mean.'

Niall laughed and gave his head a quick shake. 'You haven't changed, have you?'

She returned his laugh but there was a deliberate, humorous hollowness to it. 'I have so, Niall. It's been over two years.'

'I'm sorry. I didn't mean . . .'

He stared at her for a moment – a moment when she wondered whether all those dreams she'd had over the past two years were really going to come true. Then he snaked a hand behind her neck. She felt his hand caress the back of her neck and gently pull her closer to him. Their lips met once more, and for a moment her eyelids were lifeless, her will non-existent. The feeling of his fingertips on the baby hairs on the back of her neck made her groan inside.

And then she knew – she *knew* her dreams were still alive. As Briana might have said, *it was still there.*

They parted again, and Niall lifted her left hand, pausing to stare at the ring. 'I wanted to be sure you hadn't found . . . y'know . . . someone . . .'

Aileen's shaking head silenced him. 'I still have your letters, every last one, hidden away in the house.'

'Grand.' He nodded. 'I'm sorry I didn't write after I went to France.'

'You had more important things to be concerning yourself with. It must have been terrible there.'

'Ah, twasn't so bad – apart from the time I honestly thought I was about to die.'

'You were about to *what*?'

'Hello, Niall,' Briana said suddenly from the sidelines.

Niall dragged his gaze away from Aileen. 'Ah, Briana. Tis grand to see you again. I don't think I'll ever be able to repay you for all you've done.'

'Twas nothing.'

'And I'm sorry about . . .' He looked down to display his clothes.

Briana looked proudly at Aileen. 'You've no need to apologize, Niall. It's been a long time since I've seen my sister this happy. But . . . what exactly is it you do for a living now?'

He picked the cloth off the floor. 'Oh, I work at most of the railway stations in Dublin, but usually this one.'

'Doing what?' Aileen said.

He smiled wryly, showed them his hands, which were covered in black smudges, and took a brush from one of his jacket pockets.

'You're a shoeshine man?'

''Tis only temporary. Really.'

Aileen looked him up and down again. 'Well, that would explain the clothes.'

'You prefer me in my uniform?'

Aileen's face lost all pretence of humour. 'Don't joke like that, Niall. You know I don't care what you wear – it's just that I pictured you in your nice new suit or how you were when we first met.'

He shrugged. 'I'm no longer a soldier. But I'll get a better job than this, I promise.'

'Aach, you could be dressed as a clown or Charlie Chaplin or even a big orange carrot and I wouldn't care.' She peered intently at his face. 'Although now I mention it, a black square under your nose, a walking stick, and you're not a million miles away from Charlie Chaplin himself.'

He put on a serious frown. 'I don't have a walking stick just yet.'

'But you do have the black boot polish. We could thumb a bit on for the moustache.'

His face cracked and he leaned forward, laughing. 'Sure, you still say the daftest things, Aileen.' He kissed her again. 'And I'm glad that hasn't changed, my Mrs O'Rourke to be.'

'Ah, won't ye look at the two of yez,' Briana interjected. 'You're as annoying as you always were, and maybe a little bit more besides.' She turned to Niall. 'Anyhow, it's nice to meet you again after all this time, but I'll leave you two alone. I have another sister to see.'

'And while she does that, I thought you could show me more sights of Dublin,' Aileen said. 'Perhaps we could go to a park or walk along the riverside.'

'Ah.' His gaze hopped from one sister to the other. He swallowed, looking like he was forcing down medicine. 'I'm working until noon. I'm . . . I'm sorry.'

'Can't you get out of it?' Briana said.

Niall's hands fumbled with his polishing cloth; his head drooped forward a little. 'I took the afternoon off for you. If I take the morning off as well I won't be able to pay my rent.'

'Don't you get a day off?' Aileen asked.

'Only Sunday. I didn't think you'd want to come on a Mass day.'

'That's right,' Briana said. 'Mammy wouldn't want that.' She surveyed the station foyer, people flitting left and right before her eyes, from smart businessmen to scruffy tramps and every stage in between. 'But Aileen hasn't seen you for two years, Niall. Couldn't you . . . ?' She gave a frustrated sigh and looked suggestively at Aileen.

Aileen started opening her handbag. 'You tell me what you would have earned today and I'll give you the money.'

'Ah, no.' Niall said.

'It's for me, for us. I want to spend the day with you, Niall.'

'Please, Aileen. You must know I can't take your money.'

'Yes, you can. This is no time for being proud.'

He shook his head firmly.

Aileen stared at him, a little anger showing. 'Yes,' she said firmly.

'Aileen. I'll not be taking your money. I *will not* be taking your—'

'You *bloody well will*, Niall O'Rourke.'

He stepped back a little from her, looking just a little fearful. '*What* did you just say?'

'Just something she picked up in Belfast,' Briana said.

Aileen stepped forward and grabbed the lapels of his jacket. 'I haven't seen you in two years, Niall. *Two years.* I want to walk along the banks of the Liffey with you and stay in your arms and talk until the sun goes down and . . . and . . .' She shook her head. 'Look, I don't care where we go, but this is a special day for me. I want to make the most of it.' She frowned and tried her best to summon a tear or two. 'Please, Niall. Please.'

He paused, then pulled her in close, her arms around his waist, and his enveloping her shoulders. 'All right,' he said. 'But keep your money. I'll manage somehow.'

Aileen, her cheek on his chest, her eyes closed, said, 'I was only going to lend it to you anyhow. And at a very good rate of interest.' She felt his chest quiver with the laughter she craved. She squeezed more tightly.

Soon Briana had left to see Cathleen, leaving Aileen and Niall to head for the riverside.

'Did you say that you thought you were going to die at some point?' Aileen said as they ambled, arm in arm, out of the station.

He shrugged. 'Perhaps I was being a little dramatic. Worse things happen.'

'*What?* Worse things happen? Such as what?'

'Let me explain what I mean.'

'I think you should.'

'Well, as you probably know, we moved town by town through northern France and Belgium. We'd become entrenched, as they say, in Holland for a time. It's hard for anyone to understand, but it was horrible, dangerous and boring all at the same time. And while I was there I got the news that put it all into perspective, that made the hardships of war seem not so important after all.'

'What could possibly be worse than that?' Aileen said as he paused for breath.

She saw a few more lines around his eyes as he said, 'That was when they got the message to me that my ma had died.'

Aileen stopped walking and gasped, a hand leaping up to cover her mouth, all thoughts of how Niall had almost died whisked out of her mind. She burst into tears and threw her arms around him, trying her best to cradle his head. They stayed together for a few minutes then parted, a period of silence allowing Aileen to compose herself. Niall nodded for them to start walking again.

'I think I told you in one of my letters she was ill. Weak heart. She did well to survive for so many years after Da died.'

'Ah, Niall. It's still a terrible thing to happen.'

'Tis.' He nodded slowly. 'What made it worse was that by the time I got around to going home the war in Europe was over and I was supposed to be celebrating.'

'But you *did* go, right?'

'I did, but . . .'

'But what?'

Niall smiled awkwardly. 'By then they'd already buried her.'

'Ah, Niall. That's awful, so tis.'

'But I visited Ma's grave and went over to the cottage. I visited the landlord. I thought I might be able to keep it.'

'And?'

He shook his head glumly. 'He told me in no uncertain terms I wouldn't be welcome.'

'Why not?'

'Twas the British Army thing. The whole village knew me as a deserter. And in all fairness to the man, he'd already arranged new tenants.'

'What about your mammy's effects?'

'Ah, she had none. She didn't work, and life was hard for her after Da died. I sent most of my army pay back to her.'

'Is that why you have no money?'

'The army gave me compassionate leave to go back home, then I went back to Aldershot for another month before I got demobbed.'

'De-*what?*'

'When they let you go for good. Anyhow, by the time I travelled to see you, went again to put some more flowers on Ma's grave, paid for a few weeks' food and lodging while I sorted myself out and looked for work . . . well, I have nothing left save for my rent. But I've told you. It won't always be like that. Tis only a matter of time before my luck turns. I can work as hard as the next man.'

'I know you can, Niall, I know.' She nodded firmly. 'But tell me, what was the thing about when you thought you were going to die?'

'Ah, no.' He held a palm up and gave his head a dismissive shake, more pain showing around his eyes. 'It's not the time to talk about that. Not just now. Too morbid.'

'Well, all right. I'm just thanking God that you survived, and that the war's over and you won't be going back.'

'Me too. So now you can tell me how you got on in Belfast.'

And Aileen did. She told him about her job at the dressings factory, about the family she'd stayed with, and about the ruins of the Belfast Blitz she'd visited with Doreen. There didn't seem much point in telling him about her evenings out with Marvin. Whatever that had been, it was now in the past. But she did talk about how she was adjusting to life back in Leetown. However, toward the end the words didn't flow; half of her mind was on the day Niall thought he was going to die, the other on what he was going to do now. She was conscious that she was doing all the talking. Perhaps that was for the best – perhaps she didn't want to know what Niall had got up to. All these thoughts conspired to dry up her words.

They reached the banks of the Liffey, where they sat on a bench, neither of them speaking, just holding each other, staring out at the dark glassy water.

Niall broke the silence. 'I know you haven't been able to wear the ring at home,' he said in a slightly frightened voice. 'But if you've met another . . . I mean . . .'

Aileen poked her head up to peer along the river. 'Heck, tis a mighty beast, this thing. So much wider than the Crannagh.'

'Aileen, I'm serious.'

She turned and silenced him by placing a kiss full on his mouth. When she pulled back she put a finger against his still moist lips. 'Listen to me, Niall O'Rourke. You're mine, so y'are. Every day while you were away I prayed for you to survive this war, and now you have, you're mine. So, there'll be no more talk like that. D'you hear me?'

She took her finger from his mouth and his lips trembled for a moment. She saw him rapidly blink tears away, his face bathed in a smile of relief.

'Thank you,' he said, 'and I'm sorry. That's all I wanted to hear.'

'Well, ye heard it, ye big eejit. And that's all there is to it.'

He gave a lengthy sigh. 'You know, it's hard to believe, but there's a lot of time doing nothing when you're fighting a war – time for your mind to wander, time for you to think things aren't . . . well, things aren't as they might be. War can do strange things to a man's mind, but I'll get over it. You see if I don't.'

'You will that, Niall. You'll be grand. I'll make sure of it.'

'Ah, thank you.'

'And stop thanking me. I haven't done anything yet.'

'Ah, you have.'

They sat together for almost an hour, talking of Aileen's family, and of Niall's memories of his mother, but also not talking at all for long stretches of time.

'I didn't cry, you know,' he said after one particularly long silence.

'When?'

'At my ma's grave. I thought I would, but it just didn't come.'

'That's understandable.'

'But it's hardly right. My own ma.'

Aileen said nothing, but laid her head on Niall's chest.

'C'mon,' Niall said. 'Let's take another walk.'

Seconds later they were matching each other step for step, moving as one along the riverside. There were no nervous silences, no uncertain frowns, no self-conscious pauses. Niall wanted to know more about what had happened to Aileen in Belfast, who she'd met and what she had and hadn't liked about living there.

And Aileen was happy and excited to go into more detail about everything. Well, everything apart from the times she'd been wooed by Marvin, and especially the time he'd said he was in love with her. But Niall seemed genuinely pleased she'd enjoyed her time and made friends, relieved she was never injured, and impressed by her knowledge of the war. She didn't tell him she'd gleaned much of that knowledge from news broadcasts she'd seen at the cinema with Marvin.

Likewise, Aileen wanted to know all about Niall's experiences – what England was like, what kind of people he'd trained with and fought alongside, what it was like travelling through France, and all about his earlier campaign across the Mediterranean when he'd broken his leg. Despite all their time apart, Niall talked as if she was his best friend, colouring the picture of army life with impressions of the people he'd met, and not being afraid to talk about the battles he'd fought in.

By the time he started talking about the push into Belgium Aileen was getting cold, and so she suggested they go to one of the many cafés that peppered the city. But Niall said he preferred to sit down on a bench again, which they did for a while, giving him time to talk about the many, many times he'd thought of her over the years, and how his leg felt better than new.

At that point Aileen said, 'Niall, I'm really cold. Could we please go to a café?'

There was no reply.

'Please?' she repeated in a slightly pained tone.

'Do we have to?' he said. 'I prefer the fresh air.'

But Aileen could sense a tightness in his chest, and saw how his other arm – the one not wrapped tightly around her – was huddled to his torso. She felt his hand.

'Sure, you're frozen too, Niall. Let's go somewhere warmer.'

'There's a library just beyond. Tisn't so far to walk.'

'Ah, no. We need a hot drink. And I'm getting a little hungry too. Aren't you hungry?'

He showed her a flat smile and shook his head.

She drew herself away from him and examined his face. He seemed distant. 'Sure, you must be,' she said. 'You can't have eaten for—'

'I haven't any money, Aileen.' There was irritation in his voice. He stared at her for a moment then looked away. 'I'm sorry. But I've been telling you, Aileen. Next time. I'll take you there next time.' Then a bolt of concern hit his face. 'You . . . You will be coming here again, won't you?'

She turned and lifted her face up to his, close enough to see a heaviness around his eyes.

'Please, Aileen. Say you will.'

For a moment she was going to tell him not to be ridiculous, that she'd made plain her feelings. Then she saw not so much concern as fear on his face. She kissed him full on the lips, and felt his hand drifting around the back of her neck. The feeling made her tremble, leaving her body lifeless and yet vibrant with joy at the same time.

'I have to,' she whispered to him. 'How else are we to be planning this wedding of ours?'

The look of concern or fear or whatever it was fell away from his face, to be replaced by . . . well, it wasn't exactly a grin, but it made her heart sing.

'I was worried you wouldn't want to,' he said.

She laughed again, a warm laugh. 'What happened to the bold and cocky Niall who charmed me in Leetown?' she said.

'I'll be guessing he got knocked sideways in France and beyond. I've . . . I've seen some horrible things, Aileen. Sometimes I think I'm not the same person I was.'

'Aach, so y'are, ye daft eejit.'

He spluttered a laugh, his eyes now showing some of his former spirit. 'That's kind of you to say so. I like to think the old Niall is here somewhere and he's only needing the love of a sweet woman to bring him out.'

'I'm certain of it,' she said. 'And after all, you're only a man, so y'are.' She lifted her hand to his face and brushed away a stray curl of hair that was teasing his forehead. 'I know it's not the same thing, Niall, but being in Belfast changed me. So I understand. And in a way we've both changed together. And I'll wager we'll both keep changing for the rest of our lives – we can be sure of that if nothing else.'

He took a moment to gaze thoughtfully into her eyes. 'You have some very wise things to say, Aileen Sweeney. Did you know that?' Then his expression turned to one of concern, and Aileen knew his mind was turning to the subject she was starting to hate.

'But it's not just that,' he said. 'You know what the problem is now: your da and your brothers detest me, and I get the impression even your ma doesn't really care for me either.'

'Briana likes you. Frank too.'

'You know that isn't enough, Aileen. *You know.*'

Aileen let out a tired sigh. 'They'll accept you. I'll make sure they do.'

'And I'm already after asking around quite a few places for a better job. That should help. I just need time.'

'I know you do.' Aileen stood up and grabbed his hand. 'Niall O'Rourke, I'll make you a deal. Today I'll buy us a lovely hot pot of tea and a big slice of fruit bread each. The next time we meet, you – Mister Moneybags himself – will be paying.' She leaned back playfully to pull him off the bench. 'How does that sound?'

He looked up at her, his eyebrows shifting up like those of a puppy dog. 'That sounds grand.'

'And about time too. Let's get ourselves somewhere warm.' She tugged harder and he got to his feet, then she grabbed his arm as if it was a length of rope and started pulling him away from the riverside.

Chapter 23

A week later Aileen and Briana set off for Dublin again. They'd pulled the same trick, said they were going to make a regular thing of visiting Cathleen. Their mother was a little less keen on it this time but agreed nonetheless. And Briana even made sure Cathleen was in on the subterfuge, just in case any of the rest of the rest of the family contacted her. Cathleen understood – she was, after all, another sister.

They used the same drill, meeting Niall at Tara Street Station, the only difference this time being that the rain was coming down in sheets, so they had to run from the train carriage to the shelter of the concourse. As soon as they stopped running Aileen saw him, standing exactly where they'd met the week before, so she started running again, and very soon Briana had left to see Cathleen again, leaving Niall and Aileen together.

It was immediately obvious to Aileen that Niall was in better spirits this time. There was a brightness in his eyes when he smiled that she hadn't seen the last time. He was also wearing his suit rather than dirty work clothes, which didn't matter to Aileen but was clearly good for his confidence.

They embraced. He gently held the back of her neck again and pulled her toward him until she felt the warmth of his lips on hers. It was like a chain reaction, every muscle in her body gradually relaxing and warming. They held each other, and Aileen realized they hadn't actually spoken yet. She didn't care.

They parted, holding each other at arm's length, and now she got an even better look at his face. And it looked good. Good like a badly missed best friend. She looked down. The suit was crumpled around his ankles, and the sleeves were turned up at his wrists. It was strange – he'd looked so handsome in it before. Again, she didn't care.

Yes, this was it: he was starting to get back into civilian life. He would soon find a better job, and with it gain the favour of her family, and they would get married. The new Mr and Mrs O'Rourke would live in a cottage of their own and have a few little O'Rourkes. Yes, she'd seen a glimpse of the new ways when she'd worked in Belfast. Her eyes had been opened to the possibilities of being a working woman, which was all right while she was young and single, but would be impossible once she got married and those little O'Rourkes arrived.

'Hello again,' he said.

The words brought her out of the little bubble she'd been in, and once again she became aware of the hiss of the steam trains, the clack of heels on platform, the hubbub of conversation, and the distorted blare of the loudspeaker announcements.

He pretended to frown.

'Sorry,' she said. 'Yes, hello again.'

'C'mon,' he said, placing an arm around her. 'Remember that deal we made?'

And she did. No more words were spoken because none were needed until he opened the door to the café and they sat down. She opted for a big wedge of sponge cake with jam filling while he had a rock cake.

They settled, took sips of tea, and shared stolen smiles that got wider as the time ticked by. Aileen could feel her face blush. It was strange how she felt exhilarated and embarrassed and exactly where she belonged all at the same time.

'Didn't I tell you things would change?' Aileen said.

Niall looked at his cup with suspicion. 'The tea's certainly changed.'

'Ah, tis the rationing.' She leaned across and whispered. 'Some of these places are grand, but others put all sorts in as a substitute. We only have good tea at home because Daddy knows someone who knows someone.' She pointed to her cake. 'And the jam in this is spread so thinly it mightn't as well be there.'

'At least I'm paying this time. It didn't feel right, you spending your money on me.'

She shrugged. 'Ah, who cares about that?'

'I do,' he said, all the while maintaining his smile.

'Ah, so you don't feel manly letting *me* buy *you* a cake?'

'Something like that.'

'And does your new-found wealth stretch to taking me to the cinema?'

His smile fell away as if his face had been slapped. 'The . . . the cinema?'

'Well, I'm not keen on walking along the riverbank tonight.' She made a point of peering through the window at the rain dancing on the street outside and the umbrellas hurrying by.

'Erm . . . no, I ah . . .'

'What?' she said. 'What is it?'

He shook his head, then took a bite of rock cake, chewing and moving the chunk slowly around his mouth. 'Tis nothing,' he muttered.

'I can pay,' she said.

He shook his head again, this time more firmly.

'I don't mind paying, Niall. And I certainly don't want us to be falling out over money.'

'And neither do I. But I can't let you pay for everything.'

She reached across and grabbed his hand, gripping it tightly. 'Niall O'Rourke, just you listen to me. Are you listening?'

He nodded.

'When I was in Belfast, the house I lodged in refused to take any rent from me. I tried to insist, but she wouldn't take a penny. She made me promise to spend my money on something that would make me happy. The thing is, Niall, *you* make me happy. I have plenty of money for tea and cakes and the cinema, so I don't want to hear any more of this, d'you hear me?'

A little sadness drew itself on his face and she felt her hand being squeezed gently.

'I'm sorry,' he said. 'I have to admit you talk a lot of sense. But I'll pay next time.'

Aileen nodded in agreement, and there was a long, awkward silence before she glanced behind her, to the clock on the wall. 'We have a little time, so we do. Briana says Cathleen told her James said someone he knows told him they usually start screenings at half past seven.'

Niall snorted a laugh, and spent a few seconds desperately trying not to choke on his cake. He took a sip of tea to help it on its way down. 'What was that again?' he said.

She went to speak, but he held up a hand. 'It's all right. I think I got the gist.'

She leaned over to him and whispered. 'At least it's cheered you up a little.'

'Ah, I can certainly rely on you to do that, Aileen.'

'And as I'm paying I'll choose the film we see.'

He nodded. 'I can't argue with that.'

'And you don't mind? I don't mind if you do mind. Do you mind?'

He didn't answer at first, the pause more to control his laughter than from indecision. Eventually he straightened his face. 'No,' he said. 'I don't mind at all, and I'm sorry for being such an awkward eejit.'

'That,' she replied, 'I can get used to any day of the week.' She rested her chin on the heel of her palm. 'Now,' she said. 'Which cinema? Regal or Savoy?'

'What films are they showing?'

'I have absolutely no idea. You pick one.'

It took a moment or two, but Niall's face eventually cracked into laughter again. Then he suddenly stopped. 'Oh, Aileen, I don't know what I'd do without you.'

It was what she wanted to hear, but in a tone that hinted of desperation, which she definitely didn't want to hear.

They went to the Savoy, which was showing *Now, Voyager* starring Bette Davis and Paul Henreid. They settled together in the back row where the darkness and warmth helped her focus on the film, and, she hoped, made Niall forget whatever his troubles were, if only for a couple of hours.

It also gave the heavens time to empty themselves of rainwater, and by the time the film finished there was only a spit in the wind.

'I take it you enjoyed that?' Niall said to her once they'd left the cinema and were heading for the riverside, arm in arm.

'Ah, I'm after falling in love with that Bette Davis.'

'Who?'

'The actress who played Charlotte Vale.' She put on a fake American accent and angled her face up to the sky. 'Oh, Jerry, let's not ask for the moon when we have the stars.'

'Ah now, I *thought* you had a little tear in your eye at the end.'

''Twas just caused by the cigarette smoke.'

He laughed. 'Ah, right. So that's what it was. Anyway, I can't say that bit made much sense to me.'

'You mean, the bit about the moon and the stars? 'Twas the whole point of the film.'

'Let me put it this way. If you were to say that to me I'd tell you to have the moon, the stars, the sun and everything else up there. You should reach for whatever it is you really want. You deserve it.'

'That's very kind of you, sir.'

'And that's a grand American accent you were putting on there, by the way. I suppose that'll be listening to all them American GI fellas you met up in Belfast.'

'What? Ah, no, no. I was just . . . just copying what I heard in the cinema.'

Niall frowned as he smiled. 'It's grand, Aileen. You must have met some while you were up there. I don't mind. Honestly.'

'Listen,' Aileen said. 'You haven't shown me where you're staying.'

The words drew every vestige of humour from his face.

'We haven't the time,' he snapped.

'Why? What time is it?'

Niall started twisting his head this way and that, until he hit up on a clock above a jewellery shop.

She looked too, and said, 'Sure, we've plenty of time. It's not too far, is it?'

'Ah, well, no, tis. And you wouldn't want to be missing your train.'

'Grand,' she said, and cursed herself for putting a dampener on the evening. His place was probably in a mess and he was embarrassed about it. That would be it.

After a gentle stroll along the banks of the Liffey they reached Tara Street Station, where the ever-reliable Briana was already waiting. There was a little polite conversation concerning what they'd done that night, what the film had been like, how Cathleen was, and how terrible that downpour earlier in the evening had been, before the train arrived and Briana suggested getting on it as early as possible to get a good seat. Neither Aileen nor Niall argued with that, although there was the usual long goodbye before Niall stood on the platform, waving them off.

'So you had a good night?' Briana said as soon as the station was out of sight.

Aileen nodded. 'The film, that Bette Davis one, twas really grand. She and that Paul Henreid, they would have made such a lovely couple. But it wasn't to be.'

'Did . . . ah . . . did Niall pay?'

'Ah, Briana!' Aileen's voice was pitched a little higher than normal. 'Sure, that's a terrible thing to ask. What does it matter?'

'So, he didn't.'

Aileen stared at her sister for a few moments, then huffed out a long breath and made a point of looking away.

'I'm only asking for your own benefit, Aileen.'

Still Aileen didn't look at her sister. 'He hasn't the money just at the moment. He'll be paying next time, so he will. He has problems, but I'm sure he'll find a proper job soon.'

'You know what the real problem is, don't you, Aileen? Daddy's mentioned it enough times. Niall's down as a . . .'

Aileen fixed her with a piercing stare. 'As a what?'

Briana edged closer and lowered her voice. 'You know what I mean. He won't get a government job – not at the hospital or the council or in transport, and a lot of the non-government firms are following suit too.'

Aileen's gaze roved over her sister's face, hanging on the blemishes – the big spot on her forehead, the ever-so-slightly lumpy nose, the chip out of one of her front teeth.

'So, have you thought how he'll support the two of you?' Briana continued. 'I mean, if you . . . you know . . . if you marry him?'

Aileen narrowed her eyes at her sister. 'Briana Sweeney, whose side are you on?'

'I'm on yours, Aileen, yours.'

'And it's not *if* we get married, it's *when*.'

'But I'm just being sensible.'

'Well, just *don't*. All right?'

Briana didn't reply, but folded her arms and looked out of the windows on the other side of the train. Aileen was already staring out of the windows on her side. The two sisters didn't speak until they both got home later that night, and even then, there was a perfunctory nature to their conversation.

As usual, their mother made them a hot milk each, but Briana finished hers first and immediately got up and went to bed, saying only a soulless goodnight to the others.

'Is everything all right?' Aileen's mother said to her. Aileen nodded, still gazing at the glittering edges of peat. 'So, how was Cathleen?'

'She was grand,' Aileen said.

'Has that nasty cold of hers cleared up?'

'Ah . . . I think so. She . . . ah . . . she still has a sniffle.'

Aileen's mother didn't say anything else, but Aileen was conscious of her hovering only a few yards away. She turned her head to the side and looked up. There was a look on her mother's face that Aileen knew well. It was the same look she'd had when she found out Aileen had accidentally broken a plate some years before, or that day when Fergus had turned up with a black eye and dried blood under his nostrils and swore he hadn't been fighting.

Aileen quickly finished her milk and went to bed.

'Briana?' she whispered.

'What?' the reply came, slightly terse but not quite as bad as Aileen had feared.

'How's Cathleen's cold?'

There was a thoughtful pause. 'What are you talking about?' Briana said. 'What cold?'

'It's just . . . Mammy was asking how her cold was, while I was out there just now, after you'd come to bed. I think she was trying to catch me out . . . and . . . and I'm sorry, Briana. I'm sorry I was a bit off with you on the train.'

In the darkness Aileen felt Briana grab her hand and squeeze it. 'I'm sorry too, Aileen. I only want you to be happy. You know that, don't you?'

'Niall makes me happy.'

'I'm just being careful for you, that's all.'

'You're a good sister, Briana.'

'Will the two of yez shut up!' Fergus hissed from the other side of the room.

Aileen heard her sister giggle, then she whispered, 'Will you come with me next Saturday too?'

'Of course I will,' Briana replied, before Fergus told them to shut up again.

For Aileen, the next week went by as if someone were adding a few hours to each day, but the days did eventually pass. On the Friday evening, while the two girls were helping their mother cook the evening meal, Briana mentioned something about going to Dublin the next day to visit Cathleen again. It was a casually mentioned hope for the weather to stay fine.

'Again?' Mammy asked.

'I thought we would,' Briana replied.

'*We?*' Her mother frowned.

'Me and Aileen.'

'Ah. Right. So.' She thought for a few seconds then started poking the pork belly fat around the frying pan.

Aileen and Briana glanced at each other, and Aileen said, 'I'd better start laying the table.'

But she heard those dreaded words: 'You hold on here, young lady.'

'What?' Aileen said, her eyes hopping between Briana and her mother. 'What is it?'

Her mother flung the rag she was holding across her shoulder and put her hands on her hips. 'I'm only wanting to know if our Cathleen's well. It won't be needing the two of yez to find that out.'

'But we both like seeing her,' Aileen said, a little too quickly, she immediately realized.

Their mother peered at them with that suspicious look again.

'And Cathleen likes seeing the both of us,' Briana said.

'We're all sisters after all,' Aileen said. 'Sure, it's not fair to let one of us go and not the other.'

'And it's safer for us both to go together.'

Their mother slowly nodded. 'All right. Just this last time. And if I hear of anything . . .'

'What?' Aileen said as the words trailed off. 'If you hear what?'

Their mother pulled the rag from her shoulder, held the pan handle with it and started poking the pork belly fat again. Aileen and Briana, both slightly wild-eyed, said nothing.

The next day they both took the train to Tara Street Station again. As before, Niall met them off the train, a few words were exchanged between him and Briana, and then Briana left to see Cathleen, leaving Niall and Aileen to enjoy their time together.

As soon as they were alone, Aileen sensed that Niall was in some sort of a mood. He wasn't angry or rude or outwardly upset, just quiet and reflective. And that suit still looked as though it didn't fit. They walked arm in arm to the Liffey, and few words were spoken by either of them.

'So, have you missed me?' Aileen said as they reached the south side of the Liffey and started walking along the bank.

'I have.'

He said it. He said the words clearly, and he spoke as though he really meant it, *but was there just a little hesitation?* No, of course not, it was just the way he spoke. He was obviously rushed.

'So, are we going to the cinema again?' she said.

He looked up, then behind them. 'It's a lovely evening,' he said.

That much was true. It wasn't so bad for October, but Aileen was nevertheless feeling a little chilly around her legs. 'We can't just walk along the riverside all evening,' she said.

'Why not?'

'Ah, c'mon, Niall. Let's enjoy ourselves, do something. I don't mind paying again if that's the problem.'

He stopped walking. 'I can't let you do that, Aileen.'

'But I want to. Please, Niall. Don't you want to see a film?'

'It's not that, Aileen. It doesn't feel right, you paying all the time.'

'You're sounding like my daddy now. Sure, what's wrong with me paying?'

He shook his head. He was trying to smile, but Aileen only saw sadness. 'Nothing, Aileen. Absolutely nothing. But not every time. I can't scrounge off you forever.'

'I thought things were getting better? What with your nice suit, and you buying me tea and cake last week?'

There was a hint of anger in the way he flapped the lapel of the jacket in question. 'It's not mine, Aileen.'

'Not yours? What in heaven's name d'you mean? Didn't the British Army give it to you?'

'I sold that one to pay my rent and buy some shoeshine supplies – well, that and to treat you to tea and cake. This is only a borrowed one.'

'What?'

'I'm sorry, Aileen. I have to be honest. I can barely afford food and a roof over my head. I have no spare money. Absolutely none. I go hungry most evenings.'

Aileen glanced down, realizing that would explain why the suit didn't fit him, but holding her tongue on the matter. 'So how about this?' she said. 'I'll pay for us just this once. And I won't ask you again.'

'But you *will*, Aileen.'

'Oh, all right. Of course I will.'

He smiled warmly at her, his eyes glistening in the throw of the streetlights. 'You can fool yourself, Aileen, but not me.'

'I . . . I don't understand.'

He pointed to a bench overlooking the river. They went over and sat, Aileen's head on his chest, his arm around her shoulders.

'What do you really want to do?' she said.

'In my perfect world?' he asked.

She looked up, gave him a peck on the cheek. 'Yes. In your perfect world. Anything you want.'

'I'd like to stay here,' he said. 'Just like this. You and me.'

'You mean, all evening?'

'I mean,' he replied, 'until the Liffey runs dry.'

'Sure, you're a charming one, aren't ye?' She grinned a self-satisfied grin and lifted her hand up to admire her engagement ring. She felt cosy, and wondered how long the Liffey would take to run dry.

'But this isn't a perfect world, Aileen. And . . . and that's why this is all so hard.'

The last few words wiped the happiness from her face. She sat up and stared at him, inches from his face.

'I'm sorry, Aileen.'

'Sorry? Sorry about what? Don't be sorry, Niall. Please don't be sorry.'

'I don't mean to be so gloomy, Aileen, but there's something I have to say.'

'No. Don't speak, Niall. Please.'

'I can't do this, Aileen. It's not fair.'

'What's not fair?'

He gestured for her to settle on his chest again. She did and he held her close.

'I feel like I'm stringing you along. Tapping you for money. Taking advantage of your pity for me.'

'Niall, I can assure you there's no pity. I look *up* to you, not *down*.'

'That might be true now, but what about later? I mean, if we're to be married I need to be able to provide for you. I can't do that at the moment and . . . and I can't see a time when I will be able to. God, you have no idea how sorry I am, Aileen.'

Aileen felt wetness on her cheeks – the wetness of her world crumbling. She tried to control the shaking of her shoulders, to be brave, to grab and hold back her sorrow. It must have worked a little as there wasn't the full flood. Or perhaps it was his comforting arms – the very arms that would seem to be rejecting her. After a few minutes of silence she stopped and looked up at him.

'So, are you' – she took a gulp – 'are you breaking off our engagement?'

He gave her hair a slow and gentle caress. She felt a kiss, soft and held forever, press against her head. 'I don't know what I'm doing. I'm stuck, so I am. I want to marry you, Aileen Sweeney. I wanted that from the first time we met on the beach at Leetown.' Another kiss, then a hand behind her head, under her hair, caressing the back of her neck. She closed her eyes and felt her heart float. 'The thing is,' he said, 'sometimes you just can't have what you really want, and . . . and when I think . . .' His voice wavered, faltered, then stopped altogether.

'Things change, Niall. The world's changing. People are doing things they've never done before. Women are going out to work, having their own money, supporting themselves.'

'Not in Ireland,' Niall replied. 'And definitely not once they get married.'

They held each other and spent a few minutes watching the water find its own way downstream, occasionally meandering, breaking to whiten the dark green here and there, sometimes rushing headlong, ultimately always going one way.

Aileen pulled herself away from him, then held his head in her hands and kissed him squarely on the lips. 'Niall O'Rourke, let me take you to the cinema one last time.'

'Ah, Aileen, I—'

'Just say yes.'

'But—'

'Don't ye dare say *no*, ye big eejit. Say *yes* or *of course* or *grand* or anything else, just don't say the *no* word.'

His face seemed to collapse in, threatening a laugh. 'Ah, hell, Aileen. You don't give up, do you?'

She kissed him again. 'I'm waiting for an answer.'

He pulled away, smiling, and looking around them. 'All right, I give in. I'll go as long as you don't get us both arrested with the kissing.'

She patted his chest as if she was playing a drum. 'Yes!'

'It's a deal as long as you understand I'll be owing you.'

'Grand.'

'And you choose the film.'

She smirked. 'Don't I always?'

Chapter 24

Niall and Aileen walked out of the cinema, carried in the rush of bodies as if they were coming down the Liffey itself.

'*A Tree Grows in Brooklyn*,' Aileen said. 'Sure, that was a strange one. I didn't get the title at first.'

She threw Niall an expectant look, but he merely glanced back at her. She held on to his arm more tightly.

'Twas good though. Makes you glad you're still in Ireland and not struggling like those Nolans.' She paused, but still he said nothing. 'What did you think, Niall? Did you enjoy it?'

She felt her arm move as he shrugged his shoulders. 'Ah, twas . . .' His words trailed to a sigh.

'You didn't like it.'

'I didn't say that.'

'I can tell.'

'You can't.'

She leaned over and looked closely at his awkward smile. 'It's written all over your face.'

'Tis only a smile, Aileen.'

'Is that what it is?'

He showed her a wide grin. 'Is that better?'

'Sure, it's as if we're already married.' She jumped out in front of him and prodded a finger to her chest. 'Ah, there'll be no fooling this one about where you've been of a night.'

He stopped walking and laughed out loud. It was the first proper laugh she'd heard from him that day. It quickly died to a smile, and he muttered quietly, as though to himself, 'You're a rare one, Aileen.' And then the smile died. 'C'mon.' He nodded for them to start walking again.

They headed back to the Liffey to take in some fresh air after the smokiness of the cinema. They were both silent for a while. But when they reached the banks of the river, Niall led them to the railings, where they both leaned over, listening to the rush of the water. Niall looked straight into the river, although to Aileen his focus seemed a million miles away.

'Are you sure you're all right?' she said. 'You don't look well.'

'I'm *fine*!'

Aileen pursed her lips and glared.

'I'm sorry, Aileen. I shouldn't raise my voice at you of all people.'

She nodded glumly. 'That's all right.'

His eyes started roving over her face, settling on her eyes. 'Oh, Jesus,' he said. 'Oh, bloody hell, Aileen. What are we going to do?' He let out a sigh that lowered his shoulders an inch. He looked away, but Aileen grabbed his face and turned it back.

'Are you crying?' she said.

A slow, lazy blink let loose the drops from his eyes. Aileen pulled out a handkerchief and wiped his face.

'Ah, no. Leave me be.' He sniffed and wrestled his head free.

Aileen examined his face. Now he looked tired and weary, his jowls hanging like they never did before the war. As Aileen's father used to say, he looked like his own older brother.

'I don't mind,' she said. 'I cry all the time. Just ask Briana. Especially while you were away. I used to cry all the time then.' He didn't acknowledge the words. 'Niall, look at me,' she said. 'Please.'

He did, then said, 'Oh, Aileen.'

'What? What is it?'

'I can't do this to you, Aileen. I just can't.'

'Do what?' Her voice weakened, she felt her throat closing up. 'Oh, I see. So . . . you *do* want to break off our engagement.'

He looked straight ahead, ran the palm of a hand across his face. 'Don't make this harder than it is. I don't . . . it's not that I *want* to break it off. It's just . . . I don't want to string you along. I want you to be happy, Aileen.'

'But . . . but I *am* happy. You make me happy.'

'Ah, *now*, sure y'are. But don't you ever think about the future? I don't have any family. Your family hate me and always will for deserting. This bloody government hate me and seem hell-bent on keeping a boot on my throat. What d'you think it's going to be like in five years' time? Or ten years? What do we live on?' He pulled the stubs of the cinema tickets from his pocket and held them up to her. 'Thank you, Aileen. Really. Thank you for buying me a drink and taking me to watch a film. But you've said yourself, your money won't last forever, and I don't want you to waste what you have left on me.'

Now Aileen felt the tears overcome her, running freely down her cheeks. 'Niall. Please don't do this. I'd give you my last penny, you know that.'

'I know you would. But I don't want that.' He held her head and pulled her gently to his chest, where she nestled, wiping her tears on his jacket, snaking her arms around him and holding on like she was never going to let go. They stayed that way for a few minutes, then he said, 'C'mon, let's sit down.' At first she resisted, but soon they were on a bench, his arm around her shoulders.

'I'm so sorry, Aileen. It wouldn't be right for me to let you keep thinking that . . . that somehow everything's going to be grand when it clearly isn't.' Now he brought his arm back from around her shoulder, and she felt cold, even a little naked. 'Surely you can see that. A shoeshine man can't support *you*, Aileen, let alone a family as well.' He sighed, then ripped up the ticket stubs and threw them to the ground. 'Damn!' he hissed. 'I bloody hate meself sometimes. I wish I'd never joined the bloody British Army.'

Aileen let out a grunt as she slapped his face. 'Niall O'Rourke, just you take that back.'

'But it's—'

'Take it back, Niall. I've *seen*, remember. I've *seen* it. I'm not like the rest of my family and you *know* it. When I was in Belfast I saw the film footage, I heard the stories. I know what Germany and Japan have been doing to people. So I understand what you were doing there, what the point of it all was.' She heaved a few deep breaths, her face flushed, her eyes fiery. 'My family might not be proud of you. Nobody else in this country might be proud of you, but hell, Niall, I bloody well am. It's how I know you're a good man and it's why I love you. So you'll take those words back right now or I'll jump into this river, so I will. D'you hear me?'

He stared at her, perhaps for a minute. It felt like an hour to Aileen.

'By God, you're special,' he said eventually. 'And I suppose you're right. I shouldn't say that. I'm sorry – and I'm sorry for being so miserable. But none of that changes the facts. By the look of things, I'm going to be poor forever.'

'You're poor now and I love you.'

'Ah, thanks.'

'I didn't mean it like that. I know you'll succeed. I know you'll find something somewhere and you'll work hard and do well at it. It might not look like it now, but I have faith in you, so I have.'

'Well . . .' He took a few long, drawn-out breaths as he searched for words. 'At least one of us has.'

'Oh, hell, Niall. You're kind and you're brave and you're hard-working. That's good enough for any girl. Can't you see that?'

But Niall was staring down at the ground, motionless.

She thumped his shoulder, and then again. 'Jesus, Niall, all you need is a little more fire in your belly, a little fight. Can't ye show people what you're made of, for God's sake.'

He looked up at her. There was an expression on his face she hadn't seen before – a blank, big-eyed stare as if he was trying to tell her something, trying to pass a message on, but was also fearful of something. He looked back down to the ground again, to the same spot as before. Aileen followed his gaze. He was looking at . . . at what? *At the cinema tickets?*

'What is it?' she said. 'Niall, what's . . . ?'

He stood up again, walked toward the river and held tightly on to the railings. She followed. He was staring out again, staring at nothingness. She tugged his shoulder and he looked at her, but it was that same blank, pensive stare. He cocked his elbow and hoicked his chin up, the signal for her to hold on to his arm and follow. She did, and they strode along the riverbank promenade for a few minutes.

'Niall, you're worrying me,' she eventually said.

But there was silence.

'Talk to me, Niall. What is it?'

'Nothing. Let's head back to the station.'

She stopped still. 'No. Talk to me.'

'It's just something,' he said.

'Something?'

'Something I need to think about.'

'No, it isn't, Niall. It sounds like it's something you need to tell me about.'

'I can't, not yet.'

'You want me to beat it out of you? Is that it?'

He looked at her, gauging her. In return she raised her eyebrows, glaring at him. He smiled.

'I'm trying to be serious,' he said.

'So am I. Now, *tell* me.' She pulled his arm as she spoke.

'Well . . .' He pointed to another spare bench. They sat. 'You see, that film we just saw.'

'*The film?*' She screwed her face up.

'I didn't think much of it at the time. Or perhaps I did, but I was confused. It only occurred to me later.'

'When you ripped up the tickets and spent five minutes staring at them?'

He nodded. 'Twas something like that. And I did enjoy the film. Twas about a load of Irish people moving to New York to make new lives for themselves.'

'And?'

His only reply was for his eyes to flit to his own body, then to hers, then settle on her face.

She gasped and covered her mouth with her hand. Now it was her turn to stand and step over to the railings, gazing out over the water. She was aware of him following, standing next to her. She knew he was shrugging his shoulders as if it was obvious all along. She was also aware that words were tumbling from his mouth, but none of them registered. She only started to listen when she turned her head and looked directly at him. And now there was a little of that fight, that passion she admired so much, both on his face and in his words.

'Don't you see? It'd be grand, me and you. I can get work there – proper work because I won't be blacklisted – and we could rent one of those apartment things or even a house. The country's booming and they're crying out for workers just now. I'll be treated like a human being, and we won't have to arrange to meet in secret like we do here. We can have everything we ever dreamed of. Come on, Aileen, a new life, just you and me – a tree grows in Brooklyn for us – what d'you say?'

All Aileen could do was gulp, still focussed on his animated face, his excited eyes, his grin wider and more spirited than it had ever been this side of the war. She felt like she was swallowing her tongue, and sensed the trickle of the tears she didn't want to come.

'Oh, Niall.' She tilted her head and frowned. 'Niall, I can't do that. I . . . I can't.'

'But why not? It would solve all our troubles.'

She shook her head. 'It's too big for me. It would scare me – it scares me just to think about it. I'm just a Wicklow girl. My family's everything to me. Sure, they're a pain in the neck at times, but they're . . . they're everything I have, and my home's here.' She glanced up and down the river and behind her. 'Well, no. *Leetown's* my home, Dublin's the back of beyond, and Belfast was the end of the world. But . . . *America?*' She shook her head again.

'But . . .' Niall let out a frustrated sigh, and for a second looked as though he was going to collapse. 'Ah, who am I fooling? You're right. It was only a thought, nothing more than a stupid idea.' He held her hand, squeezing it. 'I'm sorry. I shouldn't have asked. Forget I said it.'

'It's grand, so it is. I'm flattered you asked. To ask a girl to marry you is one thing. To ask her to go to America and marry you, well, that's something else entirely. So, I'm sorry if you . . . if you think I've let you down.'

'Ah, no.' He shook his head. 'Don't apologize. It's me who should be sorry. I know I've been awful miserable lately.'

'With good reason.'

They sat in silence for a few minutes. Then Aileen said, 'C'mon. Won't you show me where you're living?'

'Tis a hell of a mess.'

'I only want to see it, Niall. I won't be living there.'

'Hah. You wouldn't fit.'

'And we can check the time on the way.'

His eyes darted around behind them. 'There,' he said.

She looked over to the clock then shot up to her feet. 'Oh heck, I was forgetting. I have a train to catch. C'mon.'

They hurried along the streets toward the station, darting left and right to avoid lovers, drunks and the occasional vagabond. Eventually Aileen shrieked as she spied her sister waiting at the platform gate.

'I was just about to give up on you,' Briana said as they approached. 'Lord only knows what sort of a fuss Daddy would make if I turned up on my own.'

But Aileen was hardly interested in what her sister was saying as they all rushed along the platform to the waiting train, Aileen stumbling once or twice as she broke into a trot. She rushed, but at the same time she didn't want to go.

The carriage door. An embrace. No, more than an embrace. Aileen allowing Niall's arms to envelop her like a warm woollen blanket on an icy winter's day, their chests pressed together, their lips locked in a passionate but painful kiss that Aileen had no intention of cutting short for a mere train ride.

'Aileen!' she heard. 'Come on.' She turned her head. Briana was holding the carriage door open.

'Please,' Niall whispered in her ear. 'Visit me next Saturday. I'll be here at noon.'

'I'll be here too,' she said. They kissed again, but slowly the embrace weakened. Even when she felt his solid hands move to her shoulders, gently pushing away, she resisted. And when he pulled his warm lips away from hers she felt weak, frightened, and not so far from passing out.

'Go on,' he said. 'You'll not be wanting to get yourself into even more hot water.'

Then, from the carriage: '*Aileen!*'

Only then did she move, but the final few steps on to the train might as well have been barefoot across hot coals. She grasped Briana's outstretched hand, pulled herself up, then closed the door and leaned out of the window. From there Niall seemed a lonely figure. It was no more than ten or twenty seconds before the whistle blew and the train jolted into motion, but for every one of those seconds Aileen was on the verge of stepping back on to the platform. As the train pulled away, she waved frantically back at Niall, who stood there with a hand aloft.

Then he was gone.

And then Aileen burst into tears.

Now it was her sister's hands – small and delicate – that were on her shoulders, guiding her away from the door and toward the compartments. The first two were full. There were only two spare seats in the third, and they took them.

Aileen's head swirled with anger and sadness at what she wanted so much but was starting to realize she might never have. Whether her sister spoke or not, she didn't know. What the other occupants were doing, she didn't care. She was content to gaze aimlessly out of the window, and soon the bright glow of the city gave way to the light-pricked blackness of rural Wicklow.

By the time the train had chugged halfway back to Leetown, the two girls were alone in the compartment, and Briana clearly felt free to talk.

'I don't understand,' she said.

'What?' Aileen replied, now shaken from her musing, and also fearing what was coming – fearing too what her own answers might be.

Briana gave her back a soothing rub. 'Twas all going so well back there on the station platform. Very touching, like Humphrey Bogart and Ingrid Bergman in *Casablanca*, or—'

Aileen shot her a stern glance.

'I'm not poking fun at you, Aileen. I was almost in tears myself, so I was. But . . . well, now I can see something's wrong. I expected a little sadness, but only a little. You're deep in thought when you should be bouncing off these walls in happiness. What happened?'

Aileen's torso heaved a couple of times as she drew in deep gasping breaths. 'It's grand, so it is. Niall has a few troubles at the moment, but it'll all come good soon enough and we'll be married next year, so we will.' She nodded reassuringly.

'Does he have a job yet? I mean, besides shining shoes.'

'And what's wrong with shining shoes?'

'Nothing's wrong with it, Aileen. I'm only asking.'

'Nothing. You're right, nothing. People will always be needing their shoes to be clean and shiny. And I'm sure Mammy and Daddy will come round to liking him soon enough. I know they will.'

Briana just stared. And stared some more.

'What?' Aileen said. 'What is it?'

Briana squeezed Aileen's hand. 'They say love is blind, Aileen.'

'What do you mean by that?'

'Well, I'm starting to wonder . . .'

Aileen shuffled to the side, distancing herself from her sister. 'Wonder what?'

'Ah, Aileen. I know you're in love, but you're making things so hard for yourself. Perhaps that's why you're upset.'

Aileen stared at Briana's face. Her forehead seemed to be carved from pity, her grimace like a twisting knife. And Aileen felt the twist. She turned away, her hand instinctively covering her eyes, and the tears started to drip from her chin.

'I'm sorry,' Briana said quickly. 'I'm sorry I said that, Aileen. I'm sure it'll . . .' She laid a hand on Aileen's shoulder and gently shook her. 'What is it, Aileen? There's more, isn't there? There's something you haven't told me.'

'He's . . .' Aileen took a long breath to calm herself. 'He's saying how he wants to go to America.'

'*America?*' Briana's jaw fell slack for a few seconds. 'But, you mean, just to try things out there?'

Aileen looked up, wiped her eyes clear and shook her head. 'For good.' A shrill scream came from her lips. 'He says there's no work for him here, says the government and all the employers have it in for him.'

'But . . . is he wanting you to go with him?'

Aileen shook her head, although it was more of a clueless roll, an accompaniment to the shrug of her shoulders. 'I don't know. He says he does, but I just don't know. And I can't bear to think of it. I can't go there, Briana, I just can't. I'm after telling him every time I see him that things will get better here. I don't want him to go, Briana. It would kill a part of me, I'm sure.'

'Oh . . . oh, God.'

'What'll I do, Briana?'

Briana went to speak once, then again, both times shaking her head as no words came. Then she glanced through the carriage window at the River Crannagh, an almost fluorescent sliver of reflected moonlight cracking the darkness. 'For now you'll just have to be pulling yourself together. We have to get off here and the last thing you need is Mammy or Daddy seeing you in this state.'

'You know, I'm not sure I care.'

Briana's eyes widened. 'Well, you better had, my little sister. I've been telling lies for your sake, and they can only stretch so far before they break.' She glanced at Aileen's hand. 'And it's time for the ring to come off too.'

More tears trickled down Aileen's cheeks.

A few minutes later they got off the train. The cool, slightly salty air stung Aileen's face at first, but as they walked to Sweeney Cottage she took deep breaths and talked with Briana of the weather, of the latest lines of food stocked at Cready's, and of Father Kinross's latest sermon – anything but where they'd just been and what she'd just been through.

By the time they were saying hello to their parents, Aileen felt as though she could be a million miles from Dublin and from Niall. It was a feeling she didn't much care for, because for the first time in years there was a contemplation of a life without Niall. It was as though any future life with him was slipping from her grasp and she felt helpless to do anything about it.

After the girls had been given a cup of warm milk, and Briana had relayed a few routine stories of how Cathleen and James were getting on in Dublin, they went to bed.

'Is it Fergus or Gerard who's snoring?' Briana whispered as they lay together and held hands.

Aileen lifted her head and aimed an ear at the far side of the bedroom. 'Both, I think.'

Briana laughed through her nose, causing Aileen to laugh too.

'At least we can talk without getting scolded,' Aileen said.

But neither of them did talk for a minute or so, and Aileen could just about hear – between snores – the ocean breaking on the beach.

'Aileen,' Briana hissed. 'I'm sorry.'

'For what?'

'I've been lying to you as well as Mammy and Daddy. At first I thought you and Niall were made for each other, so I did, but just lately . . .'

'What?'

'Well, a small part of me was thinking if you saw him a few more times you'd realize things aren't so good. For the future, I mean. And I'm sorry.'

Aileen squeezed her hand. 'You've no need to apologize. Without your help I wouldn't be seeing Niall at all. He might as well be in America already.'

'I know I was wrong, Aileen. It's not fair what they're doing to Niall, and I won't let you give up on him.'

'It's only thanks to you that my dream's still alive.'

'Ah, well, in a place like Leetown everybody needs a dream, even if it never comes true. But I hope yours does.'

'Ah, thank you.'

'Tis all part of the service of being a big sister. Now, let's sleep before we wake up Fergus.'

Aileen closed her eyes, but couldn't settle. 'Briana?' she whispered.

'What is it now?'

'I think I should apologize too.'

'Oh, dear God. For what exactly?'

'I've been awful selfish lately. You must have dreams of your own.'

'Never mind my dreams.'

'Whatever they are, I hope they come true too.'

'Thank you. Go to sleep.'

They turned away from each other, and Aileen took a few deep breaths to keep her tears silent. Very quickly her dark thoughts turned to a soft grey, and she drifted off to sleep.

Chapter 25

The next day was Sunday. And in Leetown that meant Mass, when the women of the village boasted their best dresses and the men their smartest suits, for Father Kinross expected nothing less. It was a fine morning, the sea calm and the sun as strong as it ever got in October.

The Sweeneys, as was usual for such a pleasant Sunday, separated on the walk back home. Mammy talked with the women about who was ill, who was pregnant again, and the general comings and goings of the village. Mr Sweeney and the boys returned via the pub, where they discussed the politics of the day with the other men, specifically the continuing negative reaction to Éamon de Valera's offer of condolences to Germany on the death of Adolf Hitler. Somewhere along the way Aileen got separated too, and by the time she got home only her mother was there.

Aileen's mother always wore something of a haggard expression, but today it was somehow even more weary, incongruous against her best floral dress and cream hat. She was standing at the table, and took the hat off as soon as she saw Aileen.

'I need to talk to you, Aileen,' she said.

Aileen paused, allowing her heartbeat to settle a little. 'About what?' she asked.

Her mother pointed to the chairs. 'Let's sit down.' She eased herself into a seat, and Aileen followed.

'You've . . . well, you've been seen.' Mammy's eyes were now focussed, owl-like, on Aileen's face. Aileen felt the heat of accusation course through her chest, and the room skewed sideways for a moment as if a shot of whiskey had been pumped into her veins.

'What d'you mean?' She injected a laugh, as much to calm herself down as anything.

'Someone at Mass was in Dublin yesterday.'

'Who?'

'It doesn't matter who. They saw you. With . . .'

'Oh.'

'Oh, indeed. You've been told you'll not be marrying the man, Aileen. You've been told by your daddy you'll not be seeing him again.'

It was no good. As much as she tried to control them, Aileen's tears boiled up and erupted. Her mother whipped out a cloth and handed it over. She said nothing for a few minutes as her daughter gathered herself together.

'Why are you doing this, Aileen?'

Aileen took a deep breath. 'I love him, Mammy. I can't bear the thought of not seeing him again.' She looked up, her eyes roving over her mother's face, searching for an ounce of sympathy.

'I do understand, of course I do. But you can't have everything your own way.' Her mother let out a sigh. 'You have to grow up, Aileen. You've been told you're not to see him and that'll be an end to it.'

'But why?'

'Because your daddy said so.'

'And why should he be the one to decide?'

Her mother paused, struggling to answer, eventually rushing out, 'That's just the way it is.'

'But what about you, Mammy. What do you think?'

'It doesn't matter what I think. Your daddy decides on these things and I support him.'

'And you think that's right?'

'Now, won't you stop this, Aileen.' There was a hint of a smile, one that seemed to brush Aileen's feelings aside. 'Your father deals with the politics, the money and the legal things. I take care of the house and make sure the children are fed and clothed so they grow up to be of use. He and I are as one before God, and you should know better than to think I'd go against him.'

'So, he decides who I marry and you go along with it?'

'Aach, he doesn't *decide*, Aileen. He knows what's best for you is all it is. Sure, that man wouldn't get on with your brothers, and your father has him down as a traitor to the country, so you'd be unhappy with him.'

Aileen said nothing for a few minutes, but bowed her head and looked down. 'Tisn't fair,' she muttered.

Her mother exhaled noisily. 'I know, but . . .'

As she paused, they both heard a stamping of shoes and angry words outside.

Aileen's mother sat up, her body suddenly tense. 'Oh, Holy Mother of God. I'm fearing your daddy's found out.'

The door front opened a few inches, then juddered as if it had been kicked open, swinging all the way back and smashing against the wall.

'Ah, Fergus,' their mother said, her voice now cracking.

He didn't even look at her, just stared, wild-eyed, at Aileen. He stood there in his Mass suit, looking anything but solemn. Within seconds he was at the table. 'Is it true?' he shouted.

'What?' Aileen answered.

'I'm after being told you're seeing him again, when you sneak off to the Big Smoke with Briana.'

'Seeing who?'

Fergus slapped both his hands on the table in front of her, and bore down so she could almost taste the beer on his breath. 'The deserter – the traitor to his own country.'

'I'm not far off twenty-one, Fergus. I'll see who I like.'

'Well, if you do, then someone's going to get hurt, and twould only be right too.'

Aileen sensed her fear falling away. She stood up and stepped over to him, her face slanted up to meet his, her hands on her hips. 'Is that so, Mister Al Capone?'

'The man's betrayed everyone in this country. He's a coward and deserves to be shot like one.'

'*A coward?*' she shouted out. 'Did you call him a coward?'

'Ah, don't pretend he's anything else. He's a deserter, a yellow-bellied coward and I won't have a sister of mine—'

'Don't you dare—'

Their mother now stood up and shoved an arm between them. 'Stop it, the both of yez,' she said.

But neither Aileen nor Fergus budged.

'Ah, he's drunk, Mammy,' Aileen said, her eyes not moving from Fergus's reddening face. 'He's just drunk and he can't think what he's saying.'

'Oh, is that right?' he said.

'Sure, tis. Cowards run away from trouble. Niall ran away to risk his life fighting the Nazis.'

Fergus laughed in her face. She continued.

'He fought against the Nazis, Fergus, not us. He's no coward – he's a braver man than you, and you *know* it, sure you do.'

'Ah, so now you're . . . some little girl war expert now, are ye?'

'Well, I know more than *some* do about what's happening in the world. And don't be calling me a little girl, ye big eejit.'

Aileen was vaguely aware of her mother trying to separate them again, but the two stayed toe to toe.

'Well, if you know what's *happening in the world*, you'll know that the whole war thing was an anti-Irish plot by the Brits.'

At that, Aileen stopped, her mouth agape, a despairing smile forcing itself on to her face. 'Ah, Fergus Sweeney,' she sang. 'Won't you hear yourself, the world's biggest eejit. Have you not heard about the concentration camps, of what the Germans did to the Jews? Have you not heard about what the Japanese did in the Far East?'

'Aach, *you're* the eejit, so y'are. It's all propaganda, the lot of it.'

'Ah, *Jesus Christ almighty*, Fergus. There's just no point in talking to you if all you're going to do is—'

Aileen was vaguely aware of something approaching her face, but could do nothing about it. She felt her neck twist sharply and the side of her face sting with warmth. She gasped for breath. She was, however, fully aware of her mother speaking.

'I'll thank you not to take the name of the Lord in vain, my girl.'

The room trembled in Aileen's eyes, both her mother and Fergus now staring at her, their eyes like hot knives.

'Oh, Mammy,' she managed to say, praying that she could hold the tears back, that she could show a little more strength. She failed, and her mouth clammed up. She ran into the bedroom, slammed the door behind her and threw herself on to the bed.

She heard Fergus kick the door. 'Not so bold now, are ye?' he shouted out. 'Ye Black and Tan girl, ye.'

Then she heard another slap, then Fergus again, 'What was that for, Ma?'

'Don't ever call your flesh and blood that, Fergus.'

Then she heard another voice. It was Briana. *Was she going to get the same treatment?*

Aileen jumped off the bed and opened the door to see her sister standing, confused, at the far end of the room by the outside door.

'What's happening?' Briana said, her eyes darting between her mother, Fergus and Aileen. 'What's going on?'

'And you're as bad as her,' Fergus said.

'As bad as who? What are you talking about?'

Fergus only managed a grunt, but one laden with the same disgust his frown was full of.

'We know,' their mother said to Briana.

'Know what?' she replied. Then, disappointed, 'Oh.'

'Oh, indeed. You can't have not known, Briana. And I'll bet it's been going on for weeks. All those lies to get to Dublin. I'm disappointed in you, so I am.'

Now Fergus spoke again. 'What?' he grunted. '*Weeks?*'

Their mother pointed to Briana. 'This one tricked me, said they were going to see our Cathleen.'

'I was doing no harm, Mammy.' She stepped over to Aileen and held her, checking her face. 'Are you all right, Aileen?'

'Never mind her,' their mother said. 'What d'you think your daddy's going to say when he finds out?'

'You aren't going to tell him, are you?' Aileen said.

There was no reply.

'Mammy?' Briana said.

Fergus let out a laugh. 'If she doesn't tell him then I will.' He jerked a thumb to his chest. 'And he'll whip the both of yez to within an inch of your lives.'

Their mother held a hand up. 'No, Fergus.'

'But—'

'No. Don't provoke your father. You know what he's like. He'll—'

'He'll what?' boomed a voice from the doorway.

'Dan,' she said. 'We were just . . .' She paused, unable to continue as he stomped over, unbuckling his belt.

For Aileen the next few minutes were a raucous blur. She and Briana cowered in the corner. Alcohol-soaked shouts rained down on them at first, then stinging whiplash slaps from the leather. Aileen yelped as blows caught her on the shoulder, then the knee.

'Dan!' her mother shouted, her arms on his shoulders, pulling him back, slowing down his strikes.

But this time he was in no mood to obey. 'Get off!' he shouted. He cast out an arm, as swift and strong as the wing of a swan, and his wife fell on to the floor.

Fergus knelt down and checked she was all right. Then he stood up and stepped toward his father. 'Da! Leave it.'

More lashes from the belt rained down on Aileen and Briana, both of them yelping in fear and pain. Aileen had now shrunk to a ball, her arms covering her face, but through her defences she saw the buttons from her father's best waistcoat straining as he took a deep breath and walloped the belt down again and again.

'Da!' Fergus shouted again. Then a flick of leather found its way between Aileen's arms and caught her on her cheek, the side of her jaw alive in pain. 'THAT'S ENOUGH!' she heard Fergus shout. A few grunts, a scuffle, then both men were still. Fergus rubbed his knuckles, Daddy his jaw. Daddy threw his belt down at the girls, his chest still heaving with rage. 'They've had enough, Da,' Fergus said. 'Just leave it.'

Aileen and Briana had received the biggest battering of their lives, but it could have been worse. Fergus, of all people, had prevented that.

It was only a few minutes later, with Aileen and her sister rubbing their wounds, that she made any sense of it. Young Frank and Gerard had returned from church with their father, but Gerard had wisely led Frank out of the house and away at the first sign of trouble. When their mother had been thrown down she'd hurt her head on the stone floor, but she was a tough thing, and held a wet cloth to the bruise as she sat on the chair recovering, not even shedding a tear. Their father had struck Fergus, but he'd hardly felt it. When the blow was returned, whether from the shock of his son striking him or the force of the blow itself, the beating had stopped.

The four of them sat. Daddy seemed to have come off worst – in mood at least – just staring down at the floor, his face screwed up in anguish.

'Thank you, Fergus,' Briana whispered.

'Don't you dare be thanking me,' he replied in a calm but firm voice. 'We all know who's to blame, and I swear as God is my witness, if that man ever comes here again I'll take a scythe to his legs, so I will.'

Now Daddy looked up. 'And you'll not be going to Dublin to see him,' he said, croaking the words out. 'Nobody in this family will be going there without my say-so.'

'Nobody?' Mammy said.

'Maureen, I'm . . . I'm sorry I hurt you. I shouldn't have done that. But I was angry – angry due to this one.' He threw a finger in the vague direction of Aileen. 'And I'm standing strong on this principle. Nobody goes to Dublin while that man's living there.'

'What about seeing Cathleen and James?'

'They'll just have to do the same as our Alannah and Bernard. They can visit or write. And as for you . . .' He tossed a glance at Aileen, but it was as scornful as it was brief. 'You'll never see the traitor again, and if you go against that, you're no daughter of ours, and you won't be welcome in this house.' He looked up again, his dark eyes swapping between Aileen and Briana, his lip curling. 'Now get out of the house and give us all a little respite from this nonsense. This is supposed to be the Lord's day, a day of rest. I don't want to see either of you for at least an hour.'

Slowly Briana stood up, then Aileen followed, and a few minutes later they'd left their coats and shoes just above the tide and were pattering toward the water. Neither of them spoke until they felt the cold seawater sucking the life from their feet.

'Heck, this is cold,' Aileen said, shivering.

'That'll be good for your bruises and weals,' Briana said. 'It'll cool them down a little and stop the stinging.'

'Did he catch you too?'

Briana nodded, then cupped a handful of water and splashed it on her neck. She did the same again on different parts of her body, and Aileen did likewise.

'Oh, Briana. I'm so sorry.'

'You weren't the one with the belt.'

'No, but . . . I've ruined everything for you, so I have. I've got you into some rare trouble.'

'Aileen Sweeney, don't be apologizing.'

Aileen looked over to her sister and squinted against the sun. 'Thank you, Briana. You've been grand to me. One day I'll repay you.'

Briana blushed. Then she wagged a finger at her sister. 'If I'm doing all this work and seeing you through this trouble, don't you dare be giving up on Niall, d'you hear me?'

'But I feel so confused. What am I going to do?'

'We'll sort something out, so we will. They can't tie us both to chairs for the rest of our lives.'

'But I don't understand, Briana. Why are you doing all this for me? You've got yourself into so much hot water over Niall.'

Briana thought for a few moments, all the while still soothing herself with the cool seawater. 'I suppose I want to see you get out of here. I don't want you to end up . . .'

'End up . . . what?'

'Well, like . . . never mind. I just want to see you happy, that's all. Mammy and Daddy might not understand, but I do. And I know that if a good-looking man asked me right now to go with him to America I'd be packed and ready in minutes.' She stopped and stared out to sea for a second. 'He wouldn't even need to be good-looking, if you want me to be honest.'

'It sounds easy when you say it like that,' Aileen said. 'But when someone really does ask you, it's different. Sure, when you get down to it you're the same as me, Briana. You're just a Wicklow girl.'

'How serious do you think he is about going?'

'Who knows? He almost begged me to go with him, then seemed to go cold on the whole idea, said he was only fooling himself. Oh, I hope he doesn't go, Briana. If he stays in Dublin there's a chance I'll see him eventually – perhaps when all of this has died down. But if he goes to America I'll never see him again, and I couldn't live like that. I'd rather walk into this ocean and just keep walking.' She looked out to sea and sighed. 'Besides,' she said, 'I've told him I'll see him again on Saturday.' She looked at Briana, who was just nodding slowly. 'Oh, Briana, what am I going to do?'

Briana stepped over, splashing water up on to her dress. 'Aileen,' she said. 'We've done it before and we'll do it again. By hook or by crook, you'll see him. I'll make sure of it.'

Aileen started crying, but was smiling too. 'I won't forget this,' she said, and flung her arms around her sister. They spun around, almost falling into the shallow waters.

Shivering, they put their coats and shoes back on and walked on along the beach.

Chapter 26

For the next few days in Sweeney Cottage, Aileen and Briana remained in disgrace, and looks of disgust replaced any form of conversation where they were involved.

But the sisters stood their ground, the days passed uneventfully, and Saturday arrived. After the family had shared yet another sullen breakfast together, followed by an hour working in the potato fields, it was time. In fact, it was too early, but Briana had warned Aileen the timing couldn't be perfect. Their father, together with young Frank, had gone to see a farmer about bartering some of the chickens. Their mother had gone to have a cup of tea with old Mrs Cavanagh, to 'stock up on gossip' as Fergus had put it. Fergus and Gerard were left playing cards at the table, with strict instructions to make sure their sisters didn't end up in Dublin.

Briana kept looking outside, down toward the beach. After about half an hour she suddenly stopped and walked over to Fergus.

'I'm needing a wash,' she said to him.

Fergus and Gerard both looked up. Fergus played a card and looked to Gerard to respond.

'We could just go down to the shore,' she added.

'*We?*' Fergus said.

Briana's eyes went from Fergus to Aileen and back to Fergus. 'Yes, *we*. We're still dirty from digging the potatoes this morning.'

'I'm all grimy,' Aileen said, nodding in agreement.

'You're disgusting, all right,' Fergus said.

They ignored that.

Gerard played a card. Fergus thought for a moment and placed down his response before speaking. 'I dug up potatoes too,' he said. 'And I don't need a wash.'

'Oh, you do, Fergus,' Aileen said. 'You're just used to the smell.'

Gerard sniggered.

'Very funny,' Fergus said, not looking up from his hand of cards.

'Well, we're going whether you are or not,' Briana said a little theatrically.

'Well, no, you're bloody well not,' Fergus said, mimicking her voice. 'Are so.'

He turned his cards down on to the table and nodded toward the front of the cottage. 'Touch that door and you'll have the back of my hand to contend with, so ye will.'

'Are you going to whip us like Daddy did?'

'I have a little more self-control, but yes, if I need to.'

Briana shifted from foot to foot, twice glancing at the door. 'Why don't you come with us,' she said. 'We'll be no more than a few minutes.'

Fergus looked at Gerard, who shrugged. 'I don't mind,' he said. 'I don't think it's a trick.'

'A trick?' Fergus said. 'Ha!' He stood up and pointed a two-fingered gun at Briana. 'Ten minutes. No more.'

Soon all four of them were shin-deep in the icy waters, Aileen and Briana washing their arms, knees and faces, Fergus and Gerard just standing there, trying to look casual and enigmatic, casting glances up and down the endless beach.

'Fergus?' Gerard said.

Fergus looked where Gerard was looking, at the two girls strolling along the beach toward them.

'Say something,' Gerard said.

Fergus eyed his sisters suspiciously for a few seconds. Then he turned away and shouted over to the girls, 'Hello there!'

There was no reaction from them.

'C'mon,' he said to Gerard. They started walking ashore to head them off.

Aileen and Briana couldn't hear anything after that. They knew, however, that their brothers would ultimately get nothing out of the objects of their desires, because the girls' instructions were to invite Fergus and Gerard over to the sandy beach the other side of the River Crannagh. When Fergus kept glancing back toward Aileen and Briana they sensed a little loosening of the manacles.

'We'll be grand for ten minutes,' Briana said. 'Let's get back home.'

The sisters walked out of the water and past the others, now hearing what was being said. The women were trying to persuade Fergus and Gerard to walk with them, but Fergus was having none of it. 'We have to stay here,' he said. Then he turned to Aileen and Briana. 'I'll be keeping my eye on yez,' he shouted over.

'So watch,' Briana replied.

'Anyway,' Aileen said, 'Mammy will be back any minute.'

'Sure,' Fergus said. 'Now go home and stay home. We won't be long.'

Aileen and Briana walked up the beach, shaking as much water off them as they could, keeping a discreet eye on their brothers, who were standing tall with their arms folded to show off their muscles.

As soon as Aileen and Briana shut the cottage door behind them they hurried to collect their handbags and opened the door a crack, just enough to see Fergus and Gerard in the distance – to tell when their backs were turned. They chose their moment and ran, slowing to a walk after they'd passed two or three cottages to avoid drawing attention to themselves. A few minutes later they turned into Station Road.

They knew they would be early, but that was better than not arriving at all.

When the train drew in to Tara Street Station, Aileen and Briana were surprised at how busy it was. Then again, it was earlier in the day than on their previous visits. It was harder to scan the area through the mass of bodies crossing left and right, but between them they did that, spotting two shoeshiners, neither of them Niall.

'I thought you said he'd be here?' Briana said.

'Sure, he told me he'd be working a full morning, so . . .' She slowly nodded. 'Ah, wait. He sometimes works at other stations too.'

'But he said he'd be here at noon, didn't you tell me?'

Aileen huffed. 'I can't wait until then, Briana. I can't take the risk.' She took another look around the station concourse. 'I have an idea,' she said, then she turned and approached one of the other two shoeshine men, Briana following. 'Do you know Niall?' she said to him. 'Niall O'Rourke?'

The man just shrugged.

'Jet-black hair,' she added. 'He shines shoes here most days.'

'Don't know. I'm new here.' The man waved a dirty finger across the concourse. 'You could try asking Davy over there.'

They walked across and Aileen asked the same question.

'Sure, I know him,' the man said, 'but he doesn't work here anymore.'

'Well, where does he work?' Briana asked.

He shrugged. 'I'm not so sure as he does. At least, not as a shoeshiner.' He nodded to the man Aileen and Briana had just been talking to. 'Even gave up his polish and brushes to yer new man yonder.'

Aileen's face brightened, her eyes excited. 'Has he got another job?' she said. 'I know he's been looking.'

'Aren't I after telling yez?' the man said. 'I don't know. And who are yez anyway?'

'I'm his fiancée,' Aileen said proudly.

'Sure, he mentioned you.' There was sadness in the man's words.

'What?' Aileen replied. 'What did he say about me?'

'It's the sort of thing you should really be asking him yourself.'

'Don't you have his address?' Briana muttered to Aileen.

Aileen reached into her handbag and pulled out a slip of paper. 'Do you know where this is?' she said to the man.

He squinted to look, pushing the paper to arm's distance. 'I do,' he said eventually.

They followed his directions. Across the second bridge, first right, third left, to be met with a long row of tenements of crumbling buff brick. Aileen was in shock at first: it wasn't how she'd imagined Niall's neighbourhood. Perhaps he lived in a nicer part past here. They walked on.

'What's that horrible smell?' Briana said as Aileen's eyes scanned the dilapidated front doors. Briana looked down and shrieked as she saw what appeared to be the innards of an animal discarded in the gutter, maggots squirming all over the rotting flesh.

Aileen looked too and screwed her face up in disgust.

Briana covered her mouth and said, struggling with the words, 'I think I'm going to be sick.'

'House number twenty-six,' Aileen said, taking a long stride over the gutter on to the pavement. She turned to find her sister still staring down. 'Go and wait in that café,' she said, 'around the corner and across the road.'

'And leave you on your own here?'

'I'll be grand, sure I will. It's time for your little sister to be strong now. Go and wait. If I'm not back in an hour, come for me.'

'I can't leave you here, Aileen.'

'Just go. I want to be on my own with him.'

Briana hesitated, but wished her sister good luck and hurried away to the end of the street.

Aileen hurried too, and soon found herself standing in front of tenement number twenty-six. She stood and stared up at the building that once, she assumed, had been some impressive new Georgian house fit for those upper middle classes – those British ones Daddy was forever condemning. Now it looked as though it was pleading to be put out of its misery and pulled down. Clothes – and not clean ones by the look of it – were draped from windows. Other windows were boarded up. Guttering and parts of masonry had fallen to the ground and been left there. Also at ground level, rust-brown railings had some sections missing, leaving holes in the concrete where the uprooting had taken place.

Perhaps Niall didn't live here now. Perhaps someone would tell her he'd moved to somewhere nicer. She went through the scenario in her mind as she entered the hallway and started climbing the bare wooden stairs. Yes, she would be told he'd moved, and she would go to that better place, where she would surprise him and congratulate him on his new job. He would tell her all the exciting details, then he would take her out for a coffee and cake, perhaps to the cinema again.

It would be the start of a better chapter in her life.

By now she was two floors up. She'd passed all sorts – children dressed in tatters, men laid out cold by cheap alcohol, ladies who Father Kinross had referred to as 'fallen women'. They had some things in common though: grimy, lifeless faces and rags for clothes. It was also just as cold in here as it was outside.

She stopped outside a door with the number five scrawled on it in chalk. She was about to knock on it when she heard a shout. She turned to see a man with a pockmarked face lurching toward her. He was in no way threatening, with his head bowed, his hands clasped together almost as if in prayer.

'You,' he said. 'Begging your pardon, miss. Do you have any spare pennies?' She shook her head. His saggy eyes looked her up and down. 'You look like you have.'

She knocked loudly on the door. The man turned and scuttled away. A few seconds later the door rattled in its frame and Aileen took a step back.

'Aileen?' Niall's face had an angry edge to it. No, not angry, agitated. He wore nothing but baggy old trousers and a vest under a dirty jacket. In his hand was a book. 'What are you doing here?' he said.

'I'm . . . I'm sorry I'm early, Niall. I wanted to see you.'

'But—'

'Did I do the wrong thing?'

'No. No, you didn't. Tis just the shock of it. I was hoping you wouldn't find your way here.' He sighed, looked along the corridor and said, 'Wait there a minute while I get ready. We can go for a walk. Call out my name if anyone starts on you.'

He darted back into the room, leaving it slightly ajar. Aileen leaned to look inside. She could only see half of the room, but on the floor lay three mattresses with only a walking space between them. A square wooden table with some cups on it stood next to the window, the bottom of which was broken and boarded up with wood. One mattress had a huddle on it – someone asleep, and she saw Niall place the book down on to one of the others. She squinted to see, but could only make out one of the words on the front of the book: 'America'. It made her feel nauseous.

Niall picked a shirt out of a paper bag lying on the bare floorboards. He took off his jacket, put the shirt on, then picked out shoes and put them on his bare feet. He grabbed his jacket and came to the door again.

'You had to give your suit back?'

'And the shoes.' He grabbed her hand. 'Let's go.'

They were on the street by the time he spoke again. 'I'm sorry about that,' he said. 'I didn't want you to see where I was staying.'

'Why not?' she said, knowing she was just trying to be kind. And his wry smile told her he knew it too.

'Tisn't the cleanest of places, I suppose,' she said, as they headed to a small park around the corner.

'You're right about that. There's talk of that there tuberculosis. I spend most of my time out here or in the library or railway station.'

'So, do you have a new job?'

He grimaced, almost as if he was embarrassed. 'I haven't.'

'So . . .'

'I was praying you'd turn up at the station. I was going to meet you there and tell you everything.'

'Tell me what, Niall?'

They reached the park. A couple of the benches were occupied by men sleeping, bags of possessions for pillows.

'Here,' Niall said. 'I usually use this one; it's a little sheltered from the wind.'

They sat, and Niall turned to her, held her hand. She went to kiss him but he resisted.

'I can't,' he said. 'I can't torture myself and deceive you, Aileen. You're all I've ever wanted and everything I've dreamed of for these past few years. But I've reached the point where . . .'

'Where what?'

'Aileen. When I joined the British Army I made some good friends – British friends. They defeated Hitler and his cronies. They risked their lives. Some gave their lives and won't ever come home and have opportunities of any sort. When they went back to their home towns, to their families, they were treated like the heroes they are. Their loved ones cried and told them they'd never let them out of their sight again. They got free drinks in the pubs there, a free bag of coal from the coal merchant, free milk for the little ones. They got help with being trained for life outside of the Forces.'

He took a breath, bowed his head.

'And me? Me and the other Irishmen? You've seen how I'm living. I'm bitter, I can't deny that. I can't find proper work. Anything to do with the government and they tell me they're not allowed to give me a job. The others just say they have nothing but make it clear they're lying. Even if I go back to my village I feel like a stranger. Sure, the pubs take my money but there's no smile, no welcome. And I'm not sure I'll ever be allowed to buy land even if I could afford it.'

'It'll get better, Niall. It'll all die down and—'

'No, Aileen. No, it won't.'

Aileen saw pain in his eyes, a sorrow of frustration and betrayal, and she felt the hurt reflected in her own heart.

'I've made my choice, Aileen. I got in contact with one of my pals from the British Army – someone who owed me a favour. I borrowed money from him. I've bought tickets to America. The ship sails next Friday.'

Aileen gasped, her mouth fell open, her throat choked. If her heart felt pain before, now it felt like a dead weight, falling and gone forever like a stone down a well. The picture before her of the man she loved – the man who held all her dreams in his hands – now turned to a blur. She wiped the tears from her face but more replaced them. Incoherent thoughts rushed through her mind before she could think of what to say. She found herself throwing her hands around Niall's neck, holding him tightly as she convulsed in a wreck of denial. *No*, she thought. *No, she wasn't going to let this happen.*

He said nothing either, just held her, his hands pulling her in tightly, until her rambling thoughts gave way to an acceptance of sorts. They parted, and she sat, hands in her lap, head bowed.

'You've seen the pit I live in, Aileen. Are you really wanting that?'

She opened her mouth to speak, but stopped herself and just shook her head.

'I need to get away before I go mad. If I ever want to earn a crust, I have no choice. But the most important thing is . . . I want you to come with me, Aileen.'

'But . . . ah, no, I couldn't afford it.'

'You don't need to. I bought two tickets.' He thrust a hand into his pocket and pulled out a folded-up piece of paper. 'This is yours,' he said.

'I don't want it. I don't want either of us to go.'

But she knew. This time Aileen knew it wasn't about what *she* wanted, but what Niall needed.

'Aileen, listen to me. I don't know whether I can live without you, but I know for certain I won't be able to make you happy here. So I want you to come with me. I don't know what's there on the other side of the Atlantic. I've been reading up on it, but books don't tell the whole story. All I know is that I believe in you. You can be happy there. *We* can be happy.' He put the ticket in her handbag. 'I'll understand if you can't, and believe me when I say I feel wretched for asking because it might mean I never see you again. I'd rather die than leave you, but I know I'll die little by little anyway if I stay here. Aileen, look at me.'

She did, and he took out his handkerchief to dry her eyes.

'If I stay here we'll get sick of each other – perhaps not for a while, but we will. I'll drag you down, and we'll both be unhappy. I'd prefer you to find someone else than have that. Please, Aileen, meet me on the foredeck when the ship sails at noon on Friday or we'll never meet again. I want nothing more than to see you there, but I'll understand if you decide not to, and I promise I'll never hold anything against you as long as I live.'

He stood up and held a hand out. 'C'mon, I'll take you back to the station.'

'I want to stay with you, Niall.'

'What you want now isn't important, only what you do next Friday morning.'

'We've been through this, Niall. I've told you. I can't leave Ireland.'

'Just tell me you'll think about it.'

'But can't we have one last day together?'

He shook his head. 'We'd just be torturing ourselves. I'll see you next Friday or not at all.' At that, Aileen could see tears dribbling down his face, his eyes blinking again and again.

She stood up and faced him, reached up and held his head in her hands. 'You're a mighty fine man, Niall, and a brave one. By Christ, you deserve better than this. I'm so sorry.'

'Your words mean a lot to me, Aileen. But c'mon, let's go.'

'No,' she said. 'You stay.' She reached up on tiptoe and kissed him on the cheek. 'Goodbye,' she said, 'I'll find my own way home, one way or another.'

Niall gave her a last smile, his face twitching, his cheeks glistening. 'Be strong, Aileen,' he said.

She took a few steps back, not taking her eyes off his face, then turned and walked away.

Chapter 27

Aileen appeared at the coffee shop doorway, and Briana immediately put her cup down. Aileen said nothing, but stayed at the door, just staring at her sister. Briana understood. She got to her feet, picked up her handbag and left.

'Well?' she said.

Aileen just shook her head, not slowing her pace.

'Are we going home now?'

One nod.

'Ah, Aileen. I'm sorry. Really, I am.'

Briana didn't ask for any more details, Aileen didn't offer any, and both of them spent the train journey watching the countryside speed by. It was only as they approached Leetown that Briana spoke again.

'I wonder what Mammy and Daddy are going to say to us when we get back,' she said.

'I don't care,' Aileen replied, drawling the words out.

Briana leaned across and lowered her voice. 'Aren't you going to tell me what happened?'

Aileen didn't look at her sister. 'They've got what they wanted,' she said. 'He's going to America.'

Briana stared, her mouth agape in shock.

At Leetown, Aileen pretty much marched all the way home, chin up, eyes straight ahead, leaving Briana struggling to keep up.

When they reached Sweeney Cottage, Briana hesitated. Aileen didn't; she walked straight in, unwavering and defiant. The whole family were there. It looked as though they'd just eaten, with Mammy washing up, the brothers playing cards, and Daddy cleaning his boots by the fire.

They all stopped what they were doing when Aileen and Briana appeared. All eyes turned to Daddy, who laid down his boots and brush and got to his feet. He held his head up and jerked his shoulders back, but that hint of his customary bluster dissolved as he watched Aileen walk straight past as though she were the only person in the room. Maybe it was the redness around her eyes, maybe her vacant stare, but he was unable to utter one word before she entered the bedroom.

He did, however, lay a firm hand on Briana's arm and say, 'Where have you both been?'

She shook her arm free. 'You've got what you wanted,' she said. 'Niall's going to America.' She followed Aileen into the bedroom, shutting the door firmly behind her.

As the two sisters sat next to each other on the edge of the bed they heard voices from the living room – not raised, not angry, merely puzzled.

'I think Daddy's got the message,' Briana said.

'I hope he's pleased with himself.'

They listened again, and talk from the living room soon fizzled out.

Briana broke the silence. 'Do you . . . ah . . . do you want something to eat?'

'I want to die.'

Briana put an arm around her sister's shoulders and gave her a gentle squeeze. She spoke softly. 'You know, Aileen, I'm sure it feels like the end of the world, but it won't be. And you never know, you might see him again. It's a long way, but he might come back, or you might even go over there.'

Aileen opened her handbag and plucked out the ticket Niall had given her, then screwed it up and threw it to the corner of the room.

'What's that?'

'My ticket to go with him.'

'You're kidding me.' She caught a scolding look from Aileen. 'I'm sorry, but . . .' She eyed the door and lowered her voice to a whisper. 'Why the heck are you staying here?'

Aileen took a deep breath, but didn't reply.

'Aileen? Answer me. Why aren't you going with him?'

'I've told you why, Briana.'

'But . . . he's bought you a ticket.'

'I wish I could go, but I can't. I'm just too scared. I won't be seeing him again. It's like you say, I have to accept it's not the end of the world, and . . . and . . .'

Aileen covered her face with both hands and started whimpering. She fell back on to the bed and curled up like a newborn baby. Briana pulled a blanket up to cover her, resting a hand on her shoulder, and Aileen cried until the only thing that could give her relief – sleep – floated into her mind.

For Aileen, there was a dreamlike quality to the next few days, as if she was on a boat cast adrift. She even had the nausea to go with it. Briana asked no more questions, and Aileen spoke no more about Niall and the trip he would be making to America without her. Nobody else dared speak to her due to the grief etched on her face.

She attended Mass on Sunday with the rest of the village, although her head and her heart were still elsewhere, and everyone knew it.

On Monday too, everyone was quiet, gentle and helpful with Aileen. There were no meaningful conversations at mealtimes, only polite mentions of how the clouds had unexpectedly held off that day, or how the chickens were laying well recently, or how Father Kinross's latest sermon seemed to have lasted longer than a bad winter.

Throughout Tuesday morning Aileen heard whispers behind her back – always involving her mother – and it came as no surprise when, after the midday meal, the rest of the family made their excuses and left the house, leaving the two of them alone.

'Do you want me to help you wash up?' Aileen said, loitering.

Her mother tilted her head just slightly to one side. 'Ah, no. It can wait.' She glanced to the door. 'There is something you could do for me though.'

'What?'

'Sit down.' She flicked a hand toward the table.

Aileen walked over and heard the door behind her being bolted.

They sat together, face to face, her mother holding her hands across her expansive belly.

'You've been awful quiet these last few days, Aileen. I'm worried for you.'

'I'm grand.'

She nodded. 'Well, that's good. But you only seem to be saying it. I can understand you're missing your fella, but—'

'I don't have a fella.'

'Right. I see.' A sigh of exasperation made her readjust her hands. 'You're doing the right thing putting it all behind you, Aileen. You'll find yourself a husband in time, all right. It's part of growing up, no more than that.'

'Oh, really?' Aileen was aware her nostrils were flaring, her eyes almost popping. It didn't matter. 'I suppose you'll be telling me the same thing happened to you when you were my age?'

Her mother paused, considering her reply. 'No. No, it didn't. I met your daddy when I was seventeen, married him at eighteen, and when I was nineteen your sister Alannah came along. 'Twas all very simple.'

'So, you've never known what it's like to love a man and lose him?'

'I know Briana went through the same thing a few years since. She wanted to go courting with a couple of fellas your daddy didn't approve of, and she had to give them up, but look at her now.' She pointed a hand to the door. 'She's managed to get over it all right. And so will you.'

'Perhaps I'm not my sister, Mammy.'

'There is that. And I know things are a little different now, but—'

'It's all right, Mammy. You've no need to baby me.'

A pensive frown drew itself on her mother's forehead – something Aileen had rarely seen. 'Sure, I'm not babying you, Aileen – quite the opposite. I'm trying to get you ready for being a woman. It's the way things are.' She leaned forward and held Aileen's hand. 'It's *the way things are.*'

Aileen's gaze dropped down. If she hadn't felt beaten before, she did now.

'So,' her mother continued, 'what are you going to do now?'

Aileen took a moment to think. The question was so simple, so obvious, but she hadn't given the matter any thought. She knew what she *wasn't* going to do, but no more than that.

'I suppose . . . well . . . my Belfast money will soon be running out. I suppose I need to find myself a job.' She tried to force a smile but it wouldn't come. 'Either a job or a husband,' she added.

Her mother patted her knee. 'Good girl. It'll make you feel better. I know it will.' She stood up, let out a satisfied sigh, and walked away.

Aileen pursed her lips in thought and warmed her hands over the fire. Yes, perhaps it was time to grow up – to get a job and grow up. No more silly notions of love that didn't please Mammy and Daddy and wouldn't last.

Aileen's mind was a swirl of confusion for the rest of that day, and the night was little better. She was the first one up on Wednesday morning. She was going to look for a job – first starting with Cready's, then the village pub, then the church. If those drew blanks and the local farmers didn't need regular help, she would consider working down the road in Bevanstown, where there were two shops, two pubs and a small hotel. If nothing else, the regular walk there would do her good.

She made a few promising enquiries, and it was early afternoon by the time she returned home, and noticed a strange vehicle parked outside the cottage next door. She took a second to inspect it, vaguely wondering where she'd seen it before.

She walked to her front door, but turned back for another look. It was like a car, but had thicker tyres, strange matt green bodywork and no doors. It was . . . like one of those things with the funny name that had been all over Belfast. How strange. But no matter. She shook the thought from her head and reached for the door handle.

As she opened the door all conversation stopped. The whole family were there, but before she had the chance to check the faces her mother caught her eye with a bright smile. 'Aileen,' she said, 'you have a visitor.'

All eyes turned to the one place Aileen couldn't see, the window bay around the corner from the doorway. She stepped forward and almost stumbled with the shock.

It was him – the hair was a little longer, the clothes were casual, but it was him.

'Marvin?'

He stepped away from the window and toward her, then held her gently by the arms and gave her a kiss on the cheek. 'Hello, Aileen.'

'But . . . but what are you doing here?'

He shrugged those square shoulders. 'Had some business to attend to in Dublin. Thought I'd come on over and visit an old friend.'

'You never told us you had an American friend,' Aileen's mother said. 'And he's come all the way over from America just to see you.'

Marvin smiled, slightly bowing his head to show no offence. 'Actually, I was already here, ma'am. I just haven't quite gotten around to going back yet.'

'Ma's already asked him about the film stars,' Fergus said, 'and whether he knows any of them.' He caught a glare from his mother, which only made him grin.

'I've just been talking with your family,' Marvin said. 'And a very fine bunch of people they are.'

Frank sniggered, which made Gerard snigger too.

Marvin didn't notice. He hadn't taken his eyes off Aileen since she'd come in. 'I've, uh, got a jeep out front. Thought you could show me a few of the sights – perhaps those Wicklow Mountains you told me so much about. I could take you out for the afternoon.' He turned around and gestured to the others. 'And your mother and father too, naturally.'

'Isn't he a gentleman?' Aileen's mother said.

Her husband shushed her and shook his head. Then he stood up and walked toward Marvin. 'That's grand of you to offer, Marvin. But me and my boys have things to do and people to see.'

'What things?' Fergus said.

'You'll see,' he muttered. He turned back to Marvin. 'But thank you for coming by, Marvin. It's been a pleasure hearing about New York.'

'The pleasure was all mine, sir.' Marvin nodded, turning to spread the nod to the others. 'Thank you for your fine conversation. I hope to see you all again.'

The boys and their father left the cottage.

'Mrs Sweeney,' Marvin said. 'What about you? Would you like to come with us?'

She hesitated as she eyed Aileen. 'Well . . . I suppose so, if you don't mind. It's been a while since I had a day out. Twould be grand to see a little countryside. I will, yes. Thank you, Marvin.'

'Excellent.'

'I'll butter us a little soda bread and I can buy a bottle of lemonade at Cready's, so I can.'

'Lemonade's on me, Mrs Sweeney. We can leave as soon as you're ready.'

'What about my sister?' Aileen said to Marvin.

'Sister?'

'Behind you.'

He turned swiftly, almost surprised. 'Hey, I'm sorry. I forgot about you.' He squeezed his eyes to slits. 'Diana, right?'

'Briana.'

'Oh, I'm sorry. Well, the more the merrier, I guess. Would you care to join us?'

Briana nodded.

The four of them travelled up into the Wicklow Mountains, which Aileen knew weren't very mountainous by American standards. Marvin, however, seemed impressed – or was possibly just being polite. That would be just like Marvin.

The wild and desolate moorland, broken only by the occasional lough or thicket of hardy trees, was certainly as dramatic as it was picturesque, but an open-topped vehicle allowed little opportunity to discuss the scenery. Moreover, with winter's overture in the air it was hardly practical even on the dry, sunny day they had fortunately been granted.

'Is anyone getting cold?' Marvin said as they descended a rough mountain track.

'A little,' Aileen's mother screeched, her whitened fingers holding on to her headscarf as if was the most valuable thing she owned. Aileen and Briana nodded too when he hooked his head around.

'Shall we stop here to eat?' Aileen's mother said, almost shouting the words out as a crosswind hit them.

'I got a much better idea,' Marvin hollered back. 'No disrespect to your soda bread, Mrs Sweeney, but I think a hot drink would do us all some good.'

Aileen's mother glanced at her daughters. 'I don't think we have any money.'

Marvin grinned. 'Hey, please. It would be my pleasure.' He pulled over to the side, grabbed a map from the floor and scanned it for a minute or two. 'Can you all last another twenty minutes?'

Soon they reached a small town on the edge of the mountain region and found its only café, where Marvin ordered hot tea and warm scones. They ate gathered around a log fire as big as a bed, and Marvin said they didn't have anything as old as this building back home.

'So tell me,' Aileen's mother said during a lull in the conversation, 'how exactly did you two meet in Belfast?'

'I met a lot of people in Belfast,' Aileen offered, just a little too sharply.

'We met through mutual friends,' Marvin added.

'*Mutual?*' Mrs Sweeney replied, as if she'd never heard the word. 'Is that what it is?'

Briana said, 'Ah, Mammy, she was on her own up there. She must have met a lot of people.'

'Thank you,' Aileen replied.

'But you did keep this one quiet,' Briana muttered under her breath.

Aileen could feel herself blushing, and just a tiny bit of anger welling up. '*This one*, as you put it, was a good friend to me,' she said. 'You don't know what it's like being away from home.'

'No,' Briana said. 'No, I don't. I'm sorry.'

'And she was a good friend to me too,' Marvin said, and he and Aileen took a little time to reminisce about their time in Belfast together.

Warm and fed, they returned over the same rolling hills, and were frozen once more by the time they reached Leetown, where Aileen's mother invited Marvin back into the house.

Briana piled some more peat bricks on to the dying embers of the fire, and they sat around it, Mammy on the chair, the others sitting cross-legged on the floor, waiting for the peat to catch and burn.

'So, when are you going back to America?' Mammy said.

'Oh, we only have a month or so left in Belfast,' he replied.

'That gives you time to see to the business in Dublin, I'll be supposing?'

Marvin frowned, surprised for a second, then said, 'Exactly.' He nodded and drew breath. 'Hey, it's a shame I didn't come here in the summer, huh? We could have enjoyed the drive for a little while longer.'

'Twas grand,' Aileen said. 'Mammy doesn't have too many treats these days.'

'It was a pleasure to take you out, Mrs Sweeney.'

'Ah, twas very kind of you,' she replied. 'And tell me now, will we be seeing you again before you go back home?'

'Well, uh . . .' Marvin smiled awkwardly and gave his head a quick scratch. 'I was about to mention that. It's been great meeting you all, but I have a free day tomorrow.' He turned to Aileen. 'I was wondering whether you'd like to spend the day with me, Aileen?'

'Just the two of you?' Briana said.

Marvin shrugged. 'I mean . . . if that's okay . . .' He addressed Aileen again. 'If you want to, that is. I mean, if you're free.'

Aileen hesitated, unsure what this meant for her.

'I'd understand if you'd rather not,' he said, his brow straining under a frown. 'But, you know, we might not see each other again. Ever.'

'Would you mind?' Aileen asked her mother.

'Sure, no,' Aileen's mother said. ''Tis only a day. And where were you thinking of taking her, Marvin?'

'Well, Dublin, I guess.'

'Dublin?' she replied, a hint of fear on her face as she glanced at Aileen.

'Or . . . or not. I was thinking of a whole day. Tell me if I'm missing something here, but I thought I'd pick Aileen up in the morning. We could go to Dublin for lunch, then visit Phoenix Park – you know, the zoo there. Then I thought we could take dinner and catch a show in the evening.'

'The theatre?' Mrs Sweeney asked.

He nodded. 'Why, sure.'

'Sounds grand to me,' Briana said.

'Well . . .' Her mother thought for a moment. 'You could hardly do any of that in Leetown, I suppose.'

'And all paid for,' Marvin added. He turned to Aileen. 'How about it? One last hurrah before I sail back home?'

'All right,' Aileen said. She forced a smile; it came more easily than she expected. 'You know, I think I need a little cheering up.'

'Really?' he said, his face appearing to brighten a shade. 'That'd be just great.'

A few minutes later Marvin had gone, waved away and thanked even as the jeep turned the corner and drove out of sight.

Aileen, Briana and their mother stood outside the cottage for a moment, as if Marvin was likely to come back at any minute and say he'd forgotten something.

'I'm glad you're going,' Aileen's mother said to her. 'He'll help you forget about that other one, so he will.'

'If anyone can, he certainly can,' Briana muttered, still staring up the road.

Aileen nodded thoughtfully and addressed them both. 'You do know he's only a friend, don't you?'

'Wouldn't we all love to have friends like that,' Briana said. 'He's taking you to a show at the theatre – a *show*. I've never been to a show. You have the actors right in front of you, apparently.'

'And I know . . .' Aileen's mother said, pain cracking her face, 'I know you've had a tough few weeks, Aileen. You're needing a little enjoyment, so y'are.'

Aileen glanced over to the corner around which the jeep had just disappeared. 'Maybe you're right, Mammy. Maybe a treat is exactly what I need.'

Chapter 28

The next day Marvin turned up as arranged, right on the dot, this time in a truck with a covered cabin. As Aileen's mother noticed him arrive, she remarked on how thoughtful he was – that he'd obviously learned from the chilling they'd received the day before and didn't want Aileen to get cold, or perhaps that he'd had the foresight to plan for rain.

Marvin assured Aileen's parents he would take care of her and return her well before midnight, and they left for Dublin.

After a lunch of potted shrimp and fresh bread, they whiled away the afternoon strolling between the cages of the zoo at Phoenix Park, Aileen entertaining Marvin with more stories of Leetown, but mostly Marvin telling Aileen about the life he was looking forward to getting back to. He talked about the job that was lined up for him in the city, the car he was going to look for – a Chevy Deluxe or perhaps a Hudson Commodore if he could afford it – and the food he was longing to taste again, particularly white hot dogs, grape pie, and pizza of any variety. Aileen hadn't heard of those, but the talk of food made them both hungry.

Dinner was roast beef at a hotel restaurant where the prices almost made Aileen faint, after which they queued in the rain for the theatre – although Marvin had thoughtfully brought an umbrella and held it directly over Aileen so she didn't get wet, even though she spied quite a few drops going down the back of his neck.

After Briana's mention of actors the previous day, it turned out that there were none – it was a variety show, with singers, dancers, musicians and a man telling jokes that Aileen somehow laughed at even though she didn't understand.

After a quick drink in a pub that they both said was too noisy for any meaningful conversation, they headed for the truck.

Marvin's walk was more of a lope, and he'd gone a little quiet.

'Are y'all right?' Aileen asked.

He smiled, but it was a strained smile under sad eyes. 'Just a shame it's all over. I, uh, really enjoyed the evening. Thank you so much.'

''Tis me who should be thanking you, Marvin. You paid for everything.'

He stopped walking and looked up and down the street with the air of a guilty man about to confess. He took a deep breath, then faced her directly. They were inches apart, and Aileen could sense his eyes searching her face. What he was searching for, she wasn't completely sure, although she was getting a little fearful.

'What?' she said. 'What is it?'

'Uh . . .' He ran the palm of his hand up and down the back of his head, pausing to rub his neck. 'Hey, could we meet again?' he said eventually. 'Would you . . . would you like that?'

'I thought this was a goodbye evening?'

His face flushed as he struggled to compose a reply.

'Ah, that'll be grand, Marvin. Of course we can see each other again. We're friends, aren't we?'

She grabbed his arm and held it. 'I'm awful cold. C'mon and let's get going.'

They returned to the truck and started the journey back to Leetown, first driving through the city lights, then out into the darkness of the countryside.

The shafts of light in front of Aileen – and within them the flashes of stone, dirt and insects – mesmerized her and let her mind wander for the first time that day. It occurred to her that thoughts of Niall hadn't entered her head for a whole day, and it made her smile inside with secret pride. Well, that wasn't *completely* true. In the morning, waiting for Marvin to arrive, she'd felt a little sorry for both herself and Niall, but that was only natural. And there was also the man in Phoenix Park who she couldn't keep her eyes off until he turned to face her. Only now did she realize why she'd stared: he looked like Niall from the side. Of course, she'd also thought about him when Marvin had parked close to the Liffey and she'd fondly recollected their walks, arm in arm, along the riverside. There had also been the shoeshine man across the road from the theatre. He didn't look anything like Niall, but she felt a little guilty about spending money – albeit not her own – on entertainment while some people could hardly afford to eat. The sight of him had made Niall's face pop into her mind for just a second.

So, perhaps she *had* thought of him. The point of her day had been to forget about her old love and accept that life would go on without him, and that she could still find a happiness of sorts. But that would take time. She'd only seen him five days ago after all – she shouldn't expect miracles.

A jolt from a pothole brought an apology from Marvin. It also knocked Aileen out of her reflections, and in doing so gave her an odd sensation. She had to forget about Niall, but there was a nagging feeling that . . . well, it almost felt that trying to forget him was somehow a betrayal.

She told herself not to think that way, that Niall was gone. *Niall was gone.* She just *had* to forget him. Otherwise she would end up driving herself mad. Marvin was a good man too – he'd tried his best to cheer her up.

She shuffled along the seat and rested her head on his shoulder. 'Thank you,' she said softly.

'You've had a nice day, huh?'

'Grand.' She shifted, nuzzling her cheek against his upper arm. 'Well, much more than grand.'

'Good,' he said. 'That was all I ever wanted out of today.' He glanced down and tried to flash one of his perfect white smiles.

But things were far from perfect, and in her heart Aileen knew it.

They drove on through the darkness, talking about the best parts of the theatre show – Marvin liked the musicians most as he was planning to learn to play the guitar when he finally got back home, whereas Aileen had delighted in the spectacle of the dancers with their sequinned suits and flawless make-up. The conversation stopped when they hit a patch of dense mist and Marvin needed all his powers of concentration to follow the road.

'Tis just rolling in across the sea,' Aileen said. 'Happens a lot.'

'I think I need to stop.'

By now they were travelling at little more than walking pace. Aileen peered out at the light thrown by the headlights, most of it now bouncing right back right at her. 'I suppose that's the safest thing,' she said.

Marvin said nothing, but slowed even more, eventually pulling up on to the next level patch of grass by the side of the road. He switched the engine off, gave her a smile, and looked ahead again.

'Marvin?' she said.

'What?'

'You never had any business to sort out in Dublin, did you?'

He didn't answer, just leaned back and folded his arms.

'What's happening?' Aileen said. 'You're starting to scare me a little now.'

That was a lie. Marvin was as trustworthy a man as Aileen had ever met. She felt safe with him. Always.

'There's nothing for you to worry about,' he said after a few moments. 'But . . . we need to talk. Well, I need to talk, to say something to you.'

Aileen knew it was likely to be something she didn't want to hear – at least not yet, not so soon.

'You're right,' he said, still staring ahead into the gloom. 'About the business in Dublin. I just wanted to see you again. Was that wrong?'

'Well, we're friends.'

'Sure, we are. I just wanted to talk to you, to ask you something. And, uh, I'm not sure how you're gonna take it.'

'Can't you ask me when we get back to the cottage?'

Only now did he turn to her, and she saw a little anguish carving itself on to his face: lips that twitched, eyes a little fiercer than anything she'd thought possible for 'Square Marvin'.

'You remember me telling you about Earl?'

'Earl?'

'My kid brother,' he said breathlessly.

'Well, yes, but you didn't tell me exactly what happened.'

'See, when we were young, I was always the straight one, doing the safe thing, not taking risks. When we were kids and climbed trees, he would always have to go higher than me. When we swam in the river he always seemed driven – compelled by something inside him – to go in deeper than me.'

'You must miss him.'

'Oh, sure. I'm also still a little jealous.'

'Jealous?'

'Even when we got older it was the same. He was always telling me I should live a little, let go before it's too late, before life passes right on by.'

'I can understand that.'

'Father always called him impetuous. By the time I worked out what that word meant the die was set and I knew I'd never be like Earl. Of course, his die was set too. He got used to acting without thinking things through. The opposite of me. And a few years down the line, in the war, when he was fighting in Guadalcanal . . . well, all I can say is, if he hadn't been quite so impetuous he might still be here.'

'I'm so sorry about your brother, Marvin, but surely that tells you that you're fine as you are? You're a lovely man, so y'are, and you shouldn't spend your life wishing to be someone you're not.'

He showed her a sad smile. 'Thank you, Aileen. That means a lot to me.' He drew a long breath. 'I was gonna ask – and go ahead, tell me if I'm being too personal – are you still seeing the guy who joined the British Army?'

'Niall. His name's Niall.'

'Yes. Forgive me – Niall.'

'And no. I'll not be seeing him again, so I don't want to talk about him.'

Now there was some relief on his face, those square shoulders of his settling down, relaxing. 'But what if I can have those things my brother had?' he said. 'What if I *can* change?'

'People don't change that much, Marvin. And like I say, you're fine as you are.'

'And what about you, Aileen? Could *you* change?'

She tried to blot out the question, shaking her head to throw the thought off, and settling her gaze outside. 'I think the sea mist has just about rolled by,' she said. 'Should we, ah . . .'

'You wanna go now? Is that it?'

'Oh, it's not because of you, Marvin. It's just that it's a bit dangerous parked on the side of the road like this.'

He took a long sigh through his nose, the sort Aileen's father often performed to calm himself down. He nodded, stopped as if he wasn't quite sure how to start the engine, then reached across and turned the key.

'Thank you for the talk,' he said.

'Well, thank you for the day out,' she replied.

The truck pulled out into the road, the talk ended, and Aileen told herself the lack of conversation was somehow comforting. Like best friends, she and Marvin didn't need to talk.

Twenty minutes later the truck pulled up outside the cottage.

'Would you like to come in?' she said after he walked around to open her door.

He kept his head bowed. 'I'd better scram,' he said, helping her down. 'It was, uh, a lovely day.'

'It was lovely for me too, Marvin. I . . . ah . . . I hope we can still be friends.'

'Sure,' he said, smiling but not looking at her. 'Goodbye then.'

'Oh, right. Goodbye, Marvin.'

He climbed into the truck and drove off.

Aileen watched the truck's tail lights disappear around the corner and wondered whether that was the last time she would ever see Marvin. If so, it would be a crying shame. Perhaps she should have said more. Perhaps she should have told him the reason why she couldn't talk about Niall – that tomorrow he too would be leaving for America.

It was a painful coincidence. There were two men in her life. One who she wanted to be with so badly it made her very soul weep, but who she had to forget. Another who she just wanted to be friends with, but who clearly couldn't accept that.

Both were bound for America, and she might never see either of them again.

By this late hour everyone in the Sweeney household had gone to bed, so there were no lights. Aileen stumbled in the darkness, taking careful baby steps toward the back of the house, to the toilet shed. She used it with the door open so what little moonlight there was stopped her being in complete blackness. She stumbled back to the house, dark and silent as a mausoleum – without even any snoring tonight – and got into bed with Briana.

'Did you have a good time?' Briana whispered.

'I'll tell y'about it in the morning.'

And with that, Aileen was alone with her thoughts once more.

Tomorrow was going to be hard to take. She'd hoped today would help her forget about Niall, forget about his ship leaving Dublin, but it was wishful thinking. Broken hopes and dreams would not allow themselves to be put aside so easily. Perhaps the Lord would help?

Please, God, can you make it so that tomorrow morning doesn't exist, that I sleep until the afternoon, that whenever I wake up the morning hasn't happened, that I don't have to know anything about it.

Why had her life become so complicated? Perhaps it was for the best that both Niall and Marvin were leaving. Perhaps now she could concentrate on getting a job, earning some money and helping the family survive. It had worked for Briana; *she* didn't have a man in her life and she seemed happy enough.

Of course, with Marvin – if she'd liked him 'that way' as Mammy would put it – she would never really need money. He would take care of her, would pay for everything. And he would treat her well. She was sure of that if nothing else. That was nice, what every girl wanted. He was, as Mammy and Briana kept pointing out, kind and generous as well as a handsome, fine figure of a man.

But what a mess, what a loss, and what a storm whirled around in Aileen's mind as she stilled herself in the damp darkness. The storm raged for an hour or so before, exhausted, she finally fell asleep.

Chapter 29

Aileen awoke to daylight, and within seconds her closing thoughts from the night before returned. Oh, for some respite from those thoughts, for something else to occupy her mind.

But the daylight fighting its way through the curtains told her it couldn't have been that early. She wiped the sleep from her eyes and lifted her head. She was the only one in the bedroom – Briana and their three brothers were already up.

Perhaps it was noon already.

And the ship had left the harbour.

And her love had left for good.

She hunkered back down into bed, pulled the covers over her head, and started sobbing. Some minutes later, ten or twenty or thirty – she didn't know and didn't care – the tears stopped coming of their own accord. They just stopped.

It was a sign.

She let her mind relax and almost invited more tears to come, but there were none. Yes, it was a sign of acceptance – a sign that she should forget about Niall and stop torturing herself. Yes, she could have agreed to go with him to America. She *could* have, but that was in the past. She'd made her decision and it was the right one. She couldn't leave Leetown – or at least, not for the other side of the world. Dublin, perhaps, one day. New York, never.

It was the right decision. She would wither without the support of her family, without the cosy surroundings of her birthplace. It was the right decision. No, it *had been* the right decision. It was in the past. It was finished and done with, and now she had to get on with the future.

Starting with today.

She tossed the bedclothes aside, twisted so she was sitting on the edge of the bed, and stretched. On the floor below her was a cup. She reached down and picked it up. It was water – obviously brought in by Briana. Good old Briana. What would she do without Briana? She dipped the edge of the bedsheet into the water and used it to clear the stinging saltiness from her cheeks.

There was no need to get dressed; she was still fully clothed from the previous night.

She heard muffled noises from the other side of the door. Conversation, a laugh, a concerned groan from her mother. It was time to go, time to face the day, morning or not. She could do it. She *could* do it. She stepped to the door, took a deep breath, and opened it.

'Ah, Aileen!' Her mother beckoned her in with a warm smile and pointed to the table. 'We have some bacon,' she said. 'How many rashers will ye be wanting?'

Her mother was cooking, her father was sitting next to the wireless, the boys were playing cards. Briana was helping with the cooking. It was normal, thanks be to God.

'What time is it?'

The boys took no notice. Briana and Mammy looked at Daddy.

He pointed to the wireless. 'That's the ten o'clock news just about to start.'

'Oh.'

He switched the wireless off. 'It's late enough, so tis. What are you thinking of, getting up at this hour? The rest of us have been out already and—'

'Dan,' his wife snapped. 'The girl had a long day yesterday. Won't ye button it.'

He tutted. She pulled out a chair for Aileen.

'I'm not so hungry,' Aileen said.

'But you have to eat. C'mon.'

Aileen sat, and was aware of mumbled two-word conversations, and of her father and brothers moaning. Then her father said, 'We have things to do.' As he got up he patted Aileen on the shoulder. She looked up to catch a wink from him. Then he told his three sons to *get off their lazy arses* and follow him. The men left, leaving the three women alone in the cottage.

Soon a plate of fried potatoes and bacon was placed in front of Aileen. At first she picked at them. They tasted good and, surprising herself, she devoured them and washed the lot down with two cups of sweet tea.

Perhaps, if she gave it the chance, her appetite for life would improve too. Yes, perhaps things would get better starting from today.

'Didn't I tell you?' her mother said. 'You were hungrier than you realized.'

She and Briana pulled up chairs and sat next to Aileen.

'Did you have a nice day yesterday?' her mother said. 'You know, with Marvin.'

It hit Aileen. *Oh, dear God. This was the cross-examination.*

'What was he like?' Briana said. 'Did he take you somewhere nice – one of those grand restaurant places?'

Aileen folded her arms. *What should she say? Well, what was wrong with the truth?*

She smiled, remembering scenes of Marvin and Phoenix Park and the theatre in her mind's eye. 'I had a wonderful day. Yes, Marvin took me to a lovely hotel restaurant and a variety show afterward. And yes, he was really nice to me.'

Her mother nodded almost imperceptibly. 'And?'

'And everything was grand about the day – everything from the food, to the walk in Phoenix Park, to the show, to the drink afterward.'

'He took you for a drink?'

''Tis what people do in Dublin, Briana. You should know that.'

'Yes, of course, I know that, so I do, but . . .' She looked to her mother for support.

'But what else happened with Marvin?' Mammy said.

'What else happened? He drove me home and we said goodbye, and I went to bed.'

'Oh, I see.'

Aileen took a breath and let out a long exasperated sigh. 'Aren't I after telling the both of yez, he's a friend. We're friends *and nothing more.*'

Briana and her mother glanced at each other and took a moment to give doubtful nods.

'Well, yes,' her mother said. 'That's grand, so it is.'

'Of course,' Briana added. 'We know what you mean.'

Her mother collected the knife, fork and cup on to the plate and stood. 'Yes,' she said. 'Yes, well, that's all right then.' She walked off.

'What's wrong?' Aileen whispered to her sister. 'Why are you and Mammy acting like a pair of eejits?'

'Ah, Mammy and myself are thinking the same, that you and Marvin are, y'know . . .'

'Well, you're wrong. We're not – *y'know.*'

'If you say so. But he's such a lovely man, so he is. You'll struggle to find better.'

Aileen bowed her head and slowly shook it.

'Are you still thinking of Niall?'

She looked up. 'What are you talking about? I haven't mentioned Niall.'

'No,' Briana said. 'No.' She put a hand on Aileen's knee and patted it. 'Whatever happens, I'm glad you had a nice day yesterday. I think you needed it, so you did.'

'Thank you, and I'm sorry if I'm a little grumpy.'

'So, what'll you be up to today?'

'I think I might be looking for a job again, helping Mammy do a little washing, and I should really . . .'

Aileen's words trailed off as she heard a familiar sound – one that made her anxious. It was the sound of a truck pulling up outside the cottage. They stared at each other, Briana looking as worried as Aileen felt.

Aileen bounced up and ran to the window. 'Dear God,' she said. 'Oh no.' She turned to Briana. 'It's him – it's Marvin.'

'Marvin? But . . .'

'What the heck is he doing here?'

Briana frowned. 'What's wrong with him being here?'

There was a knock at the door.

'I'll get it,' their mother said.

'No,' Aileen said, not thinking – not *having time* to think.

Her mother showed her a look of disdain, then went over and opened the door.

'Marvin?' she said. 'How lovely to see you again. Come in, why don't you.'

He stepped inside, said nothing, but his eyes locked on to Aileen and he strode straight over to her. 'Aileen,' he said. 'I really need to talk to you.'

Aileen looked him up and down. His clothes were crumpled. Even his *face* looked crumpled. His hair was uncombed, which wasn't like him at all.

'I don't understand,' she said. 'Where have you been?'

'Well . . .' He sighed and rubbed a hand up and down his tired face. 'I, uh, spent the night in the truck. Parked it up a few miles down the road. I've hardly slept.' He eyed the seats.

Aileen sat back down. Briana instinctively rose from the next chair and sat cross-legged on the floor nearby, leaving Marvin to take the vacant seat. Aileen looked across to her mother, who was standing by the washtub.

'Ah . . . perhaps I'd better see to the chickens,' her mother said. She glared at Briana, but Briana showed no signs of moving, so she picked up the plate of leftover scraps and left.

Marvin turned to Aileen. He seemed unable to control his breathing, gasping and gulping as he tried to speak.

'Calm down,' Aileen told him. 'Tell me what happened.'

He shook his head. 'Nothing happened. But . . . well, yesterday happened. Yesterday happened and I planned it all, Aileen. I wanted to ask you something. I wanted you to have the most wonderful day of your life, and then I planned to ask you something.'

'What? Ask me what?'

'Just hear me out here. Just listen.' He reached out and held her hand in both of his. 'Aileen, you probably don't remember the first time we met, but I do. I remember telling you how I fell in love with you the first time I saw you, even before I got to know you. I meant every word of it. That glorious waterfall of auburn hair; your eyes, emerald like the stone and many times as enchanting; the button nose, pretty as anything; the perfectly judged smattering of freckles; and, oh heaven, your smile – when you smile that's exactly where my heart goes, *heaven*. I know all that might sound corny to you, but they're the truest words I ever spoke.'

'Oh, Marvin.' Aileen's face creased, but in pain, not pleasure.

'Please, Aileen. Just listen to me.'

Aileen tried to hold it back, but it was no good, the tears had a life all of their own and raced down her cheeks.

'Some days I thought you were out of my league, or that maybe we wouldn't get on, but as I got to know you none of that mattered to me. Something else just clicked, like I'd been tied down and then something let me free to float among the clouds, and it was exhilarating. There's something about you, Aileen. Even in wartime you were fun to be with, you brightened up my life, and . . . and . . . look, when you left Belfast I tried not to think about you, to forget I'd ever known you. But it didn't work – this thing inside me wouldn't let me forget. Every time I saw a pretty girl I told myself there were plenty more besides, but this same thing – *whatever the hell it is* – kept reminding me of your face, your smile, your giggle, your sense of humour, the smart replies, the way you just say it as it is, and I knew I never wanted any of those other girls. So, I had to come here to see you, and to know whether I still felt the same way. And I do, Aileen, *I do*. I can't explain it, and I've tried to make all the excuses to myself, but I just wanna *be* with you, goddammit.'

'Oh, Marvin. I knew that you . . . I mean, I *thought* that . . . but why didn't you tell me all this before?'

'Believe me, I've tried a hundred times, but I was always I worried I'd turn you away, that knowing the way I felt would scare you off and I'd lose you forever. In the end I just couldn't control this thing – I had to tell you. I meant to come out with all this yesterday. I planned it that way, but it just didn't work. Like I told you, I always wished I had the courage of my kid brother. Perhaps I've changed. Perhaps now I do. Aileen, I want you. I just want to be with you forever.'

'What are you saying, Marvin? I'm not sure I can—'

'Aileen, come with me back to New York. Come back and marry me. I can't promise you the world, but I can assure you I'll give it my best shot, that I'll love you as good as any man could and that you'll have the best time ever. I got a good job waiting for me back home and you'll want for nothing. I'm certain you'll love my family and they'll love you. *I can make you happy*, Aileen.'

Aileen's lower jaw gaped, her lips twitched. A fog of confusion gripped her head.

'Oh, Aileen. I don't have a ring for you just yet, but I'll make up for that, honestly I will. Please make me the happiest man alive and agree to be my wife.'

Chapter 30

Manhattan, New York City, 1995

Arturo's isn't one of New York's finest restaurants; it's not even the best on Ninth Avenue. But it's Aileen's favourite of many years. That's *many, many* years.

They're seated in a quiet corner away from the draught of the entrance, but not too close to the kitchen.

'Have you decided what you're having?' Aileen says.

'Probably my usual steak,' he says. 'You?'

'I don't know if I'm in a fish or a chicken mood.'

'Oh, I think you probably do know. You have chicken every year.'

'I guess so. Another reminder of the past.'

'Talking of the past . . .'

'Here we go,' Aileen sings.

'What?' he says. 'I was only going to say they should name a dish after us. When I think back to the late forties, when we first started coming here . . .'

'Oh, Marvin,' she says. 'You always were the dreamer.'

He shrugs. 'It's only nostalgia. What's wrong with that?'

'Now you'll start getting all misty-eyed about when we got married.'

'And what if I do? It's good to look back, to think how far we've all come.'

'And how dumb we all were back then?'

Marvin hesitates. 'I'd say more innocent than dumb. But I know what you mean. We know so much now, but I'm not sure we're better off for it. There's something about that innocence, don't you think? It's almost like the knowledge is a burden.'

She laughs. 'I always said you should have been a poet, Marvin.' She sits back and glances at him. There's a knowing smirk, but one that holds the warmth of years. 'I can remember when you turned up on our doorstep at Leetown just after the war. You said you had to go home soon and wanted to bag an Irish bride and take her back.'

'Hey, come on. I'm a poet, remember? I put it better than that.'

'I'm sure you did.' Aileen takes a sip of drink. Just water. With her seventieth birthday rapidly approaching, she knows she has to start cutting down on her beloved wine. 'Tell me, Marvin. While we're being a little nostalgic, and while there's just the two of us, would you say you had any regrets?'

'About us? About what happened in little old Leetown just after the war?'

'You don't have to say if you . . .'

He gives his head a brief shake to halt her. 'That's okay. I guess we never much talked about it in all these years. Do I have any regrets? Well, I have to say I did for a few weeks – but not after . . . well, you know.'

'I do know. I remember it well.'

'It was right, the way it turned out for the two of us. It was for the best. Definitely.' He takes a breath, then says, 'What about you?'

'Do I have any regrets?' she says. 'About running away from my home and family to a land of opportunity, freedom and fresh bagels?' She stares into space for a moment. 'A lot of sadness. A *lot*. You can't help that. But regrets?' She shook her head. 'None whatsoever.'

'You know something, Aileen? I thought not.'

'No. If I'd stayed in Leetown there's no way I'd have travelled like I have, or had four wonderful children with the man I still love, or done so many other things that make me truly happy. And I know you're the dreamer, but I often think back to that day – the day you changed my life.' She shot him a glance. 'And I'm still grateful.'

Her eyes dwelt for just a second on those teeth, still all present but now a uniform yellow, and his hair, now thinning and more white than blond. In her mind, just for a moment, the teeth were that pure white again and the hair full and blond with youth.

Leetown, County Wicklow, 1945

Inside Sweeney Cottage, Marvin was now on one knee, his outstretched hand holding Aileen's, the lazy peat fire casting a soft glow on one side of his face.

'I know I'm not the most dynamic guy in the world, but I promise to love you more than I love life itself. If I need to ask you a thousand times, just say so and I will. Please, Aileen. Please come back to America and be my wife.'

Aileen felt the atmosphere, full and heavy with expectation, stifling her very breath. She could see nothing but his half-amber face, soft-hearted, gentle and kind, staring back at her expectantly.

'Oh, Marvin. That's so nice of you, but . . . I . . . I can't leave.' She sniffed a few tears back. 'I could leave Leetown, but not Ireland.'

He held her chin between his thumb and forefinger, steadied her, then spoke slowly and deliberately. 'I know you. And you could. You really could. And you'd be able to visit here. It's not like you'd be cutting yourself off for good. It's America, not the moon.'

She shook her head. 'No, Marvin. I'm too scared.'

He held her hand tightly, clasping it to his chest. 'Well, *don't* be scared, goddammit. You're a beautiful, intelligent, confident woman. You *are* confident, you just need to believe it. You can do this, Aileen, I know it.'

'But, it's too . . .'

'Too what?'

'Too far away. Even the thought of it scares me.'

'But, wasn't Belfast scary at first?'

'Ah, it's not the same thing.'

'And what exactly are you scared of? Scared of missing Leetown? Or scared you'll settle in a place, that it'll feel like home before you want it to?'

Aileen's eyes fell to one side, to Briana. There was an urge to ask Briana what she would say, but her throat was jammed and Briana's face was as placid as a midsummer lake.

She returned her gaze to Marvin. 'But . . . America? I'm sorry, Marvin. It's all too sudden. The more I think about it, the harder it becomes.'

Marvin's voice started to strain. 'Well, *don't* think about it, just *do* it. You can come back here and visit. Okay, so not every week, but every year, and they say you'll be able to fly here pretty soon. I told you, it's not the moon, it's America. And heck, I'll be able to afford it. I got a good job waiting for me. You'll want for nothing.'

Aileen stared down, her hand rubbing her forehead. There was something in his words. The thoughts were racing around inside her head like caged wild wolves, because there was definitely something in what Marvin had said.

Marvin then talked about not putting excuses in front of everything, but Aileen wasn't listening. She was thinking of the moon.

The moon.

It wasn't the moon.

She started mumbling to herself. 'America isn't the moon,' she said. 'It's not the moon.' Then she was back in the cinema, with Niall, listening to Bette Davis talking of the moon and the stars. And then, with her breathing halted, she was outside the cinema, listening to Niall. He was telling her to have the moon, the stars, the sun and everything – that she should reach for whatever it was she truly wanted.

Aileen gasped, then shut her eyes tightly. 'Oh Jesus. Oh my Lord.'

'Aileen?' he said. 'Please tell me, will you marry me?'

She wiped the tears from her face and looked into his eyes, good and honest, but sad and desperate.

'Thank you so much, Marvin.' She stood up and kissed him on the forehead, holding on until her tears ran on to his face. She let go, then kissed him again.

He narrowed his eyes. 'So, is that a yes?'

She shook her head. 'No. It's a no, and I'm more sorry than I've ever been in my life. But I can't thank you enough for this, Marvin. And I'll never forget it.'

'I don't understand. What did I do wrong?'

'Nothing,' she said, sniffing and drying her eyes. 'Listen to me, Marvin. You've done absolutely nothing wrong, and one day you'll make some girl a wonderful husband. But it won't be me.'

She bolted for the bedroom.

Briana was still sitting on the floor, still looking up at Marvin, who now had his head in his hands. Noises from the bedroom made her wrench her attention from him. 'Aileen?' she shouted out. 'Aileen? What're you doing?' She got to her feet and went into the bedroom. 'What's happening?' she said.

Aileen had taken her mother's suitcase out from under the bed and was throwing all her clothes into it. When Briana appeared, she stopped, groaned as if upset, and flung her arms around Briana. The girls hugged for a few seconds, then held hands, face to face.

'Oh, Briana, I'm all a mess. I don't know, I'm not sure – then again I am, I am, I am sure, I'm so sure it hurts.'

'I don't understand, Aileen. Are you going where I think you're going?'

'I am.' She scattered a few more items into the suitcase. 'I haven't much time, but I know I have to do this. If I don't go I'll spend the rest of my life regretting it.'

Briana beamed a proud smile. 'I know, Aileen.'

'You do understand, don't you?'

'Oh, I do, Aileen, I do. I know exactly how hard it is. I only wish I was as brave as you.'

'Brave? Ha!' She let go of her sister and started rummaging around in her handbag. 'Have I got enough time? What's the time? I'm late, I know. Will I make it?' She cursed. 'Where in the name of God did I . . . ?'

Briana reached for her handbag, opened it, and pulled out the ticket. 'Here. You'll be needing this.'

Aileen grabbed it, stared at it, almost in tears. 'But . . . my ticket. How did . . . ? You kept it?'

'I had an idea you'd need it – maybe a hope. Like I said, you're a braver woman than me. I knew that all along.'

'Oh, Briana, I'm so lucky to have such a romantic fool for a sister.' Aileen threw herself around her sister again and held on. 'Oh God. I'm so scared, Briana. I don't know if I'm doing the right thing. Am I doing the right thing? What d'you think?'

Briana pushed her away, holding on to her shoulders and looking her in the eye. 'Yes, my little sister, you *are* doing the right thing. It's just . . .'

'Just what?'

'You're just going to go off without saying goodbye to everyone?'

'I don't know. Should I stop awhile? I'll just cause arguments. And I don't have the time.'

Briana thought for a moment. 'You're right. You have to go while you have the nerve. Go to the station, catch the next train to Dublin, and whatever you do, don't look back.'

Aileen chewed her lip and nodded. 'Yes. Right. What's the time? D'you know what the time is?'

'No, but it can't be eleven yet. You have time.'

'Yes. Right. Grand.' Aileen hugged her sister and squeezed. 'Oh heck, I'm going to miss you.'

'I know, I know. Now, c'mon.'

Aileen stood back. 'Yes, yes.' She quickly tucked in the clothes that spilled over the edges of the case and shut it, then stepped toward her sister, arms out. 'Awww, Briana. What in heaven's name am I doing?'

'Whatever you're doing, just do it. Believe me, you don't want Mammy catching you – she'll only try to talk you out of it. Now go.'

'Right.' Aileen nodded to herself. 'Yes. Yes, you're right.' She took a deep breath, slung her handbag over her shoulder, and grabbed the suitcase. 'I'm doing it. I'm going now.' She took two more deep breaths and marched out into the main room, where she gave Marvin's lonely, hunched form a final glance as she headed for the front door.

Briana wasn't far behind. 'Now, are you sure you don't want me to come to Dublin with you?'

Aileen opened the door and they both stepped outside. The door shut, its thump giving Aileen encouragement.

'I could if you want,' Briana said. 'I could come along on the train.'

'No, Briana.' Aileen gave her head a firm shake. 'No. I'll only know if I really want to do this if I do it all on my own. And I know that makes me sound like an eejit, but . . .' She hugged Briana once more. 'Oh, Briana. I'll write, I'll visit, I'll use one of those telephone things if I can get hold of one. Most of all, I promise I'll see you again, one way or another.'

Releasing her sister, Aileen shook her head and sighed. 'Ah, dear God. It's no good, Briana. I can't do it. I can't go without saying goodbye to Mammy. I haven't it in me.'

'No. Right. I understand. But you'll have to hurry.'

Their mother was filling a basket with eggs from the chicken house. She stopped and placed the basket down when she saw Aileen and Briana hurtling toward her.

'What is it?' she said, only mildly alarmed. 'What's going on?'

'I haven't much time, Mammy.' Aileen put the case down.

'What is it, Aileen? Tell me.'

'Mammy, it's no use trying to talk me out of it. I'm going. I'm getting on that ship to America, and I'm going to marry Niall.'

Her mother said nothing at first, through shock or confusion – her face was always hard to read. 'No,' she said eventually. 'Oh no.'

'Yes, Mammy. Oh yes.'

Her mother stared at her for what felt like an age, before nodding slowly. 'Ah, well, if you truly feel like that, Aileen.'

'I do. And I'm not arguing about it.'

'No.' She looked at the case. So did Aileen.

'And I'm sorry, I have to borrow your case again.'

'I don't care about my case. I care about my daughter. But I suppose tis good. Tis good that a little of me goes with you.'

'I'm sorry, Mammy. I never meant to . . .'

'Shh,' her mother said, and held her arms out.

Aileen threw her arms around her mother, and felt that hand caressing her hair – the hand that had lovingly and selflessly fed her, washed her, clothed her and brushed her hair over so many years. Aileen pulled back and looked her mother in the eye. There was a calmness she didn't expect. There was love, there was concern, but most of all there was acceptance.

'Aileen, I get the feeling I wouldn't ever be able to change your mind. And that's a *good* thing. I remember . . . I had this sort of talk before with your sister.' She glanced at Briana, standing behind Aileen. 'And I'm still not sure I did the right thing. But I'm here to bring up my little ones as well as I can, so they grow up good and strong, so they can survive out of the nest, and so they'll know when it's time to go.' Tears started to pool on her lower eyelids. 'I think that job's done as far as you're concerned.'

'Oh, Mammy. Oh heck, I'll miss you, Mammy.'

'Not as much as I'll miss you, Aileen. All my little ones fly off, and my heart never stops aching for them. But your time's come. Just be sure to look after yourself.'

'I will, Mammy. I promise you.'

'And . . . and look after this Niall fellow too.'

Aileen pressed her head against her mother's chest again, and felt the warmth of her embrace, knowing it might be for the last time.

'Aileen, I know how you feel about Niall, and I know he's a good man despite what all the men who run this country think. I really mean that. So, if you want my blessing to go and marry him, then you have it. Good luck and God bless the both of you.' She squeezed Aileen once more.

'What about Daddy?' Aileen said.

'Leave your daddy to me, Aileen. And listen to me. Don't you go judging him too harshly. Remember that I knew him for many years before you were even born, and we've been through a lot together. He's a good man too, in his own way.'

'Mammy, I have a lot of good memories of him to take with me. But I have to go now.'

She released her daughter. 'Of course. May God bless and protect you, Aileen.' She swallowed as if in pain, and wiped a few tears away.

Aileen turned, gave Briana one last hug, then grabbed her case. 'Goodbye!' she shouted as she ran off. 'I'll miss you both!'

Then she was gone.

Chapter 31

Aileen's tears only stopped coming once she'd settled herself down in the carriage at Leetown Station.

As the train pulled out and away from the village – Aileen's village – she kept telling herself not to look back, just as Briana had said, but she couldn't help herself. She found herself staring with both uncertainty and fondness at her own beginnings until the train rounded the bend.

She took a few deep breaths, dried her face, and forced herself to smile. The smile faltered, but she fought to keep it there, and within minutes no effort was needed.

There would be no more tears.

She'd been happy in Leetown – and lucky too. But this would be the start of a new happiness – one in a new and exciting country, and with the man she loved.

Rows of long, wood-panelled benches filled the whole centre section of the foredeck, and Niall was sitting on the end of the second one from the back.

This was where they'd arranged to meet. At least, if Aileen had decided to come. He was nervous enough for himself, leaving his homeland for another country. All right, he'd been to Britain, France, Belgium and Holland, not to mention sailing through the Mediterranean. But this was another *continent* – one *five days* away. As if that wasn't bad enough, he was doubly nervous for not knowing whether Aileen was going to make it.

But no, she would make it, he was sure of it. She would change her mind and come to America with him. She'd probably just left it late – that was like her, a right Miss Unpredictable.

He allowed himself a slight smile at that.

From here he could just about see the occupant of every seat. He could mostly see the backs of heads, but that would have been enough. If Aileen were sitting there right now he would know, he would definitely know.

An image of her lustrous hair – that distinctive blend of brown and red, as wavy as the sea just beyond the handrails – was flowing through his mind along with all the other memories he held from their times together.

But memories alone were no good.

He stood up and glanced around, scanning heads and faces, then stepped to one side and peered around the side deck. Did he tell Aileen to meet him on the foredeck? Of course he did.

Calm down, Niall.

And was there more than one foredeck? If so they might not meet. She might even go to the other one, not find him and, distraught, get off the ship.

He shook his head. More than one foredeck?

Don't be stupid, Niall.

However, it was a chilly day. Perhaps not so much on land, but definitely here above the ocean where there was a salty whip to the wind. So she could have decided to sit elsewhere and just keep checking the foredeck now and then.

No, Niall. Just sit and be patient.

He sat and thought on. Could he genuinely be so sure she'd be here? It hadn't seemed promising the last time they'd met, when she'd told him she couldn't do it – couldn't leave Ireland and her family behind – and had said goodbye for the last time. But *surely* she must have had time to reconsider.

He turned his attentions to the people around him, wondering how many of them were ordinary Irish sorts just like him, striving and sacrificing in order to discover a new and better existence on the other side of the world. Just like him. And there were a few women too, just like Aileen.

He patted his hands on his knees, took a few strengthening gasps of the cool air, and scanned all the unknown heads before him once more. He folded his right leg on to his left knee, sighed and mumbled a curse, then took his right leg down and reversed the position. He turned to the man sitting next to him, who was immaculately dressed – and well educated, judging by the newspaper he was reading.

'Excuse me,' Niall said, leaning in to him, 'do you happen to know the time, please?'

The man frowned. 'I'd say it's about ten minutes later than the last time you asked me.'

'Ah, yes, I'm sorry. So I did – I forgot. Sorry. A lot of people look the same here.' He gave the man an apologetic smile, which was wasted as he'd already turned back to his newspaper.

Niall told himself not to worry about the time. Aileen's timing wasn't in his hands. He imagined her walking along that wobbly gangplank, and wondered how she would cope with it. The ship rocked around in the quay – not much, but enough to make anyone boarding hold the handrail tightly and look where they were going, so Aileen would also see the rush of seawater lapping and rushing back and forth along—

He jumped to his feet. The gangplank. *Of course.* If she wasn't yet on the ship he could watch out for her getting onboard. He turned and hurried there, swimming against the tide of his fellow passengers, quite a few of them looking as worried as he felt.

Yes, there was a vantage point, a position on the handrail he could cling on to and claim as his own. He looked directly down at the grey-tinted sea slopping around as if it was probing the hull for a way in. There was a definite stink of oil and sewers, but it only registered for a second before he locked his eyes on to the gangway just a little further along and below and started checking the trail of passengers teetering as they boarded.

There!

He felt like shouting it. *There* was one who looked like – but no, she turned her head: much older than Aileen. A few minutes later he held his breath as he spotted another woman with the same colour hair as Aileen. But the hair was longer, and she was holding hands with a man. Not Aileen. It was going to be a long, boring journey. He needed a little company, a familiar smile to bring joy, a friendly ear to listen. Aileen would be perfect. And the perfect accompaniment to his new life in America too.

No, Niall, no. He didn't need company and a smile and an ear. *He needed Aileen.*

He needed her and her alone to be his friend, his lover, his wife and his helper. Aileen should be his everything to share everything with. He wanted her here and by his side forever – to have, to hold, to love, to cherish.

Oh heck. Thoughts of Aileen – a life without her – were making him feel sick and bringing tears to his eyes. Only now was it dawning on him. He needed her, but he'd been too bold, too confident, too sure of himself. The trail of people boarding slowed to a trickle, stragglers who hadn't noticed the time, and drinkers who wanted to slake their thirst on the last of the genuine black stuff right up till the last minute.

She wasn't coming. *Damn it!*

He should have seen her again. To hell with her family. He should have gone to Leetown again and pleaded with her to come with him. He should have given her more time to decide. *Or perhaps he should have dragged her to the docks and on to the ship.*

Then even the trickle of passengers stopped. Niall had an urge to climb over the railings, scale down the hull and insist they leave the gangway in place for another ten minutes. *He needed another ten minutes.*

But no. The gangway was taken away, the artery between ship and land had been severed, and now only ropes connected the floating town to the quayside. Niall watched as they too were pulled on board. He had an urge to jump ship, his unshakeable confidence of the previous week gone, like a rug pulled from under his feet.

He'd changed his mind. He didn't want to go to America. He was Irish and wanted to stay in Ireland. *Good God, this was more frightening than setting sail for occupied France* – at least there had been a purpose to that, and he'd been trained and felt part of a team.

Only now, as he backed away from the railings, did he notice how tightly he'd been holding them. His hands were tired, his knuckles white under taut skin.

He wiped the tears from his face and told himself to have a little dignity. He'd made his decision, booked the tickets, packed what few possessions he had, and said goodbye to the few friends he'd made in Dublin. He'd done all of that with a stoicism that had come so easily. Even when he'd given Aileen her ticket there had been no hesitation, no thought that this was a mistake and he might have been better off staying in Dublin.

But now, when it was just too damn late, there was hesitation. The quayside buildings got smaller as the rumble of the engines got louder and the beast of a craft was manoeuvred around and further away from land. Niall found himself staring and told himself to stop trying to judge the growing gap below – to stop weighing it up against his very average swimming skills.

So.

Aileen hadn't made it.

For whatever reason, she wasn't here. He was on his own. He'd been sure she would change her mind, but he'd been kidding himself all along. He would just have to live with the consequences.

The horn sounded. That gap to the quayside might as well have been a whole ocean now, and the anxiety was filling his head.

'Are y'all right, m'lad?'

Niall turned away from the salt breeze, and was met with an old man's face, crooked pegs for teeth, a pitted bulbous nose, carved cheeks.

'Only, you're looking fair queasy there if you don't mind me saying.'

Niall gulped, almost glad someone had stopped to talk to him, to break him away from his nightmare. 'Actually, I do feel a little ill.'

The old man winked. 'You'll get used to it, so you will. Tis easy for me. I've been back and forth more times than I can count on my hands. I'll wager tis your first time?'

'Tis.'

The man looked toward the foredeck, where Niall had been sitting half an hour before. He casually nodded in that direction. 'Try a seat on the front. Sit down there and keep your eyes on the horizon. Twill help.'

'I'll try that, thank you.' He held his hand out to the man. 'My name's Niall, by the way. Niall O'Rourke.'

The man gave Niall's hand a strong shake – he was clearly in good health for his age. 'I'm Ed Mahoney,' he said. 'Well, twas O'Mahoney. Life in America's been a little simpler since I dropped the "O".'

'But tell me, Mr Mahoney, has life been good for you over there?'

'Ah, it has.' He nodded gravely. 'Tis very much, as they say, a land of opportunity.'

'You found what you went there for?'

'I found a good job and a grand wife. The rest seemed to slot into place.'

Niall nodded. 'Good for you, sir.' His knees almost buckled as the ship dipped and rose with the ocean swell.

The man eyed the seats on the foredeck. 'Niall, I think you should go and sit yourself down over there.'

'I will. Thank you. And I might see you again.'

'Please God, you will,' the man said as Niall walked away.

So, perhaps he could cope on his own after all. There were other people besides Aileen. Life would go on without her. The thought made him weak, and he clung on to railings. He let go and tried to will strength into his body as he rounded the corner leading to the foredeck and scanned the area for a spare seat. A woman and her husband moved up slightly to give him room to sit. Yes, there were other people. He sat down and tried to calm himself.

But no. *Heck, no.* He didn't want 'other people'. He didn't want to cope on his own. And he definitely didn't want to find a wife in America. It was clear in his own mind what he wanted. He wanted *Aileen*, dammit.

It was then that he heard his name being called.

The first time he heard it he thought it must be the old man – the only person there who knew his name.

The second time he realized it was a female voice, and he felt a power strike through him.

The third time he felt faint and tears pooled in his eyes.

She was two rows away. That joyful smile, the welcoming emerald eyes framed by that set of auburn locks.

He gulped, unable to speak.

Then she was there, standing in front of him.

And then they were standing together, locked as one, words irrelevant and unnecessary. He lifted her off her feet and swung her around. They kissed, then leaned back to look into each other's eyes.

'I've been looking for you everywhere,' Aileen said. 'I'm sorry for being unsure, Niall. I'm so sorry.'

'That's all right,' he replied. 'It's grand. All I care about is that you're here – that in the end you believed in yourself and you believed in me.'

'But I always believed in you, Niall – always. Twas only myself I wasn't so sure of, and I'm sorry I didn't have the confidence. I can't promise you I'll be the best wife in the world, but I'll try.'

'No apology needed, Aileen – *my Aileen*.'

Aileen went to speak but stopped herself. She frowned and ran a finger over the redness on his cheeks. 'Have you been crying?'

He shook his head and laughed. '*No!*'

'I got on half an hour ago. I had to take my suitcase to my cabin but then I came right here, where you said to meet, but you weren't here.'

He shrugged. 'Sure, I was about, I just had to stretch my legs for a while.'

'So you knew I'd come?'

'Twas never in doubt in my mind,' he said.

She frowned and gave him a sideways glare.

The corners of his lips were twitching. She carried on glaring, his face reddened, and seconds later he broke into a laugh and said, 'Well, twill teach me to take you for granted, so it will.'

Aileen ran her fingers through his hair, combing back the dark mop that sat tight and thick. She gave him a kiss and grabbed his arm. 'C'mon,' she said, stepping away.

'Where?'

'The back of the boat.'

He pulled her close and lifted his head higher, to look down upon her. 'You mean the *bow* of the *ship*, I think.'

She raised an eyebrow.

He cracked a grin. 'You mean to tell me you've never been on a ship before?'

'Look at you, *Captain O'Rourke*. Whatever you call the back end, let's go there.'

'What for?'

'For one thing, if we're to be married you've to get used to doing as you're told. For another, I want to wave goodbye.'

'To who?'

'To Ireland.'

He spluttered out a laugh and shook his head. 'You're daft.'

'C'mon.' She pulled and he followed, both of them laughing and darting along the side deck like a couple of schoolchildren who'd just pulled a prank.

Ten minutes later Aileen wasn't laughing. Apart from the odd trip on a small fishing boat she'd never been to sea before. The quayside was fast fading to a mere detail of the land, and that brought a new and unsettling loneliness.

She told herself she wasn't alone, that there must have been thousands on the ship – one of them her husband-to-be – but the thought didn't reassure her. She could see that the island full of people she knew was no longer within reach; its long beaches, friendly towns and rolling green hills were no longer just a hop away. And there was nothing she could do about it.

'Aileen. Are you all right?'

She didn't look, unable to wrest her gaze from the land, her eyes holding on to the sight as long as they could. 'I'm already missing it all,' she said. 'Our cottage. Cready's. The Crannagh and the wooden bridge over it. Mammy and Daddy, Little Frank and Gerard, even Fergus, and the chickens too – their fresh eggs and even their clucking on a dewy morning.' She groaned and turned to Niall. 'But most of all I'm missing

Briana. Oh heck, Niall, I'm really not sure I can live without her. She's been so good to me, so she has – we're best friends and I don't think I can—'

Niall pulled her in close and held on to her, keeping her head on his chest, running his fingers through her hair.

'Aileen,' he said, 'remember that you can stay in touch. But remember too that life in New York will be grand for us. I'll make sure of it. I can work hard over there. I know leaving makes your heart ache, and in all fairness it does mine too, but it'll be worth it. It's a new world over there; it's up to us to make it a *better* one.'

Slowly, and with a jitter and a gulp, she nodded in agreement, wiping away the single tear that trickled from her cheek on to his shirt.

'That's it,' she said. 'No more.'

'What? No more what?'

'No more bad thoughts and no more tears. We'll survive – no, we'll do more than that, much more.' She felt the touch of his lips on her head, his hot breath on her forehead, and she smiled to herself. 'You know I had the most stupid of all bad thoughts just now, Niall.'

'What was that?'

'I was looking out there, at the quayside and the ocean, and I was thinking of . . .'

'Thinking of what?'

'I was thinking whether I could swim to shore if I jumped off.'

He kissed her head again. 'You're beautiful, Aileen. But aren't you the daft one sometimes.'

They held each other for another few minutes, both watching as the thin whisper of land that had been their home became an insignificant line on the horizon.

'You'll be grand, Aileen. We'll be grand. I'll be here for you. From now on there'll be no more secret stolen days here and there when we can manage it. From now on I'll be here for you every day the Lord blesses us with.'

Aileen felt his hand reach to the back of her neck, where the wisps of soft hair lay waiting for him. His fingertips ran lightly over her, and she felt that delicious warm tremble again.

And she knew she would have that feeling for as long as they both lived.

Chapter 32

At Arturo's, Aileen and Marvin stop talking as another man sits down at the table, directly opposite Aileen.

'Hey, Niall,' Marvin says. 'We were just talking about you.'

'About how I need the john every five minutes these days?'

'No.'

'About my balding head?'

Marvin chuckles and glances at Aileen. 'Not quite. I think the words your wife used were "beautiful children with the man I still love".'

Aileen leans across the table. 'But in my heart I was thinking about your balding head, my darling.' Then she whispers, although so loudly the next table can hear, 'And let's be honest here, it's more *bald* than *balding*.'

'How can you say such a hurtful thing?' Niall says, drawing his face down to mock sadness. It quickly recovers and a few words of the old Irish spark from his tongue. 'Ah, I'm after forgetting. Sure, you're my wife, aren't ye. That'll explain it.' He picks up a menu and his accent switches back. 'Have either of you decided what you're having yet?'

Aileen glances at Marvin, but he's clearly elsewhere.

'Are you okay?' Aileen says to him.

He shakes himself back to the present. 'I'm sorry, I was still miles away.'

Niall leans across to him. 'A bit like this one in the cab on the way here.' He aims a nod at Aileen. 'All the way she was gazing out of the window, in a world of her own.'

'And I told you,' Aileen says. 'I like to reminisce, especially on our wedding anniversary.' While Niall tuts and runs his finger down the menu, she turns to Marvin. 'Are you back with us yet?'

'Just about,' he replies. He slowly brings his eyes to set upon hers, and stares. 'I was just thinking of that day in Leetown again.'

'You mean, when I . . . let you down?'

'You didn't let me down, Aileen. Far from it. Yeah, okay, I was sore for a while, but I *was* a bit of a jerk in my younger days, and it all turned out for the best. You know I'm happy. I've been happier than I could have dreamed of ever since that day.'

'Good,' Aileen said.

Leetown, County Wicklow, 1945

After Briana and her mother had watched Aileen run off around the corner to the railway station, her mother sighed and continued collecting eggs from the henhouse. When she finished, she glanced at Briana and her solid frown.

'Don't hold your face like that, Briana,' she said.

Briana took no notice.

'Are you worried?' her mother asked.

'I am. About Aileen.'

'She'll be grand,' her mother said. 'Sure, tis a big step for her, but she's a confident girl, always has been.' She gave Briana a resigned smile.

'I know my daughters, and you were always the dreamer, so you were. Then again, that can be a virtue.'

'What do you mean by that?'

'I think you know what I mean, my girl. I've noticed the way you look at . . . well, I won't say.'

Briana let out a gasp – hurt by her own transparency as much as anything.

'And I never really did say sorry, did I?'

'For what?'

'Ah, just the business with, you know, the fellas you were courting way back. I know you liked them, and perhaps I should have . . .'

''Tis grand, Mammy. You don't have to say it.'

Her mother's face took on a stern but sincere expression. 'Right. But you know, don't you?'

'I do. And thank you.'

'It's just that . . . some of my little ones need more help than others, and some people need a bit of guidance as to what's best for them.'

'I'm not sure what you mean, Mammy.'

'Briana. I'll stay here a while longer, giving my chickens and my thoughts a little attention. Why don't you go back inside?'

'Right.' Briana looked toward the cottage and took a gulp. 'I'll be off back indoors then.' She turned and left.

Once inside the cottage, Briana shut the door behind her and leaned her back against it. Marvin was still sitting next to the fire, gazing into the peat which was now barely glowing. Briana didn't move until he lifted his head and looked over to her. His face was expressionless, as blank and bland as the sand outside.

'I thought you'd forgotten about me,' he said.

Briana stepped forward and sat on the floor next to him, where she'd been before.

'Actually, I haven't, no.' She looked up to him, now seeing the red rims of his eyes. 'How are you feeling?' she said.

'Guess you think I'm an idiot.'

'Now, why would I be thinking that?'

His lips were closed, but Briana could see his teeth were gritting behind them, the joints of his jawbone twitching. Then he took a long breath. 'Well, an idiot is exactly what I feel. I just don't understand. I mean, what did I do wrong?'

'You did nothing wrong, Marvin. Twas nice.'

'Nice?'

'Twas lovely, what you said to Aileen.'

'Yeah, well, it wasn't nice having it all thrown back in my face. I feel awful – so stupid. I certainly don't feel nice.'

Briana stayed still and silent, looking up at him while he tutted and huffed to himself.

'I mean, was I *too* nice? Am I too nice? Is that it? Is that what's wrong with me?'

'Ah, don't be torturing yourself, Marvin. If Aileen wasn't in love with you after all you've done for her and all those beautiful words you said, then it simply wasn't right and it wouldn't have done either of you any good.'

'Beautiful words?'

'Well, apart from the bragging about money.'

'You think I do that?'

She grimaced. 'Just a little.'

'Oh.'

'But you're also a very kind man.'

'Kind?'

'Being kind and nice gets you a long way, Marvin.'

He pulled his gaze away from the glowing peat bricks and toward Briana. She smiled at him but only got a scowl in return. She got up, went over to the cabinet tucked away in the corner of the room and opened it. This was Daddy's own cabinet, the one she hardly ever touched, and definitely not while he was around. And she *never* touched that bottle – even Daddy only touched that bottle on special occasions. This moment wasn't exactly special, but Briana felt there was an outside chance it might turn out that way.

A few seconds later she brought over the bottle, together with a small shot glass.

Marvin looked at it suspiciously, then his expression softened. He smiled. It was an awkward smile, as if something he didn't like the taste of had forced its way into his mouth, but it was a smile. 'I don't really touch hard liquor,' he said.

'And I never touch Daddy's best whiskey, but I have today. Here, hold this.'

She put the glass in his reluctant grasp, and within seconds it was full to the brim.

'Go on,' she said.

He let out a sigh. 'Oh, what the hell. Guess I could do with a drink.' He threw the dark brown liquid into his mouth, gulped it down, and handed the glass back to Briana. He twisted his head to one side and gave a single hoarse cry.

'Feel better now?'

All he could do was nod. But now there was a hint of a better smile.

'Marvin, would you care to take a walk along the strand with me?'

'The beach? Well, I . . . uh. . .'

'Ah, c'mon, Marvin. You can kick off your shoes and socks. If a little Irish whiskey helps you, then some freezing cold Leetown seawater on your bare feet is guaranteed to help a heck of a lot more.'

'It won't be enough,' he said. 'I feel wretched.'

'I know, but it'll be a start. Please don't leave here just like this. Come for a walk with me.'

He thought for a few moments then slowly got to his feet. 'Well, I guess I could do with some fresh air. Thank you, Briana. That's very kind of you.'

'It's my pleasure, Marvin.' She aimed her most alluring smile at him.

Manhattan, New York City, 1995

At Arturo's, the waiter brings four glasses of champagne over to the table where Aileen, Niall and Marvin are sitting, and says it's good to see them all again.

As he leaves, the fourth person seats herself at the table, opposite Marvin.

'We were just reminiscing, dear,' Marvin says to her.

'Well, *he* was reminiscing,' Niall says to her. 'You were in the bathroom, he was on another planet.'

'Let me guess,' Briana says to Marvin. 'These two were fooling around.'

Marvin nods. 'You're right about that. It *was* very entertaining though.'

'They always were – right from when they were young lovers. A natural double act if ever there was one.'

Marvin reaches across and holds Briana's hand. 'Actually,' he says, 'I was doing some of my own fond reminiscing about how I found my beautiful Irish bride.'

Briana purses her lips and struggles to control her tight smile. Then she draws breath, and looks at Marvin, Aileen and Niall in turn. 'I propose a toast.'

'I think we all know what's coming,' Aileen says.

Niall reaches for his glass. 'No point breaking an annual tradition.'

'Okay,' Aileen says, reaching for hers. 'And I *do* like just a little corny sentimentality before I eat.'

'Less of the sarcasm, little sister,' Briana says. 'A joint wedding was a pretty rare event, even in 1946. Call me a fool but I think it's something to be proud of.'

'It is,' Aileen says, her tone matching her earnest expression. 'I'm only fooling and you're right.' She reaches across and places her hand next to Niall's. He covers it with his. They hold their glasses up and clink them together.

Marvin and Briana do exactly the same, and then all four glasses clink together above the centre of the table.

'To the Leetown days,' they all say.

It's almost a quarter to eleven. Marvin and Briana have returned upstate, while Aileen and Niall are back home on Long Island, digesting the evening's food and conversation with the help of a small cup of cocoa each.

'Shall I put the TV on?' Niall says.

Aileen shakes her head. 'Don't let's spoil the moment.'

His eyes bob up to the ceiling.

'And don't be doing that thing with your eyes, please. One day they'll stay up there inside your head.'

When Niall stops laughing he takes a careful sip of the steaming sweet liquid. 'You know I'm joking.'

'Of course I do, but you know me – any excuse for a traditional Irish nag.'

They exchange a look and a hint of a smile.

'You know,' Aileen says, 'I never really did work out what I saw in you all those years ago. I guess I was just young and innocent. Didn't know much about the world.'

'Ah, well. That was your loss.' Another sip of cocoa. 'And my gain.'

'You say such charming things.' Aileen sighs and lifts her cup to her mouth.

Niall holds his hand out, resting it on her knee. She holds it. For a few minutes all they hear is the clock in the hall ticking, and their own sips and slurps.

'If I can be serious for a moment,' Aileen says. 'Do you have any regrets?'

'Mmm . . . Not going for the pizza?'

'I said *serious*.'

'I *am* being serious. That lasagne's laying a little heavy.' He swills the half-inch of cocoa remaining in his cup. 'Regrets?' he says. 'You mean real big ones?'

'Humdingers.'

He thinks for a few seconds, then says, 'Only the two you know about. Not many people manage to miss both their parents' funerals.'

She gives his hand a squeeze. 'That's pretty impressive, I have to admit.'

There's a jolly angle to his voice as he adds, 'I only hope I don't miss my own.'

She giggles, almost spilling her drink. 'Is that it?' she says. 'Is that the full extent of things you'd change if you could go around again?'

'You know, Aileen, it is. It really is. I feel so lucky.' He takes a deep breath. 'Did I ever tell you about the time I was in France, when the fact I was Irish saved my life?'

'Not this year. But it's only February.'

'Ah, you've heard it?'

'Come on. I'm whacked. Let's drink up and go to bed.'

Ten minutes later, teeth cleaned, they get into bed. They both say, 'Goodnight, dear.' They kiss and turn the lights out.

A few minutes of silence follows. Then Aileen speaks.

'There was something else I was getting at,' she says.

'What?'

She hesitates, then says, 'Have you ever regretted . . . Oh, it sounds stupid.'

'Go on. What?'

'Well, Briana and myself have been back home a few times over the years. And I'm so glad we both made peace with Mammy and Daddy.'

He sniggers in the darkness.

'What?' she says. 'What did I say?'

'It's just how you still call them that. I'm sorry. And I'm glad too. I know getting things straight with your parents was important to you. What is it you were going to say?'

'Well, you never went back. Never. Not once. Did you ever regret being Irish?'

'Jeez,' he says. 'Heavy question.' He takes a moment to sigh. 'Hell, my accent's hardly recognizable now. I'm way more American than Irish.' He pauses for thought again. 'But honestly? No way.'

'Really?'

'You know as well as I do. That country made me who I am. I wouldn't change it for anything. And when I think of us two back then, and how we are now, we've done okay, haven't we?'

'Sure,' she says. 'We haven't done too badly for a couple who ran away together halfway round the world with hardly a penny between them and no parental backup.'

'Yeah,' he says. 'Yeah, you're right. And I haven't done so bad for a cowardly deserter.'

Aileen reverts to her full – or slightly heightened – Irish accent. 'Aach, will ye shut yer face, ye big eejit.'

In the darkness, he slowly leans across. She senses his warm breath on her face, feels his hand on the back of her neck, and then the tender flesh of his lips on hers.

But the most exquisite of these sensations is his hand on the back of her neck, his fingertips gently teasing those baby hairs. The thrill isn't quite as delicious as it once was, but it's there.

It's still there.

AFTERWORD

Somewhere between fifty thousand and a hundred thousand men from the Irish Republic voluntarily joined the British Forces during World War Two. Women numbering around twice that figure left their country to work in UK armaments factories. Almost five thousand of those volunteers were men who deserted the Irish Army to join the Allied war effort.

Many of the men who went to fight alongside Great Britain freely admitted that their motives were either financial or the lure of adventure. Regardless, the Allied forces owe them a great debt: many returned home injured, some not at all.

However, these men were not treated well when they returned to the Republic of Ireland. Indeed, the five thousand who had previously been in the Irish Army were branded as traitors, denied pensions, blacklisted by state employers, and publicly ostracized. Even their wives and children were repeatedly told they should be ashamed of them.

In fairness, it has to be remembered that technically these men were indeed deserters, and in many other countries might have suffered a worse fate. But in hindsight, they were brave men who volunteered to risk their lives in battle when they could easily have chosen a far safer life away from the hostilities.

In 2012 the Irish government officially apologized for the way the government of the day treated them.

In 2013, even though only a few still survived, all 4,981 were granted official pardons.

ACKNOWLEDGMENTS

The inspiration for this novel came from my memories of childhood family holidays in various parts of Ireland, so firstly I owe a huge thank you to my parents for taking me there.

Secondly, in terms of fine-tuning the manuscript, I have to thank Monica Byles for her excellent copyediting skills (the word 'thorough' isn't enough here) and Elizabeth Cochrane for her equally excellent proofreading. I'll also take the opportunity to thank the whole Amazon Publishing team, but especially Sammia Hamer, Victoria Pepe and Bekah Graham for their help and advice over the last few years.

But the most difficult parts of any book project are its conception, initial development and getting that crucial first draft produced. In that respect, I have to say that this book, more than any other I've written, owes everything to the encouragement and support of Maria, who told me it was the best thing I'd ever written. So an extra-special huge thank you is due to her.

ABOUT THE AUTHOR

Rachel Quinn has published many novels under various pen names, most notably as Ray Kingfisher, and lives in Hampshire in the UK.

An Ocean Between Us is Rachel's first historical romance.

For more information on the author, please visit www. raykingfisher.com.